**HELLO AND
GET READY**

WRITTEN

BY

BILL
SHARROCK

**BEFORE
WE GET STARTED...**

CHAPTER #1
ANNA-SEKA

She stared. Nothing. The shapeless mist rose up in front of her like a frosted curtain, hanging lank against the pale light and stirring in the slight, chill breeze. Nothing.

She moved. She paused. She moved again. She was like a ghost against the mist, her eyes wide, her head tilted to catch the slightest sound. All about her the air was heavy with silence, drenched, cold and unknown. She stepped forward, carefully measuring each stride. Her boots sounded in the emptiness as they sank up to the lacings in the sodden turf, and then squelched as she eased them clear.

There were two broken pillars hung with rusted iron work, directly ahead of her. They loomed out of the mist like ancient sentinels. She approached and they let her pass. Again she paused.

Just in front of her, it must have been no more than three spear lengths, she could make out several huddled shapes almost lost against the greyness.

She waited yet again: watching, listening, sensing the chill against her cheeks and fixing the shapes in her gaze. Still, there was nothing, no movement at all.

'Well, all right,' her lips moved in a whisper. At the same time, one hand slid to the hilt of the sword at her hip, and she eased it carefully out of the scabbard. 'No sense taking any chances.' She glanced to the left and right. It was still day but there was not enough light in this broken place to catch her polished blade and warn someone of her approach.

Once more she moved. The shadows did not stir to meet her coming, nor did they melt back into the mist. They stayed where they were, motionless almost lost and unknown.

She crept forward as a hunter.

And as she came towards them, like figures in a dream the shapes revealed themselves. With a slight gasp of relief, she saw that they were statues, no more than statues. But they were strange statues: squat, rounded, colourful and weirdly childlike.

Despite herself, she smiled, reached out and touched the painted surface of the nearest one: it was ice cold to the touch. For a moment she studied it: the statue of a unicorn, its paint chipped and worn but with eyes that were big and round, black on white and edged with red and gold. The twisted horn of this abandoned unicorn had been broken near the top, and the carved mane, once purest white, was stained with mud and the touch of many little hands.

She smiled again, but unwilling to be distracted, and then straightened and looked around. What was this place?

As the breeze rose and the mist stirred and swirled, more shapes appeared. Some she recognised, some she didn't, and those that she recognised were only vague memories from books that she had found among piles of rubbish in empty houses on empty streets: an elephant, a camel, a zebra with one leg missing, and a crocodile with a carved seat moulded onto its back.

At last the sun pushed through the gloom, glowing like a mirror of polished pearl and making dull shadows beneath the silent figures.

Anna-Seka of the College of Scouts, lifted her sword and rested it across her shoulder. Was this a temple, or was it a burial place? She shook her head. No one would bury their dead like this, nor would they gather priests here and make sacrifice.

A branch cracked, and she looked to her left. Out of the melting mist something living appeared. It was a deer, a young deer, dappled with the coat of early spring and wide-eyed to see a stranger in its world. They stared at each other: human and forest creature in a lost world of statues. And then in a moment the deer was gone, searching out the grey cloak of mist with a turning step and a toss of its head. Gone.

'Well, there goes supper,' muttered the young scout and crouched down for a moment. She peered into the tree-lined edge of this abandoned and mysterious place she had come across. There was, she thought, always a chance another deer might choose to stray across her path. Slipping her sword back into its scabbard, she un-slung the bow from across her shoulder, took an arrow from the quiver at her hip, and carefully nocked it.

How long she waited, she could not tell, but she did not relax the bow until the mist had risen to the tree tops. Slowly it broke up, drifting like skeins of silk among the jagged spires of the shattered towers of decaying concrete that lay beyond. Nothing.

She sighed, straightened once more, and for just a moment, leaned on the bow stave.

It was that slight movement that saved her life.

The barb-tipped bolt that had been fired at her head, grazed the back of her neck, struck the unicorn high on the shoulder in a shower of plaster chips, and careened away into the gloom. With the skill of practised reflex, Anna-Seka sprang to one side, reached again for an arrow, and raised her bow. But even as she did so, she knew that it was hopeless. Several figures had appeared from the tree line. They were all armed with cross-bows, and all making ready to let fly. There was not much time.

Slowly, deliberately, Anna-Seka lowered her bow, then sank to one knee. She raised one hand in the sign of peace, paused, then put her finger to her lips. It was a movement that she hoped would be instantly recognised by these outlanders and might even save her life: the sign of a stranger come in friendship.

Outlanders or Stainers: that was what these bowmen were. They were members of the strange and scattered tribe that dwelt outside the great city in the wild and desolate region men called the Stain Kingdom. One of them stepped forward as she waited: a giant of a man, but stooped and ragged, with a straggled beard and a gaunt chiselled face that had seen more than a score of seasons of sun and rain and snow. He gazed at the woman in front of him.

'What brings ye here?' he said, his voice heavy with the local dialect, common among outlanders.

'Give me your name, and I'll give you my name and my reason,' replied Anna, trying to keep her voice steady.

The man smiled. 'It's my bolt that nearly knocked your pretty head off those shoulders of yor'n,' he replied. 'I think ye owe me your name before I give you mine.'

Anna did not return the smile, but she sensed herself to be safer than she was a moment ago. 'My name is Anna-Seka,' she said. 'I am a scout of the Great City.'

The man shrugged. 'A viper, then, and come to rob poor folks of what little they have among these ruins.'

Anna frowned. 'I steal from no man. We are sent to find that which is abandoned and bring word to our masters. This is a lost city. No one owns it.'

'Aye, but we live near it.' The man turned to gesture towards the men and the woman who waited behind him, and Anna saw the telltale stain running across his neck.

Anna nodded. 'Then that is well. We are taught and trained not to take from those folk we may come across, and to leave them in peace.'

The man gave a harsh guttural laugh, secretly taken by her unexpected beauty. 'Well, they do not teach ye very well, lassie. Only last week we came back from a hunt to find that our stores had been raided, and half of our grain supplies taken.'

'They were scouts from the City?'

'They were, and as my name is Bepsi of the Loca clan, we caught up with them before they reached the crossing point.' He frowned. 'We made them pay a price they won't forget.'

'You killed them?'

The man shrugged. 'I'm not sure, but they carried away three of their number on their backs, and left our grain where it should lie.'

Anna frowned. She had heard only yesterday that one of the city patrols had been ambushed near the Crossing. 'I steal from no man,' she repeated.

The man smiled again. 'I can tell from your eye that you are telling the truth, Anna-Seka, and that will be enough to make sure that you live to breathe another day.' He laughed again, but without bitterness. 'Faith! For some strange reason I am glad now that I missed ye!' He paused. 'Where are ye bound?'

Anna looked around. 'Well, I'm not sure where I am, so I've no idea where I'm going.'

To her surprise, all the Stain folk laughed. And then the man called Bepsi-Loca came forward and offered her his hand. 'Come with us, lassie. We've a camp nearby, and food to share. You've no business out here, wandering around on your own. This is a cursed place, and only the cursed stay here.'

Anna took his hand. It was a firm, calloused grasp. 'I have been in other cities and waste spaces before, but I have never seen such a place as this. What was it?'

The man shook his head and turned again to wave the other folk forward. 'We are not sure, but we think that children once, long ago, played here. We have found their toys and dolls scattered about, and even a cradle on wheels. It was all twisted up and half buried.' He pointed. 'Just over there.'

Anna shrugged. 'Nothing worth the taking, then?'

'Aye, a forsaken place.' Bepsi-Loca smiled. 'A good place to leave, and better to forget. If you are looking for things to take, we can show you.'

Anna paused. 'Not far from here?'

'Far enough to know that we will be left in peace, but close enough to make it worth your while,' the man replied. He put his fingers to his lips and whistled:

'Nike! Come here now, and bring Leviss with you.'

A young woman with a lad perhaps slightly older at her side, came forward. Their crossbows were slung from their hips, and their studded puffer jackets were crossed by baldrics worked with silver-gilt wire. Anna could not help but notice that they were heavily stained on one side of their faces and their hair was unwashed and tangled. But although their knee length boots almost covered leggings that were torn and ragged, they walked together with a stride that would have matched any guardsman: even one from the High Citadel.

'A brother and a sister?' she asked.

Bepsi grinned and nodded. 'Little demons from the day that they could walk,' he replied, 'but born hunters from the first year of their youth.'

They came, bowed together, straightened and smiled.

'Uncle,' said the young woman, 'What's to do?'

'Well, first show yourself civil and give your hand to our visitor, Anna-Seka from the great city. She has lost her way, and is looking for something to take back home to her masters.'

For a moment the girl named Nike, scowled, but then she suddenly brightened. 'Can we play a trick on her, uncle, and lead her into the Badlands, and leave her there for the Wasters?' She glanced at Anna as she spoke and cheerfully winked:

'Do not fear, Anna-Seka. You are safe with us. A friend of my uncle is also mine.' She turned again to Bepsi. 'There are some strange mechanical things in the Glass Tunnel down by the Water Pit three stadia beyond those high towers.' She pointed. 'We could be there in two hours, and back in time for supper.'

'Is that so?' Bepsi frowned even as he smiled. 'Well, I'll take a reach to the left beyond the precinct and meet you on the other side somewhere between here and home. Make sure you are clear of the iron thickets by sundown. We've lost folk there before y'know.'

Nike nodded. 'Don't worry, uncle,' she said. 'We won't be taking any risks.' She waved as the man called Bepsi-Loca moved away and then she glanced at Anna. 'Are ye handy with that bow?' she asked.

'Handy enough,' replied Anna, and without pausing she reached for her bow. In an instant an arrow was nocked. She lifted the bow in one smooth movement and let it fly. On the other side of the open space where there was a low brick wall, a large buck hare was just about to clear the wall and hop away into the undergrowth. The arrow struck it at the base of the neck and it was dead before it flopped to the ground.

The Stain Folk stared for a moment. 'You'll do,' said Nike, and she gave her brother a wink. 'What d'ye think, Leviss?'

Leviss grinned. 'I think I know nothing more than what we're having for supper,' he said. 'Come on, let's be going.'

An hour later, Anna-Seka found herself on the eastern side of the city. She scarcely knew how. The two young outlanders had led her on a narrow, twisting and almost hidden route. They had stayed away from the main streets, tracked across piles of rubble, made their way through the lower floors of abandoned buildings, and found their way along narrow, winding alleyways and covered passages. Twice they went down broken concrete steps into the darkness of subways lined with ancient tiles that curved above their heads and glistened with water. Strange lettering decorated the walls, and coils of thick and coloured wiring hung from the ceiling, or trailed across the broad hallways. Once they climbed down onto a narrow iron-railed track and followed it into a tunnel for a short distance before Nike thought better of it and ordered them back. 'Wild folk live down there,' she had muttered. 'I can smell them.'

It was a relief to Anna when at last they made their way back to the surface and found themselves in a kind of open square lined with bare trees, and strewn with rubbish.

'Not far now,' said Leviss. 'The iron thickets are just ahead. Mind how you go now, and not a word.'

Anna had been in other quarters of this city, but she had never come this far, nor seen anything like 'the iron thickets': it was a wall of twisted metal, about two spear lengths in height, and stretching at least a hundred yards either side of where they had emerged.

'What is it?' she asked.

Leviss shrugged. 'Who knows,' he said, 'but if you look closely you can see wheels in among the wreckage, and cables, and ribbed panels and all sorts of strange things.'

Anna-Seka gazed at the metal hedge. 'It once moved,' she said slowly. 'See, those iron bars, held by wooden beams? They make a road for it. Just like we saw in the tunnel back there.'

'You think so?' Leviss put his head on one side, studied the wreckage and smiled. 'Well, whatever it is, or was, it's nothing but a nuisance now. We have to climb through and over it to get where we are going. Don't touch those cables, by the way. They have something in them that will strike you down, and burn you up from the inside.'

'And sometimes even the iron itself,' added Nike. 'Only touch what I tell you to. Leave the rest alone.'

Anna swallowed hard. 'Lead on,' she said.

It took them half an hour to work their way through the thicket, a distance of no more than twenty paces. Twice Nike had to shout a warning when Anna was about to reach out and grab a steel girder, and twice they had to stop while Leviss checked some cables and moved them to one side with the butt of his spear.

But at last they emerged safely on the other side and found themselves in an open yard with a large building on one side.

'Are you all right?' asked Nike, offering her hand to Anna as she stepped beyond the last of the iron entanglements.

Anna nodded. 'Thank you,' she said. 'We never did anything like that in training.'

'Training?'

Anna unslung her bow, and looked around. 'Yes,' she said, 'training. Every scout from the Great City, from Serenity itself, must undergo a year's training in the School or College for Scouts. After that we are each assigned a mentor, an experienced scout who will take us on our first patrol, and thereafter be our constant companion and closest friend.'

Nike raised her eyebrows. 'But your mentor, he is not here now?'

Anna shrugged. 'He may be, he may be not, but he will know exactly where I am.'

The outlander girl gave a short laugh. 'Is he a magician then? Some sort of wizard from the olden times?'

Anna shook her head. 'It does not work like that.' She paused. 'I cannot explain. It's difficult to understand, but,' and here she hesitated, 'it is all about friendship, and training, and trust.'

Leviss, who was impatient to move on, tapped his spear on the ground. 'We need to get going,' he said. Without waiting for a reply, he began to move away across the yard, and the others followed him. He pushed on ahead, looking to left and right, and walking steadily with a slight crouch and spear held at his hip. Nike came alongside Anna:

'This mentor you speak of, what is he named.'

For a moment, Anna hesitated then she replied:

'He is called Hartley, lord Hartley and there is no better scout in all of Serenity. He is to me as a father. I would follow him anywhere.'

Nike shrugged. 'But here you are now, all on your own and following two strangers into the heart of you know not where.'

Anna did not reply at first.

But as they approached a line of battered, rusting vehicles, she nocked an arrow once more, paused and then spoke: 'Lord Hartley sent me on this mission. He knows the risks, but he also knows me. He would not have sent me if he thought I was not up to it.'

'I would like to meet this Hartley. Is he like our warlords, do you think?'

Anna had heard of the northern warlords. They were fierce warrior-leaders of the stain-folk and outlanders and they ruled over different areas of the stain-lands. There were five chief warlords, called the Big Five, and they ruled the lesser warlords who in turn ruled over the folk below them. Although they never tried to come near Serenity itself, they resisted any groups from the city who came into their territory. She thought for a moment:

'Hartley is not a warlord, but he is a man of high honour and status within the city. My parents told me I was very lucky that my name had been chosen to be mentored by lord Hartley. Names are always chosen by ballot. There is no personal favouritism or special influence when scouts are assigned their mentors.'

Nike shrugged again and then gave a low whistle. Leviss turned round. She raised one finger, and he replied with three, then went on. Nike smiled. 'Three more stadia until we arrive,' she muttered. They walked on together past the vehicles, some of which were burnt out, and made their way down a broad street between two towering buildings.

'Our warlord is Delsea,' she suddenly said.

'I have heard his name, but I have never seen him.'

Nike knelt down, studied some tracks that ran across the dust covering the tarmac, and then straightened: 'It is better to hear of him, than to see him,' she said quietly. 'Much better.'

'You keep out of his way then?'

'I doubt if he knows we exist, Anna-Seka.' Nike studied the flawless beauty of the woman in front of her: she was so like a child, and so unlike any of the folk that Nike knew. 'He rules this area with an iron fist, but he pays tribute to the great warlord: Chesterman,' she added.

'Tribute?'

'Aye, taxes: mostly in form of food and weapons, but sometimes in the form of military service. Such a service has not come to our village in my lifetime, but every year the lots are cast, and a village is chosen to send their young men and women to the stain capital.' She stopped for a moment, scanned the area in front and behind them, and then gestured to Anna to walk on. 'Once there, in the city, we call it the Burgh or Brokinburgh, they are taken through a training and selection programme. The lucky ones are chosen to join the outlander army that Chesterman himself leads.'

'And the rest are allowed to return?'

Nike frowned. 'Those who have managed to survive are allowed to return home.' She glanced at the sun as it dipped lower, throwing deep shadows across the street. 'Last year, the settlement next to us sent thirty of their young people to the city. Seven returned.'

'That is a heavy price,' said Anna, watching as Leviss just ahead of them, gave a wave and disappeared down a narrow alleyway.

Nike shrugged. 'There is no alternative. That is the price, and it is the price we pay to keep these lands safe. It has always been so.'

'Ever since the Great Burning, the time that the sky caught fire and the lands melted,' replied Anna quietly.

'Just so,' said Nike. 'The Burning was a day of fury and a time of madness, as my father used to say. My grandmother told me that the sea itself boiled and the deepest lakes and rivers ran dry.'

'Perhaps it is just a legend,' said Anna as they entered the alleyway. Leviss was silhouetted at the alley-end, about thirty yards ahead.

With a shake of her head, Nike put her hand to a half-scorched wall of broken brick and cracked plaster. It crumbled to her touch. 'Myth or legend or history, it matters not. Whatever happened, there was fire and this is what it has left us.' She paused. 'Come on! I don't want Leviss to get too far ahead. This place is not safe.'

They did not catch up with Leviss until they had cleared the buildings of the wide street, and found themselves in a strange parkland. Most of the trees had been reduced to blackened stumps, and what bushes that remained were little more than dried and stunted patches of undergrowth. But it was what lay beyond the parkland that caught Anna's eye. It was a large, tunnel-like building made of glass and iron. It gleamed in the fading light, and its soaring, polished sides appeared perfectly preserved.

Anna stopped. 'I don't understand,' she said.

Leviss, who had stopped to let the other two catch up, laughed. 'Well, you should understand,' he said. 'It was built by your people, and not so long ago neither.'

Anna stared. 'A resource centre!' she said. 'It's a resource centre.'

'Hah! Is that what ye call it? We called it the Eater, 'cos that what it does or used to do.' He smiled at the girl's confusion, and yet he still wondered at the smooth perfection of her face and form. 'Your people from your city came here about ten years ago,' he went on. 'They built this monster and sucked the land dry hereabouts until we drove them out.'

Anna looked around. 'There was fighting here?'

'Aye, but before my time. I was too young to serve, but my father and brothers fought in Delsea's legion. One brother did not come home, and my father was wounded, but when the fighting was done, this land was ours once more and your Serenity had crept back to lick its wounds.' He raised his spear as if saluting the Glass Tunnel. 'There are strange machines in there,' he said, 'All smashed, but still strange. No one goes there now.'

'Except us?' Anna-Seka smiled nervously.

Leviss chuckled. 'Are we no one? I think not. We are the children of Delsea. Besides, we have a daughter of Serenity to guide us.' He glanced at Nike. 'Shall we press on, sister? The day is slipping away on us.'

Nike sighed. 'It has taken us longer than I would have liked, but there is little point in turning back now. Besides, once we clear the Tunnel, there's an easier route home by the Water Pit, and we might still make it before sunset.'

The entrance to the Glass Tunnel was partly blocked by a fallen tree and the wreck of a burnt-out bus, but with Leviss leading the way they squeezed between the obstructions, pushed open the entrance-door and entered.

Although it was still light outside, the interior of the building was almost lost in shadow. A heavy, damp gloom pushed out from the depths of the tunnel despite the huge glass ceiling, and the high, over-arching pillars of polished steel. The first thing Anna noticed was the smooth, ice-white floor, strewn with debris but still gleaming softly in the shadowy light. And then as her eyes adjusted, she saw the familiar shapes of processors, generators and storage silos. She looked around uncertainly. It was just like being in one of the giant Resource Centres that lay just beyond the great city itself. During her training programme she and other recruits had visited such places. And she remembered the time when Hartley was mentoring her only a year ago: he had taken her to one of the larger centres that lay many miles from Serenity. It was far from the city but still came within the borders of the Safe Lands in the northern province of the kingdom. She had not enjoyed that day.

'These are your reason for living,' Hartley had said to her as he showed her around the machines. 'Such machines cannot supply Serenity with processed resources, unless the college scouts tell Rebuild where to find the raw materials. You find them, you report back, and the working parties will retrieve them.'

Anna-Seka remembered how many folk there were in that particular Resource Centre, working quietly around each machine and so intent on what they were doing that they seemed almost unaware of her presence, and only ever looked up when Hartley spoke to them. The air was filled with the gentle hum of the generators, and the deep rumble of trolleys weighed down with materials and being pushed or dragged by teams of white-coated workers. They looked, all of them, hollow-eyed and weary. She felt uneasy and did not like what she saw, but accepted what her mentor had told her, even if she promised herself that she would try and avoid entering such a place again.

But here she was now, on her own except for two stain-folk, and standing in the heart of an abandoned Resource Centre. It was like being in a tomb.

'Any use to you?' asked Nike.

Anna hesitated. 'I never knew that we had built centres so deep in the . . .'

Nike smiled. 'The stain-lands? Yes, don't worry. We know what we are, and what you think of us.'

For just a moment, Nike and her brother noticed how the girl blushed and dipped her head. 'I am sorry,' she said.

'Ah, don't be lassie!' laughed Leviss, still fascinated by her unmarked complexion, but at the same time seeing in front of him someone who was in so many ways just like them.

'There's nothing to be ashamed of,' he went on, 'we are who we are, and that ain't gonna change. Some of us outlanders were born this way, and some of us had the stain come upon them when they were younger and living as citizens of Serenity itself.' He paused. 'And before you ask, both of us here were born as stain-folk, but our parents were from the great city.'

Again, Anna-reddened. 'That must be difficult,' she said quietly.

'Hah! There you go again! Apologising, and ducking that sweet head of yours. Look up now, and tell me what you see. My sister and I don't say sorry to no one, and don't expect the same from anyone else neither.' He grinned. 'but if you catch us staring at ye for longer than we should, it's perhaps because we t'aint seen anyone like ye before.'

Anna looked away, looked back, and smiled. 'Let's check those machines,' she said.

Even as she spoke, unknown to any of them, a silent watcher was studying the entrance to the Glass Tunnel, and the doorway they had just entered.

He also was a scout, but not of Serenity. His forehead carried the stain, and his armour and weapons set him apart as a soldier of one of the higher warlords. He also carried something not often seen, a spy glass, and it was this he had been using when he spotted Anna, Nike and Leviss crossing the open ground towards the Glass Tunnel.

'My lord Chesterman will be interested in this,' he muttered, easing himself to a better position behind the pile of discarded rubbish, and putting the spyglass to his eye once more. He could just make out the shadows of the three scouts moving about in the Glass Tunnel. The evening sun caught the sheets of polished glass and lit the interior of the tunnel for at least part of its length. He watched and he waited. The minutes crept by, and then the shadows all at once disappeared.

Cursing under his breath, the stain-scout stood up. 'What are these kids up to now?' he muttered to himself, and picking up his crossbow, set off down the mound of debris where he had taken up position, and headed for the entranceway to the tunnel. He had to go carefully. The sloping mound moved under his steps, and all sorts of broken and abandoned rubbish threatened to trap his ankles, or wrap itself around his boots. And he knew that if the others heard him coming, they would either put an arrow in his chest, or vanish away into the depths of this building they were exploring.

He reached the doorway, slipped a feathered bolt into his crossbow, and eased the cable back. A soft click told him it was ready. Taking a deep breath, he entered the Glass Tunnel.

All was quiet within. And still. He knelt down and put his ear to the floor, listening for the sound of distant footfalls. There was nothing.

Working his way carefully between the machines, he peered into the darkness looking for any clues that might tell him where these strangers were now, or where they were headed. But there was not a sound, not the least movement, and not even the distant echo of booted feet, nothing that would tell him of their presence. And so for a time that was longer than he was comfortable with, he stood stock still and waited. The gloom deepened, and the dust hung like golden curtains over the machines in the last copper glimmer of sunset.

'They've taken the dark way,' the scout whispered to himself. He knew he should follow, but he feared to. The dangers of the outside world he could endure, and even look to be part of, but not the deep, dark fastness of the Tunnel. He should light a torch, he knew that, but it would only give away his presence, and make him an easy target for an unseen crossbow, or a sudden dagger thrust. 'Well, all right,' he thought to himself and stepped back, 'I will report back to my lord Chesterman. I lost them in the Tunnel, but they must come out on the great eastern road, and we have scouts aplenty on that route.'

He glanced around again. The machines slept, the light of day was all but gone, and it was time to leave.

Even as the stain-scout left the Glass Tunnel and cut away across the barren parkland and into the night, Nike led Leviss and Anna-Seka up the long flight of steps that led to the far exit.

'We're here,' she said.

Anna shook her head. 'You must have eyes like a cat. I couldn't see a thing back there.'

Nike smiled. 'Perhaps that is why they call me Missy Cat,' she said. 'I sometimes think I see better in the night than I do in the day.' She put her hand on the polished handle of the door. 'Watch how you go now. This quarter is not always friendly. Chesterman counts this area as his and his alone. He does not take kindly to intruders, whether stain-folk like himself, or people of the Great City.'

'Aye,' whispered Leviss coming up alongside them. 'The beautiful people can expect no mercy if they fall into the hands of our lord Chesterman.'

Anna-Seka frowned. 'And yet you have befriended me. Why?'

Leviss shrugged. 'You interest me,' he said. You're the first creature of Serenity I've seen close up, and . . .'

'And likely the last, if you keep wittering,' hissed Nike. 'Come on! We can't stay here any longer. The Eastern Road will be watched for sure, so we must keep to the shadows and move quickly. The moon will be rising soon, and the road we must take will be lit for miles.'

They left the Tunnel, followed a sloping track-way between two ruined buildings, and then skirted a large pool, inky black beneath the dark sky. For the first time that day, Anna felt tired and hungry. Perhaps it was because there was at last the prospect of safety, and a warm fire and a meal among folk she could almost trust. She wasn't sure of anything in this place, but if her sudden weariness dragged at her legs, her hunger spurred her on. She followed after Nike, with Leviss close behind, keeping a watch in case they were being tracked, or had been spotted by wild folk or some hostile scouts.

At last with the Glass Tunnel far behind them and the large pool now lost in the darkness, they moved shadow-like along the empty streets, turning this way and that as Nike led them steadily east, then north east and finally on a direct line with the pole star which gleamed above them. All was quiet, except for the occasional call of a hoot owl, and once the faint sound of scrabbling as a jackal darted away in front of them and disappeared.

With the moon now rising bright and full against a star-pocked sky, they hugged the edges of the buildings, and crept along beneath any awnings or covered ways they came across. Glass from shattered windows was strewn across the pavements in this quarter of the city, and it slowed their pace as they stepped carefully to avoid making any noise and drawing attention to their passing. Then, with the second hour of night almost passed, they cleared the broken canyons of high-rise buildings and found themselves in an abandoned, low-roofed suburb of ruined houses.

'Another mile and we're home,' whispered Nike, and Anna-Seka gasped with relief. At least, she told herself as they pushed on past battered shop-fronts and burned out homes, she would have something to show Hartley and the resources committee for her latest reconnaissance: the position of The Glass Tunnel, and the state of the machinery still intact inside it. If she made it back safely, that is. Otherwise, she would just be another scout that had disappeared without trace in the wastelands of the northern kingdom.

For it was true that not all scouts returned from such expeditions, and there were occasions when whole patrols simply vanished and were never seen or heard of again. Although Serenity itself was safe behind its multi-walled defences and watch-towers, the border-regions had never been less than dangerous, and the interior of Stain-land was seen as a continual threat. The king of Serenity, as ever, was confident of 'ultimate victory' over the warlords of the Stain-kingdom. He constantly assured the people of this in his feast-day speeches, and the courtiers and palace officials were practised at seeming calm and confident as they moved about the city, But everyone knew that despite the northern wars, there was a single ominous threat which hung over every citizen of Serenity and led to a constant but unspoken fear: the stain-plague. Or put more simply: the Stain.

No one, high-born or low-born was immune to that disease, and although it was rare within the boundaries of the kingdom, there was not a citizen, young or old, who was not aware that it could strike at any time and without warning. Once a stain appeared on the surface of the skin, there was no cure, and therefore no prospect of recovery. And accordingly, no treatment was offered to those unfortunate enough to catch this plague. The worst affliction, of course, was the stain that appeared on the face or neck, visible to all and instantly recognizable. But any stain was bound to be found out at the compulsory health checks held every six weeks by the Graders. The reaction of the authorities was always swift. The sufferer was sent for diagnosis by medical staff, then committed to an official trial. The court judges always delivered the same sentence. It was not a death sentence, but the alternative was almost as bad: instant and summary imprisonment or sometimes banishment without right of appeal. All property became the property of the state, and all relatives were themselves likely to suffer long term quarantine within the massive prison complex beneath the central tower of Serenity itself.

The victim, if banished, was given three days rations, escorted to the borderlands by a small detachment of the security forces and abandoned to the barren emptiness of Stain-land, or the outlands.

It had always been that way and, as Anna-Seka had been taught from her youth, it would always continue to be so. It was a question of beauty. Beauty was the touchstone of virtue and therefore beauty must be protected at all costs. 'The beauty of the city, is the beauty of its people' as one of the official mottos read: the same motto which was inscribed on the walls of the civic temple, and over the gates of the imperial palace. At the entrances to the schools, universities and colleges another motto was often seen: 'Power is beauty, and beauty is power.'

All honour lay in beauty, and every citizen's duty was to defend and uphold that honour. It was enshrined in law, and most perfectly expressed in the presence of the king himself, and the royal family.

Anna had always understood that, and along with her sister and her cousins had always accepted it without question. But ever since she had become a scout, and particularly since she had been brought under the mentorship of Hartley, she had come to see that the world was not as simple and straightforward a place as she had at first believed.

After all, the stain-folk themselves had for the most part originally been citizens of Serenity, or at least their ancestors had been so. And they were not like the wild folk, not totally alien and hostile. They were simply abandoned, cast off, rejected, and spilled into the outlands: that strange country she herself had been sent to scout. So, here she was now, in the company of stain-folk, dependent on them, trusting in them, and even admitting to somehow liking them. Well, almost.

A sudden sound brought Anna out of her thoughts. Ahead of her, Nike had given a low whistle, and stopped, half crouched, with her crossbow raised. Leviss knelt and waved Anna down. Moments later, he looked beyond Nike, then raised three fingers and smiled.

'They have come for us,' he said. As he spoke, three figures emerged out of the darkness. It was Bepsi-Loca and two other stain folk. They carried their spears at the hip, and their bows were slung across their shoulders.

'You're late,' said Bepsi, smiling as he came up to them. 'Mother has kept the soup cooking longer than she would wish, and the fire has no more than two hours left unless I can persuade these idle nephews of mine to go and scavenge some more wood.'

Nike gave her uncle a hug, stepped back and nodded to the other two men. 'We were delayed,' she said. 'at the Glass Tunnel.'

Bepsi-Loca grunted. 'That's no place to idle about in,' he said. 'The whole area is crawling with Chesterman's scouts.'

'Is that so, uncle? Well we didn't see one, did we, Anna-Seka?'

Anna smiled. 'Is camp far?' she asked.

For just a moment, Bepsi gazed at her. 'You look tired, lassie,' he said. 'Come on! It's not far, and there's food in the pot, and a warm bed awaiting ye. It's little enough, but it's home, and we are happy to share it with you.'

CHAPTER #2
THE FEAST

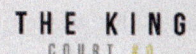

Meanwhile, far away across the vast and trackless wastes of the borderlands and beyond the Fence and the plains of the southern kingdom to the great city of Serenity itself all seemed to be peaceful. If you stood on the outer walls of that city and looked inwards to its heart you would be able to make out in the upper distance, the many-towered spires of the palace all brightly lit for the evening watch and hung with flags and banners.

Today was a feast day. It was a feast day in honour of the king, and many of the important nobles had been invited to the palace to help the king celebrate.

Although the king, renowned of course for his beauty, was respected and loved by many of his people, it was only on rare occasions that he appeared in public. On such occasions, his appearances were only brief, and usually to give a prepared speech, or award medals and decorations to members of his council, the armed forces or perhaps the security services. He was something of a recluse, isolated in his exclusive royal apartments clouds above the rest of the city, and even if there were few who dared to doubt his power and authority, there were a significant number among the highest rank of citizenry who whispered that he had perhaps passed the best of his days. As long as anyone could remember, the throne room remained empty, except for the ceremonial guardsmen who stood before the throne itself. But no one talked of abdication, or if they did it was in secret. Any criticism of the king invited arrest at the hands of the secret police, the feared Triple S.

As for the rest of the royal family, they had for the most part disappeared from public view, and only the upper courts of the city knew what had befallen them.

But today was a happy day. It was a feast day, called as it was every year to celebrate the last great battle. It was a battle which had seen the defeat of the enemy, and the destruction of the Old Town all those centuries ago. Stained and unstained parted. And with that victory had come the dawning of the age of Serenity. Of all the feast days, it was the only one to rank above Glamgel Day: the feast which honoured GlamTech and celebrated the discovery of the apparently miraculous formulation that had transformed the lives of almost every citizen of Serenity. While the common folk would celebrate any feast day as best they could with gatherings in market squares and food and drink shared from house to house, the higher ranks were required to attend more formal events held within the precinct of the palace itself. The activities went on for most of the day with displays by military bands, teams of marching girls, and choruses of specially trained singers all dressed in white robes. There were also strictly organised dances where dozens of competitors from each district whirled and pirouetted in elaborate routines before a panel of grey-masked and velvet-cloaked judges.

In Upper Town, which was divided into the four different 'courts of the nobles', separate ceremonies took place, designed to celebrate and emphasise the differences between each 'court'. It was here that the relative strength and influence of the great 'colleges' of Litra, Rebuild and Glamtech were most on show. The rivalry was obvious, and each college strove to make its presence felt, but the singular dominance of Glamtech was difficult to miss. It was even suspected that the king and his royal officials encouraged that rivalry, while making sure that no one college became too powerful in its own right. The pre-eminent status of Glamtech, however, was perhaps no better indicated than in the unexplained and unchallenged determination of the senior technician of Glamtech, lord Shadwatch, to go everywhere without a mask.

The wearing of masks by all citizens was written into law, and rigidly enforced with only one or two statutory exceptions. For example, if a member of the nobility was a contestant in an 'outshining', he did not wear a mask, and this always caused a stir of interest and gossip. Everyone was keen to see a celebrity unmasked, and an outshining was just such an opportunity. Also, at a particular event known as the 'day of the domes', nobles and celebrities appeared unmasked for a short time within the protective shelter of glass domes. Their 'beauty ratings' could then be observed, discussed and of course, admired by the normal citizenry who were encouraged to buy tickets for such events. Teams of officials called 'Graders' visited every house at least twice a year to assess every citizen's rank and beauty. During these compulsory 'beauty checks', DNA samples along with information sheets about each individual were relayed to a centralised bio hub called the Gene Pool, the rumoured heart of the city's bio-security system. It ensured the cleaning of the citizenry's beauty pool and lessened the chances of staining. Each new batch of Glamgel contained an updated formula that was then rationed at a friendly cost. 'Re-gradings' were not uncommon, and certified in law. And the mask was a symbol and badge of rank within the city.

But lord Shadwatch went everywhere unmasked, and no one, not even the security services or imperial police tried to intervene or arrest him. And no one was ever heard to comment. It was simply accepted, even though the mask was perhaps the pre-eminent symbol of Serenity and its declared independence.

Now, on this particular feast day, the factories were closed for one full shift and only the military units tasked with manning the defences of the city remained on duty. Street vendors in their merchant-masks roamed the crowded squares and high lanes selling all kinds of food and drink, as well as trinkets, silks and precious spices from unknown places far beyond the walls of Serenity.

As expected the weather was fine, but if you had climbed to the topmost tower of the palace citadel and looked to the north and west, you would have been able to see in the distance, on certain days, a dark and lowering cloud that hung over a high mountain on the borders of the Stain kingdom or outlands. It was from seasonal scrub fires, lit to keep the immediate area north of the Fence clear of vegetation. Today was such a day. But that did not dampen the spirits of the people of Serenity. Especially the spirits of those of the highest rank lucky enough to have received an invitation to the Royal Feast to be held in the great banqueting hall of the imperial palace that very night.

To be invited was a great honour. To attend was a great privilege. To be looked upon by the king for even an instant, was a memory to be treasured. But to be spoken to by the king or to see his face was a dream that few beyond the inner circle of the court ever realised.

And so when the trumpets sounded at sunset from the speakers on the ramparts of the central interchange, the guests in all their careful finery and matchless beauty (but with their faces concealed and protected by masks according to rank and to law) made their way from the outer wards. They passed through the Lion Gates, across the Court of Peace and into the elevators which led to the closely guarded sanctuary of the palace-basilica itself that often sat above the clouds.

Normally – and this was a long standing tradition – masks were to be worn throughout any royal feast, despite the impossibility of eating or drinking while wearing a mask. Food was always served, and it was always of the highest quality, but it was only there to act as a symbol of royal wealth and generosity. It always remained untouched throughout the feast, and guests had to content themselves with the pleasures of conversation and occasional entertainment.

Every so often, however, this tradition was suspended at the discretion of the king. No explanation was ever given, and the announcement was always made at the last minute.

And so on this particular day the guests arrived as usual in their festival finery and masked for the feast. However, some of the more favoured guests had already heard, by messages discreetly passed to them by senior officials of the royal household, that indeed on this night at this particular feast, the king had issued a 'feasting decree'. He decreed that when the feast commenced no masks were to be worn: for a period of no less than thirty minutes, and for no longer than an hour.

At every gate, at every entrance way, at every turn of a corridor or crossing of a bridge, the guests had to have their palms checked and the rankings of their masks verified by members of the Serene Security Service or Triple S. At this point they were then told that this particular feast was to be mask free. Accordingly, all food served at the feasting tables could be eaten. Of course it was seen as only a formality, but all was excitement, chatter and smiles as one by one, or in husband-and-wife pairs, the guests, with their masks now temporarily removed – according to the announced protocol of the palace for this particular feast - made their way to the outer reception area of the banqueting hall itself. There they assembled, and waited in hushed expectation for the moment when the high chancellor of the Chancellery and the supreme head of Glamtech (the developer and manufacturer of Glamgel) invited them to enter and take their places. At last the members of the inner court arrived, nodding to the waiting guests as they filed past them and into the hall. After them, came the high officials of Litra and Rebuild, the academic and engineering colleges of the Serene Kingdom, and second only to Glamtech. Then, when all were received, the chancellor resplendent in his robes of office, and escorted by two torch bearers arrived and gave a short speech of welcome. Moments later they were all seated about the long table in the centre of the glittering chamber called the 'high banqueting hall'.

The golden chair at the head of the table remained empty: the king would arrive later. At a signal from the Governor of the Feast, servants brought the first course, while musicians seated to one side on a raised platform, quietly played traditional harvest songs and country tunes. For a long time, no one spoke. Everyone knew the procedure. Only the king could break the silence, and the king was not present.

Nor was the queen present. The queen had not been at a royal function for some considerable time. Nor had she been seen outside the palace precinct. Nor within it.

The queen had gone, disappeared, vanished. And she had vanished along with her children and immediate family. But no one dared speak of this: certainly not within earshot of the king or his officials. Rumours abounded in the lower quarters of the city, but within the Upper Town and the palace precincts it was well known what had happened: the queen had been arrested, put on trial and exiled. Some claimed a worse fate had befallen the queen, but such stories were simply not believed. Not even the king would allow such a punishment. The queen had been exiled to a remote corner of the kingdom: that was customarily agreed among the nobility, most of whom knew exactly where she was, but there were few who dared to talk about it in public.

But, back to this particular feast:

The second course came and went. The musicians played on. The mask free edict was still in place. A certain nervousness grew among the guests, even as they ate: hushed whispers, sidelong glances, and an awkward stirring in seats. Only towards the head of the table, where the highest officials sat, was there an atmosphere of relaxed calm. And those guests, at the lower end of the same table, if they dared to glance towards the golden chair, would have noticed a particularly beautiful couple, a young man and woman, sitting opposite each other. The woman, of noble birth, was called Talessa. She was the daughter of Akton, the high chancellor. Even among the courtiers, her flawless beauty was renowned. Her name, in the ancient tongue, meant 'Sunrise', and her family was well-known and honoured throughout Serenity. The man, also a noble, was called Barvarik, a name popular in certain quarters of the Upper Town. He was known and well spoken of among the upper circle of courtiers, and his reputation rested on his prowess as a warrior. His name meant 'Strikes like a bear', but his tall, angular frame belied such a title. It was only the fierce light in his jet black eyes that revealed the measure of this soldier, and his strength. But now, as he leaned forward, cradling his wine cup and gazing at the woman opposite him, he whispered softly to her as if to someone he held in deep affection. And there was only gentleness in his expression.

It was a gaze that she returned, and anyone close enough to where they were sitting could tell at a glance that they were very much in love.

'Our Talessa has lost her heart to that young man,' whispered the high chancellor to his wife, as he flashed yet another look towards the doors to see if the king had arrived.

'And he to her,' replied his wife, hiding her comment behind her napkin.

There was no more time to reflect on this, for she had no sooner spoken than there was a sudden, crisp blast of megaphone speakers, the main doors swung open and the king at last entered the banqueting hall, escorted by his bodyguard. He wore no mask.

Everyone stood, saluted with right hand to left breast, and bowed their heads as the king swept past them. It was only when he arrived at the head of the table, that he acknowledged any of the guests or courtiers. He nodded in the direction of some Glamtech officials, paused to smile at the chief of staff, and his wife, and then at the last stopped and extended his hand to the High Chancellor.

'Is all ready, Akton?' he asked in a voice so quiet it could scarce be heard beyond a few paces.

The high chancellor took the king's hand, knelt and kissed the golden ring on the royal forefinger. 'All is ready, my lord,' he replied and then stood.

'My apologies for my lateness,' muttered the king, glancing towards Talessa for a moment. 'Affairs of state, you know.'

'You were not late, my lord,' said the high chancellor quickly. 'As you see, we began the meal on the hour,' he paused, 'as you instructed.'

The king grunted, waited for his bodyguards to take their station behind the throne, and then took his seat. For a long time, he sat motionless staring down at the table in front of him, as if waiting for something to appear. Then, suddenly he sighed, raised his eyes, and sat back. 'Continue,' he said.

Everyone, except the high chancellor sat down, but still no one spoke. A deep quiet, quieter even than the one that had preceded the king's arrival, filled the hall. Even the servants who had come up from the kitchens to serve the third course waited silently to one side of the entrance way. Somewhere, far along one of the corridors, a dog barked and its master called it to silence. The echoes died away. No one moved.

Then Akton, as chancellor, raised his cup. 'Welcome to this happy evening,' he said. 'And welcome to this great celebration of our great city in honour of our mighty king.' Then he nodded to a servant who stepped forward and filled his cup:

'A toast to our king! Who will call the toast?' The governor spoke and rapped his staff of office against the floor.

At first no one moved. At last, further down the table, a middle-aged and slightly stooped man got to his feet. He was of the merchant class, chosen for his wealth and skill in trading, but clearly less handsome than those above him. His name was Elfraed, and he had a reputation for plain speaking. It was not lost on the king, nor anyone else at the table, that Elfraed had left his cup on the table, and ignored his wife's nervous gesture that he should pick it up.

'My lords,' he said, his booming voice echoing around the gilded walls, 'let us toast our good king.' He paused. 'But let us also add our heartfelt wish that one day soon the queen and the rest of the royal family might one day return to Serenity and grace us with their presence. He paused again, and that the queen herself might sit alongside her husband once more in the throne room of Serenity.'

There was a gasp that ran along the length of the table. The guards that lined the walls straightened as one and brought their weapons to their chests. The king stared, his eyes dark beneath furrowed brows and his hand clenched about his own cup. Everyone of the guests knew, or at least suspected that their queen along with the rest of the royal family had been banished to a place called The Island some years before. It was an event that it was unwise to speak of, not even in the streets of the city, let alone within the palace, and in the presence of the king himself.

The high chancellor stepped towards the king and leaned forward as if to whisper to him, but was waved away. 'Hold your peace, Akton,' muttered the king. 'One of my citizens has spoken before you.' Then, without taking his eyes off the merchant Elfraed, the king slowly stood and raised his cup:

'To absent friends,' he said, and drank.

As one, the guests repeated the toast and raised their cups. The king nodded, and then gestured for Elfraed to be seated. 'I see that you have not forgotten our queen, Elfraed,' he began, 'and neither have I. Nor have I forgotten the reason for her departure, and the reasons which prevent her return.' He glanced down at his cup and then looked up again. 'Do you trust your king, Elfraed?'

The merchant looked surprised to be addressed directly by the king. He scrambled to his feet. 'Yes, my lord,' he said quickly. 'I would trust you with my life.'

The king gave a thin smile. 'Would you? Well, you may indeed have to entrust your life to me one day, especially if you let that wine in your cup do all your thinking for you. Do you understand what I am saying?'

The merchant gave a hasty bow, painfully aware that the captain of the king's guard was glaring at him. 'Yes, my lord,' he replied. 'Of course, my lord.'

Again the king smiled. 'Then tell me what I am saying, sir merchant.' He paused. 'And choose your words carefully.'

The merchant felt his wife's hand touch his, but he did not look down. He took a deep breath. 'My lord king,' he said carefully, 'you are saying that the queen and her household offended against the laws and constitution of Serenity, and therefore according to those laws, the queen was banished to The Island until such time as the high court might determine that she is able to return.'

This time the merchant lowered his head when he had finished speaking, and did not attempt to sit down.

The king grunted, and turned to his high chancellor. 'What should we do with this fellow, Akton? Tell me now.'

The chancellor did not hesitate. He looked up at the king. 'You are the law, sire. As you speak, so we do. But you do not have a rebel here, my lord. I am sure of it. He is of good family and good reputation. As you have rightly observed, the wine has become his master this night. Deliver him back into the hands of his good wife, and doubtless she will box his ears, and remind him how close he came to the gallows. That should make him one of your most loyal subjects.'

The king sighed. 'Ah, mercy. You offer me mercy as your answer.'

The chancellor nodded. 'Mercy is the gift of princes, my lord. It is more precious than the jewels in the royal crown.'

Now the king gave a short, bitter laugh. 'By the heavens, Akton. I look for judgement like a thunderbolt to sweep this simpleton away, and yet you counsel mercy.'

Again the chancellor nodded. 'Are we not taught that great kings place mercy over judgement, and you are without doubt a great king.'

'Am I? Am I so? I had not noticed.' At last the king sat down. He slumped back in his chair, and gazed up at the golden banner that overhung the table. 'Give me music, and give me wine. I need laughter. Not wisdom.' He gave a careless wave. 'This hall echoes like a tomb.' The high chancellor nodded to the chief steward who clapped his hands, and pointed to the musicians. Almost instantly there was music: a happy, tavern tune that fell strangely across the silent banqueting hall until at last the guests, relieved that at least no one had been arrested, began to talk quietly. And then after a while, they began to chatter amongst themselves and even laugh. The third course was served.

Talessa, who was seated within earshot of the king, took advantage of the welcome hubbub to lean across the table to Barvarik:

'Have you ever seen such courage?' she whispered, glancing in the direction of the man called Elfraed.

He smiled, and leaned forward himself, noting that the king had been distracted for a moment by the chancellor. 'Courage, you say?' he said softly. 'I saw a man who decided to play the fool, and ended by telling us all the truth.'

Talessa's eyes widened. 'Have a care, Barvi,' she replied, using the familiar form of his name. 'The king has shown you favour, but that will all be forgotten if he hears one word . . .'

She stopped, as Barvarik gently put a finger to her lips:

'Hush, Talle,' he said. 'And do not fear. I am all discretion.'

At that moment, a maid appeared carrying a silver dish of pastries. She nodded to Barvarik and then turned to Talessa:

'My lady,' she said, 'can I interest you in some of our cook's finest creations?' As she spoke, she presented the dish and placed it on the table between them. It was that movement that took Talessa by surprise. Normally, the dish would be held, and the pastries served with silver tongs or a slide, but instead, before Talessa could sit back, the dish had swept in front of her so that the edge caught her on the forearm. It was the lightest of touches, but Talessa felt a scratch, and when she looked there was just the trace of a red weal on her snow white skin.

'Oh, my lady!' The maid let go of the dish, and put her hand to her mouth. 'Forgive me!'

Talessa shook her head, content with the look of alarm on the maid's face. 'Think nothing of it,' she said. 'It is a scratch, no more. A little bit of Glamegel before I go to bed this evening, and it will be gone by the morning.' She paused. 'You are perhaps not used to serving at table?'

The maid blushed and lowered her head. 'I am from the Lower Town, my lady. We were sent for by the steward's commissioners, my sister and I as well as some of our friends. My parents were told that there were not enough palace servants this year to wait on table for the feast day. My father is an apothecary. I work in his shop.'

'I see.' Talessa smiled. 'Well, rest easy. I will not be reporting you to anyone, least of all the steward.' As she smiled, she glanced in the direction of the king, who was still talking with her father the chancellor. Then she turned to look at Barvarik

'What say you, my lord Barvarik. Shall we forgive this poor girl?'

Barvarik pretended to frown. 'Well, I don't know,' he said. 'She gave those pastries a fright, and if I hadn't caught them . . .' He smiled. 'No harm done. All is well.'

The maid smiled gratefully, and curtsied. 'Thank you, my lord.' She reached forward and picked up the tray. 'I must get back to the kitchen,' she said and disappeared.

'She was a strange one,' said Barvarik, then he touched Talessa on the arm. 'Is it serious?' he asked. 'We should get that scratch looked at. The medical team at the palace will want to check you out.' He paused. 'We can't be too careful. You know that. An injury like this, no matter how slight, can lead to a downgrading. You know the Graders, and how they operate. They are trained to ignore all background reasons for an incident. They simply assess on the basis of the incident and the incident alone. If any of them even suspects that you might have suffered a "flesh breach" as the Grading Department calls it, both you and your parents will be issued with a grading summons.'

Talessa blew on the scratch. 'I'll live,' she said lightly. 'The poor girl was just nervous. It's a mercy that she didn't hit me over the head with that tray.'

But even as she spoke a medical team, alerted to the incident, came up to the table, bowed to the king and then turned to Talessa:

'You are wounded, my lady?' said one of the team, a Glamtech nurse.

'It is nothing,' replied Talessa, 'just a scratch.'

'We will be the judge of that, my lady,' the nurse answered crisply, and coming forward, quietly took hold of Talessa's arm at the wrist and examined it. 'It is as you say, a scratch,' she said, 'but we must treat it in accordance with regulations.' Without waiting for a reply, she waved to a paramedic who quickly brought a medical bag to the table.

Moments later, with the treatment complete, the medical team left, after giving Talessa a stamped form with a pass code to show to security personnel at any checkpoint she had to pass through during the next three days.

Barvarik watched them go, and then turned to Talessa:

'It is just as well that scratch wasn't any deeper,' he said, 'or you'd be in a hospital treatment bay by now.'

They both laughed, the evening drifted on into happy conversation, and the incident was soon forgotten.

But a young man sitting on his own further down the table, had seen what had happened. From the moment that the maid had appeared he had not taken his eyes off her, and only when she had brushed passed him and gone on towards the entrance to the kitchens, had he switched his attention back to Talessa.

The young man was Shadwatch. He bore an old clan name from before the Great Burning and was well known as the senior technician at Glamtech. Next to the palace and the court administration, the department of Glamtech was the most powerful in the kingdom. It was said that all that was good and all that was evil came out of Glamtech. This was of course an exaggeration, but Glamtech had a fearsome reputation for developing and producing all kinds of innovations: tools, weapons, lighting and medicines. Glamgel was its most famous and utilised invention due to its anti-ageing properties, and this in the minds of many gave Glamtech, or Glamtech, pre-eminence over the other government departments, including the commissariat and security services. Most of Glamtech's work was top secret, and its top officials reported directly to the king and no one else, not even the high chancellor.

Of course Akton, working within the chancellery had his own network of spies and informers so there was not much that emerged from Glamtech that he did not already know about. Nevertheless, there was an unspoken tension between Glamtech, the palace administration and the chancellery. Moreover, the talk in the marketplace was that Glamtech had more influence in the affairs of state than was healthy for the kingdom. But with the sole rights to Glamgel firmly in Glamtech's grasp there were few folk who were willing to challenge their authority and influence. Of the other two departments or 'colleges', Litra worked more closely with Glamtech, and was even capable of producing its own technical innovations, such as the solar encapsuled Litra-light, widely used to power most of the kingdom.

But all that is an aside: the fact is that on this particular evening the young Shadwatch had recognised the maid when she first entered, and seemed puzzled to see her. He also took an interest in what was going on, because he had a deeper and secret interest in Talessa. They had grown up together, and had come to know each other well over the years, despite the restriction of so often having to meet and talk from behind the anonymity of masks. And although circumstances had drawn their paths apart some years before, he had never forgotten her. She was beautiful, but then so was everyone in the upper quarter of the city: breathtakingly beautiful. That was understood. Beauty was the passport to anywhere that mattered. However with Talessa, her beauty was quite something else. It was not simply the physical beauty of form, of complexion, of graceful movement. No, it was the beauty that springs from deep within: a beauty of the soul that wells up within a person and shines out of their eyes, and is heard in the very words they speak and the way that they speak them. And this was what Shadwatch saw and heard in Talessa. In short, he was fascinated by her, and quietly amazed that almost no one else had seen what he had seen in this noblewoman. Almost no one. Yes, there was the rub. In that single word almost, there lay the rub. One other man had discovered what he, Shadwatch had known for so long, and now that man, the object of Shadwatch's resentment and the man they called Barvarik, was Talessa's close friend. If something was not done about it soon, Shadwatch decided, this Barvarik would within the year become her chosen man. He knew, because he knew so much, that Talessa had first noticed Barvarik when she was only twelve and he was no more than fifteen. She had once passed a fleeting remark to Shadwatch about Barvarik when they had met in the market precinct one day, and he knew instantly that she was secretly drawn to the young warrior and his shy ways.

And so the lord of Glamtech ground his teeth as he watched the young couple. Well, he decided, if he could not stop the wedding, at least he would never attend it, even though all such high-born events were always graced by senior Glamtech officials, as a matter of form and government compliance. Someone tapped him lightly on the shoulder and he looked up: 'Mother,' he said quietly.

His mother, tall with raven black hair and milk-white skin, smiled and sat down next to him. 'We were hoping you might leave your place and join us,' she said, gesturing along the table to where a group of palace folk, men and women, were chattering and laughing.

Shadwatch turned away to look towards Talessa again. 'I am perfectly comfortable here, mother,' he said, his voice cool and drained of emotion.

She reached out and touched his hand. He pulled it away. 'You still miss your father,' she said quietly.

Without shifting his gaze, her son replied; 'I will miss him until the day he is avenged, mother.'

'The king's brother?'

'He murdered my father, mother. You know that. I will not rest until the debt is settled.' He paused. 'Blood for blood.'

'The blood of a prince?'

'The blood of a murderer.' Shadwatch drummed his fingers on the table. 'Go back to your guests, mother. Leave me to my unhappy thoughts.'

The lady Jetta, that was her name, tossed her head and smiled sadly. 'You have the same stubborn courage as your father.' She stood. 'Use that pretty head of yours before you act, Shadwatch. It was never proven that prince Marlin killed your father, even though it does seem likely.' She hesitated. 'But whatever you may think, that prince whose blood you desire has now fled the kingdom and lives somewhere among the stain-folk.'

Jetta's son frowned, and at last he looked at her. 'The king's brother will return, mother. He must. I know him. And when he returns, I will be waiting.'

Jetta glanced along the table, and gestured towards Talessa: 'She is beautiful, isn't she?'

In that moment, Shadwatch's expression softened. 'There is no greater beauty in this room. I would die for her, mother.'

Jetta gently squeezed her son's shoulder and turned away. 'You may have to die for her my son. I fear that her heart belongs to another.' She bowed to the guests sitting opposite, and moved away.

For a long time, Shadwatch stared at nothing. The music played on, the guests ate, drank and talked, but he sat alone, motionless and lost in his own world.

It did not go unnoticed. The king leaned towards Akton, the High Chancellor. 'Our young Glamtech lord seems distracted tonight,' he whispered.

'You mean Shadwatch, sire?'

'I do. He sits alone, scarcely acknowledges his mother when she speaks to him, and spends more time than is wise staring either at me or the noblewoman Talessa, I cannot tell.'

Akton smiled, and dipped bread into his wine. 'He is now of the age, sire when he will far more readily stare at a beautiful woman than he will even glance at a king.'

The king chuckled. 'Perhaps you are right. So even a man who seems to have nothing in his heart but science, and invention and endless formulae can find room in some corner of his thoughts for something we lesser mortals might call love?'

The High Chancellor nodded. 'Just so, my lord. He is of marriageable age, and since his father died . . .' His voice trailed away as he saw the king suddenly frown. 'forgive me, my lord,' he said hastily, 'I did not mean . . .'

The king waved his hand. 'I know exactly what you mean, chancellor, but fear not, you said nothing to deserve my displeasure.' He paused, and glanced again in Shadwatch's direction. 'Your words reminded me, that's all.' He looked up at the gilded rafters of the ceiling. 'Shadwatch's father was a good man: brilliant, loyal, trustworthy and hardworking. That's a rare combination these days, and we lost him to that rogue brother of mine. Cut down he was, without mercy, and all because of my brother's thirst for power, and his rage against the law of this land and the traditions of our fathers.'

The high chancellor took a deep breath. 'It was never proven, my lord.'

'Hah!' The king slapped the table, and several of the guests looked up. 'You always were the lawyer, Akton: so careful with legal niceties, and apt to miss the uncomfortable truth when it's staring you in the face.'

Akton nodded. 'Certainly the evidence weighed heavily against prince Marlin, my lord. On the same night that Shadwatch's father was murdered, he fled the kingdom, and has not been seen since.'

Raising one hand, the king studied his fingernails, then smiled. 'We send our scouts into Stain-land on the first day of every week, and on the last day they return and make their reports.'

'They do, my lord.'

'And yet, although they bring us all manner of information about all manner of people and places, not one of them, not one!' (for a moment he raised his voice) 'has been able to bring me any news of that brother of mine.'

'Lord Hartley tells me that he is confident of success, and expects to be bringing good news to the palace any day.'

'Does he now? Does he indeed? Well, perhaps he knows more than my own spies know, but I see precious little sign of this good news he talks of. Where is he, by the way? I expected to see him tonight.'

Akton coughed nervously, and glanced towards the doors as if hoping to see Hartley come marching into the banqueting hall. 'He sent word, my lord, that he had been delayed. There's a patrol come in late from the north-western quadrant of the Stain-lands. He was keen to see them the moment they had arrived.'

The king grunted. 'He's a hard worker is Hartley, I'll give him that. He knows where his duty lies. No lounging around here among all these over-fed creatures of the courts and Upper Town. What say you, chancellor?'

Akton looked steadily at the king. 'It is a formal celebration, my lord king, decreed by the will of the assembly, and upheld for generations. Your people have come to do you honour.'

'Yes! Yes!' The king waved his hand. 'I know all that, Akton, but look at them man. They've come for the food, and they've come to be seen. They can sit here before me with their masks off, simpering away like so many fish in a bowl, and hoping they might catch my eye and be tossed some morsel of what-have-you.' He glared at the table. 'Well, all that is going to change.'

'To change, my lord?'

'Yes, to change and to establish something new by royal decree, and decree absolute.' He paused. 'From this day, all formal festivals of feasting at the palace and within the royal precincts will require that guests wear masks throughout, according to our precious tradition.' He paused. 'The royal protocol known as mask free is to be withdrawn on a permanent basis. From tomorrow it will be as if such a protocol and mark of favour on my part never existed. As I am sure you will agree, masks will henceforth be worn on all occasions as a mark of respect to myself, the king.' Again, he paused, then went on:

'We need to tighten things up, chancellor. These people have grown fat, sleek and over indulged during these past months.'

'My lord!' Akton lowered his voice, and leaned forward. 'If the people hear you, they will not understand.'

'The people, you say?' The king gave a short laugh but then lowered his voice. 'The people? You know them, Akton. Look at them, now! They are all of royal blood or the first three ranks. There are none here below noble rank, apart from one or two hangers-on from Litra.'

'Hangers-on, my lord?' Akton glanced around nervously.

'Yes, hangers-on: simpletons brought up from the lower city on supposed scholarships and sent to do courses at the Litra Halls of Learning. You should know, chancellor because it was you who introduced the whole idea.'

'And it bears your seal of approval your majesty,' replied Akton holding his gaze.

The king stared back. 'So it does. So it does.' He hesitated. 'Tell me, high chancellor, are these scholarships of yours bearing fruit?'

Akton risked a frown. This conversation was not going well. Was the king already drunk after so little wine?

'My lord,' he said quietly. 'Only yesterday the dean of Litra academic studies told me that all the Fourth Rank scholars, both men and women, were excelling in their courses.'

The king smiled and filled his cup. 'Well, that's lucky then,' he muttered, and looked away as if wanting to end the conversation. But even as he turned he caught sight of a figure who had appeared in the doorway at the far end of the hall. It was a man, tall and broad-shouldered, with almost pure white hair hanging straight to his shoulders. He wore the deep blue cloak of Rebuild, and carried a golden staff in one hand. He had already removed his mask, and the king who had the eyes of a hawk, recognised him in an instant.

'Ah,' he said, and clapped his hands. 'Calmeron. Here's an honest fellow, come all the way from the outer defences to pay homage to his lord.'

Akton nodded: 'There is much to do on our border defence works, sire. The scouts of the stain-folk are getting bolder, and even some of the wild folk have been spotted near one of our border forts. The Rebuild engineers have been busy.'

'Rebuild has all the resources it needs?' asked the king raising his eyebrows.

'Yes, sire. Calmeron met with me last week. He presented his latest construction programme, and said that his men had built a new highway to bring supplies and salvage from the interior of the north-western quadrant.'

'We can afford this, Chancellor?'

Akton shrugged. 'We don't have any choice, my king. If we stop building, and cut back on our expeditions into the outlands, we will soon become vulnerable to attack. It is just as well that the assembly voted through the extra taxes and tribute levies last month.' As he finished speaking, Calmeron, who by now had made his way along the length of the banqueting hall, approached the king and saluted.

'My lord king,' he said crisply, I bring greetings from the high council of Rebuild.'

The king acknowledged his salute, and gestured for him to sit down. 'And where are the council of Rebuild based at present ?' he asked.

Calmeron took his place by the king. Reaching into his tunic, he pulled out a flask and carefully poured it out so that the contents slowly spread on the table. A map slowly appeared in the pool of Glamgel liquid. It was an accurate, detailed and colourful map. Without hesitating, Calmeron carefully turned it so that the king could see it better, and stabbed with his finger at a point part way up the map towards the centre.

'See, my lord,' he said to the king. 'We have established a new Rebuild site just beyond the Great Wall or Fence in the third quadrant, due north of our main base at Arx. It overlooks the imperial highway that we finished constructing last spring.'

The king leaned forward and frowned. 'That must be at least two kilometres north of original Fence-line. Is it safe?'

Calmeron smiled. 'Perfectly, my lord king. It has four high towers, curtain walls twelve metres thick and two defended gateways.'

'And a permanent garrison?'

'Of course, my lord. And we have increased the number of master-armament technicians and weapon specialists. It also has the latest Glamtech searchlight batteries complete with Litra lighting systems..'

'You have done this because members of the high council are based there?'

'Precisely, my lord. The high council is keen to be at the sharp end of things, so to speak, and the imperial highway runs directly into the heart of Stain-land for at least forty kilometres now. Whoever controls the highway, holds the key to the ancient kingdom, or what's left of it.'

Leaning back, the king smiled. 'Ah, at last! Some good news: progress on the northern borders, and the first clear sign for months that we have a foothold in the third quadrant.' He looked at the High Chancellor. 'What say you Akton?'

Akton nodded to the king, reached out and slid the map closer. He studied it, rubbing his chin thoughtfully, and leaning forward for a moment before sitting back. 'It looks reasonably secure,' he said, 'but I think we should get some experts from Litra to go with Calmeron to assess it. If we let the council at Arx know, they should have no objection.'

Calmeron raised his eyebrows but said nothing. The king shook his head. 'What do those stargazers and philosophers know about defence systems,' he said, clenching and unclenching his fist, a sure sign that he was irritated to the point of anger.

The gesture was not lost on Akton. He gave a slight shrug, 'As his majesty pleases,' he said, his voice level. 'Litra has a well-established department of technical and military studies, and supplies Glamtech with specialist research on weapons development, but that of course is no reason for them to have an opinion worth listening to.'

There was an awkward silence. At last Calmeron spoke. 'The high council of Rebuild welcomes any assistance endorsed by the palace,' he said quietly, 'but it is my opinion, and also that of the Arx administration, that this particular Rebuild base is well resourced.' He paused. 'We have already had an inspection by officials of the SSS, who came with the approval of the royal secretariat and the interior ministry at Arx. I understand that they liked what they saw.'

The king gave a short laugh, and slapped the table. 'Well, that's decided then! No need to be disturbing the councillors of Rebuild. If those foxes in the Triple S are happy . . ."' He hesitated, and looked at Akton: 'We are agreed?'

The high chancellor nodded and pushed the map back towards the king. 'As your majesty wishes,' he answered.

Little had been heard of this conversation. Most of the guests were too busy enjoying the freedom of the feast, and the opportunity to meet and talk without having to wear their masks. Even most of those sitting close by did not hear what the king was saying to the two officials. Nor did the servants hear. They were occupied with making sure that the last of the food and drink was served before the governor of the feast – usually the palace steward – declared festivities to be at an end. And besides, these servants had been trained from their youth to be deaf to whatever was not intended for their ears.

But two of the guests had heard. Both Talessa and Barvarik had stopped talking to one another some moments ago. They were still leaning forward, facing one another as though they were deep in conversation, but they had not uttered a single word for some time. Even as they looked into each other's eyes, they both knew that they were over-hearing a conversation that it would surely be treason to repeat within or without the palace walls.

As the high chancellor pushed the map towards the king and the conversation came to an end, Barvarik winked at Talessa, touched her lightly on the hand and whispered: 'All is not well in this part of the forest, I think.'

Talessa smiled nervously, but did not reply. She sat back, and wiped her lips with her napkin. It was that slight movement that caught the attention of the king. He looked at Talessa, gave a puzzled frown and then smiled:

'Is this feast to your liking, my lady?' he asked.

Talessa looked at the king, blushed and then inclined her head. 'It is, my lord king,' she replied.

'Then that is well,' said the king. 'It is just that I thought you perhaps looked a little unwell.'

Talessa's blush deepened. 'I thank the king for his concern, but I can assure you, my lord, that I am quite well.'

The king stared at the young noblewoman for a moment. Again, a frown flickered across his brow, then he shrugged and turned to the high chancellor:

'Time for me to go, I think, chancellor. I believe this feast has run its course. Tell the people. The mask free is over."

The high chancellor took his cue with a resigned shrug. He stood, and signalled towards the steward who stepped forward from his position by the doors. Then he raised his staff of office and rapped it three times on the marble floor. The hall fell silent.

'The mask free ends! The king will retire,' said the steward, his parade-ground voice filling the room.

Everyone put their masks on and stood while the king, with a discreet bow, rose from his chair, pulled his cloak about his shoulders and walked the length of the hall towards the doors. His bodyguard closed around him, without a word being spoken. They escorted the king through the doors and down the long, gilded corridor towards the royal apartments.

Although it was accepted that the feast might have continued for a little while, the steward noted the customary nod from the high chancellor and struck the floor again with his staff:

'And that concludes the feast,' he said. 'Guests may leave. Remember, if you have not done so already, to re-apply your masks with the code clearly visible before leaving the hall. Security checks will depend on it.'

It wasn't long before Talessa and Barvarik found themselves crossing an inner courtyard between the banqueting hall and the main gate. They put on their masks before the first security check, and joined the stream of guests heading for the guard of honour which had been drawn up at the great tower which guarded the entrance to the palace and the inner courts. The court masks, with their engraved number and code, concealed their faces but were necessary to pass through the frequent checks of the SSS personnel.

Everyone understood that within Serenity the wearing of masks in public was compulsory, except for military personnel on active service. Developed by Glamtech, the court masks were exclusively designed for the nobility. They were strapless and by technology only know to Glamtech, simply hung on the wearer's face. The chrome-like full face covering offered protection against any accidental blows or scratches which might mar the beauty of the wearer, but still allowed enhanced vision, the ability to breathe and speak freely and a certain air of mystery not enjoyed by the folk of the lower sections of the Lower City. Masks worn in the Lower City were by law much more simply and crudely made. They were cheaper and less inefficient than those of

Upper Town and the courts.

Barvarik took Talessa by the hand as they walked across the cobbled courtyard. 'You should get that scratch seen to,' he said quietly.

'I told you,' whispered Talessa, 'but if it helps you to stop worrying, I will go to the medical centre tomorrow and get it checked.'

Barvarik gave an unseen smile. 'Thank you,' he replied, and paused. 'I worry for you.'

They were approaching the guard of honour, when Talessa spoke again:

'I am more worried by that conversation we overheard,' she said. 'The king and my father seem to have their differences.'

'They are not always the best of friends,' said Bavarik, lowering his voice, 'but they are both committed to the prosperity and safety of Serenity.' He released Talessa's hand as they came up to the gateway, and saluted the honour guard which had come crisply to attention, weapons held at 'present', and heads erect.

Passing between the guards, they offered their palms to the SSS officials who quickly scanned them, and code-checked their masks. They were waved on and soon found themselves in the outer precinct of the palace court along with the other guests. Carriages, chariots and other vehicles had arrived to ferry the guests back to their homes, and the whole area was lit by the bright white lights of the Litra Energy System.

Barvarik looked up at the stars. 'Beautiful,' he said. But even as he spoke, there was a trumpet blast via the court speakers, and rockets of every colour filled the sky. The annual fireworks display had begun. This night it was even more spectacular than the displays that had come before. With signs of trouble brewing on the borders the king had ordered that the fireworks be as dramatic and awe-inspiring as possible. Glamtech had not let him down.

The people gasped as they lifted their heads to the streams of coloured rocketry, the multiple bursts of blue, red, orange, white and green, and the fiercely glowing flares which fell like radiant blossoms above the city.

Between the echoing thunder of explosions as the rockets rose, weaved and spread their lights across the sky, both Talessa and Barvarik could hear the distant cheering of the folk of the lower city who had come out into the streets to watch the display.

'We have a great city,' said Barvarik.

Talessa nodded. 'I wonder if they can even see this from the borders,' she replied.

CHAPTER #3
THE WAY HOME

In the heart of the third quadrant of the outlands, Anna-Seka sat by the camp fire and gazed up at the stars. It seemed so peaceful. As she lowered her gaze and looked towards the south, she could see a faint glow on the distant horizon. It seemed to pulse and flicker in the darkness. She nodded to herself: 'The festival,' she whispered.

Someone tapped her on the arm. It was Nike. 'Thinking of home?' the Stain-girl asked.

Anna-Seka smiled. 'I like it here,' she said. 'I am among friends, I think.'

There was a silence. The others seated about the fire had stopped talking and were looking at her.

'That's a rare thing to hear someone from the Great City say,' said Bepsi-Loca, putting down his cup. 'You do us honour, lassie.'

Anna shrugged. 'It is easily given. You found me as a stranger, you helped me, even though you are stain-folk and I am . . .' she paused, 'of the City. And now you have given me fire and food and shelter.'

Bepsi-Loca smiled. 'It is our way,' he said. 'You gave us your trust, we give you our fire.'

From the other side of the fire, and almost lost in the shadows, Leviss leaned forward and tossed a branch into the flames. 'Not all the city-folk who come our way are so deserving,' he said. 'They come to spy and to steal, so we welcome them with our arrows and our spear-points.'

'I have heard of this,' said Anna quietly. She looked up at the stars again. 'We can share the stars, why is it that we cannot share the land beneath them?'

Someone laughed, but there was sadness in the sound. 'There is a hunger in your city that cannot be satisfied,' came an aged voice and Anna looked to see one of the elder-folk gazing at her across the fire. His grizzled face had seen many winters, and his shoulders were stooped with years of work in open fields. But his eyes shone in the light of the flames, and his hands were strong about his cup.

'Go on, father,' said Anna-Seka using the term kept for the older citizens of her city.

The man nodded to acknowledge the courtesy, and tipped the dregs of his cup into the flames: 'Your king wants what we cannot give him, so he sends his soldiers to take it from us,' he said. 'And his desire is without end. It is long since that his hunger became greed, and now his greed becomes cruelty. The more he takes, the more he wants. His belly is never full, so that the harder we fight to keep our own, the more fiercely he raises his hand against us.' He reached for a branch and stirred the embers at the edge of the fire. 'It is a kind of madness, I'm thinking.'

'We have many people, father,' replied Anna. 'The streets and markets of Serenity are crowded, always crowded. They have to be fed, and our farms are too small and our cattle and sheep are too few. Where should we go, else we starve?'

'Somewhere else, lassie,' answered the elder. 'And where ever you go, you should think to ask before you take, and not to take the very best. It's better that way, for everyone.'

'It's a common enough courtesy,' added Nike, 'and it keeps the blood of innocent folk from the dust.'

For a while Anna did not reply, but stared at the glowing embers and thought of home. At last she looked up. 'I will not speak against my people,' she said, 'nor will I hold to what you say about my king.' She paused. 'But I will never forget your kindness to me. You could have easily treated me as an enemy, and no one, neither of Stain-land nor of Serenity would have found that strange.'

'And so?' Bepsi-Loca gazed at Anna-Seka with a faint smile.

Anna returned his gaze. 'Tomorrow, I must return to the Great City. I will report to my commander, and I will tell him what I have seen.'

'You will tell him everything?'

'I will tell him everything he needs to know.'

'Which is?'

It was Anna's turn to smile. 'I will tell him this: that the area of the quadrant that I scouted as assigned is nothing but a wasteland, burnt out, devastated, and deserted. No one walks these lands, I will say, and the land itself is diseased. The smell of death hangs heavy in the air, and all the wells and streams are poisoned. Only vultures remain, and they do not stay for long.' She hesitated as those listening to her, took in her words, and the meaning of them. 'I will tell my commander that the land is cursed, and there is nothing worth the taking.'

Bepsi-Loca stood up. 'You would break your oath to your commander?'

Anna-Seka lowered her head. 'I would do what I must and keep faith with my friends.'

'Friends are we? Twice you have said it now, and yet you hardly know us.' The Stain-captain frowned.

'I know that you are stain-folk and that you have every reason to hate me, but instead . . .'

'Perhaps we mean to betray you at the end?'

'I did not see that in your eyes, captain, nor in the eyes of any of your folk here.'

It was Bepsi-Loca who now fell silent. He turned away took two, then three paces into the shadows, and then returned. 'You are a strange one, lassie,' he said at last, 'but I can't help but like ye.'

Anna smiled sadly at the flames and then looked up: 'Then give me leave to return to the border tomorrow. If I leave at first light, I should make the first border-post by noon, and if fortune favours all of us, you will neither see me again nor hear any more of me. Nor will I suffer my people to trouble you in your lands.'

The captain gave a shake of his head and grinned. 'This is a rare gift you offer us, and all for a handful of kindness: a kindness so light on the wind that it could blow away like chaff before the thresher's flail.'

'A handful of kindness,' repeated Anna quietly. 'That is beautiful.' She paused. 'The city I come from prides itself on its beauty and the beauty of its citizens, but you never hear words as beautiful as that in our streets.'

'Hah!' Bepsi-Cola grinned again. 'Then it is a poor city you come from, lassie, despite its shining towers and streets of gold.' He turned to Nike. 'You'd best get some rest, youngster. You and Leviss will escort our guest to the border tomorrow.'

Nike nodded. 'All the way to the border?'

'Only as far as the Shuppin Xenta. You know it, don't you. It's just off the main highway and about five kilometres from the northern most watch tower.'

'The highway the Serenity-folk built last spring?'

'The very same. Don't go near it mind. That highway tower has a spyglass that sees everything.' He paused. 'We have lost folk there before.'

'I know it,' said Nike, 'but don't worry. We will see her safely past the mantraps and briar swamps, and only turn back when we see the signal flags of the tower.'

Bepsi-Loca nodded. 'See you do, my lass. I'm only sending you because you're the best at your trade in our family, and I know you won't go anywhere without that brother of yours.'

Nike laughed. 'He has the eyes of a hawk and the appetite of a buck beaver, but sometimes he comes in useful.'

Leviss swallowed the piece of pie he was chewing and looked up. 'Ho, little sister,' he said, 'let me take my bow with me tomorrow, and I will find you a young stag to bring home for supper.'

They all laughed, someone threw another branch on the fire, and one by one they pulled their cloaks about them and lay down to sleep.

Only Bepsi-Loca and another man stayed to keep watch. Anna waited until everyone had settled and then found Bepsi-Loca who was sitting at the base of a rocky outcrop just beyond the camp. She sat down beside him, and without saying anything, pressed something into his hand. He opened his hand, and glanced down. It was a golden locket.

'What's this lassie?' he said.

'It's a token,' she said, 'a token of my family. Anyone in Serenity who sees it, can tell at a glance the rank of its owner. If you turn it over, you will see some markings. That's my family-code and status.'

'A dangerous thing for an outlander like myself to carry?'

Anna-Seka shrugged. 'It's called a gift-token,' she said. 'We give them to those we trust, and those we wish to reward. If you give my name, as you show the token, it becomes a passport.'

'And if I forget your name?'

Anna smiled. 'Then you are a dead man.'

Bepsi-Loca smiled in return, grunted, and hooked it onto the chain around his neck next to some relics from the old world. One resembled a tag with the engravings 'Visa Gold'. 'I thank you, lassie, and it's a fine honour you show me.' He leaned back and looked up at the stars. 'But there's nothing on this earth would make me want to go within a day's march of that great city of yours.'

'Sometimes our fortunes take us down paths we do not wish to tread,' said Anna. 'My father told me that.' She hesitated. 'I miss him.'

'He has passed to the long sleep?'

'He works in the palace. It is not often that he is seen beyond its gates.'

A nightjar called somewhere in the darkness, and Bepsi-Loca instinctively gripped his crossbow. He stared for a moment, and then relaxed. 'Only one call,' he said, 'Ye need to get ready when someone answers.'

'Someone?'

'Aye. That bird only calls to mark its territory. It does not expect an answer.'

'I never knew that.'

Bepsi-Loca glanced at the girl. 'Your father: he is an important man, then?'

Anna gave a shrug. 'Some folks would say so. He speaks to the king.'

'Does he now? And does the king listen?'

'Papa never says, and I never ask.' Anna gave a little sigh. 'I should get some sleep.'

'Aye, lass. So ye should. Tomorrow will be a longer day than most, and you will need your wits about ye.'

The girl-scout stood. 'Thank you again, for that you have done.'

Bepsi-Loca looked up at her. 'And thank you, lassie, for all that you are thinking to do.' He paused. 'For us, mind.'

As Anna-Seka walked back to the fire, she heard the Stain-captain get to his feet, and give a low whistle. From somewhere in the darkness away to the right there came another whistle. The other guard was in position and all was well.

In the morning, before the sun rose, Anna-Seka set off for the borders with Nike and Leviss. It was still dark, but the sky was lightening in the east, and a fine day was promised. Bepsi-Loca had got up early to see them clear the camp, but apart from the two guards of the dawn watch no one else was awake.

No one spoke, even in farewell. All was done with nods and smiles, and at the end a swift embrace. Only as they disappeared into the thin morning mist did Bepsi-Loca speak, and this only to himself. 'The heavens keep ye,' he muttered, but they didn't hear. Nor did they turn, and in a moment they were gone. Putting his staff across his shoulder the Stain-captain walked slowly back to the camp. Breakfast first, he decided, and then we'll take a wide reach to the north and west, circle back and be here again by supper time. Hopefully, he would have a fire lit and the pottage-pot bubbling by the time that Nike and Leviss returned.

It was towards noon, that Anna and the others reached the low scarp that crests near the imperial highway and looks south towards the first of the border-forts. They had made good progress. The skies were bright and clear, but it was not hot, and a slight breeze at their backs made the journey easier. Only once had they stopped, and that was for a quick drink at a fast-flowing stream that cut down through the foothills. They had time to take a brief meal of bread and cheese before pressing on.

They saw no one, but kept close to tree lines and undergrowth just in case. Once Leviss scrambled up to the top of rocky outcrop to scout the way ahead, and also to check if they were themselves being followed, but he saw nothing.

'As empty as a clean pot,' he said as he slithered back down, and brushed his hands. 'Not even a carrion crow or a plains rabbit.'

'That's good then,' replied Nike, 'but keep a sharp eye. The closer we get to the border, the more dangerous it will be.'

'Wild-folk?' asked Anna as they set off again.

'Any folk,' said Nike. 'There's none friendly in these parts. We are well beyond our tribal lands, and anyone we meet is bound to have a reason not to welcome us.'

'Even my people?' said Anna.

'Huh!' Nike quickened her pace. 'Especially your people. They will come after us because we are stain-folk. They will come after you simply because of the company you keep.'

And so at noon, they stood atop the scarp and studied the way ahead. The sun was arcing across the sky high to the south, and the breeze that had been at their backs all day suddenly swung to the west and strengthened.

'Best be on our way,' said Nike. 'We'll be standing out sharp and clear on this ridge, and any scout worth his salt will pick us out easily.'

Leviss nodded and pointed away to his left. 'And, see, look now! There's clouds a-rising on the western hills. If I know that breeze, it'll be bringing a storm our way before too long.' As if all had been agreed, he shouldered his spear and began to lope away down the steep slope of the scarp.

Nike watched him go, and smiled. 'There goes my brother,' she said, 'choosing the way ahead without thinking to ask.'

Anna shaded her eyes and studied the track he was taking: it led down between two boulders and past a stand of heath-land birches. 'Your brother has chosen well,' she said.

Nike shrugged. 'He has that, and I shouldn't be surprised. My uncle taught him well.' She slung her crossbow, and loosened the dagger at her belt. 'Come on,' she said.

They followed Leviss down the scarp, turning across the slope at its steepest points, and scrambling down among the heather and long grass. The valley floor lay far below, and Anna reckoned to herself that it would be at least an hour before they reached its shelter. There was still no sign of life apart from some circling birds, high up and away to the east. Anna was puzzled. This was good land, she said to herself, well set to the sun, and well grassed, but no one seems to have lived here for years, or even passed this way.

She stopped and looked around. There was something wrong. It was too quiet. That was a lesson Hartley had taught her. 'The quieter it is, the more dangerous it is,' he used to say to her when they were tracking along the practise routes just inside the border. 'The eye of a hawk makes no sound, and it's the eye of a hawk that will find you out.'

'Anna-Seka!'

Anna looked down the slope. Nike was waving to her. 'Come on!'

She hurried down to where the stain-girl was waiting for her. 'Sorry,' she said as she came up to her. 'I was just taking a second look.'

Nike grinned. 'You feel it too? Too quiet, isn't it? My father, who was trained in tracking by the warlord Chesterman, always used to say that silence is the first cousin to trouble when you are in open country.' She gestured towards the valley beneath them. 'See that stand of trees down there? When we reach it, choose a place to hide out for a bit, while Leviss and I scout the way ahead. The border fence is closer than you think, and there could be patrols almost anywhere south of that valley.'

Anna nodded. 'Do you think we'll reach the fence and tower by nightfall?'

'Not if we stand here talking, we won't.' Nike smiled and slapped Anna on the shoulder. 'Not long now. Once we get ourselves across the valley, we're as good as there. I won't be taking you right to the fence, mind. Just as far as Shuppin Xenta. You'll be able to see it from those trees.'

'And the highway?'

'Aye, and the highway, but we'll steer well clear of that. Anything that comes along that road is seen in an instant, and marked as enemy or friend.' She laughed. 'If you are a friend, they'll feed ye, if you're an enemy,' she paused and drew her hand across her throat, 'that's all ye'll get.'

Again, Anna nodded. 'Let's go,' she said.

They came to the forest within the hour. Anna sat down gratefully in the shelter of the trees while Nike and Leviss made ready to scout the way ahead.

'We'll be back before you know it,' said Nike. 'I'll whistle twice, you reply with one whistle, but don't show yourself until you see us for sure.'

Anna nodded. 'I'll be here,' she said.

She waited until they had crossed an open meadow beyond the tree line and disappeared in among some rocky outcrops covered with brush. For a moment she thought of closing her eyes and resting. Just for a moment.

Even as she closed her eyes, she tried to open them again, telling herself that even if she only slept for a minute, it could be fatal. 'The forest can be your friend,' Hartley used to tell her, 'or it can be your enemy. You can never trust it, no matter how much you think you know it.'

And so she sat and waited, finishing the last of her water, and rubbing some on the back of her neck as she stared at the way Nike and Leviss had gone. And as she stared she began to count the minutes as they slipped by. 'Stay awake,' she told herself, 'you must stay awake.'

She waited for an hour. There was still no sign of them. The sun touched the top of the ridge beyond the rocky outcrops and threw shadows across the meadow. She stopped counting. There was no point. Nike and Leviss were late, and that was that. Standing up, Anna strung her bow, and nocked an arrow.

'No point in staying here,' she muttered to herself. 'If they have struck trouble, I'm no use to them where I am now.'

Looking around and stopping for a moment to scan the meadow, she stepped out of the forest and into the meadow. As she began to cross the meadow, all weariness left her. She walked freely and like a hunter: crouched, head raised, her bow brushing the knee length grass and making it sigh as she passed.

Almost immediately she caught sight of a long, low concrete building streaked with rust and partly overgrown with creepers and brush.

Large letters of painted iron, some twisted, others broken formed part of a long lost name or title.

'Shuppin Xenta,' she whispered to herself, and moved away from it, keeping to the middle of the meadow, and heading for the outcrops which lay about a bowshot south of where she now was. After she had taken no more than another twenty paces, she glanced to her left and saw something beyond the concrete building that made her stop, go down on one knee and then lie full length in the grass.

It was the imperial highway, and it was no more than a kilometre away. To Anna it was a magnificent sight. As the roadway approached the border and the first of the great towers, a series of pillars and arches raised it above ground-level to a height of at least fifty feet. All the brickwork was plastered over with a shining white covering developed by Glamtech. It was said to be able to resist or deflect any missiles fired at it by stain and wild folk, or any other invaders. Leastways, that is what Hartley had told Anna, and as far as she knew, he never lied.

But what most drew Anna's attention to the highway was the sight of groups of people walking along it. She could not tell if they were armed, but she supposed that they were, and even at that distance she could see that they were nearly all marching in ranks. At least two of the groups carried battle standards at their head, and Anna could just make out some men on horseback. Something made her keep down, and only raise her head to the level of the grass-top. She knew that the folk she was watching were her folk, but she was equally certain that if she was spotted, alone and in the open on the wrong side of the border, she could expect to be shown no mercy. Only when they had retrieved her body would they realise that they had accidentally killed a city scout, and a member of Serenity's nobility. And then of course there would be an enquiry, and perhaps even a trial and some sort of retribution, but that would be of little use to Anna and her family. She smiled to herself. How Hartley would laugh when she finally made it back across the border, reported to him and told him of all her adventures. She could hear him now:

'Anna, Anna, how often have I told you? Keep to your chosen path, and stay on your own when you are north of the border. You are a lone scout, not a squad-scout. That is how I have trained you. And I certainly didn't train you to mix with stain-folk.' He would frown, and lower his head as he spoke. He always did that. And Anna always knew to wait. At last, if she waited, there would come a pause, a long pause, maybe five seconds. Then he would slowly straighten and look at Anna with those deep, dark kindly eyes of his:

'O daughter of Serenity,' he would say – how clearly she could see it! – 'I care for you as if you were my very daughter, and I am as happy to see you come safely home with that silly head of yours on those young shoulders as I am about anything else this day.'

And then at last he would smile, look up at the windows of the office and laugh. 'We'll not be putting this report in writing, will we?'

And that would be all.

Anna-Seka leaned to one side and looked at the outcrops and the ridge beyond. Where had Nike and Leviss got to? There was no sign of them. She watched the shadows cast by the setting sun creep across the meadow. It was only a matter of time: soon she too would be covered by shadow, and that would be her chance to slip away and make for the shelter of the outcrops.

She waited, half expecting to see Nike and Leviss appear at any moment, but another hour passed and there was nothing. That hour had given her time to think. If they had got lost, they would understand that she could not wait for them beyond sunset. And if they managed to make their way back to where they had left her, and found her gone, they would reach the same conclusion. But if they had been taken prisoner, then there was nothing more that she could do for them, nor they for her.

As the vast shadow of highway passed over her, she stood, confident of its shelter. To get home: that was all that was left to her. Crouching once more, and drawing her bow to a quarter-draw, she made her way towards the outcrops.

A short while later, as the darkness of early evening deepened, she cleared the outcrops, found a deer trail and followed it towards the border. The going was easy as the path wound its way through scrub and bracken, and she soon found herself approaching the border fence. The moon rose, lighting the way ahead, and the storm that they had feared never came. The night sky was clear and bright. For a moment she paused to check that no one was following her, and then she pressed on. The Fence or Wall seemed impossibly high to her as she neared it. The huge steel pylons loomed above her, their tops lost in darkness. Sheets of metal, riveted in a great curtain, held in place by massive cables and anchored by a series of concrete supports made the Fence appear more like the wall of a fortress. But it had always been called 'the Fence' in the college of scouts, and it had always served as an apparently impregnable barrier between the kingdom of Serenity and the outlands.

When she was within a bowshot of the Fence, Anna stopped, unstrung her bow and rested it across her shoulder. Carefully she studied the barrier ahead of her and the terrain in front of it. She could see the light from several watchtowers away to her right, but what took her attention most was the vast squared monolith of the Great Tower, standing out against the first of the evening stars to her left. That was where the imperial highway, atop its mighty viaduct, passed through the Fence via the Great Gates and on into the kingdom itself.

Of course she could go there, somehow, present herself to the guards and be taken to the SSS Border Office for questioning. Processing would follow and – with luck – she would eventually be released with a pass for the city. That seemed simple, but it was not recommended. Not for a lone scout in the service of a mentor like Hartley. The risks were too great.

'You are a ghost, Anna,' he used to say to her. 'You have been chosen and trained to pass unrecognised into the outlands, and to return unseen. That is our way. We are effective because folk on both sides of the Fence scarcely know of our existence. SSS patrols they know, scout squads they know, and military units they know, but for the most part they are blind to the lone scouts. The king knows, as do his advisers. The head of Glamtech knows, and the senior command of the SSS, but they do not talk of what they know. Over the years, vague rumours have sometimes slipped out and these have slowly changed into wild stories of a legendary circle of elite warriors who roam the outlands at will, defending the helpless and watching over the borders. No one really believes such tales, and they are encouraged not to enquire any further. Our mystery is our greatest protection, and our best asset. That is why you must always use a 'sally way' when crossing the border.'

And that message was written on Anna's heart. Indeed, although she knew Hartley as her mentor, she knew none of the other recruits she had been trained with. Friendships were not encouraged, personal names were not allowed, and after the initial induction week, she did all her training in strict isolation. She ate alone, slept alone, exercised alone, and her sole instructor was Hartley. In this way she had no idea how far she had progressed in the lone scout course, or how close she was to a full initiation until the day that Hartley told her that she would be entering the outlands on her own, and would return in the same way.

And so here she was, at night, on the wrong side of the border, staring up at the Fence, and pondering her next move. The lights of the watch towers gleamed like stars against the top of the wall, and she could just make out the shadowy figures of guards moving against the night sky. A chill breeze stirred the grasses at her feet, and made her pull her cloak about her shoulders. While she remained here, she had the protection of darkness unless a foot-patrol came her way, but once morning came her only shelter would come from the forest, and that would mean retreating back the way she had come.

Biting her lip, she took her bow-stave in both hands and gazed along the fence line. Well all right, she said to herself, there is nothing for it but to find a 'sally way'. These were doors set into the solid facings of the Fence, and disguised to look like riveted panels and nothing more. Hartley had told her that there was one for every kilometre of fence line, and on more than one occasion he had shown her where one was and how to find it. 'Look for a faint discolouration on the surface of the panel,' he had said. 'And then count the number of rivets on the panel. If it's an odd number, you are in luck: it's a sally way.'

He had then shown her how to open it.

Silently, she set off along the fence line, keeping low, and trying not to disturb the brush and bracken that grew at the base of the wall. In the moonlight, it was difficult to look for any discolouration, but it was not impossible. Twice she thought she had found a panel, and twice she was deceived, but on the third try – almost an hour later – she found a panel with an odd number of rivets. She sank to one knee, looked cautiously around and then began the process of opening the sally way. What was it, Hartley had told her?

'Push with one hand on the spot where the missing rivet should be. With the other hand, press hard against the rivet that is directly opposite.'

Holding her breath, she did as Hartley had told her. At first there was nothing, and then from behind the panel came a soft click, and all at once the whole panel pushed out gently towards her. Then, just as Hartley had told her, she leaned back and allowed the panel to come free, attached by two sprung-loaded arms. Its movement was as smooth and silent, as she had hoped it would be. Only once had Hartley shown her how to open a sally way, and he had warned her that if it had never been used before it would probably open with a dangerous squeaking sound – something Rebuild had never been able to solve.

But all was well. To complete the process, she reached behind the projected panel, found a small handle and twisted it downwards. The panel detached on one side, and swung back: the way was clear.

Carefully, she peered inside. There was nothing to be seen. It was as dark as the deepest, clouded night, and the moonlight only penetrated the interior for a couple of paces, no more.

'Some of the tunnels have scorpions and rats, as well as other creatures,' Hartley had warned her. 'Watch where you put your hands.'

Anna thought for a moment, then reaching inside her tunic pulled out a pair of archer's gloves. She slipped them on. They were hardly thick enough to withstand the strike of a viper-scorpion, but they would give her some protection against the teeth and claws of a rat.

With a last glance over her shoulder, she entered the tunnel, took a deep breath, and closed the panel behind her.

PREMONITION

Meanwhile back in the heart of Serenity, Anna-Seka's sister, was not sleeping well. Talessa had gone to bed early, feeling unusually tired, and had woken with a slight fever and a cough. She was not unduly alarmed. She had suffered colds before, and had found them to be uncomfortable for a few days but nothing more. This was of course not the season for colds, but then the weather had been unusually chill lately, and the folk at Litra had put out a general warning that stormy weather was coming down from the north.

At last, towards the midnight hour, she got up, slipped on her silk dressing gown, and went out onto the balcony of her apartment.

There was a refreshing breeze, and she turned her face towards it, feeling better almost straight away. The sky was clear, the moon was full, and the stars shone like fireflies against the night sky. Far below her, the city slept. Avenues of light, some golden, some brightest white and some pale blue drew lines like straightened necklaces across the city, marking out the high lanes, quadrants and courts of the Upper and Lower Towns. Here and there, almost lost against the glow of the lights she could make out pinpoints of flickering light moving this way and that in small groups and clusters. They were SSS patrols, visor lights beaming, checking that the streets were safe and all was secure. It was comforting to see. Occasionally, Lower-Towners strayed beyond their quadrants, and despite the strict requirements set by the Graders who established everyone's rank and place within the city, there were always some who seemed determined to test the age-old restrictions and boundaries that lay at the heart of the civic constitution.

Talessa let her gaze drift along one of the avenues towards the walls of Upper Town. She noticed an unusual gathering of torchlights just beyond an open square which she recognised as the entrance to an area of parkland called the People's Garden. It was not a particularly beautiful park, and nor was it very popular except on those festival days when an outshining took place. And then of course, it was packed. Outshinings were very popular, and although they were sometimes restricted to the folk of Upper Town most of the available seats were filled even before the first contests took place, usually just before noon on the day appointed.

The People's Garden was not the only arena in the city where outshinings were held, but it was certainly the biggest. It was built to hold an audience of about twelve thousand, while the other arenas were considerably smaller and held no more than a thousand people, and sometimes less than five hundred.

Talessa leaned on the balcony rail and studied the torchlights. There must have been about fifty of them and they were moving back and forth between the entrance of the parkland, and the arena which lay at its centre.

'They make ready,' she said to herself. 'There will be an outshining soon, perhaps even tomorrow.'

She was not sure that she liked outshinings. There was something disquieting about them, something unreal in a world where everything else seemed so ordered, so safe, so as it was meant to be. It was not that spectators were only allowed to attend if they were wearing masks, and masks of the correct rank. That, of course was expected. It was something else. Perhaps it was the way that the fighting cages overhung the arena, swinging slowly back and forth on the giant gantries that lowered the captured opponents into the arena where the challengers waited. To Talessa the people in the cages seemed like victims even before they began each contest. They were not expected to win, and although there were legendary occasions when a stainer or convicted criminal had held his own for a while, Talessa could not recall any occasion when the result of an outshining had ever gone against a citizen of Serenity.

After all, an outshining was really an exercise in intimidation, a mind game and a contest where the more beautiful and confident nobility intimidated and overwhelmed the weaker contestants. The winner retained their rank and status, or added to it, while the defeated citizen was stripped of his or her status, and condemned to the lowest social rank of Lower Town. As a consequence, one family was honoured, the other family was shamed. Both honour and shame were carefully recorded in the citizenry files of the Commissariat Records Office.

Outshinings were also opportunities for political advancement, particularly for younger citizens of Upper Town keen to gain the recognition and favour of members of the higher courts of nobility. If, as sometimes happened, a noble was formally challenged to solve a dispute at an outshining, that noble could nominate a champion to enter the outshining cage on his or her behalf. To take up such a role as champion at an outshining was seen as an act of bravery and selfless loyalty. It was always well rewarded, if the champion was successful. Defeat was something else entirely.

Ever since she could remember Talessa's family had taken her to watch these events, as a privilege and as a duty. She even recalled being hoisted on her father's shoulders so she could see better what was going on, and then clapping her hands and shouting when everyone else shouted, but scarcely understanding why.

Unlike the terrible arena contests of the Old World, no one was ever hurt at an outshining, she told herself. Not physically, leastways. The challengers always came away with their beauty untouched and their faces unmarred. It was very rare that any blood was shed. In the case of a drawn contest, or one that was deadlocked after an extended period, the umpire could rule that the matter be resolved with a formalised and strictly controlled sword fight. This hardly ever occurred, and was seen as an exception and not the rule.

But from her early teens Talessa understood that after every contest at least one of the contestants would leave the arena broken in spirit and reduced in a way that made her feel a deep sorrow for them. It was true that there were times when the defeated contestant, man or woman, declared 'outshone' by the judge, would simply turn and walk away with a perfunctory bow to the victor. However, most often they limped towards the edge of the arena, shoulders slouched and heads bowed as though they had been beaten with a stick.

And then there were times that they crawled towards the safety of the rearmost bars of the fighting cage, groaning as they went, or even sobbing. Always they went alone. Always they were abandoned. As for the stainers and outlanders among the defeated contestants, they were, without exception, led away in chains and mocked. Any criminals selected for an outshining were treated in the same way. To Talessa, the contests seemed always weighted in favour of the nobility, and the results were certainly predictable, despite the frenzied betting that often attended an outshining.

No one seemed to mind. The crowd cheered the victor, but they ignored the defeated ones, not even offering them a careless shout of sympathy as they left the cage or granting them a sad shake of the head.

The most unusual contests were those in which a citizen of Serenity challenged another citizen of equal rank. It was allowed under the rules, but it was rare. Most often these particular contests were conducted before a smaller, exclusive audience drawn from immediate family members and members of the ruling classes of Litra, Glamtech and the Chancellery. Although it was not always clear why such contests took place, Talessa understood that they were most often called to settle disputes between citizens over property, marriage or simply status. And with these disputes came ever present but scarcely acknowledged fear of de-grading.

And Talessa had to admit that once, despite her rank and upbringing, she had felt the tears come when she saw a young lad, not much older than herself, broken in a fighting cage and driven from the arena by a seasoned warrior of the royal household. Although the lad was from the Lower Town and of the lowest grade, he had entered the contest proudly, standing upright, and looking his opponent squarely in the face despite the other's reputation. Within a matter of minutes he had been crushed, almost as though he were of no account, and scarcely worth the warrior's notice. Staggering towards the edge of the fighting cage, the lad had caught her eye, and he ducked his head in shame. That was all, but it brought the tears to Anna's eyes. Her father had rebuked her, and her mother had hurried her away, shushing and tutting until they reached the gates of the park. There they both passed through security. When they found themselves in the broad and almost deserted street that led back towards the heart of Upper town, her mother had stopped, put her hand on her shoulder and looked hard at her.

'Remember who you are,' she had said. 'Tears are not your portion.'

She had not replied to her mother, but she had tried to remember those words: 'Tears are not your portion.'

After that particular contest, all the subsequent visits to an outshining, whether in the Great Arena, or at one of the smaller ones, were always difficult for Talessa. However, she was adept at covering her emotions, and was grateful that whenever she went to the arena that she could wear her mask and retreat behind its impassive gaze. Of all the folks she knew in the Upper Town and Imperial Precinct, it was only Barvarik who guessed her sorrow. She loved him for it, and loved him more when he kept her painful secret, and often whispered his understanding in her ear whenever a contest began.

And so this night, she leaned on the balcony gazed at the torchlight preparations, and comforted herself with the thought that Barvarik would also be at this outshining, and that throughout it he would never leave her side.

She heard the sound of her bedroom door being opened, and turned to see her mother.

Talessa darling,' she said, coming in. 'I saw your light on, and came to see if everything was all right.'

Talessa nodded, and stepped down into her room from the balcony. 'All is well, mother,' she said. 'I was hot, but the night air has cooled me. That is all.'

Her mother swept forward, with a worried frown. She put her hand on her daughter's brow. 'You must be careful, dear. There is fever in the Lower Town. Some of the folk down there are very poorly. They waste away and look terrible.'

Talessa smiled. 'Now, how would you know that, mother? As long as I can remember you have never visited the housing quarters of Lower Town. Have you been talking to those ladies of yours, who you meet for afternoon tea at the Cascading Gardens? If someone so much as looks pale, or gives a little cough, they declare a pandemic and send frantic messages to the medical commissariat at Litra.'

'Oh, tut! Tut! And away with you!' laughed her mother, and she hugged her daughter. 'Now off to bed with you, before you catch a chill.' She stood back, peered at her daughter for a moment then shook her head. 'You know, you are looking a little pale, Talessa.'

Talessa laughed. 'Mother, you are such a fusser! I am perfectly fine. Think of Anna, away on her scout-training, and probably half-starved and lost somewhere in the middle of nowhere.' She paused and kissed her mother on the cheek. 'But as your dutiful daughter, I will take myself to bed, sleep till morning, and see you at breakfast.'

Smiling, her mother returned the kiss, and wished her goodnight. Talessa climbed into bed, and moments later was asleep. Outside, and far below the preparations for the outshining went on.

THE TUNNEL

E ven further away, beyond the city and across the many miles of the kingdom to its northern borders, her sister Anna-Seka was working her way along the tunnel that she hoped would bring her to safety. It was difficult going. When she had first crossed the Fence, all that time ago with Hartley, it had been during daylight hours, and a pale light shone down through the grating above her head in the walkway they had found. But in this tunnel, it was impossible to see anything clearly. If only she had thought to recharge the glow necklace her mother had given her before she left, but it was too late to be thinking of that, and of course the guards would probably have taken it off her, anyway. She felt her way along the tunnel. Its sides were smooth, but its roof was low. Much lower than the tunnel she had used before. In that tunnel, she had been able to walk upright, with her head just below the grating. But here, in this tunnel in the dark, she had to stoop and sometimes crawl, and as she went she tensed herself for the touch of something other than smooth, cool tiles: perhaps fur, perhaps scales, perhaps the barb of a scorpion's sting.

Slowly, she made her way forward, eyes wide open and straining for the merest chink of light. Surely, she told herself, she must soon be coming to the entrance. But the minutes passed, and there was no sign of an ending to the darkness. Twice the tunnel veered away to the right, then back to the left. Once, it sloped upwards for a short distance, and then back downwards as though it was clearing an obstruction. She wondered if it was a maintenance tunnel, intended only for workers, and not for scouting parties. Why it seemed so much longer than her earlier crossing with Hartley she could not tell.

At last, when she was almost persuaded that she had somehow found a sally way that led along the Fence and not through it, she noticed the merest glimmer of light far ahead. For a moment she thought it might be a glow worm, or perhaps the faint gleam of an animal's eye, but as she held her course, she noticed that the light flickered like a distant star. And then, to her joy and relief, she sensed a lightening of the air, and the merest hint of moonlight filtering down from above her head.

Scarcely pausing to feel for the sides of the tunnel, she scrambled forward. Something scuttled away in front of her and was gone, but she herself scarcely paused, even though she gasped for an instant before pressing on. The light grew. Soon she could make out the tiled surface of the tunnel about ten paces ahead of where she now was, and there, directly ahead, the dim shadow of a door. A cool brightness streamed down through the grating above her and she breathed in the freshness of the night air.

'Made it!' she gasped.

It took her only a moment to find the handle of the door, turn it and then push against the riveted plate. With a faint click, the door gave way beneath her hand. Just as before, it thrust forward on its sprung-loaded arms, and then with hardly any effort she was able to swing it open.

The first thing that she noticed were the stars shining across the full arc of the sky, and at their heart, like a pearl of great price, the moon. She smiled at the beauty of what she saw, and stepped clear of the tunnel. All about her was silent, still and untouched. The tree line was about twenty paces away, but the undergrowth had pushed forward almost to the base of the pylons of the Fence. She could just make out a narrow track way winding away into the darkness between clumps of broom, but it seemed as if no one had been near this sector of the Fence for some time.

Turning for a moment to ease the sally way closed, she looked about for a moment, took off her gloves and began to head towards the trees. Although, technically she was now in the northern realm of the southern kingdom, and therefore safe, there was in truth little that was safe about these border lands. Hartley had repeatedly warned her, during her training days that lone scouts were easily mistaken for intruders by security patrols, and nervous guards were inclined to shoot first before they had properly identified their targets.

'You have no friends in these parts,' he used to tell her, 'and no one will call you comrade until you reach the outer precincts of the city itself.'

And so she crept forward, head low and bow-string nocked with a war arrow. There were even rumours that some wild folk had managed to cross the Fence, and that they had the mysterious ability to scale the highest of walls without making a sound, nor leave a trace of their passing.

Reaching the trees, she glanced back the way she had come, and then plunged into the shadows.

Hartley had taught her well. Even in the faltering darkness of the forest, Anna was able to keep up a good pace, stay on the track-way and check that it was still heading southwards towards the city. Whenever she came to a clearing she did her best to check her position against the stars, just as she had been shown in the first few weeks of her training. It gave her a sense of confidence and for the first time since she had set off for the borders with Nike and Leviss, she began to tell herself that she would soon be home. She was tired, hungry and very thirsty but she knew that this was no time to stop. The further she could travel in the hours before sunrise, the safer she would be.

At last, Anna cleared the forest and came out on a broad, sloping plain running from east to west and stretching to the horizon beneath the moonlit skies. A faint glow far to the south told her that was where her route lay to the first quadrant and find Serenity. Promising herself a rest after she had reached a river that she could just make out, a mile or two ahead of her on the plain, she set off once more. As she went, Anna was surprised yet again by the silence and emptiness of the land she was passing through. Earlier, when she had come with Hartley to the borders, they always seemed to pass through settled lands: not crowded, but well occupied with farms and roads and small villages. But here there was nothing. There was no sign of a building, not even a shepherd's hut or a field-barn. There were no fences, no gates, no roads nor footpaths. The track-ways she came across were so narrow and uneven that she thought them to be pig-runs or deer-tracks. Every so often there was a stand of trees or low bushes, but there was little to show that they had been deliberately planted or cultivated. This was a wasteland.

At last she reached the river which flowed sluggishly between reed banks and wound its way slowly towards the western horizon. It glowed darkly in the moonlight, making Anna-Seka pause before she attempted to cross it.

'I will rest on the other side,' she promised herself, as she stood on the near bank and gazed across the river. It was less than a spear-cast wide, but it looked deep, and the swirling eddies in the current warned her that there were hidden traps beneath the peaceful surface of the current.

But it was a river that needed to be crossed.

Anna had just taken her bow stave and was beginning to test the depth of the water close to the bank, when she heard a sound. It was a human sound: the sound of a boot against dry leaves. And it was behind her.

Dropping down, she turned, drawing her broadsword and dagger at the same time and raising them to 'point of guard'. In that instant as she turned, Anna saw what least she expected to see: it was Hartley.

He was standing facing her, no more than five paces away, and smiling in that way he had whenever he met her.

'Anna,' he said softly.

She did not reply at first, so taken by surprise at his sudden appearance.

'Anna-Seka,' he spoke again, this time using her more formal name.

'My lord Hartley.' She bowed, then raised her head and slowly stood. 'I was lost,' she said.

'So I see. You have crossed the Fence due north of here?'

'I have, my lord. I found a sally way and managed to make my way through a tunnel.' She paused. 'It was not easy. I see now why some folk call it The Wall.'

He nodded, still smiling. 'The sally ways on this sector of the border are old, out of date, and scarcely used these days.' He shrugged. 'Nonetheless, I see you have survived. Come now, we will walk while you give me your report. There's a roadway not far from here to the east. We can find a staging post there, and with any luck arrange for a pair of horses to get us home.'

'But the river my lord. How do we cross it?'

Hartley chuckled. 'Ah, Anna! We don't cross it here. It's too deep, too fast and full of tangles. There's a bridge just down the bank away. There are guards there, but they know me, and you won't even have to show your pass.' He paused. 'You look tired. Here!' He slipped a water bottle from his belt and tossed it to her. 'Drink up now, but not too much mind. We'll get you a meal at the staging post.'

'Thank you, my lord.' Anna-Seka drank eagerly from the bottle and handed it back. 'Are we far from the city?'

'Not if we can get ourselves a couple of horses. Two days should see us there.' He glanced over Anna's shoulder at the way she had come, nodded and then gestured towards the river bank. 'We'll follow this river to the bridge. Go softly now. I'll tell you when you can speak and only then tell me what you've been up to.'

And so they headed away, keeping to the river bank as it headed east and south. Hartley led, Anna followed, and as she had been taught she turned briefly every ten paces or so to see if they were being tracked.

At last they reached the bridge. The guards watched them as they came, and saluted Hartley when they were within a spear cast. Hartley returned the salute. 'We have passes,' he said as he and Anna reached the bridge.

The guards stood back and presented arms. 'You may pass, lord Hartley,' the elder of the two said. 'All is peaceful here. Nothing has happened since two stainer-prisoners were brought this way.'

Hartley nodded. 'It was my men who brought them. They will be on their way to the city by now.'

'Just so, my lord,' replied the guard, and they both saluted again as Hartley and Anna-Seka crossed the bridge.

Anna said nothing, but she now believed what she had feared to admit: both Nike and Leviss had been captured and were on their way to trial and judgement far to the south in the courts of Serenity.

In the city itself, it had been announced by the palace that the outshining planned for the great arena had been delayed. No explanation had been given. No one thought it strange that such a delay had been declared. Outshinings were seen as unpredictable events and subject to the whim of the palace, as well as the numerous conditions set by the commissariatand the SSS. 'The safety of the public', was the often declared motto of the Security Services, and this tied in well with the policy of the commissariat, inscribed in marble above the doors of that department: 'Beauty through Truth, Truth through Beauty.'

So an outshining could be cancelled at a moment's notice, or even without warning. There was never an official apology. And why should there be? All actions taken by departments such as the commissariat and the SSS, as well as Glamtech, Litra and even Rebuild were invariably in the public interest, and for the welfare of all the citizens of Serenity, no matter what their grade and status. The king himself, in his prepared speeches on festival days, usually paid tribute to the ruling council and senate, saying that they regarded all citizens as equal under the law, and saw no difference between the folk of the Lower or the Upper Town.

Stainers, or stain-folk of the outlands of course were a different matter. They were, by reason of their sheer disfigurement and isolation, beyond the protection of the law, and therefore fit for only two things: imprisonment or exile. Execution was only invoked if the courts decided that a stainer had also been found guilty of treason against the state, or incitement to rebellion.

Sometimes, stain folk were chosen for an outshining. They were always matched against warriors or nobles of outstanding beauty and flawless appearance, and although a result in such a contest could never be guaranteed, it was considered unthinkable that a stainer could ever possibly get the upper hand against a Grade A Imperial citizen or a noble. The king usually attended such events, and it was also considered unthinkable that the head of the royal household be allowed to view anything so distressing as a defeat for one of the representatives of the Upper Town courts or perhaps the Palace Precinct.

BEAUTY
THROUGH TRUTH

In the city itself, it had been announced by the palace that the outshining planned for the great arena had been delayed. No explanation had been given. No one thought it strange that such a delay had been declared. Outshinings were seen as unpredictable events and subject to the whim of the palace, as well as the numerous conditions set by the commissariat and the SSS. 'The safety of the public', was the often declared motto of the Security Services, and this tied in well with the policy of the commissariat, inscribed in marble above the doors of that department: 'Beauty through Truth, Truth through Beauty.'

So an outshining could be cancelled at a moment's notice, or even without warning. There was never an official apology. And why should there be? All actions taken by departments such as the commissariat and the SSS, as well as Glamtech, Litra and even Rebuild were invariably in the public interest, and for the welfare of all the citizens of Serenity, no matter what their grade and status. The king himself, in his prepared speeches on festival days, usually paid tribute to the ruling council and senate, saying that they regarded all citizens as equal under the law, and saw no difference between the folk of the Lower or the Upper Town.

Stainers, or stain-folk of the outlands of course were a different matter. They were, by reason of their sheer disfigurement and isolation, beyond the protection of the law, and therefore fit for only two things: imprisonment or exile. Execution was only invoked if the courts decided that a stainer had also been found guilty of treason against the state, or incitement to rebellion.

Sometimes, stain folk were chosen for an outshining. They were always matched against warriors or nobles of outstanding beauty and flawless appearance, and although a result in such a contest could never be guaranteed, it was considered unthinkable that a stainer could ever possibly get the upper hand against a Grade A Imperial citizen or a noble. The king usually attended such events, and it was also considered unthinkable that the head of the royal household be allowed to view anything so distressing as a defeat for one of the representatives of the Upper Town courts or perhaps the Palace Precinct.

And so, the citizens of Serenity, well used to 'reading between the lines' of Palace announcements and decrees, did not openly discuss the decision to delay the outshining, but privately it was whispered that perhaps some stain-folk, or even wild-folk had been captured and were being brought to the city for a festival event.

In the dwelling quarter of her court, Talessa had slept in late. She awoke with the sun streaming into her bedroom from the balcony windows, and a gentle breeze stirring the fine white curtains. She felt so much better. Getting up, she washed, dressed and sat down in a reclining chair to wait for the maid to come and attend to her make-up and dress her hair. Today would be a perfect day for a visit to the mall. Perhaps her mother might accompany her, and they could buy trinkets and silken scarves for one another, and she might even find a keepsake for Barvarik.

At length the maid came.

'Ah, mistress, you are awake,' she said. 'I checked earlier but you were asleep.'

Talessa did not bother to turn her face from the sunlight, but waved the maid forward. 'That is not a problem. You did well to let me sleep. Come now, and attend to me. I have a busy day ahead.'

The maid, carrying a tray of Glamgel cosmetics, lotions and perfumes, bowed and hurried forward. 'I will dress your hair first, mistress and then attend to your make up.'

Talessa sighed. That meant of course that she would have to shift from her reclining chair and move to the dressing table and mirror on the other side of the room. 'As you please,' she said. 'You know best.'

As she sat down at the dressing table, the maid placed her tray on a side table, and leaned forward to draw a braid of her mistress's hair back from her cheek and neck. As she did so, she paused and then gasped. Her eyes widened and she stepped back.

'Mistress!' she said, and put her hand to her mouth.

Annoyed, Talessa looked around. 'What is it? What is all this fuss?'

For a time the maid could not reply. She began to shake, and then pointed. 'Mistress!' she repeated. 'Look, mistress!'

'At what, woman? At what?' Talessa started to get to her feet but the maid shook her head:

'No! No!' she replied, almost shouting. 'Your neck, mistress. Look at your neck!'

Turning back to the mirror, Talessa looked, and sat back with a gasp.

CHAPTER #4

OUTSHINING AND EXILE

B y the time that Anna-Seka and Hartley reached the staging post, she had made her report, and he had told her about the capture of the two stainers.

She assured her mentor that the area she had scouted was diseased, barren and without value or profit.

'So you wasted your time?' said Hartley glancing at her as they walked together.

Anna-Seka took a deep breath and nodded. 'There was nothing.'

'Nothing?'

'Nothing worth the concern of Rebuild,' she replied, hating herself for the deception, but hoping that Hartley would not sense it. 'It was a wasteland. I doubt if even the SSS would consider such a place to be any more than a blank area on one of their maps.'

Again Hartley glanced at her. 'But you saw the Glass Tunnel?'

Anna looked surprised. 'How did you know that I saw the Glass Tunnel?'

He smiled. 'It lies in the heart of the quadrant you were sent to. You cannot have missed it.'

Taken aback, Anna nodded. 'I did see the Tunnel, my lord. In fact I entered it, and traversed its length.' She paused. 'There was machinery there, I admit, but it was smashed beyond repair. Wild folk, I guess.'

They walked on for a while.

'If you have traversed the Glass Tunnel on your own,' said Hartley at last, 'you are worthy of a promotion, or at least a mention in my report to the chancellor.'

Anna struggled with how she was now feeling. It had been difficult enough to lie to her mentor about the area that Bepsi-Loca and his stain-folk lived in, but the more the conversation went on, the more she began to feel that Hartley had doubts about her story anyway. She decided however to defend her deception to the last even if, as seemed likely, Nike and Leviss had been captured by Hartley's patrol, and might well have already confessed their friendship with Anna. The interrogation methods of the Security Services, and their deadly efficiency were well known to most citizens of Upper Town, even if such methods were not openly spoken of.

'Are you familiar with the Glass Tunnel yourself, my lord?' Anna asked, trying to sound casual.

Hartley chuckled. 'Well, yes, as it happens, I am. But it is some time since I have been that way. The machines you mention were intact when I scouted that area, but I accept that they could well have been destroyed by now.'

'You accept, my lord? You doubt my report?'

The staging post was just up ahead. Hartley stopped, and put his hand on Anna's shoulder. 'Why should I doubt your report, Anna-Seka? You are my pupil. You are one of my best pupils. I sent you on this mission because I trust you.'

Anna reddened. 'I am sorry my lord. I did not mean . . .'

'Hah!' The scout-lord gave a short laugh. 'Think nothing of it. You are right to insist on the truth of your report. After all, haven't I just said that I trust you?'

'You have my lord.'

'Then think nothing of it. I am happy with your report, and will get it sent on to the Chancellery along with a recommendation that you be approved as a certified Lone-scout.' He paused. 'Technically, you will be under the control of the Chancellery, but you will always report directly to me.'

'Thank you, my lord.' Inwardly Anna sighed with relief, but deeper down still hated herself for deceiving the man she most respected among the officials of the City.

Again Hartley smiled. Then he gestured towards the Staging Post. 'Look, we are nearly there, and see! There are guards leading horses out of the stables already. It's almost as if they knew we were coming.'

Less than an hour later, they were ready to leave the staging post. With their encoded court masks now on, they swung into the saddle and began the long ride back towards Serenity. Their route would take them directly past Cornus, the supply city that lay only a kilometre or so south of the Fence, and a sister-settlement to the great Rebuild-centre of Arx that lay nearby on the other side of a river. But they would not turn aside, even though both cities were an important if not vital part of the kingdom's defence and resource system. Arx was the second principal town and headquarters of Rebuild, that mighty construction department of the new kingdom. In size it was only a fraction of the size of Serenity, but some of its buildings were of more recent construction and equipped with a dazzling array of equipment for the processing and dispatch of salvage and resources extracted from the outlands. Its technical defence systems were also unmatched by any other city.

Hartley had only once or twice taken Anna-Seka into Cornus during their training missions, but on each occasion she had been awestruck by its magnificence and scale. However, it was - as its name indicates – an industrial complex rather than a city in the sense that Serenity was a city. Arx was much the same, except on an even grander scale.

'To work in Cornus or Arx is an honour,' Hartley said to her once, 'but I do not think it is a privilege. If you stay there too long, you begin to wonder if you are a human that behaves like a machine, or a machine that behaves like a human.'

After her visit to this supply city, Anna had understood exactly what he meant. While the folk were friendly enough, they always seemed a little cool and distant, and moved with precise, co-ordinated gestures and movements that indeed gave them a machine-like quality.

And so she was happy to by-pass the gates and towers of the Cornus, and ride on southwards with Hartley as they made their way towards the hills that lay beyond the great plains of the northern borderlands.

They made good progress, and spoke little, until the sun dipped towards the western horizon. As they approached a walled hostelry set aside for imperial officials, Anna suddenly asked:

'My lord, tell me more of the two outlanders you captured.'

Hartley eased back on the reins and they both slowed their horses to a gentle trot. 'What would you like to know?' he asked.

'Anything you can tell me, my lord. Anything that might help me when I return to the outlands.'

Hartley thought for a moment. 'Well, let me see,' he said. 'They were both young, about your age,' he smiled, 'a man and a woman.'

'They fought?'

'They had the good sense not to. We were upon them before they realised it.'

'That was lucky, my lord.'

Hartley shook his head, and stared towards the hostelry. 'There was no luck about it,' he said. 'We saw them from about a mile away. They came over a low ridge east of the highway, trying to keep in the cover of a stand of trees, but my men were on duty on one of the watch towers by the highway. They spotted them immediately.'

For a while Anna said nothing. The hostelry was now no more than a bowshot away.

'I guess they will be sent to the main prison below the palace precinct,' she said at last.

This time Hartley just shrugged, and for a moment Anna thought he had lost interest in the conversation. But then he spoke:

'I will leave their fate to the judges of the Common Court,' he said 'but if I had my way we would be making an example of them.'

Anna-Seka felt a shudder run through her body, and hoped that her mentor had not noticed. 'You mean forced labour in the prison-factory on the lower levels of the imperial penitentiary,' she replied quietly.

Hartley looked at her. 'You almost sound sorry for them, Anna-Seka, and yet you do not know them. They are nothing but stainers, and stainers who have come into the kingdom contrary to the law.' He flicked his horse's reins. 'They do not deserve mercy, nor do they expect it.'

'Of course, my lord,' answered Anna, and she too urged her horse to a canter. No more was said until they reached the hostelry.

Showing their passes to the guards on the gate, they entered an enclosed courtyard and handed their horses to a stable lad. They were about to make their way to the checking office and main building when Anna noticed a prison wagon drawn up against a barn on the other side of the yard.

'One of ours?' she asked.

Hartley nodded. 'See the code? That's ours all right, and if I'm right it will have those stainers we captured.'

Anna longed to walk across and see if she could catch sight of Nike and Leviss, but she knew that it was best not to arouse any suspicion. And so she gave a casual shrug. 'I could do with a hot meal, a wash and a place to sleep,' she said.

Hartley chuckled. 'Well, you could well get all three here, but I can't guarantee the quality. This hostelry is run by a sub-department of Rebuild, and they are not generous with their funding beyond the City.'

But to Anna's relief she found that her quarters were comfortable if not comparable to those of Serenity, and the meal that was brought to her door was far better than anything she had eaten since she had set off from the City all those days ago. Except that is, for the meal that she had shared with the stain-folk around that camp fire on the night before she, Nike and Leviss had set off for the border.

In the evening, she went out into the courtyard for some fresh air, and took a brief moment to stand and then to look up at the stars. The prison wagon was still there on the far side of the yard. She was wondering if she might not stroll over towards it, when Hartley suddenly appeared at her side.

'I had the same idea,' he said.

'My lord?'

'The stars, I like to see them on a clear night. Reassuring, they are: so bright, so clear, so constant.' He looked at Anna, and continued:

'Do you trust me, Anna-Seka?'

'I do, my lord.'

'Then don't. Trust no one, Anna. Not even me, your mentor. No one. It's safer that way.'

For a time Anna did not reply. She gazed at the stars. They were so beautiful and beyond counting. 'It may be safer, my lord,' she said after a while, 'but surely it is lonelier.'

Hartley nodded, stepped down off the step into the yard and stared at the prison wagon. 'You are a Lone-scout, Anna Seka. You are called to be lonely, trained to be lonely.' He paused. 'Do you have the heart for it?'

Anna thought hard. She was aware of distant chatter and snatches of laughter coming from the hostelry kitchens. From somewhere beyond the gates a guard-dog barked and was silent. 'I have the heart to serve the kingdom,' she said after a while. 'Is that enough, my lord?'

Hartley gave a slight shrug. 'It is a start,' he said, and he glanced towards the prison wagon.

'Would you like to see these stainers?' he asked suddenly.

Anna felt herself tense and momentarily redden. 'Is it necessary, my lord?' she asked.

Hartley shrugged again. 'You seemed to take an interest in them before, or was I mistaken?'

'No, my lord,' Anna replied quickly, as she herself stepped down into the yard. 'You were not mistaken.' Again she hesitated, her mind crowded with thoughts of what might happen if either Nike or Leviss gave her away and confessed that they knew her. 'Is it safe, my lord?' she went on, uncertainly. 'They are stainers. They might be infectious.'

'Ah, dear Anna-Seka!' Hartley smiled. 'Who have you been talking to? Even the folk at Litra and Glamtech as well as the head of the Medical Research Centre himself, tell me that they are still unsure how stains develop.' He nodded to himself and continued: 'What we do know however is that the condition we call stains or staining can be inherited and passed on from one generation to another, and that such folk are not infectious.' He smiled again. 'One of the very few things we learned from those two young outlanders in that wagon is that they were both born with stains. They are brother and sister, y'know. One carries a stain across the face to the neck, and the other is stained around the left eye and back.'

Anna's heart sank. Any faint hope that she might have had that the prisoners in the wagon were not Nike and Leviss, faded away to nothing. She lowered her head. 'We could perhaps take a look,' she muttered, and felt Hartley stare at her for just an instant. Then he put a hand gently on her shoulder:

'You are a strange one, Anna-Seka. High born you are, with a father who has the ear of the king, and a mother who is renowned throughout the city for her beauty, and yet you constantly surprise me.'

Anna looked up. 'I disappoint you, my lord?'

Hartley shook his head. 'Pouf! No, of course not. On the contrary, you fascinate me.' He looked at Anna. 'I see something in you, something I do not see in others.'

'My lord?'

'I see honesty, plain speaking and a willingness to take your own path, and not to blame others for the consequences.'

At last, Anna felt herself smile. 'You remind me of my father, my lord.'

'Hmm! Then my job is done. Your father is a man I have always respected. We do not always agree, but we respect each other's opinions.' Hartley glanced again at the prison wagon. 'Come, let us check on these fellows.'

It was already quite dark as they approached the wagon. Clouds had moved in from the west, and only the light from a couple of wall-mounted lanterns illuminated the barred windows of the wagon. The glow-tech systems so widely used in Serenity were not yet being used so near to the borders, except in the supply cities, and the great towers of the Fence.

Hartley peered through the bars. He grunted. 'They are both asleep,' he said. 'Should we wake them?'

'Let them sleep my lord,' she replied, and coming forward she rested her face against one of the windows and looked into the gloom. Leviss was shackled to one side of the wagon, and Nike to the other. They each had a rough blanket across their shoulders, and a straw mattress to lie on. Their eyes were closed.

Hartley nodded. 'Let them sleep? Why not? That's a small mercy considering what lies ahead of them.' He slapped the side of the wagon, but they did not stir. Anna stared at them for a moment longer, then turned away. 'They are so young, my lord,' she said. 'Are they for the arena, the prison or the galleys?'

Stooping, Hartley picked up a stick that lay beside the wagon, and drew in the dust: three circles, overlapping each other. 'See!' he said. 'Three judges that sit on the three thrones in the high court. They will decide. One judges for mercy's sake, one judges to uphold the law, and the third judge listens and makes the decision.'

Anna looked at her mentor. 'I never knew that.'

'Well, you know now.' He gave a brief, taut smile and began to walk away. 'It seems a pretty idea, and almost just in its way, but whatever you do, don't fall into those judges' hands.' He paused. 'They have hearts of stone.'

For a second, Anna could scarcely believe what she had just heard: an open criticism of the high court, and therefore the palace and the kingdom itself. She looked around. No one was listening. No one had heard, beyond herself.

Even as Hartley walked away, she stayed where she was staring after him, and wondering what had moved him to say such a thing.

He reached the step that led to the main building, and turned. 'Are you coming?' he said.

They left early in the morning, just as the sun was rising, but the prison wagon had already left. One of the guards at the gate told Hartley that it had pulled out of the hostelry at the beginning of the fourth watch, with an escort of Security Services cavalry. 'Can't think why they are in such a hurry,' said the guard.

'You didn't think to ask them?' replied Hartley, as he swung into the saddle and turned his horse's head towards the entrance.

The guard grunted. 'You don't ask those fellows anything, not even the time of day. I've never met any of them yet who gave me more than yes or no, and a sharp look.'

Hartley frowned. 'They're just doing their job soldier, and I thank you for doing yours.'

The guard saluted and waved them through. 'If you're bound for the City, the roads are clear,' he said, 'but I wouldn't stray from the highway. We've had reports of strange folk hereabouts.'

Hartley returned the salute, nodded to Anna, and set off through the gates down the spur road that led to the imperial highway. Soon, as their horses awoke to their task, they rose from a trot to a canter.

Snorting in the morning air and fresh after a night's rest they took to the road at full stride and quickly covered the distance to the highway. There, as they expected, they came across a roadblock and a routine inspection. The officer on duty recognised Hartley's mask but stared hard at Anna and checked her palm-pass twice. At last he nodded, and stepped back:

'Go well,' he said, and don't stop until you reach the next hostel. We've had one or two incidents along this stretch of the highway.'

'Anything I should know?' asked Hartley, casually.

'No, my lord,' answered the officer. 'Just be careful, that's all.' He signed to a soldier to lift the toll-bar and watched them as they led their horses through the check-point and onto the highway.

'I wonder what he meant by that?' asked Anna as they swung back into the saddle.

Hartley smiled. 'He meant nothing at all,' he said quietly. 'This talk of strange folk and one or two incidents along the highway is a rumour. We put such stories about every so often in the border zone near the Supply City. It keeps any travellers just a little afraid, and discourages them from leaving the highway for whatever reason.' Clicking his tongue, he leaned forward and patted his horse's neck. 'A little bit of fear goes a long way in these parts,' he added.

They rode for three days, only stopping to camp for the night in farming settlements, and once at an imperial staging post. Towards the noon on the fourth day they crested a low rise on the highway, and there before them, about five miles away, lay the city of Serenity. It was almost lost in the distant haze, but they could make out the high towers of the Upper City, and the four beacons that marked the four courts of the imperial precinct and palace.

Hartley reined in, stood in the stirrups and shaded his eyes as he looked southwards. 'All quiet ahead,' he said. 'It's almost too quiet. There seems to be nothing on the road between us and the outer gates of the city.'

'Is that strange, my lord?' asked Anna as she too stared towards her homeland.

'It's not strange, Anna, but it is unusual. My guess is they they've cleared the way ahead to prepare the route for the outshining.'

'There is to be an outshining, then?'

Hartley smiled. 'Did I not say? Perhaps not. There is to be a special outshining pageant in honour of the king. The imperial council has ordered that stain-folk captured during this season be brought to the arena as contestants.' He began to ride again, easing his horse to a steady trot, and Anna followed.

'Will they fight against each other, my lord?' she asked, coming up alongside him.

Hartley glanced at her with a look of mild surprise. 'Against each other? Why, no. Where's the fun in that, and where's the point? No, they will be matched against our finest and most beautiful warriors.'

'It is a "proving-time", then, my lord?'

Hartley nodded, but did not reply.

As they rode, Anna noticed that all the trees had been cleared from both sides of the highway for a distance of about one hundred paces. Surely, she wondered, the Security Services did not fear bandit raids and ambushes along this part of the highway so close to the City itself.

As if Hartley guessed her thoughts, he answered. 'The king is concerned about the number of reported sightings of wildfolk and outlanders this far from the city walls.'

'But that cannot be, my lord Hartley,' replied Anna her voice rising. 'Surely they could not wander so close to the city and hope to escape.'

'Precisely, my young scout! They may think they are free, but they are in fact broken and under imperial service.' He paused. 'But still they come, drifting in across the Fence, or The Wall as some folk call it. They crawl, they run, they hide, but in the end they come out of the shadows '

'Because they are discovered?'

'Hah! Because they are starving, weak and scarcely able to stand. The land will not feed them, the farming folk drive them away, and the villagers keep them on the move.'

Anna nodded. 'I remember now. As a child I saw some stain-folk being herded along the road in chains. They looked like scarecrows.'

'Scarecrows? That's a good word for it. Good for nothing they are. Not even the prison gallows or the treadmill could find a use for them. We have to fatten these rogues up, y'know, before we let them loose in the cages of the arena.' Leaning to one side, he spat neatly into the undergrowth. 'But we do not feed them too well.' A dark smile crept across his face. 'Folk do not go to an outshining to see beauty undone by ugliness.' He hesitated. 'That's unthinkable,' he said.

'Unthinkable,' repeated Anna. She had never heard her mentor speak this way before. It worried her. He was not an unkind man. She knew that, but for the first time she was hearing him say things that were harsh, cruel and unworthy of a college scout.

'You must be tired, my lord,' she suddenly said. 'It has been a long journey, and you have so much responsibility, and so much to do.'

Hartley was taken by the reply, almost surprised. No one had ever spoken to him like that before, let alone one of his students. This girl was young enough to be his daughter, and had scarcely entered the service of the imperial college of scouts. And yet – he shook his head – and smiled, she was risking all by telling him exactly what she thought, and yes, almost rebuking him.

'I like you, Anna-Seka,' he said slowly. 'You will make an excellent scout one day, but if you want to survive long enough to make a respectable career in the service of the king, you must learn to think more carefully before you speak, and even then determine to say only a little more than nothing at all.'

'Deeds not words,' replied Anna-Seka, repeating one of the mottos of the college of scouts

'Just so, just so,' said Hartley, again surprised to find himself relieved that what he had said about the outshining had only momentarily alarmed this young woman.

'We will make the city by evening at the latest,' he said. 'I have business in the second court of the Upper City. I want you to go to the duty office of the college and make a provisional report.' He paused. 'They are expecting you.'

'And then, my lord?'

Hartley shrugged. 'And then your time is your own. Stable your horse and then make your way to the college hostel for some well earned rest. In three days you can go to the outshining and after that you will be put on a week's home-leave. Your family will be pleased to see you. They have been somewhat anxious for you, y'know. Your first mission, and one taken with a mentor in only remote support.' Again he paused. 'You did very well. I am pleased with you.'

Anna smiled. This was the mentor she knew. 'Thank you my lord.'

They rode on in silence into the first quadrant towards the city, and did not speak again until they were no more than a mile from the Great Gates of the outer defences, and the first of the close-security patrols met them at a road block.

'This is a Glamtech unit,' said Hartley as they approached. 'Leave the talking to me. They always want to know more than they need to.'

Anna risked a chuckle. 'My father always says that, my lord.'

Hartley glanced at her and winked so that his mask glowed softly. 'Does he now? Well, he's a good man, your father, so it's good to hear that his judgement is also my own.'

They trotted their horses up to the roadblock, swung down from the saddle, and presented their passes to the officer of the guard. He glanced at them, registered their masks, nodded to Hartley, and handed the passes back.

'You're the first scouts we've seen all day. This section of the highway has been sealed off for the outshining. What have you been up to?'

Hartley looked disinterested, and half turned away before he answered. 'Just a training exercise,' he said. 'Border testing, and a fixed reconnaissance, that's all.'

'Nothing more, my lord?' The officer's tone was flat and cool.

Hartley turned back and held the man with a mask-stare that made Anna tense, and for an instant her hand instinctively slipped to the hilt of her sword.

'Perhaps you and I should meet in a cage of your choice, my friend,' he said. 'That way both of us would discover if you are indeed worthy to ask such a question.'

The guards on either side of the officer straightened, and one of them began to lift his weapon, but the officer waved him down. 'That will not be necessary, my lord,' he said to Hartley. 'You may pass. No further questions.'

Moment later they had cleared the roadblock and were lifting their horses to a canter once more. 'Rogues,' said Hartley under his breath, but then grinned at Anna. 'Don't look back whatever you do,' he said. 'If you do, they'll shoot you out of the saddle.'

'But they are Glamtech, my lord. How is that possible.'

Hartley threw back his head and laughed. 'Ah, my poor Anna Seka! How innocent you are, and yet so beautiful and high born. This is not the city you know and love. Outside the walls of Serenity there is another reality. Have you never noticed? Here, security is everything. That, and the resources and supplies we bring to the City. We bring them so that the City might live, and the steady flow of such resources are only made possible by hard-edged folk like those we have just been chatting with. In their own way they are pirates and a law unto themselves, but it is their very arrogance and carelessness for the law that makes them so good at their job.'

'You mean they have to sometimes break the law in order to protect those who live by it?'

'Precisely. This land is not entirely what it may seem to be. There is peace and there is prosperity, but it is bought at a price. The walls of Serenity are high and they are strong, but it is the dark strength of those that keep watch beyond the walls that allows the villagers and farming folk to sleep safely at night, and bring their produce to market without fear of attack.'

Anna looked ahead at the walls of the City that rose to meet them as they cantered along the road. 'A dark strength,' she repeated quietly to herself. Here was something else that was new, and on this journey to and from the outlands she had learned so much that was new to her. How beautiful the walls of the city looked. They glowed in the evening light, and the reflector towers and armoured bastions along their length shone even more brightly with the glo-tech lamps and floodlights that were built into the masonry, and anchored to the battlements and ramparts of each tower and defence-work. Moreover, the massive double gates that marked and protected the entrance to Serenity gleamed with polished fittings of bronze, lacquered plastic, silver and gold. Such beauty! Such strength! But if Hartley was right, they were no defence at all without that 'dark strength' he had described to her.

'Will I see you at the outshining, my lord?' she asked.

Hartley nodded. 'Of course. It is my duty, and also my pleasure. If what my men say is correct, there will be some fifty stainers chosen for the cages in three days time. I can hardly miss that, nor would I want to.' He paused. 'I might even place a wager on the outcome of one or two of the contests.'

Anna could not help the shudder that ran through her body. She knew that Nike and Leviss were bound for the cages of the arena, but the thought that bets might be exchanged and money won or lost over the result of their outshining, made a sick feeling well up inside of her.

They passed through the gates as the sun set. They did not even have to show their passes. The guards clearly recognised Hartley by his court one mask and waved him through.

Anna breathed deeply as they clattered over the bridge that spanned the inner ditch and hotplate. She was home.

Three days later the city, with Anna among them, came to the outshining at the great arena. By midday every seat in the arena was taken, and by the second hour after noon when the first contest was due to take place, even the standing area was thronged with folk from the Lower Town and the tradesmen and their wives of the lesser courts of Serenity. By custom, masks did not have to be worn at an outshining by the contestants, and the spectator-folk, themselves masked according to the law, crowded in to see their personal favourites appearing without masks. Those who dared to come without a mask, either enjoyed the very rare privilege of an official mask-pass, or were summarily turned away along with an instant fine.

Anna Seka had a place in the grand viewing stand which overlooked the 'shining ground' on its north side. It was reserved for the higher nobility and their families. She had been given a pass to match that of her step-father, the High Chancellor, who was chatting to a nearby official and happily took her place beside him. She noticed straight away that her sister was not there. And her mother, who was said to be suffering from a slight fever, was also not present. Her place had been offered to Hartley, as Anna's mentor.

Shadwatch of Glamtech was also there, unmasked as usual and sitting on his own as was his custom. He ignored all but the most direct greetings, even from senior officials, but seemed happy to chat to his attendant glambot, Teevey Blue-Ray.

The king was absent. No one was surprised. His attendance at outshinings was at best infrequent, and although he did not openly disapprove of them, it was whispered in the inner circle of the palace that he found them at times tiresome even if they were politically useful if not required. However, Akton the chancellor had come in his name, and even carried the royal sceptre to denote his status as regent, and to announce the beginning of the afternoon's entertainment when the moment came.

Anna also noticed that the three judges of the imperial court were present, and next to them, Barvarik. But there was no sign of her sister, Talessa. Barvarik's expression straightway told Anna that something was wrong. His features were taut, and both hands clenched the arms of his chair.

She turned to her step-father. 'My lord,' she said, not even sure that he had noticed her, and conscious of the formality of the viewing stand, 'I see that lord Barvarik is not himself today.'

Her father turned, raised his hand in greeting and then nodded sadly. 'Ah, daughter, you have come! It is good to see you. We were worried, you know.' He paused, then lowered his voice. 'Yes, Barvarik, as you can see, he has suffered, and we have suffered too, a blow not one of us expected to see.'

'Talessa?' Anna sensed that the tone in her step-father's voice meant that tragedy had overtaken her sister.

He nodded again. 'My daughter, and your sister is no longer one of us. She has become a stainer.'

Anna gasped. 'Father, that cannot be!' Behind her mask, tears filled her eyes.

Akton reached out and took his step-daughter's hand. 'Hush now, Anna. It is as yet not commonly known what tragedy has befallen our poor girl and we ourselves.'

'What do you mean, father?'

'Apart from the royal household and the imperial judges, Talessa's fall from beauty has been kept a closed event. I would ask that you tell no one else.' He paused. 'Your mother's heart is broken.'

Anna shook her head in disbelief. 'How can this be?' she whispered. 'Our family has no stain cells. We have been tested, all of us.' Again she shook her head. 'I don't understand.'

When her father did not answer, Anna risked a glance at Hartley, but he did not seem to have overheard the conversation. He had turned away and was talking to the nobleman on his right hand. Again, she looked at her father. 'I will say nothing,' she said, her voice trembling and then once more whispered: 'Can nothing be done, father?'

Akton gave a slight shake of the head, and looked fixedly ahead and down into the arena where the cages of the first contestants were being lowered. 'The best Litra physicians assure me that nothing can reverse her condition. Our dear Talessa has been declared a stainer and assigned a capsule in the main prison.' He paused and looked away. 'I never thought to see the day when our beautiful child would be assigned one of those dreadful contrivances.'

Before Anna could reply, there was a blast of trumpets from the arena speakers. Her step-father, impassive, stood with sceptre in hand, to begin the outshining.

And so the pageant began. It lasted through the rest of the afternoon, with a short break for refreshments, and then continued on into the evening. As expected the contests were almost exclusively between captured stain-folk and nobles drawn from the upper courts of the imperial precinct. To be chosen to compete was considered an honour, so long as you were a citizen of Serenity. If you were a stainer on the other hand, it was considered a punishment and a mark of degradation.

Anna, like her sister, had never particularly liked outshinings but she watched this particular pageant with a renewed and fearful interest. Already she had spotted Nike and Leviss suspended high above the arena in two of the cages among those of the other contestants, and she knew it was only a matter of time before at least one of them was called to a shining.

By the end of the first hour, all had gone according to plan as far as the imperial planning committee were concerned:

Five stainers had been set against citizens of Serenity, and all five had been defeated. And contests had proceeded according to the strict rules of an outshining. It went this way:

After a single trumpet note, guards on the gantry above the arena would lower a chosen stainer-cage into the centre of the arena. Then the umpire, resplendent in robes of green and gold would call for a challenger. That was the signal for a noble to remove his mask (which always produced a murmur of excited chatter) and step forward. As the noble neared the cage it was also the signal for a loud burst of cheering from the waiting crowd. When all had gone quiet, the umpire would strike the ground three times with his staff, and step back.

For anyone unfamiliar with an outshining, little would appear to follow this elaborate beginning. The noble would enter the cage, the door would be swung shut, and the contest would begin. At first, to the untrained eye, nothing appeared to happen. The two contestants would merely stand opposite each other at about three metres distant, and stare fixedly at their opponent.

And so it would persist in this manner: a combat by presence, as the imperial handbook on outshinings described it. It was a simple collision of wills, a test of confidence, and above all a 'beauty contest'. It was firmly believed throughout the kingdom that physical beauty gave an individual man or woman the unique power to assert themselves as superior to an opponent. And superior in every way.

'An enemy inferior in appearance must inevitably surrender and submit to the superior beauty of his or her opponent,' as the festival handbook put it.

To the spectators, well versed in such festivals or pageants, such an occasion made for fascinating viewing. It was permitted by the chancery for citizens of Serenity to bet on each contest. They could place bets in two ways:

(a) The length of time required for a contestant to overwhelm his opponent

(b) Which opponent would be the victor.

Anna knew only too well the signs of victory and defeat: one of the contestants, almost invariably a stainer, would begin to look away, then shake. Sometimes it was no more than a faint trembling of the hands, or a subtle swaying of the shoulders. This could go on for minutes. Then a tremor would appear to run through the whole body, and the contestant would begin to convulse and tremble uncontrollably. At the last, they would slowly sink to their knees, and either bow their head, or rock sideways and topple to the sand-covered floor of the cage.

The moment this happened, the umpire would raise his staff and the crowd would roar their approval and stamp their feet. A pause would follow, the noble would step out of the cage, which would be raised again with the defeated stainer lying motionless in the sand or kneeling.

And so it went: no blood, no broken bones, no death cries. But in its own particular way an outshining had its own form of brutality. It was a crushing place where will was broken and personality was reduced to total submission.

Anna watched as one by one the captured stainers were broken down to the status of victims: lying twisted and convulsed were they fell, or crouched over, tears streaming into the sand. She had hoped that she might have been able to leave during the refreshment break, but neither Nike or Leviss had been called. They remained in their cages. Anna knew she would have to wait. At least, she told herself, it could not be much longer. Apart from Nike and Leviss, there were only two other stain-folk left, two young men who at first glance looked like brothers.

And so she stayed, hating each moment of raucous victory, but talking quietly with her father when the crowd settled down to the next contest, and nodding whenever she thought any onlookers expected her to. Hartley had disappeared, slipping away when she was not looking. She did not wonder why he had left the outshining, and she had long since learned not to ask such questions. Lord Hartley came and went as he pleased, and no one seemed to challenge his decisions, or question his presence or his absence. Not even her father.

At last, just as the umpire entered the arena once more, and the excited babble of the crowd began to die away, Hartley returned and sat down next to her with a smile that lit up his mask. 'It is all arranged,' he said to Anna as he sat back in his chair.

'What is arranged, my lord?' she asked, only half interested.

'You will see, Anna Seka,' he replied. 'You will see.'

The umpire waited longer than usual, until there was not a sound from the crowd, and the faint birdsong in the trees beyond could just be heard. Then he raised his staff:

'And now for something special,' he said, his deep voice echoing across the arena. He paused for dramatic effect, then raising his staff pointed towards the grand viewing stand:

'Lord Hartley has graciously agreed to demonstrate the power and authority of Serenity, by challenging two contestants at once.' He waited for the buzz of excitement to die away, and then went on. 'Two stainers will challenge lord Hartley simultaneously: the beauty of the kingdom versus the barbarous might of the outlands.'

As the applause flooded around the arena, Hartley nodded modestly, and got slowly to his feet. He glanced at Anna. 'Wish me luck, Anna Seka,' he said, and turned away before she could reply.

Slowly he removed his mask. There were gasps of admiration. His legendary beauty, almost never seen, stirred the arena. Smiling, he made his way down from the viewing stand, with every eye upon him.

Moments later he was in the arena, standing on the fighting platform and facing the two young men of the outlands, who, because of their duality, were both now themselves standing outside their lowered cages. Slowly the applause died away, and the contest began.

It was soon clear that this was not to be a foregone conclusion. The young men, clearly fiercely determined, well built and fit, had determined to make a fight of it. They stood about a metre apart from one another, so that Hartley could not focus on both of them at once, and Anna noticed that they also swayed slightly from side to side in an effort to disturb his concentration.

For a time it worked, and Hartley struggled to assert himself. A nervous hush descended over the crowd, and for the first time there was no calling out of bets or offers of odds on a quick victory. Several minutes passed, and for just a brief pause Anna found herself hoping that the young men might turn the tables on her mentor, and bring him to his knees.

But Hartley was not going to be so easily defeated. Although it was against the rules to shift from your 'shining point', Hartley moved slightly, almost imperceptibly to his left. Holding their ground, the two men followed his gaze, and so aligned themselves with his full focus. And there he held them, as a serpent holds its prey in its deadly glance. They could have moved, but they did not. Perhaps, in their courage and pride, they held their positions and returned his stare. Anna sighed, and looked down. Soon it would all be over. Two minutes later, no more, there came a shout from the crowd, and she raised her head. The two young men were kneeling together in front of Hartley, eyes clenched shut and shoulders shaking. Defeated. Crushed.

Hartley looked at them for a moment, shrugged and then did something almost never seen before in the arena: he drew his sword. Slowly, deliberately he tapped both stainers lightly on the head with the flat of the blade, and turned away with a brief bow the umpire. The crowd which had begun to cheer, suddenly fell silent. At the same time, the umpire who was a man of renown in Serenity, stepped up to Hartley, frowned and said something to him.

Anna watched as her mentor paused, glanced towards the viewing stand for an instant, and then turning back, replied to the umpire. There was a hesitation on the umpire's part, and then he nodded uncertainly before raising his staff:

'A fair contest,' he said. 'There is no dispute. And now as the rules allow, my lord Hartley is allowed to choose the contestant for the next outshining.'

It took Anna some time to realise that her name had then been called.

Her father tapped her on the arm, and she started. 'Papa?' she said, using the term of close affection and at the same time staring down into the arena. The umpire, his mask pulsing and aglow, stared back up at her.

Akton smiled unseen through his mask. 'I know, my daughter' he said. 'This is your first outshining. Count it an honour and a privilege to be chosen. Do it in memory of your sister.'

'But papa . . .' she started to protest but he smiled again and took her by the hand. 'Do not worry daughter. Hartley, your mentor is down there, and the crowd will be with you. Choose the stainer boy. Do you see him up there in the cage? He looks the weaker, and younger too. See how he stands? He is defeated already.' He smiled again, and squeezed her hand. 'Go now, and Serenity be with you.'

Anna found herself on her feet. She took off her mask. The crowd all around her melted away, as she made her way down the steps and into the arena. Hartley met her, smiled warmly and put his hand on her shoulder. 'There you are, little scout. What a day this is! First, I am pitted against the two most stubborn stainers I have ever come across, and now you have been chosen to complete your first outshining.'

'My lord,' whispered Anna. 'Am I ready for such a thing?'

He laughed, turned and winked at the umpire. 'No one is ever ready inside of themselves. It is your appearance that makes you ready. That is all. Think of that. In your beauty is your strength.'

Anna nodded, and then remembering the formalities of the contest, turned and bowed to the umpire, who returned her bow and motioned her forward.

'Come near, step-daughter of Akton,' he said. 'This is your moment, and here is your place to take a stand.'

She came forward, aware that the viewing stands around the arena and fighting platform had fallen silent, and that both Nike and Leviss, with their cages lowered, were on the other side of the contest-area, waiting to see whom she would choose. They had recognised her. Of course they had. Leviss's eyes were wide with surprise, but Nike was looking at her with a strange smile. It was a smile of recognition, yes, but what else did it say?

'Choose your contestant,' said the umpire quietly, 'and make ready to begin.'

Anna found that her mind which had been a confused whirl, full of doubts, fears and uncertainties, suddenly cleared. She knew now what she must do. It was far more than perhaps was expected of her. And what is more, her head told her heart that what she was about to do was madness. But she would do it. She would. She had to. Tensing for a moment, she took a deep breath: her heart had ruled her head and there was no turning back.

'My lord umpire,' she said, raising her voice and trying to keep it from shaking, 'you do me great honour to summon me here, and my lord Hartley has done this city great honour by defeating two opponents at once. As I am his chosen pupil, and as he is my appointed mentor, I will return the honour by also facing two contestants at the same time.'

For a moment, the umpire was taken aback. He stood open-mouthed behind his mask for a second, then recovering himself, turned to Hartley. 'This is very irregular,' he said. 'This girl is still a trainee is she not, and not yet proven in the arena?'

Hartley was quick to reply. 'She is a lone scout, my lord, and as such has been taught by me to think for herself, and to take measured risks, not foolhardy ones. But she has also been taught to place daring over safety.' He paused. 'This is very unusual, I grant you my lord umpire, but it is in keeping with our code.'

An excited hum ran about the crowd as the news of what Anna-Seka was about to do filtered up to the higher parts of the stands and to the grand viewing stand itself.

The umpire thought for a bit longer, frowned and then raised his staff. 'So be it!' he said, and struck the ground.

Hartley did not leave the arena, nor did he replace his mask. He was fascinated by Anna, and surprised to even find himself defending her before the umpire, and in front of the crowd. She had courage, he could not deny that, but then so did many of his pupils, and yet they did not move him as Anna did. Indeed, he could hardly remember some of their names. But this daughter of Akton, this Anna-Seka, had a mystery about her that he was drawn to, but could not yet fully understand.

He watched as the last two cages were lowered together, the doors opened and the stainers were led out.

Anna, her mask removed, had taken her stand about three metres away from where Nike and Leviss now stood. She saw the recognition in their eyes, and the hope. She also saw friendship. They did not call out. They did not betray her. Their silence reassured her, but at the same time nearly moved her to tears. Clearly they expected her to show mercy, to perhaps turn away from the fight and refuse the outshining: to rescue them by taking upon herself the shame of a refusal.

But she knew that that could never be. She returned their pleading looks with a cold, hard-edged pitiless gaze. It was to be an unrelenting outshining: dark, deep and unfeeling. Drawing on all her strength, and all her training, she focussed, made wide her eyes and held her friends in the grip of her mind, as a snake holds its prey under its deadly hypnosis before it strikes.

Leviss was the first to fall. Overwhelmed and painfully aware of his inferior demeanor, he opened his mouth to say something, shook his head slightly and then toppled into the sand. Nike looked at her brother, for a moment reached out for him and then turned to face Anna again. The pleading in her eyes had now become defiance. She returned her friend's gaze with all the hate that she could muster. But it was not in her to hate. Her head told her to hate, but her heart told her that she could not, not even in the face of a seemingly merciless stare. She began to shake: her glance fell, her hands clenched, unclenched and then at last hung by her side. Moments later, her head began to drop, and her shoulders stooped. With one last supreme effort, she lifted her gaze.

Anna-Seka saw in front of her an expression of deepest sorrow, an expression that she had never seen in the eyes of any other creature: her friend was broken, and she, Anna Seka, had broken her.

With a sob that made her whole body shake, Nike bowed her head and sank to her knees. It was a movement that made Anna want to rush forward, catch her up, and hold her in her arms. But she knew she could not. What was done, was not yet done till all was done. So she held her gaze: motionless, proud and pitiless. With all the appearance of a terrible beauty that was entirely without compassion, Anna fought back the tears, and smothered the deep groan that welled up within her.

At last, the umpire struck the ground and shouted: 'We have a victor! Anna-Seka of the Upper Town and the imperial precinct has won against two opponents recruited from stainland.' He struck the ground again. 'That concludes the outshining.'

'My lord!' Anna had spoken. She had spoken precisely when she was expected not to speak. All that was required of her under tournament rules, was for her to hold her peace, bow to the umpire, acknowledge the crowd, and then leave the arena, putting on her mask as she left. But she had spoken, and loudly enough for all in the spectator-area to hear. Up in the grand viewing stand, Akton leaned forward. 'What is my daughter up to now?' he muttered under his breath.

But it was the umpire who broke the silence:

'Why do you speak?' he asked.

Anna bowed. 'My lord, is it not written in the rules of outshining, that a victor in their first contest may claim a boon or favour from the umpire in the presence of the assembled citizens?'

The umpire coughed. He had not expected this. 'You have read this in the rules, yourself?'

'My father read it, my lord. He told me when I was no more than nine years old, but I know him for an honest man, and I trust that the rules have not changed since then.'

For a long time the umpire did not answer. He was aware of Hartley coming up on his shoulder, but he waved him back. The crowd held its breath. Hartley was not a man to be dismissed by a gesture, but on this occasion he complied. Even the guards whose task it was to take the defeated stainers back to their cages, did not move, but remained in their places on the far side of the arena. Anna was facing the umpire, but she was careful not to look directly at him. Instead she kept her gaze lowered. After a while she heard the umpire clear his throat and begin to speak once more:

'Your step-father, the High Chancellor, is right of course,' he said. 'According to the rules, you are entitled to ask a favour of myself as umpire of this outshining.' He paused: 'Ask what you will, and I will listen to your request.'

Bowing again, Anna spoke: 'My lord umpire, I ask only this: that the two stainers I have just defeated be delivered back to the outlands,' she paused, 'back from whence they came.'

There was a silence. The umpire grunted, frowned and then grunted again. 'What's that you say? You are asking that we let these prisoners go free?'

Anna-Seka shook her head. 'No, my lord. Not set free, but banished. Cast out, returned to the wilderness.' Again she paused. 'I will take responsibility for their return. I have recently returned from the outlands with my lord Hartley. I know how barren and diseased those lands are. I am not offering these outlanders freedom, but am instead releasing them so that they do not remain a burden on our city.'

As she spoke, Anna caught Hartley's eye. He still had not put his mask on, and he was studying her intently, his eyes giving away nothing but intense interest, and a slight puzzlement.

Again, the umpire coughed, and now his mask glowed. 'Most irregular,' he said, 'most irregular.'

'But it lies perfectly within the rules of an outshining contest, my lord,' interrupted Hartley. 'See, the high chancellor and his secretary are present are they not? Can they not adjudicate?'

The umpire scowled, and his mask now glowed a deep red. He did not appreciate being lectured on protocol by Hartley. What's more, as this elected officer was himself a Glamtech official, he was not keen to involve the high chancellor and his department, especially in a decision regarding an outshining.

'That will not be necessary, my lord,' the umpire said quickly. 'We will grant this request, but only on one condition.'

'And what is that?' asked Hartley risking yet another interruption.

'Why no more than this: that you yourself accompany these stainers and the chancellor's step-daughter to the outlands, and report back to the outshining executive of Serenity before the next full moon.'

'Ten days, my lord? We will have to be swift, I am thinking.'

With a wave of the hand, the umpire turned away. 'You are lonescouts, are you not? Ten days is more than enough time.' He now turned to Anna:

'Your request is granted, Anna-Seka of Akton. The prisoners will be delivered into your custody at the great northern gate tomorrow morning, at the first hour of the dawn watch. Do not be late, or the arrangement is forfeit.'

'Thank you, my lord,' replied Anna. Only now did she risk a glance towards where Leviss lay sprawled on the ground. Nike was still kneeling, head bowed. She longed to go to them, and offer some comfort, and perhaps even a whispered explanation, but she dared not. Anything more than cool detachment, and an indifferent glance, was likely to be seen as sympathy: then all would be lost. She looked at Hartley. 'And thank you also, my lord,' she said, bowing more deeply than was usually expected.

Hartley shrugged as he replaced his mask. 'I will expect to see you at the northern gate tomorrow morning. Do not be late.'

CHAPTER #5
MARLIN

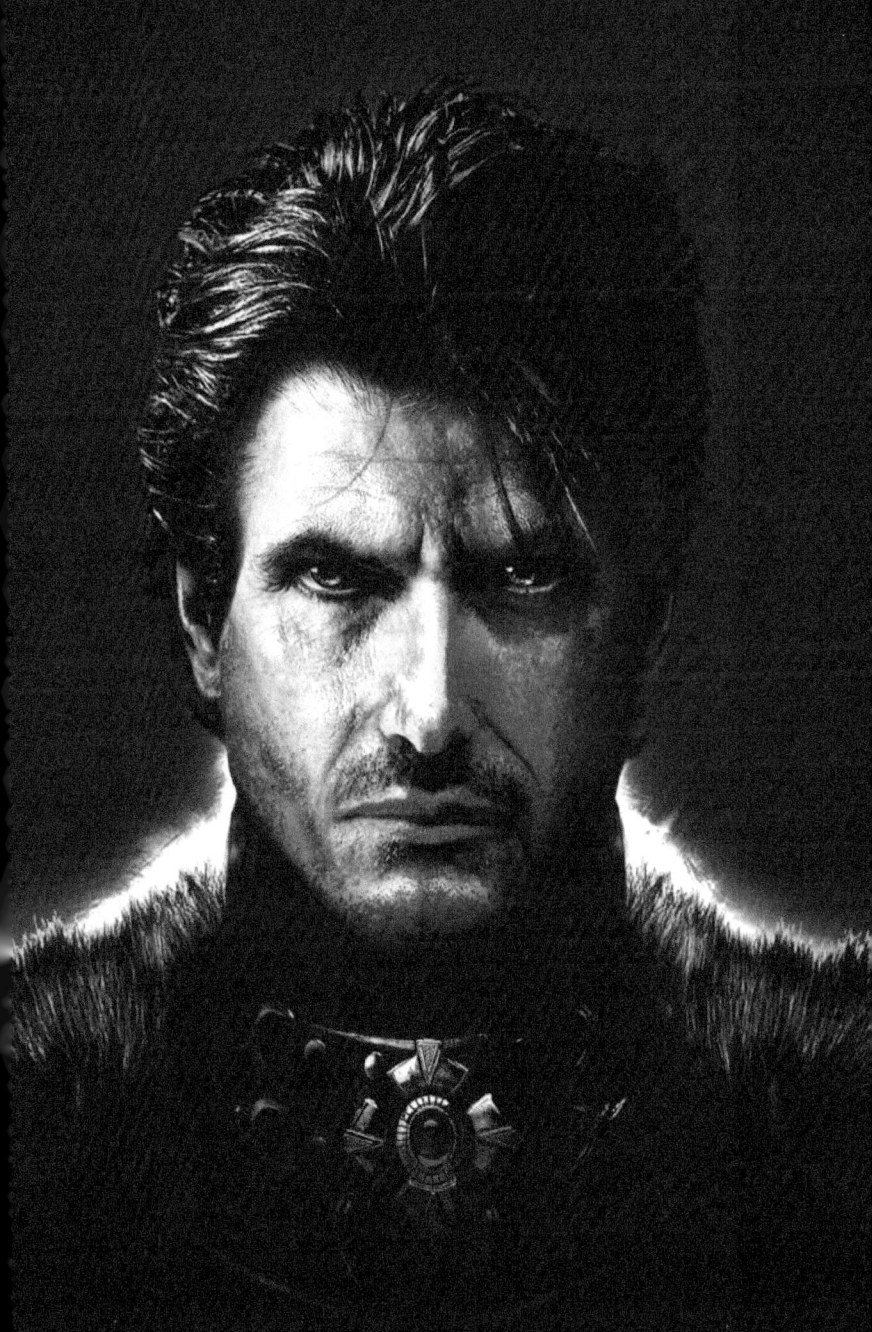

Anna did not sleep well. She woke early, two hours before sunrise, and got ready to leave. Her father was in the kitchen-courtyard to see her off. He had arranged with the servants for a small pack to be added to her usual kitbag.

'It might come in useful,' he said, pressing it into her hand and kissing her on the cheek. 'Don't forget your mask now, and go careful on your way to the gate. The streets aren't as safe as they used to be.'

She thanked him, and half turned to leave. 'Is this a good idea, papa?' she asked suddenly, staring through the window into the darkness.

Akton smiled. 'Your trip to the outlands? A good idea? It is neither good nor bad until we see the result of it, but I trust the heart of the girl who thought of such a thing.'

Anna gave her step-father a hug. 'Look after mama, papa. And give her my love.'

'I will daughter, I will. Now, off with you now, or you'll be late. I'll send our doorkeeper with you as far as the first guard-post of Low Town.' He kissed her gently on the brow. 'Go well, Anna, and the peace of Serenity go with you.'

Twenty minutes later, Anna was hurrying along the deserted streets of Low Town, dimly lit by the latest Glamtech glow lamps set high on the walls of the houses and shops. Hartley came up alongside her as she neared the northern gate. She startled with surprise.

'My lord,' she said quickly. 'I did not hear you.'

He nodded. 'You were not meant to, little scout, but I am pleased to see that once again you had drawn your sword even as you turned to see me.'

'You have trained me well, my lord.'

He shrugged. 'Have I? I am not sure. Time will tell.' Then he gestured towards the guards waiting by the gate:

'Shadwatch's men, and two security agents as well, I see. They will have brought your stainer friends with them.'

'My friends, my lord?' Anna tried to look puzzled.

Hartley looked hard at her for a moment, then gave a dry laugh: 'A joke, Anna-Seka, a joke. Of course they are not your friends, but they should be. You have done more for them, than anyone else in this fine city would have thought to.' He took a couple of steps forward, and stopped. 'I see them now. In the shadows, over there. See?'

Anna peered into the gloom. She could just make out, some distance away, the huddled forms of two people, but could not say for sure that it was Leviss and Nike. Hartley, she decided, must have eyes like a hawk.

Then her mentor slapped her on the shoulder:

'Come on!' he said. 'I have ordered horses for us. I hope these outlanders can ride.'

Anna was not the only one to rise early that morning. Barvarik had also slept badly. In fact he had hardly slept at all since Talessa had been judged 'stained', and taken away to Level Four of the grand imperial prison. He still could scarcely believe what had happened to his betrothed. Suddenly she was gone, and there was every chance that he would never see her again.

Despite the pleadings of her mother and father, the king's secretary had signed the warrant for Talessa's arrest, trial and transportation. It had all happened within the same day. By early afternoon she had been taken from the hospital ward where she was being treated, put to trial in the general assizes of the imperial precinct, and finally sent down to prison. The length of her sentence was to be confirmed later at the next meeting of the High Council. Such a meeting was to be held in secret, and Talessa's father had been asked not to attend, even though he was the chancellor.

For a brief but mad moment Barvarik had thought of somehow rescuing his Talessa, and trying to escape into the fields and forest beyond the outer walls of the city. But when he saw the armed escort which surrounded her, he abandoned the idea. Any intervention on his part could only end in disaster. All he could do was wait, and hope that when some time had passed he might be able to get permission from the chancellery to visit Talessa in prison.

But in the meantime, he could not sleep. And even as Anna-Seka, Talessa's step-sister was heading for the great North Gate and the road to the border-lands, he was standing on the balcony of his room overlooking the city and wondering what more he could do. The city below him seemed so peaceful, so undisturbed. And yet he sensed that all was not well within Serenity, nor without, and that sooner or later his skills and commitment as a warrior of the Imperial Guard would be called upon. It had been many years since the armies of Serenity had gone to war, and many years since there had been an armed invasion of the kingdom, but the storm clouds were definitely gathering, and all was not well in the outlands, and the borderlands to the north.

There was talk that Arx itself might be under threat, and earlier this year several cohorts of regular troops had been sent to that city to reinforce the garrison, and protect the king's highway where it passed close by to Arx and ran on to the Fence and the Great Tower.

But the Imperial Guard had not yet been chosen to go. His regiment was tasked with the defence of the western walls of Serenity, and only several days before he had been grateful for such a commission. But now, with Talessa taken from him, he found himself wishing that he might be sent out of the city to a trouble-spot where he might perhaps lose himself in the action and danger of a military campaign. He even envied Anna-Seka for her mission to return the two stainers to the outlands. Of course she had fought well in the arena – surprisingly well – and she had every right to claim her privilege from the outshining executive. And of course the fact that she was Hartley's student, and the High Chancellor's step-daughter clearly carried some weight. Too much, perhaps. Such a swift rise to notice among the high councillors of Serenity was always –and had always been – both dangerous and unwise. There was little doubt that she would need Hartley's protection for some time to come.

He leaned forward on the balcony rail and stared at the dim watch lamps along the royal avenue that led down from the Upper Town. Soon it would be dawn, and the first of the morning patrols would be appearing in the streets.

He knew what he had to do. After breakfast, he would go to the central commissariat of the main prison and make application to visit Talessa. Then, he would make his way to the third court where his regiment had its barracks. Once there, he would report to his senior officer and apply for a seconded transfer to a border patrol. He knew that he had a good chance of acceptance. Transfers to the borders were not popular, and there was always a need for extra troops in that area. It would only be a temporary transfer, perhaps six months no more, and by then his prison application would have been processed, and all going well he might be granted leave to see Talessa. Although prison sentences, especially for stainers, were often years, even decades in length, after the first six months visits by relatives and close friends were actively encouraged.

Only last year, the uncle of a close friend of Barvarik's had been sent to level two of the prison for some kind of offence. After a period of isolation, the uncle was encouraged to invite his family to visit him. Barvarik was also invited, and while he was in the prison visitors' area, the duty officer told him that the High Council had found that prisoners worked better and for longer if they were able to see relatives and friends on a regular basis.

But of course, as the prison authorities had intended, Barvarik had hated visiting the place. Yes, it was clean, it was tidy and it was well lit. The facilities for the prisoners, based on a series of capsules, suspended from gantries and pulleys into narrow shafts, although designed to be lowered deep underground, were well equipped and even comfortable. But that was only half the story. From the moment that Barvarik entered the east wing of level two where capsules hung from their cables like weird, oversize fruit on a vine, he saw that the area he had entered was as much a factory, as it was a prison. There were, beneath the clustered capsules, production lines, assembly areas with landing stages, maintenance units and dispatch centres. Guards stood around in their distinctive SSS uniforms, but there were also works managers in white coats, engineers in overalls and specialist tradesmen in the drab uniform of the Lower Town. The air was filled with the sound of machinery, and a pale dust hung over the work-bays and assembly lines.

It was not a good place to be, and yet this was only the second level, where prisoners convicted of lesser, temporary offences were kept. From his childhood Barvarik had been taught that the lowest levels of the main prison, dug deep down into the rocky foundations of the city, were places without hope, and that to be sent to the third or fourth level was the equivalent of a death sentence.

Barvarik stepped back from the balcony of his apartment and stared at the emptiness. His betrothed had been sent to the fourth level, and so that was that. He might at some stage be able to visit her, as would her family, but there could be no release for her from the sentence she had received, and she would almost certainly live out the rest of her life without ever seeing the light of day again. Where was the justice in that? He struggled to answer that question. He had never bothered to ask it of himself before. Not until his Talessa had been taken from him. But he was asking it now, and try as he might, his conscience would not reply.

Going back into his room, he took his sword from where it hung from the scabbard rack above the fireplace. Slowly he turned it over in his hand, feeling its familiar weight, relaxing the grip, feeling the balance and admiring, as he always did the chastened blade and its steel-blue edge. One day, he said to himself as the words slowly and painfully formed in his mind: one day there will be better laws in Serenity: laws that set men and women free, instead of enslaving them.

There was a knock at the door, and he looked up. It was his early morning call.

'Thank you!' he said, raising his voice and then listening as the footsteps of his man-servant retreated down the hallway. He sighed again, glanced at his sword once more and slid it back into its scabbard.

'Breakfast and then the commissariat,' he muttered to himself, and made ready for his day.

By the time that Barvarik had finished his breakfast, Anna-Seka, Hartley, Nike and Leviss were well clear of Serenity and galloping their horses across the open plain that led to the northern borders. Hartley had been impressed by the horsemanship of the two outlanders, but had said nothing. Anna was relieved, and it gave her the opportunity to speak to Nike and Leviss without giving away any clues that she might have met them before.

What she didn't know was that Hartley had already guessed that Anna knew them, but was now planning to use it to his advantage. He was disappointed by Anna's deception, but found himself respecting her for it. He knew that she was instinctively loyal both to himself, and the City, but she had shown a special kind of courage in defending these two outcasts, even at risk of her own imprisonment or even execution. Somehow they had formed a bond: the two stainers and his dark-eyed student-scout, and it was a bond he was not inclined to break. Not yet, at least.

He listened to Anna as she chatted away to the girl-stainer, trying, as he listened, to build up a picture of their friendship, and what they might yet be planning. But little was given away, and again Hartley found himself admiring her for it. So he shrugged as they eased to a gentle canter and began to work their way down a slope towards a staging post. It would be such a pity if he had to turn Anna over to the SSS interrogation squad, and the Middle Chamber of Enquiry. This girl-scout had real ability and a greater degree of resourcefulness he was yet to discover in any other member of his reconnaissance division.

As for Nike and Leviss themselves, on this particular day they felt nothing but gratitude for Anna. At the outshining, they had both been convinced that Anna had cruelly betrayed them for a reason that was totally beyond their understanding. Until, of course, she had spoken to the umpire and the other citizens of Serenity, just as the contest had ended. At first, they had been too overwhelmed and disoriented by their defeat to fully understand what was happening. However, as they recovered their strength and their wits in a cell in a guard-house near the northern gate that night, they were able to talk to each other at last. Then, and only then the nature of Anna's plan took shape in their minds.

'She means to get us back home,' Leviss had said after a while, as he sat in the straw of the cell with his back against the stone wall. 'She is our friend after all.'

Nike had nodded. 'She is,' she had replied under her breath, 'but keep your voice down. If we are overheard, then she is lost and we with her.'

And now, the following day as they rode together across the great northern plain of the first quadrant with a Security Services officer at their backs, Anna at their side and Hartley directly ahead of them, the two outlanders were more determined than ever to keep Anna's mission a secret between themselves. As for the senior escort officer, they recognised him from the outshining, and could tell by the badges on his shoulder that he was of a dangerously high rank, and unlikely to show mercy if he suspected treachery.

And so they went on, Leviss holding his peace, while his sister talked easily with Anna, and Hartley guided his horse just in front of them, always just within earshot.

Three days later they came to the border, and crossed at the great northern gate, where the senior security officer was to leave them and return to Serenity. There were some puzzled looks from the border-post guards, but they did not challenge Hartley's mask, nor the signed warrant he carried. Soon they found themselves across the Fence-Line and cantering along the imperial highway. It was shortly afterwards that Hartley drew his horse alongside that of Anna. He leaned towards her. 'We will stop soon,' he said. 'But know this: our paths must separate for a time.'

Anna looked at her tutor, impassive behind his mask. There was nothing in the tone of his voice to tell her of his true intentions. She nodded. 'I understand, my lord,' she said, and then turned to look at the road ahead. It was empty, which was hardly surprising. These were toxic lands and in recent years had been well cleaned over by Rebuild's divisions and working parties. There were some ruined buildings, hardly any trees and few signs of habitation beyond a few broken down stone walls and an occasional commercial complex, empty and abandoned since the Great Burning. Near these buildings Anna also noticed rusting sign posts and the occasional battered roadside hoarding. To her they seemed to show that there had once been scattered townships in these lands. How many folk, she wondered had once lived here, and where had they all gone all those years ago?

About a mile ahead where the road climbed a low scarp she could see a beacon-cairn and guessed that was where Hartley would choose to stop.

She was right. They pulled up on the crest of the scarp, almost next to the cairn.

Hartley pointed away to the north and west. 'That is the quadrant where the Glass Tunnel can be found, and I guess it is also where these stainers have their home. Am I right?'

Anna was careful not to answer, but turned and looked at Nike and Leviss. 'Is that so?' she asked.

Nike grinned and then replied. 'It is, or near enough. Our family moves about, y'know. We are hunter-gatherers, and do not stay in one place for long. As long as we keep to the territory ruled by our warlord, then we feel we have a home.' She turned to Leviss. 'Am I right, brother?'

Leviss nodded. 'If you let us go now, we will not bother you anymore, and nor will our warlord. He will not have to send men to look for us.'

Hartley sat up in the saddle and stared at Leviss until his mask glowed. 'Though I do not fear this warlord of yours, I would know his name.'

Leviss hesitated. 'The name of our warlord is not ours to give, but I will tell you the name of the high-lord who rules all of these lands from the Ice Mountains to the Fence and Tower.'

'And?'

'His name is Chesterman.'

Hartley shook his head. 'I am unmoved,' he said. 'I have heard that name, but do not find it worthy of any note.'

For just an instant Leviss's eyes flashed, but he bit his lip and held his peace. Hartley waited for a moment, as if he hoped that Leviss might yet have something more useful to say. Then he gave a dry laugh, which echoed strangely from behind his mask.

'Get you gone,' he said. 'Both of you. And count yourselves lucky. But if I or any of my men find you within a mile of the Fence, you won't be shown the mercy you have been shown this time. My scout here will accompany you for a short distance, and then return to this cairn.' He paused. 'If she does not return safely, we will raze the land between here and the northern edge of this quadrant. There will be no survivors. Do you understand?'

Leviss said nothing, but Nike nodded. 'We understand,' she said. 'Your scout will be safe with us.'

With a shrug, Hartley turned to Anna. 'Go no more than half a day's march, then leave them. I will meet you here tomorrow at noon.'

Anna gave a slight bow. 'You are camping here, my lord?'

Hartley shook his head. 'I have business to attend to,' he said crisply. 'It is a matter of general security, nothing more, but it needs to be done.' He turned his horse's head, put his heels to its flanks and began to ride away. 'Go now!' he called over his shoulder. 'The day moves on!'

Anna-Seka, Nike and Leviss watched him go. When he was about half a mile distant, and little more than a vague shape on the horizon, Nike sighed with relief:

'Thank goodness that one's gone,' she said. 'I don't like his voice and I don't like his mask.'

Reaching up, Anna took her own mask off. It was standard practice for lone scouts to remove their masks once they were more than a mile north of the Fence, but if they were in a patrol of two or more scouts, masks had to be worn at all times, except in times of war.

Again, Nike sighed. 'It's so good to see you properly again,' she said, 'and to know that you are our friend and not an enemy.'

Anna clicked her tongue, flicked the reins and began to trot her horse forward. The others followed. 'I am sorry for what I did to you in the arena,' she said as they caught up with her. 'It seemed to be the only way to set you free.'

Nike grinned. 'I see that now, but at the time I didn't know what was going on. It didn't seem like you at all.'

'It wasn't,' said Anna simply. 'It wasn't me.'

Leviss looked puzzled. 'How do you mean, little sister?' he asked, using the term for a close friendship.

Anna smiled. 'It was a pretend me, and I was half scared to death in the doing of it. If the umpire or even lord Hartley had sensed what I was up to, all would have been lost,' she paused, 'for all of us.'

'Hah!' Leviss almost shouted. 'You played the game well. My uncle will give you the best of suppers if we manage to find him and the encampment before nightfall.'

'Where away, then?' asked Anna. 'I guessed north, but I have no idea, really.'

With a laugh, Leviss turned and winked at Nike. 'North will do fine just now. Uncle Bepsi moves about don't y'know. He chases the good pasture, a fair wind and fresh water. We will ride as blind as maybe, and look for nothing more than smudges of smoke on the skyline. That will do us.'

'Smudges of smoke?'

'Aye, camp fires. For good or ill. My uncle has organised and led wagon parties in very much the same way for years. You can tell his camp fires at a thousand paces, y'know: simple and friendly, but well protected from attack by bandits and wildfolk.' Leviss paused. 'That's his way, and that's the way we will find him.'

Glancing at Nike, Anna frowned. 'Does that make sense?' she asked.

Nike grinned. 'Not really, but for all that it's the right thing to do.' She slapped Anna on the shoulder. 'Cheer up, little scout. All is forgiven, and there's nothing to forgive. You have brought us safely to this place, and now it's our turn to get you safely home.' Leaning forward, she whispered in her horse's ear and stirred it to a canter. Leviss and Anna followed.

If they had looked back, they would have seen in the distance by an outcrop of rocks, a lone rider. He had a farscope held to his eye and was studying them intently. At last he lowered the 'scope. 'As I thought,' he muttered to himself, then turning his horse about, began to gallop along a grassy track towards the north and east. It was Hartley.

By the time the sun set on that day, Anna, Nike and Leviss had ridden for several hours and at last had caught sight of a camp fire about a mile away near a forest.

'Do you think it's your uncle?' asked Anna reining in.

Nike shrugged. 'Hard to tell, but since there are no other fires about, we may as well take the chance.'

'It's Uncle Bepsi all right,' said Leviss. 'See how he has pitched that fire? Near those woods, and with an open slope on two sides? Perfect, ain't it?' He put heels to his horse, making it rear for just a moment. 'You can box my ears if I'm wrong.'

He wasn't.

They came up the slope to the fire, coming out of the evening shadows and calling out the peace-cry as they swung from the saddle. Several figures appeared, and in among them a man carrying a war-spear. It was Bepsi-Loca.

RENEGADE

At the same time, many miles to the north and west, Hartley had reached a strange, sprawling building at the head of a narrow, shadow-filled valley. It was unusual to see one in this quadrant of the outlands, and it was well hidden to all but a practised eye. Or one who knew where to look for it. To anyone from the lost generations, familiar with the ancient architecture of the days before the Great Burning, it would have had the appearance of a football stadium. And that is what it was.

Hartley knew it well. It was the dwelling place of the king's brother: Prince Marlin of the House of Beau-John. Marlin the Exile, Marlin the renegade and outcast, and the one who, according to local legend had sworn to wreak revenge on the royal house of his birth. When his own wife and family had been struck by the stain-plague and cast into prison to await the prospect of execution without trial and without mercy, unable to set them free, he had fled the kingdom vowing to destroy Serenity. But before he left, he had stolen a poison formula from the central laboratory of Glamtech. It was an act that left Grim-Ace, the father of Shadwatch, dead, after he had attempted to stop Marlin from escaping.

Soon the king's brother had gathered around himself similar exiles and outcasts of Serenity, some coming with their families, others coming on their own, but all coming with this single idea: to find shelter with the king's brother. In return for his protection, they acknowledged him as their lord, and lent their skills and efforts to the task of transforming the abandoned stadium into a fortress. It had taken some years, but slowly and surely, with the building works mostly complete, Marlin had built up his military strength. He created hidden outposts in the barren lands of the western wasteland, and then reached out to the folk of the Stain kingdom in the provinces which lay to the north and east. He carefully avoided open confrontation with Serenity, but all the while used his inside knowledge to search out contacts and any sympathisers within the city itself. And that is how he had found Hartley, and how Hartley had found him.

Over the months and then the years, they constructed a network of spies, scouts and agents provocateurs that stretched from the halls of the Stain kingdom to the inner gates and high towers of Serenity and even to the corridors of the imperial palace itself.

For Marlin knew that secrecy was the imperative of his survival. If the king suspected that he, Marlin was planning an imminent attack against Serenity, he would not hesitate to launch the combined might of the Security Services and their military divisions against the outlands.

And Marlin knew his brother well. He knew that this high-king would not cease in his searching of the outlands until he was completely satisfied that he had at last destroyed Marlin along with all his supporters and their families. Their mutual hatred for one another burned bright in the quiet corners of both kingdoms and drifted silently across the lands that lay in between. On the king's part it was a hatred born of past memories and deep unspoken fears. For Marlin it was a hatred nourished by all that he knew to be true, or believed what must surely be so: his family had perished at the hands of his brother.

'One day!' That was the thought always at the back of Marlin's mind, and whenever he met with Hartley, that was ever the greeting he used to welcome him. For Hartley was his chief co-conspirator, a man who seemed as eager to betray his own king, as Marlin was desperate to bring that king down.

As for Hartley he never of course spoke openly of his reasons for supporting the king's brother, not even when he was north of the Fence, but time and again he had proved his loyalty to Marlin. Using his influence and contacts as a senior official within the palace, Hartley had provided Marlin with valuable information about everything from the passwords of the Lower Town patrols, to the security networks of the innermost sanctums of Litra, Glamtech and Rebuild.

And so together they had devised and planned and put into action their plot to reach deep into the heart of the palace itself and strike at those believed to be most secure and most honoured within Serenity. It was simply this: a poison plot. Using technology stolen from the top secret laboratories of Glamtech, they trained a select band of poisoners from among the Lower Town folk who had seen their families suffer at the hands of the king and his officials. Their desire for vengeance was a guarantee of their loyalty to Marlin, even though they themselves had no idea that it was Hartley who had identified them and drawn them into the web of this poison plot.

Thus it was that the little maid of Lower Town had been recruited, trained and then given the pilot-task of carrying the first dose of poison against the noble-woman Talessa, daughter of Akton, the High Chancellor. Neither Marlin nor Hartley were sure that the poison would work, or what effect it would have. It was simply an experiment, a dangerous experiment, but to their darkened minds an experiment well worth the risk.

It was only when Hartley had overheard Barvarik talking to Akton at the outshining about what had befallen Talessa, that he realised that the attack had been successful. He had almost cried out with joy – a rare betrayal of emotion for one so cool under even the most severe pressure – but he had bit his tongue, held his peace, and determined to get word to Marlin as soon as possible. Anna-Seka's performance in the arena of the outshining had played perfectly into his hands. When she had set the stainers free after her victory in the arena, it was easy for him to volunteer as her escort, without arousing suspicion. In fact it added to his status as an upholder of the law, and a protector of his own people.

He smiled to himself as he thought over all that had happened in the past weeks. Slowly, everything was moving into place. It was almost as though the fates had decreed it. Of course, he didn't believe in the 'the fates', but strangely he liked the idea and turned it over in his mind. Somehow, he decided that it had been decreed by some unknown and unseen power, that he was destined to rule Serenity, or at least be its kingmaker.

He reined in his horse about a hundred yards from the entrance to the stadium, and waited in the gloom. It was better that way. To ride straight up to the gates without giving warning, was to invite a crossbow bolt in the chest, or a shower of pulse-balls about his head.

He did not have long to wait. A figure appeared on the walls above the gates, and then another: two armed men. Someone stepped between them and climbed up onto a platform. Even at that distance, Hartley could tell that the lord of this place was now looking down at him. He raised his arm in salute:

'My lord Marlin!' he shouted, so that his voice echoed across the narrow valley.

The other man stared at him for a moment then raised his arm. But he said nothing.

Hartley nodded to himself. This was so like the king's brother. He shrugged and spoke again:

'I come in peace, lord Marlin, and I come with news.'

The king's brother signed to one of his men, who shouldered his crossbow and disappeared from the ramparts. Moments later the gates swung open, and a group of spearmen appeared. They marched towards Hartley, who swung down from the saddle to meet them.

A short while later he found himself in a large open area which now acted as the courtyard of the fortress. Marlin had also come down from the ramparts and was waiting for him. Again, he did not speak, but simply gestured towards Hartley as if he wanted him to approach.

But Hartley did not move. He held his ground, something he had planned to do earlier. He was determined to show Marlin that he could not be treated as one of his hired servants. If he could not persuade the king's brother that he was at least his equal in their enterprise, then he, Hartley, would go his own way.

For longer than was comfortable, both men held each other in a common gaze. Hartley was wearing his mask, but Marlin was bare-headed. The guards, helmeted and armed, stood stock still, not taking their eyes off Hartley, and waiting for a command from their lord.

At last Marlin spoke:

'The day draws on, lord Hartley. Will you take supper before we speak together?'

'I would tell you my news first, and then you can decide if I am worthy of such an honour,' replied Hartley, his voice strong and clear in the evening air.

Again, Marlin stared at Hartley. He had recognised the man in front of him, both from his mask and his voice. He also knew him by the way he stood: tall, confident and like a king. Marlin found it slightly troubling, but he knew that this official of Serenity had already proven himself to be a useful ally, and could even yet offer more. At last Marlin nodded. 'Speak with me as we are escorted to the main hall. That should give you more than enough time to say your piece.'

With a shrug, Hartley led his horse forward and handed the reins to one of the spearmen. 'Take good care of him,' he said. 'He's a good horse, and I will need him to carry me back to the border.'

The man bowed and led the horse away. Together, Marlin and Hartley walked across the courtyard towards the steep flight of steps that led up to the main hall.

'Well, my lord,' said Marlin. 'What news?'

Hartley lowered his voice as he spoke:

'Our plan, my lord. It has worked.'

Marlin glanced at Hartley. 'And we are not betrayed?'

Hartley shook his head. 'There is not even the least suspicion that it was anything more than an unfortunate infection. The formula you supplied acted precisely as you hoped it would.'

Marlin looked at the masked figure. How he hated those masks. No one in the stain kingdom wore them, although closed helmets were popular among the warrior class. Masks told you nothing of the man or woman who wore them. They were meant to shield the beauty of the wearer, but to Marlin's thinking they shielded the soul. Nothing for good or evil ever showed through the implacable gaze of those masks. Hartley could be smiling at him now, or sneering, he could not tell. And yet in his own expression, he, Marlin, held nothing secret. 'The eyes are the window to the soul', his mother used to tell him, 'If you can hold an unmasked man in your gaze for long enough you can read him as if you were reading a book.'

He turned away and looked out over the courtyard, the walls beyond, and there in the distance the faint outline of the towers and turrets of the Stain-City, known in those parts as Brokinburgh, or more simply, the Burgh.

'Who suffered the formula?' he asked after a while. 'Who did we strike down?'

Hartley's reply was crisp and without emotion. 'Talessa, daughter of Akton.'

Marlin frowned. 'Talessa? Talessa has been imprisoned? I did not think . . .'

'What did you not think, my lord?' The faintest tone of scorn crept into Hartley's voice.

With a sigh, Marlin turned to look at the mask again. 'Talessa is one of the few nobles in the palace that I do not have a quarrel with. Her father, yes: gladly would I see him suffer, but not his daughter.' He hesitated. 'But no matter, it is done, and what is done cannot be undone.'

'Just so. Just so.' Hartley took a step towards the hall, then turned. 'We are ready to strike again, you know. All our agents are in place. If you give the word, I can make sure by the end of next week that another twelve citizens of Serenity will be mysteriously infected with the stain, and find themselves in the imperial prison.'

'By the end of the week?'

'I return to the border tomorrow. Three days later I should be back in Serenity. I will issue the code and the attacks will begin.'

'And then?'

Hartley looked towards Brokinburgh, the Stain City. 'That is simple, my lord. Once I am sure that panic and fear are spreading through the streets of both Upper and Lower Town, I will leave Serenity, and make my way back here.' He gestured towards the city in the distance. 'I believe it is time to bring your little army and the forces of the warlords out of the shadows,' he paused, 'and to bring them down on the borders.'

'What, already?' Marlin looked surprised.

Hartley chuckled. 'A plague within the city, and a hostile army without: is that not the perfect dish to satisfy your appetite for revenge?'

The king's brother shook his head. 'You laugh at me, my lord?'

With a grunt, Hartley put his hand to his mask as if to apologise for wearing it. 'Why, no my lord. I do not laugh at you, but with you.'

The two men walked together into the hall, the guards pushing back the great doors, and saluting the lords as they passed. It wasn't until they were seated at supper that Hartley spoke again:

'Now we have started this plan of yours, prince Marlin, we must finish,' said Hartley, removing his mask and breaking some bread. 'If we move quickly, we can break the spirit of Serenity even before our troops reach its gates.'

Marlin studied Hartley. At last he could see the man behind the mask: read his eyes and hope to read his mind. What he saw reassured him. Hartley returned his gaze with an ice-cool honesty that told Marlin all that he wanted to know: this man of Serenity with whom he had entered into an alliance, was just as single-minded and ruthless as he hoped he himself had become.

'What do you propose?' he asked, reaching for the wine.

Hartley spoke without hesitating: 'When I return from Serenity, we should ride to Brokinburgh. I know you have a good number of troops at your disposal already, but we will need all the war bands of the Stain-lords if we are to have any chance of crossing the border, let alone attacking Serenity itself. Without the Big Five, we are powerless.'

Marlin raised one eyebrow. 'Not only do you speak as if you know that those five warlords will come with us, you also seem to think that a simple invasion will be enough to bring my brother's kingdom down. You should know better. Most men understand how well designed the defences of that kingdom are.'

Hartley nodded. 'I do, my lord and what I know, I know because I helped to design those defences.' He paused. 'I know their strengths and I know their weaknesses.'

Marlin nodded. 'And you have sufficient people on the inside?'

Hartley crumbled a piece of bread between his fingers. 'I believe so, my lord, but as always there is no guarantee of success. Fate is a fickle fellow, and no one's ally. In the end, anything can happen. All that we can do is to try and narrow the gap of uncertainty.'

Signing for a servant to bring some more food, Marlin leaned back in his chair. 'Ah, yes, the gap of uncertainty: we have no pledge as yet from the Stain-lords that they will follow us into battle.'

'There is one Stain-lord that will bring his army, and if he comes the others will follow.'

'Chesterman?'

'The same.' Hartley smiled. 'The one who wears the motorcycle. I can rely on him.'

'As a brother?'

Hartley shrugged. 'We understand each other.'

Again Marlin stared hard at this imperial official who was so willing to betray his king and so confident that his betrayal would bring success. He gave a faint smile. 'It is all in the masks, I think,' he said.

Hartley smiled back. 'Masks are such useful things,' he said. 'They separate and they conceal. They inspire fear in those that look upon them, and they instil courage in those that wear them.'

'So long as the mask fits, my lord.'

'Ah!' Hartley shook his head. 'So long as the mask appears to fit, that is all.'

A trumpet sounded on the walls. It was the beginning of the night watch. Soon the watch beams would be turned on. Getting slowly to his feet, Hartley picked up his mask, put it on and bowed to Marlin:

'My lord, I must leave early in the morning if I am to reach the border by noon. If you would show me to my quarters . . .'

Marlin smiled, stood and clapped his hands. A servant appeared. 'Show the lord Hartley to his rooms,' said Marlin, 'and tell the stable-master that his horse must be ready at dawn tomorrow.'

Hartley had just reached the door when Marlin suddenly spoke:

'How will I know that you have returned from Serenity and have crossed the border once more?'

Hartley nodded. 'I will light the beacon at Far Ammon. I will use a pale green fire. When you see it lit, you will know that I am only a day's journey from this place.'

'That is well, then.' Marlin grunted and returned to his supper. 'Take your rest now and travel well in the morning.' He smiled, 'I would ask you to bring my greetings to the fair citizens of Serenity, but I can think of none who would welcome them.'

Turning, Hartley gave a casual wave of the hand. 'My lord, you have more friends within the walls of that city than you know.' Without waiting for a reply, he left and followed the servant down the narrow, gloomy corridor that led to his quarters.

CHAPTER #6
POISONINGS

Hartley was true to his promise. He left Marlin's stadium-fortress early the following morning, rode hard for the border and met Anna-Seka at the stone cairn. She told him little of her journey with Nike and Leviss, except to say that she had seen them both safely to a stainer encampment some miles to the north and west. She did not mention that she had been welcomed by all the stainers including Bepsi-Loca, and had also been given their hospitality and shelter for the night. Nor did she mention that she had promised to return, next time that she was sent on a reconnaissance to that quadrant of the outlands.

But Hartley had guessed, and had said nothing, choosing instead to simply tell her that his mission had also gone well, and that it was important that they both return to Serenity without delay.

Within a day they had reached the border, and three days after that they reached the northern gates of Serenity. Leaving Anna to report to the Security Services commissariat, he hurried away to his contact in the chancellery, making sure on the way to leave a brief message with a palace official that the mission to return the two stainers to the outlands had been safely accomplished. He knew of course that Anna-Seka, with her report completed, would soon make her own way back to the imperial precinct and her family home. What she would tell her father, the high chancellor, he could not say but he was not concerned. Already he had decided that Anna's loyalty to the palace, the kingdom and to the king himself would keep her discreet, and sworn to secrecy in her own heart, even if it was a secrecy not sworn to himself.

'I have taught her well,' he muttered to himself, as he climbed the steps to the chancellery. 'She may not like me, but she trusts me and that is all I require.'

He frowned at the thought. Anna was not like the others, and he held her in some regard. But it was more than regard, it was affection. Yes, that was it, affection: an emotion he was unused to. He shook his head as if to free himself of the idea, and went on up the steps.

He reached the top and came out on a paved landing. A guard at the entrance to the chancellery saluted, and stepped back, as so often only taking the slightest of glances at his pass, and not even bothering to test his palm. For a moment he thought of rebuking the guard for this lapse of security, but he thought better of it. After all, the man was only demonstrating his loyalty and in these days of conspiracy and shadow politics, that was no bad thing.

And so, returning the guard's salute he passed through the entrance and into the chancellery. He soon found his contact, busy at his desk and surrounded by the paperwork of the imperial administration. It only took a moment for Hartley to place the coded message on the desk in front of the official. Without looking up, the man's hand slid over the message hiding it instantly. With a subtlety Hartley admired, the man kept working as though he had not even noticed the presence of the masked noble, and only confirmed that he understood what he had just received, by giving the merest nod.

As Hartley moved away, he heard the scratching of the pen on the pale paper of the chancellery, and smiled with approval. That man was an official he could rely on. It had taken him some time to persuade the fellow to throw his lot in with this particular palace conspiracy, but once persuaded he had shown a cold, calculating efficiency that was sure to reap a rich harvest in the coming days. For all concerned.

As it turned out, within five days Hartley's expectations had been fully realised. News spread through the palace precinct and the three main courts of the Upper Town that twelve more nobles, both men and women, had been declared stainers after sudden and unexplained infections or 'poisonings' and sent to the lower levels of the main prison. In two of the courts where multiple poisonings had occurred over several days, people began to apply for residential transfers, and some even abandoned their houses even before official sanction had been granted. In the marketplaces it was openly said that the authorities were losing control of the situation. Several secret petitions were lodged with the Commissariat, and the walls of quieter streets in Lower Town were daubed with anti-police slogans.

Triple S patrols were stepped up, and armed guards put at the entrances of every public building.

In order to allay fears and stop panic from spreading through the city, Hartley, along with other high ranking officials made a point of attending a number of festivals, notably the Frozen Bride auctions. These were always supervised by Glamtech, but commissariat officers made sure that proper procedures were followed, and that all successful bids were logged through their department, and the appropriate class of purchaser was assigned to every 'bridal consignment'. They were particularly popular, and useful for distracting the citizenry.

Hartley, though clearly not interested in bidding at these auctions, was able by his mere presence to reassure key people in Upper Town that the spate of poisonings or unexplained stainings was not something to worry about. And so his plan unfolded, and he was able to watch its course without arousing any suspicion.

Meanwhile, the laboratories of Glamtech were busy testing samples taken from the victims to see if such infections were in fact poisonings. And as always, Glamgel was used as a baseline component of any research into an anti-dote. At the same time, Security Service personnel swarmed throughout the palace, searching rooms and interviewing all citizens and residents: from cooks and stable lads to high councillors and even members of the royal household. But nothing was discovered and no arrests were made. In the meantime the Graders continued about their business, screening the citizenry and assessing their status.

Hartley himself was summoned to assist in the poisonings investigation, and for a week he even worked alongside Akton the chancellor and Shadwatch of Glamtech to try and track down the cause of this calamity that had so swiftly overtaken the city.

It was, for a different reason, an anxious time for Hartley. He had contacts throughout the Upper Town, and while these contacts were no doubt useful if not vital to the success of his plans, none of them had yet been tested by the more advanced interrogation techniques used by the SSS. It would only take one to crack under questioning, and all would be lost.

And so he held his breath, kept his counsel and tried to discreetly persuade Mackinsson, the head of the Security Services, not to be too aggressive in his conduct of interviews, especially when interrogating Litra personnel.

'These Litra folk are sworn to loyalty, and brought up from the cradle to honour and defend the king,' he said to Mackinsson at one briefing where the king himself was present. 'Of course we have to interview them, but I believe the cause of this plague lies elsewhere.'

There were few men that Arbut Mackinsson trusted, but he trusted Hartley. They had come through the training school together, and had later become brothers in arms during the Winter Wars, the wars which had raged along the borders to the north all those years ago. And so he had nodded, albeit reluctantly, and given instructions that his agents were to 'go easy' on anyone from Litra, but to report back on even the least suspicion of anything less than absolute loyalty.

And so, as Hartley had hoped, nothing was discovered, and no one was accused. It was then that Hartley played his card, as the ancient saying went. He tabled a report in a meeting convened by Akton, again in the presence of the king. In it he claimed that there were reports from one or two of his scouts that there was particular unrest on the north and north western coastal borders of the kingdom, as well as the region of the third quadrant. He asked leave to investigate.

'I believe,' he said, 'that there may be a connection between this unrest, and the apparent poisonings the city has suffered.'

'So you believe that we are indeed dealing with poisonings?' asked the king, expressionless behind his mask, and his voice giving nothing away.

Hartley had hesitated as if thinking through his answer. 'We cannot be sure, sire,' he said at last, 'but what we are experiencing has all the hallmarks of a carefully planned attack. Of course we have never been sure as to how staining occurs when it occurs naturally,' he hesitated, 'but I am reliably informed that researchers in both Litra and Glamtech are beginning to suspect that outlanders hostile to Serenity have been hard at work developing a venom or poison that closely replicates staining.'

'Replicates?'

'Reproduces, my lord. Reproduces would be a more exact term.' He looked at Shadwatch: 'Would that not be correct my lord Shadwatch?'

The technical head of Glamtech frowned, and stared at some papers in front of him. As was his unchallenged custom, he did not wear a mask: 'It is too soon to say for sure, but it is possible,' he said after a while. 'After all, our research laboratories have been breached by forces hostile to the kingdom once before.'

'My brother,' said the king, and a shadow fell across his mask. 'You speak of lord Marlin my brother.'

Shadwatch bit his lower lip, and then nodded. 'I do, my lord. All the evidence for that breach points to prince Marlin.' He paused. 'As you know, sire, I believe that it was in fact your brother who killed my father in the Glamtech laboratories and stole the formula.'

The king grunted. 'You credit my brother with too much daring and too much guile, Shadwatch. He is a rabbit, and always has been. A scared rabbit. He ran like a rabbit when his family was arrested and hid like a rabbit when they were sentenced. Kill your father, did he? He has neither the stomach nor the skill for such a thing.'

Shadwatch started to say something, but the king waved him to silence and went on:

'Whoever raided the laboratories and attacked your father, was no more than an opportunist who saw his chance and took it. Raw cunning? Yes, I grant you, and a degree of nerve mixed with some resolve,' he glanced at Hartley, 'but that is all: cunning, nerve, resolve. These are three things that my wretched brother has never had. He has fled, abandoning his wife and children to their fate. I have no doubt he is skulking somewhere in the outlands, feeding off the land and begging from passing strangers.' He paused. 'What say you, lord Hartley?'

Hartley tilted his head to one side, appearing to ponder the king's question for longer than was usual. Then he straightened:

'My lord king,' he said, 'you are right not to concern yourself with your brother, but nonetheless I believe there is a real threat to both you and your kingdom, and I believe it comes from others in the outlands.'

'The third quadrant, you said?'

'I did, my lord.'

The king shrugged. 'Then the solution is clear. We lay it waste. It is as simple as that. Send in the elite regiments of the imperial guard. Three regiments should be sufficient. Glamtech will provide the logistical support, and Rebuild can give us what engineers we need. We will turn that region into a smoking ruin, and leave it as a warning to all other stainers and wildfolk who might plot to challenge the kingdom. I leave it in your hands lord Hartley. No prisoners, mind. No mercy, no prisoners. Simple.'

Before Hartley could answer, Akton had got to his feet. 'My lord king,' he said. 'May I speak?'

The king looked up at his chancellor. 'If you feel you must, my lord, but keep it brief. This meeting tires me.'

Akton now did something that surprised everyone in the room, and not least, Hartley. Reaching up, he slipped his mask from his face. Carefully, he set the mask down on the table and faced the king. His eyes were darkly bright, and his brow was furrowed. When he spoke without the mask, his words rang strong and clear about the room:

'Your majesty,' he began, 'We do not have the resources for such an undertaking. Even if Rebuild and Glamtech committed all their expertise and manpower to such a campaign, they could not hope to complete the task.' He paused. 'The third quadrant is too vast, and although there is plenty of open land and desert, there is also no shortage of forest, swamp, and hill country. An entire army could disappear within a month, and leave no trace of its passing.'

The king studied Akton's mask on the table in front of him, as if expecting to see its owner looking from behind it. 'What's this, Akton?' he said quietly. 'Is this fear I hear? Fear from my high chancellor.'

'No, my lord,' Hartley interrupted. 'Your chancellor offers sound advice. We should not be making war against the countryside. It is not the land that attacks us. Instead, we need to find the actual source of these attacks on our citizens. Isolate that source and then extinguish it.' He rubbed his hands together slowly. 'Give me leave to return to the borders, sire. I will find out who is behind this threat, and then bring you word.'

The king turned to Akton. 'What do you think?'

The chancellor nodded slowly, then replied. 'There is wisdom in that, my lord king. Wisdom, and yet great danger. Lord Hartley speaks as if he would go alone. We have few friends north of the great tower, and none that I know of in the third quadrant.'

The king shrugged. 'Well, I never heard of a halfway decent plan yet that didn't involve some sort of risk.' He paused, and drummed his fingers on the table for just a moment. 'But neither have I ever known lord Hartley to be rash or foolhardy.' He turned again to Hartley. 'Am I right, my lord?'

Hartley did not answer at first. Part of his mind was still focussed on why Akton had removed his mask. The rest of his mind was consumed with the idea that the king did not trust any of his advisers. At last he spoke:

'There is risk, your majesty, but it is a risk that has to be taken and taken alone. I know the borders well. I can pass unseen into the outlands without too much difficulty, but if I took so much as a squad of cavalry with me, or a troop of scouts, we would be spotted straightaway.' He stood up. 'Give me leave, sire to head north tomorrow, cross the border before the end of the week, and then return. I pledge to be back here with news in ten to twelve days, no more.'

Even as he finished speaking, it was as if the king had meanwhile lost interest in what he was saying. Looking away, and gesturing with his hand the king dismissed him. 'Get you gone, my lord,' he said. 'Do what you must. Speak to no one about this meeting, and we too will hold our peace.'

With a bow to the king, and a brief salute to both Akton and Shadwatch, Hartley left the chamber. He would not have made his way so confidently down the corridor towards the main entrance if he had heard what Shadwatch was now saying:

'My lord king, lord Hartley has an appetite for the outlands that does not rest well with me,' Shadwatch said, sensing that the king wanted to bring the meeting to a close.

The king grunted. 'It is his job, Shadwatch. His job. He loves the shadows, and shuns the light. He is a scout. Without him and his fellows, we are blind.'

Shadwatch gave the slightest of frowns. He dared not cross the king or challenge him, but neither did he trust Hartley. 'Still, he said to himself, Glamtech can look after itself. It does not need the likes of Hartley to keep it strong, nor is it dependent on the favour of Litra or Rebuild, but will always rely on the favour of the king. After all, he decided, we have Glamgel.'

And so he bowed to the king. 'My lord,' he said quietly, and then turned to acknowledge Akton who had put on his mask once more and was preparing to leave. 'We should meet for supper, my lord chancellor,' Shadwatch said. 'I have some matters of Glamtech security to talk through with you.'

Akton returned his salute. 'That will be useful, lord Shadwatch,' he said crisply. 'I will send my secretary with a list of suitable dates, and then we can perhaps agree on a time.'

By the time the chancellor had finished speaking, the king had also got to his feet, and was gathering up the scattered pile of papers that were still awaiting his signature. 'Gentlemen,' he said, 'you are dismissed. I will see you here at noon in three days times.'

They all left the meeting hall separately, each man with his armed escort, and the king with his banner bearer going before him. As Akton reached the top of the steps at the entrance overlooking the courtyard, he saw Anna-Seka hurrying towards him.

While he waited for her to climb the steps, he paused to look out over the city below: so peaceful, so calm, so apparently free of trouble. And yet . . .

Anna reached the topmost step. 'Father,' she said. 'Here you are! I was hoping that I might meet with you.'

Akton smiled. 'A problem?' he asked.

'Not really papa, but something I thought you should know. I met lord Hartley in the lower court. He has reassigned me.'

'Reassigned?'

'Yes. Well, I think so. I am not sure. He has asked me to stay back in the city, even though I am meant to be permanently attached to his patrol until my initial training is complete.'

'I see.'

Anna shrugged. 'Well, I'm not sure that I see, papa,' she replied. 'He has asked me to report to the College of Scouts today and pick up transfer papers for a city-defence regiment in the second court of the imperial precinct.'

'He gave you no explanation, then?'

Anna shook her head. 'That's just it, papa. I know he doesn't have to, but he usually tells me why he is asking me to do something, no matter how unimportant.'

Akton looked at his daughter. He was proud of the way she had conducted herself in the outshining arena the other day: it left him a little puzzled perhaps, but nonetheless, proud. She had shown decisive leadership and strong, clear thinking. It was no wonder that she had been confused by Hartley's sudden decision to put her on a transfer list.

'Did lord Hartley explain what he was doing, and what mission, if any, he had in mind?' Akton asked.

'No papa, but when I watched him go, I noticed that he was heading down a side path that leads to the Border Commissariat. He is returning to the outlands, I think.'

Behind his mask, Akton was content not to give anything away. He gave a slight nod. 'That is a possibility,' he said, hoping his voice would not betray his concern.

Anna looked at her step-father. She sensed his hesitancy, something she could not recall having ever seen in him before.

'Is everything alright, papa?' she asked.

He coughed and turned his head to one side. It was a slight and swift movement, but it told Anna everything. She scarcely listened to his answer when it came. She knew the truth.

'All is well, daughter,' Akton said, hating himself for the deception.

'There is nothing to worry about.'

Anna stepped to one side as if to let her step father pass, but then put her hand on his arm. 'Papa,' she whispered. 'You trust my lord Hartley, don't you?'

Akton sighed. 'My daughter, the only one I truly trust in those palace corridors behind us, is the king.' He paused. 'And that is because I am sworn to.'

The chancellor could not see his step daughter's eyes, but he guessed that they must have widened with surprise, and there were perhaps even tears starting. Reaching up he gently touched the side of her mask:

'Ah, daughter,' he said, 'do not fear. My colleagues here, we may not entirely trust each other within the palace, but we do honour each other as brothers, and remind ourselves every day that without a common purpose and unity, we cannot hope to survive.' He sighed again. 'It is the enemy without that makes all of us friends within.'

Anna nodded. 'Then all is well, papa. But know this, although I trust lord Hartley, I trust you more, more than life itself.' She squeezed his arm, and stepped back. 'I must away now. They will be expecting me at the College, and I need to report to my new regiment before sunset today.'

'Then I can go at least part of the way with you, daughter. Your mother is expecting me to take her to the mall at the Cascading Gardens this afternoon. The best way to the College from here will take us past our front door will it not?'

Anna laughed, and her father rejoiced to hear it. 'Oh, papa! You know these city streets better than I do, and I am the one who is training to be an imperial scout.'

They laughed together, and set off down the steps arm in arm: father and daughter. As they went they did not notice the figure in the shadow of the pillars that flanked the top of the step-way. It was Shadwatch. Waiting until the chancellor and his step daughter had almost disappeared, he emerged and stared after them:

'Interesting,' he muttered to himself, and turning went back into the palace.

Four days later, Hartley crossed the northern border alone. He did not cross at the great tower and terminus of the imperial highway. Instead, he used a lesser known military crossing point about five miles to the east. It was manned by half a dozen bored-looking guards from one of the Lower Town militia units. When they saw Hartley approaching from some distance away, he looked like no more than a local farmer, or travelling merchant who had lost his way. So they remained where they were, lounging on the porch outside the guard-post, and talking quietly among themselves.

It was their sergeant who at last realised that they had made a mistake. Hartley was no more than twenty yards from the guard-post, when he suddenly leapt to his feet, shouted at the others and ordered them to attention.

Smiling behind his mask at their scrambling confusion, Hartley rode up to the crossing point and swung down from the saddle. He did not return the sergeant's hurried salute.

'If I had been a stain-warrior,' he said, 'you would have all been dead by now.' He paused, waiting for them to finish forming up in line of attention. 'What's your unit?' he asked the sergeant.

'We are a detachment of the 3rd company/Twentieth Regiment Lower Town, my lord,' the sergeant answered, without a mask and visibly sweating.

'A militia unit, then?'

'Yes, my lord. We have been here for some time.'

'Too long by the look of it,' replied Hartley, his voice icy cool. He stared down the line of men, their weapons held across their chests, and their caps at last straightened. 'Any activity?'

'None, my lord. Or almost none. You are the first traveller we have seen in a week.'

Hartley showed his pass, and then offered his palm to the scanner. 'I need a fresh horse and a meal. When I have both, I will cross the border here. Understood?'

'My lord.' The sergeant saluted again, and this time Hartley returned his salute. 'And when will you return, my lord?' the sergeant asked.

Taking the saddle bags from his horse, Hartley shook his head. 'I am not returning because I never crossed,' he said. 'You understand? You will not log this crossing. It never happened. You have no recollection of this incident.' He looked along the line of men again. 'None of you.'

The sergeant knew better than to question a man who was clearly a senior officer of the imperial high command. He nodded. 'Only the horse will know, sire,' he said, risking a slight smile.

Hartley ignored the comment. 'Get me a meal,' he said, and walked slowly across to the main door of the guard post.

An hour later he had left, riding through the narrow gateway of the Fence, and heading northwards across open countryside.

Back in Serenity, Barvarik had come to a decision. He had made up his mind: He would not leave on his military service transfer and northern posting until he had tried at least once more to see Talessa. There was little doubt that the commissariat would turn him down. After all, six months was the usual wait before permission was granted to visit prisoners who were convicted stainers. Nobility counted for nothing. The law was clear: to become a stainer was to become a non-citizen, or an un-person, an outcast. Indeed, even to apply to visit a person who had become stained was to invite suspicion, if not disgrace. It was not uncommon for stainers to be openly and publically rejected by their own families, even in the instant that the court pronounced sentence, and the victim was hurried away.

But Barvarik was sensitive to none of that. He simply had to see Talessa before his posting, and if that were not possible he would at least be able to tell himself that he had tried. And even if he were rejected, he might just be able to persuade one of the officials to at least hand a note to Talessa so that she would know that he had come to see her.

He crossed the marble courtyard of the commissariat building, climbed the long flight of steps and entered the gold and white halls of Serenity's most feared building. Here were the guardians of the law, and the executors of its justice. And here were the grey-faced men with their grey-faced masks, who said little, wrote much, and moved like ghosts among the pillars and galleries of this soaring temple.

Swallowing hard, and adjusting his regimental mask Barvarik crossed the foyer and went to the 'office of reception'.

An official seated behind a large wood-carved desk looked up as he came in:

'Yes?' He stared expressionless at Barvarik.

'My name is Barvarik.' He offered his palm. 'I have come to see the lady Talessa, daughter of Akton,' he paused, 'Recently sent to level four.'

The official shrugged. 'The one you speak of no longer has that name. She has been reassigned a number. Would you like me to read it out to you?'

'I would like to see the lady Talessa.'

This time the official sighed. 'I will give you her number, and then you can leave by the way you came in.' He reached for a desk file. 'That is the law.'

'You already have my written application. I am posted to the northern border. For six months. I thought perhaps . . .'

It was rare for officials to remove their masks for any reason, but occasionally they would do so to express their contempt for anyone they were interviewing. It was called an 'outshining of the commissariat'. And on this occasion, that is exactly what the official did. He reached up and removed his mask.

'I did not ask you to think,' he said, his pale grey eyes staring fixedly at Barvarik, 'I asked you leave.'

There was a moment, a mere breath, and Bavarik's sword cleared its scabbard and swept in a gleaming curve above the official's head. It sang as it came down and stopped less than an inch from the side of the man's jaw.

'If my blade should slip now,' said Barvarik with no trace of feeling in his voice, 'there would no longer be any need for you to wear a mask.'

'You threaten to kill me?' replied the official, as he shrunk back, his shoulders hunched and shaking.

Barvarik grunted. 'If I thought to kill you, your head would be on the ground now at your feet. No, my friend I am just reminding you that the gentle kiss of my sword, should it so choose, would open your cheek to the bone and your state would be worse than that of any stainer.' He paused. 'Unless you would prefer a real outshining?' He moved the blade slightly so that it rested on the side of the official's jaw. 'Do I need to repeat myself?'

The official did not move. For a moment his eyes moved to see if there was anyone else in the foyer, but no one had come in. Slowly, he reached up touched the sword and pushed it away. 'Let me check your records,' he said.

Shortly afterwards, Barvarik was making away along one of the lower corridors that led to the level four capsules and lifts of the main prison wing. He had the pass in his hand written for him by the official and stamped with the royal crest. He showed it at every check point until at last he came to a door set into a pillar of polished steel. It was the entrance to a staff-capsule. A guard showed him to the door which slid open as he approached. The moment he entered, the door closed, the room he was in glowed with a pale green light and then with a gentle whirr, the capsule began its descent.

Above his head, through the ceiling of polished glass Barvarik could see the bright white light of the upper level staging area growing steadily smaller as he dropped down into the depths of the prison. Looking through the translucent walls of the capsule, he could make out, swinging from cables at fixed heights, a number of capsules used exclusively for prisoners. He knew that the capsule he now occupied was an access-lift for visitors and security personnel. The prison blocks on each level were little more than groups of capsules suspended within the massive shaft, each capsule containing a prisoner. They could be efficiently raised and lowered to whatever level the prison superintendent might decide. Above was light, below was darkness. And so down and down Barvarik went until the light above him was no more than a distant pinpoint. At last the access- lift came to a halt with a high-pitched hum. There was a pause and the lift door opened. It was level four.

Another guard met him, and showed him to a platform, lit by the same pale light that had filled the lift. Suspended just above the platform was a single prisoner capsule. The guard gestured towards it:

'It's this one,' he said. 'You have seven minutes.'

'Seven?'

The guard shrugged. 'It's the rules. I'll tell you when.' He walked over to a hatch on the floor and punched in a code. A cable dropped from the impossibly high ceiling into the shaft as the hatch swirled open. Seconds later, a trigger echoed from the depths and the capsule imerged. The guard unlocked it. Then he knocked twice against a polished brass plate. There was a pause, and the door swung open with a low hum.

'Thank you.' Barvarik took hold of the entry rail and entered. The door closed behind him. He stood for a moment, his eyes adjusting to the gloom, but even before he could see clearly, he heard a voice:

'Barvi, is that you?'

He stepped forward, and heard the door shut behind him. 'Talle?' His voice echoed softly.

A figure huddled one corner, stood slowly and came towards him. 'You are here,' Talessa whispered. Her voice was cracked and dry. She took his hand, and he took her in his arms, embraced her and then stepped back.

'What have they done to you?' he asked.

Talessa put her hand to the side of her face. The characteristic mark from the infection had spread across her left cheekbone almost to her jaw. 'The stain, you mean?'

Barvarik shook his head. 'I see no stain,' he said. 'No, what have they done, putting you down here in this hell-hole and leaving you all alone in the darkness?'

She tried to smile. 'It's the rules,' she said, and took hold of his hand again. 'I'm a stainer now,' she looked around, 'and this is what they do to stainers.' Brushing back a strand of hair, she tried to smile. 'All I have to do now, is obey the rules.'

'Rules! All I hear in this place is that word.' He squeezed her hand. 'You should not be here,' he added, and drew her to himself again. They kissed.

Talessa stepped back and smiled up at him sadly. 'I know I should not be here, but here is where I am, and here is where I stay until the king says otherwise.'

Frowning, Barvarik ran his hand gently where her hair fell across her neck and shoulder. 'Once the high court has made a decision, I doubt if our king gives it another thought,' he said and paused. 'Perhaps I should remind him of his duty.'

'Oh, Barvi, do not make things any worse than they are already. One of the other prisoners told me that anyone who makes trouble is put on permanent hard labour in lower-level four, and once you are down there you are forgotten.'

'You can speak to the other prisoners, then?'

Talessa shook her head. 'We only meet in groups of five once every three days when we are inspected by medics from the hospital corps, and our capsules are sanitised. No one is meant to speak, but if you are lucky you can whisper.' She hesitated and glanced towards the door. 'I am learning.'

'You shouldn't have to, Talle.' Barvarik looked back towards the door. The spy-plate in the centre of its polished surface was still closed. 'We need to get you out of here.'

'Oh, Barvi,' Talessa barely held back a sob. 'That is not possible. No one escapes from this place. No one. They say that only those who have lost their minds attempt to escape. And always they are quickly caught and never seen again.'

Leaning forward, Barvarik whispered in her ear. 'Leave it to me, my love, and do not lose hope. I will not leave you to waste away in this place.'

'But how? How?' Talessa shook her head again. 'It is impossible. The walls, the guards, the endless capsule locks and lift bars.'

Barvarik smiled grimly. 'They are designed to hold you in, that is true, but can they hold me out?'

There was the sound of a key in the door and the heavy lock turning.

'Do not despair, Talle.' Barvarik hugged Talessa, kissed her lightly on the cheek and stepped back as the door swung open.

'It is time,' said the guard.

Acknowledging the guard with a brief salute, Barvarik turned to Talessa:

'I will be back,' he said, 'I am posted to the borders for a short time, but I will be back.'

Talessa nodded. 'Give my love to my mother and father,' she paused, 'and if you see Anna-Seka tell her the same. Tell her, I miss her.'

Barvarik smiled. 'I will. Stay well. I will not fail you. Promise.'

The guard grunted. 'It is time,' he repeated. He reached up to take Barvarik by the arm, but was met with a glance that told him that such a move would not be wise. He let his hand fall. 'You must go, my lord,' he said quietly.

Moments later, Barvarik was outside the capsule and heading across the platform towards the lift. He heard the door to Talessa's cell-capsule close with a deep, metallic thud, but he did not turn to look back. Soon he was back in the visitors' capsule, and heading up the shaft and past the lower third and lower second mid-levels. At last he found himself gliding to a halt at an upper middle reception platform, pushed the release button and stepped out. As he set off towards the main corridor, he counted the number of steps and noticed that the first check point of the principle exit route lay just beyond two intersecting side corridors. He showed his palm as well as his written pass and the guards waved him through. After that, each check point lay in full view of the preceding one, and when he reached the staircase that led up to the level above, there was a doubling of the guard with a senior officer present.

The same process was repeated as he moved towards the topmost level, and by the time that he crossed the foyer that led to the outer court of the commissariat, he knew that escape was not going to be an easy option. On his way to the barracks, he stopped by at Talessa's house to let his parents know that he had just seen their daughter, and that all was as well as it could be. They were grateful for his news, but saddened to hear that conditions in the prison were as difficult as they had feared.

Akton knew that the prospects of mercy for his daughter, and an early release were not good. In fact they were highly unlikely, but he had not shared this with his wife. He knew that it would be more than she could bear.

With the visit at an end, he walked with Barvarik to the entrance of the house. Once there, Barvarick quietly asked him if he believed that there was anything more that could be done.

Akton glanced at the young officer as he put on his mask once more. 'Within the law, my son? There is nothing more that can be done beyond an occasional visit, and perhaps a letter if the commissariat allows.'

Barvarick paused. He had not yet put his own mask on. 'And without the law, ly lord? What recourse do we have without the law?'

'I fear there is none,' replied Akton. 'And besides, we are bound by the law, are we not?'

Staring hard at the young knight, Akton nodded slowly, and then put his hand on Barvarik's shoulder. 'You are headed for the borders with your regiment? Good. Go well and send word of your return when you are posted back to Serenity. We should like to meet with you again.' He watched as Barvarik returned his salute and made his way down the steps to the avenue that led across the precinct and towards the barracks.

'That young man will not let the matter rest there,' Akton muttered to himself and went back inside.

Two days later, the regiment although delayed, left Serenity with Barvarik riding among them at the head of the second cohort.

A CHANGE OF PLANS

At the same time, further north, Hartley was just arriving back at Marlin's fortress deep in the heart of the outlands. He had made good time, but was keen to press his advantage. The weather had turned bad, with storm clouds driving in from the east and bringing curtains of drifting rain and hill mist. He rode his horse through the open gates, and swung down from the saddle. The rain streamed from his cloak and mask.

Marlin met him in the inner courtyard. 'Come in, my lord,' he said. 'We've been expecting you. There is time to dry out and take a meal before we discuss our plans.'

Hartley nodded. 'If we leave on the morrow, all will be well.'

'And if this storm does not slacken?'

'Then we get wet.' Hartley grimaced and handed his horse to the stable lad. He turned to Marlin. 'Delay is our chief enemy in this matter. If we do not make haste I believe we will lose our chief advantage.'

'Which is?'

Hartley glanced upwards at the drifting storm-clouds. 'Our advantage is that at this moment no one suspects what we are about to do.' He shrugged. 'But that cannot last. As more and more of the Serenity citizens fall to the stain, the efforts of the Triple S to find the source will redouble.'

Together, the two men entered the relative calm and shelter of the main building.

'I will leave you here in the care of my servants,' said Marlin, 'and meet you in the conference suite within the hour.'

And so it was that the king's brother, prince Marlin and Hartley the 'shadow-master' of the College of Scouts met together and drew up their plans for the following day.

Two days later, with plans made, they had ridden almost half way to the Burgh. Two days after that they approached its walls.

Marlin was known to the guards. They saluted and waved him through. Lord Hartley, wearing his mask, followed on ignoring their puzzled and hostile looks.

After about a quarter of a mile and just inside the walls of an old festival precinct, Marlin led Hartley to a large building of panelled glass with Visitors and Guests inscribed in faint lettering above the doorway. 'You will wait here for me,' he said to Hartley. 'I will find the warlords, the Big Five. My contacts tell me that Chesterman has not been seen in Brokinburgh for some time, but he is rumoured to be close by.' He paused. 'Don't be tempted to leave this safe-house for even a short walk. Without my protection you are a dead man.'

Hartley looked out at the tumble-down buildings, clustered at one end of the vast courtyard. It was clear that they had been built some time after the precinct itself had been built, and almost certainly after the 'Great Burning'. But they had been constructed almost entirely out of the ruins and abandoned equipment of the earlier city. There were parts of plane fuselages, typically called 'MIGS' or 'Boeings'. These were often used as the bases for haulage carts or personal ox-drawn transport. Railway carriages and upturned shells of automobiles and truck cabs were most often used as shop fronts or piled up for multi-level living quarters and warehouses. Hartley even noticed the burned out body of a bus converted into some kind of eating house. There were also several larger buildings built out of battered metal panels, dressed concrete blocks and tubular steel. These buildings leaned at every angle, and seemed to be held together with rusting cables and wooden props.

The main street that ran from the central gate of Brokinburgh to this precinct was roughly cemented with an open drain running down its centre. Stray dogs gathered there in search for scraps of food and dispersed as a hollowed 'F1' vehicle carrying goods tugged by a donkey passed. Clusters of cables hung down walls and high poles then ran along the ground. They stretched over the rooftopss like a giant net in the direction of the main warlord Fortress that overshadowed the center of the burgh like a colossus. Stainers, both men and women of every age, were moving up and down the street in small groups. Many drifted into the area around the safe house. Some were clearly traders, others were family folk, and a few were soldiers. All were dressed in an assortment of leather jackets, jeans, ancient-times sportswear and sneakers. Some wore faded sweat tops with strange logos and inscriptions from another era, and another world. Many wore dull-coloured baseball caps and battered tunics of riveted leather. They chattered as they went about their daily tasks, and a few that passed close to the safe-house paused to glance at the masked figure staring out at them, and even gestured towards him. But those same folk clearly knew Marlin, and either smiled in his direction or saluted.

'They treat you as a citizen of this place,' said Hartley, wrinkling his nose at the smell that came from the drain, and made its way through cracks in the panelling.

Marlin chuckled. 'That's because I am,' he replied. 'When I left Serenity, these folk took me in as though I was a brother, driven in on a storm.' He paused. 'They shared my sorrow, and breathed in my desire for revenge.' He hesitated. 'They understood my anger.'

'Your family was taken from you?'

'Hah!' Marlin stared along the street for a moment, and raised his hand to acknowledge someone. 'My children, a son and a daughter, were stained. I hid them as best I could, but not even a king's brother could keep such a secret from the Security Services for long.' He shook his head. 'And so I lost them, and my wife besides: sent to the deepest corner of the imperial dungeons and left to await execution.'

Hartley nodded. 'The law is a harsh mistress.'

Marlin's eyes flashed. 'It was not the judgement of the law. No, it was the deliberate deceit of the king, my brother, and the low cunning of that running dog, Akton who calls himself the high chancellor.'

For a moment Hartley thought that the man in front of him was going to start shouting, but the prince suddenly seemed to recover himself, bit his lower lip and forced a smile:

'What is done, is done,' he said, 'but it is not forgotten. And I will have blood. I will have the blood of a king, and judgement upon his chief servant.' He closed his eyes. 'And upon his family.'

Hartley was keen to get deeper inside the safe-house. His presence in the atrium or foyer of this strange bits and pieces building, this relic of the past, was attracting too much attention. For just an instant he reached to the side of his mask as if about to take it off, but then seemed to think better of it. 'We are running out of time,' he said.

'Of course.' Marlin went to an inner door and knocked. Almost immediately it opened. A serving girl in smock and apron stared out at them.

'Ah, Chanella!' Marlin greeted her. 'You have waited for us. Good! Now away with you to the high hall, and tell any warlords you find there that I am coming.'

The girl curtsied, glanced suspiciously at Hartley and then moved quickly away and down the street.

Pushing the door open, Marlin showed Hartley inside. 'Make yourself comfortable, but keep out of sight. Don't even go near the windows. You can see already that it attracts attention. I will be back as soon as I can.'

'You will bring the warlords with you?'

Marlin shrugged. 'Those that I can find, and those who will come,' he said. 'But follow my lead. I will let you know when to speak, and when to hold your peace. The more of them who will listen to your story and the more who decide to trust you, the better our chances of success.' He grinned. 'And the better your chances of staying alive.' He pointed at a chair by an open fire. 'Rest up now. I'll away to my lords.'

Hartley took a pace towards the chair, and then turned. 'Chesterman? Will we see him today?'

'Who knows?' Marlin shrugged again. 'If we do, pray that he's in a good mood. If he decides he doesn't like the look of you, then all is lost.'

Not waiting for a reply, Marlin left. Hartley thought of sliding the bolt on the door, but then decided against it. He went to the fire, spread his hands to the flames, and then sat down. Outside he could hear the noise of the town as folk bustled back and forth. 'Much like Lower Town,' he thought to himself, and smiled at the memory.

Marlin was delayed in his return. Not all the warlords were waiting for him when he arrived at the high hall, and those that were there insisted that no decisions be reached until sufficient of their number had gathered.

In the end, although about thirty men - all with gaudy neckties - were crowded into the meeting room at the far end of the hall, Chesterman – their acknowledged leader – was not among them. After about an hour of discussion it was decided that without Chesterman there could be no agreed conclusion regarding lord Hartley and so the meeting was brought to a close. But there was at least an agreement that they would all meet again when their leader, lord Chesterman, next appeared in Brokinburgh.

So, Marlin was disappointed but not surprised. He knew that Chesterman was not one to hurry to a gathering he himself had not called, but equally he knew that in the end this leader of the warlords would put in an appearance. On his own time, and in his own way. But he would come. After all, Marlin himself had met up with Chesterman on more than one occasion, and at every such meeting they had got on well enough. Admittedly the meetings had been brief, workmanlike affairs but there had never been any tension between the two men. Even though Chesterman always wore his closed war helmet, the one men called the Motorcycle, and though he wore it as if to hide his persona, he seemed to be almost friendly in his manner.

At least that is what Marlin told himself as he hurried back through the streets of Brokinburgh to the safehouse.

But as he neared the house, he saw something that surprised him, even if he was not at first alarmed by it. A small crowd had gathered outside the door. They were all armed retainers, talking quietly among themselves, but taking care to keep any curious passers-by back from the front of the house.

In the centre of the crowd was a tall, well built and helmeted man, wearing a long leather cloak, and resting a curved single-edged sword against his right shoulder. Although the man had his back to Marlin, he recognised him at once. It was Chesterman. There was no other man in all the kingdom or the lands beyond, who wore such a helmet. And no one would dare to.

'My lord!'

Chesterman turned round and the crowd fell back. His distinctive necktie of polished silk, caught Marlin's eye. He was in no doubt. And it was not just because of the tie, which Marlin knew was of a type only worn by the most senior warlords : it was of course the helmet.

Chesterman's close-fitting Motorcycle helmet was the more unusual in the outlands because most stain folk did not wear that style of head protection. Instead of the customary eye slits of a closed or semi-closed helmet, Chesterman's helmet had a thin, glowing strip of red lights which somehow allowed vision, but concealed the eyes.

'My lord, you have come after all,' Marlin went on, hurrying up and offering his hand.

Chesterman ignored Marlin's outstretched hand. 'You are late,' he said, his voice strangely disembodied through the micro-speaker of the closed helmet.

For a moment Marlin was confused. 'My lord, I do not understand. I have just come from a meeting with the other warlords. We were expecting you,' he paused, 'We were hoping you might come.'

Chesterman swung his sword down and rested its point against his boot. 'I came here first. Your maid servant met me on the way to the hall, and told me where you were.' He turned and looked at the door of the house. 'I knocked but there was no answer.'

Marlin frowned. Why was Chesterman telling him this? He walked to the door and knocked on it loudly. No one came. And then one or two of the men with Chesterman chuckled. Another looked away and spat.

'Lord Marlin, you are wasting your time. There is no one inside. My men have checked.' Chesterman's voice was level, almost disinterested.

Marlin shook his head. 'That is not possible my lord. Forgive me, but I left lord Hartley here. It was agreed that he wait in the safe-house until I returned.'

'And so he did,' replied Chesterman, smiling from within his helmet at Marlin's confusion. He waited briefly for the king's brother to reply, and seeing that no reply was coming, he went on:

'As you know, every safe house in Brokingburgh has an escape door. This one is set precisely here.' He gestured to one of his men who hurried forward and pressed one of the relief carvings set into the side of a window frame. All at once a narrow door swung open.

'When the front door is bolted, we must enter by another way,' said Chesterman, his voice flat and without emotion.

A sense of dread came over Marlin. What had Chesterman done? Almost as if he had understood Marlin's alarm, the warlord added:

'I found your man Hartley, and having found him,' he grunted and looked away, 'I slew him.'

Marlin gasped. 'You did what?'

'I killed your man. It had to be done.' Chesterman shrugged. 'So I did it.'

For a moment Marlin was too surprised to reply. At last he spoke. 'Hartley was an ally, a friend, a mighty lord of Serenity. And yet you say you killed him?'

Chesterman remained unmoved. 'Lord Hartley was not my ally, and he was barely your friend.'

Shaking his head in disbelief, Marlin again struggled to find the words to say. 'But this is madness,' he said, his voice raised. 'He trusted us, my lord. I led him here to the Burgh with the promise of a meeting before the council of warlords, and now we have killed him.' His voice faded away. 'It is a betrayal, my lord. A betrayal.'

There was a stir among the warlords.

Chesterman sighed, and raised his hand. 'There is no betrayal in putting down a mad dog. He may have trusted us, but I never trusted him. He is the king's man, and always has been. Serenity is in his blood. We all know that. Whatever, he may have seemed to be offering, it was just a concealment, a sleight of hand. These kingdom-citizens are all the same: mere politicians, masked fools.'

Staring hard at the eye-slits of Chesterman's helmet, Marlin muttered:

'So you don't trust me, then, my lord?'

The helmet moved slightly as if Chesterman were measuring the distance between himself and the Marlin:

'Oh, I trust you, lord Marlin. If I didn't trust you, you would have been dead a long time ago.'

'So what is the difference between myself and the man you have just killed?'

'It's simple,' replied Chesterman. He gave a slight gesture, which told his men including the four other senior warlords to move back out of earshot. 'You have thrown in your lot with us, lord Marlin. You have no love for Serenity, and that place has no love for you.' Pausing, he gazed at a team of horses pulling a cart made out of a metal tubing with the inscription Aer Lingus painted along its length. As it rattled by, he noticed that the drover, a heavy set man with long, braided hair and a baseball cap, had an ancient music sounds player slung across his shoulder on a plastic strap. The staccato beat of what was once called 'rap' filled the air. As he passed, the man turned, saw them, and with a broken toothed grin raised a clenched fist in the air. Then he was gone.

'And Hartley?' asked Marlin staring after the cart. 'What of him?'

Chesterman sighed. 'As for Hartley, he lived on both sides of the Fence. His loyalty was divided, and neatly so. Too neatly for my liking. And his betrayal of his countrymen was also too smooth for me to ever trust it.'

'How can you know that, my lord?'

The warlord chuckled. 'You would be surprised at what I know, Marlin, and how I come to know. But rest in this: Hartley lived in his own world, no one else's. He made his own rules, and pretended all else. He had to go.'

'That's more than harsh,' replied Marlin, then paused: 'but what's done is done.' He was aware that Chesterman was surrounded by his own men, and that he himself as a renegade prince of Serenity, was not welcomed by every man or woman of Brokinburgh. 'Shouldn't we at least give this man a burial fit for a noble of his standing?' he asked quietly.

Chesterman walked up to the door which had already been opened from the inside, and pushed it. It swung open. 'You'll find nothing in here,' he said. 'A squad from the sanitation department has been already and taken the body away. See that smoke over the rooftops? That's the city furnace, and the last resting place of your friend. In a place like this the dead cannot be left to rot.'

'You were quick about it then,' replied Marlin calmly. 'A swift execution.'

Chesterman nodded, strangely patient with the man in front of him. 'Even before my warlords here arrived, all had been done that needed to be done.'

For a moment, Marlin thought of going into the house, but he knew that there would be nothing to see. Everything would be as if Hartley had never been there, and the murder had never happened. The reputation of the Brokinburgh sanitation squads had spread well beyond the walls of the Burgh itself.

'You know that this means war,' he said, turning to Chesterman, still risking a confrontation with the warlord.

'Something we were already committed to, I think,' answered Chesterman quietly. He took a pace towards Marlin. 'Are you with us, my lord?'

Marlin did not reply. In his mind he was still turning over the thought that Hartley, a high ranking official of Serenity, head of the college of scouts and a supreme lord among the nobles of that city, was suddenly dead, murdered, and reduced to ashes. And somehow, he himself, a prince of Serenity, had been involved and part of the trap.

Together, Marlin and Chesterman climbed up onto the back of a chariot-bus pulled by three pairs of oxen. They sat down on the empty bench just ahead of the tail-plane shell of an abandoned fighter jet that made up the rear of the bus, and were driven slowly along the street towards the fortress. Chesterman's men followed behind them. As senior warlord of the outlands, Chesterman seemed content with Marlin's silence, for the time being at least.

At last they came to an intersection, where the chariot-bus came to a halt. They both climbed down from the bus and walked together. Stride for stride they moved past and among the market folk, then headed on by the clutter of buildings and barricades that made up Brokinburgh's main thoroughfare.

A short while later they neared a market square, overhung with a weird array of street lighting, powered by humming generators and antiquated steam turbines. The square itself was lined with stalls and full of street traders and basket-laden housewives.

Marlin sensed that he had been silent for long enough:

'Did he die well, my lord?' he asked.

Chesterman fixed his gaze on the way ahead. 'Lord Hartley, you mean?'

'I do.'

'Why do you ask?'

'It is important to me.'

Chesterman glanced at the man beside him. 'He really was your friend, then?'

Marlin shrugged. 'We understood each other. I enjoyed his company, though I scarcely knew the man before I left Serenity.'

Chesterman nodded. 'I see. Well, your friend did not die easily, but he died well.'

'Sword in hand?'

'Aye, sword in hand, and it was a useful hand he had.' Chesterman pushed by a market trader and a townswoman haggling over a side of bacon. 'I had hoped to take him by surprise, but he was more acute than I thought.'

'How so?'

'He read me like a book when I came towards him, my hand outstretched in the sign of peace. This deception meant nothing to him. I think he saw my intent in the way I moved. I was measuring the distance between myself and him until I found a sword's length.'

Marlin grunted. 'And your sword was still in its scabbard?'

'Aye, but loosened in the sheath. Y'know, I think he even noticed that little trick of mine. His blade was half drawn even as I drew mine. We came to blows before a single word had been uttered.'

Marlin lowered his head, and thought for a moment. He could see it now, and so clearly: two lords in a narrow and darkened room, their swords gleaming in the half light, and each man moving like a wild cat, striking, and retreating, then striking again.

'A long fight, then?' he asked.

'Long enough. He slipped.' Chesterman paused, turned around and waved his men forward. 'He slipped, and that was enough. The edge of a carpet, that's all it took to bring such a warrior down. It almost seemed a shame to take advantage of it.'

'But it had to be done?'

Chesterman touched the side of his helmet, and the lights flickered, then grew brighter. He nodded. 'Aye, it had to be done.'

A chariot-bus pulled to halt nearby, and several soldiers in leather jackets and jogger-pants clambered out. At the same time, Marlin noticed that Chesterman's men had gathered around him. Instinctively, he straightened and put a hand on the hilt of his sword. If these outlanders of the Burgh were now under orders to finish him off as well, he would at least take a few with him.

But they didn't move any closer.

'So, my lord Marlin,' said Chesterman, as if he didn't notice. 'Are you with us, or are you not?'

The king's brother thought hard. He was aware that his life did not so much depend on the answer he gave to that question, as to the way that he gave it. Any sense of doubt or hesitancy and he was a dead man.

'I am with you, my lord,' he said crisply. 'Your enemies are my enemies, and your friends are . . .' he smiled, 'my brothers in arms.'

'You say this to save your skin?'

'Of course, my lord, but also to advance my cause.'

Chesterman threw back his head and laughed:

'At last, an honest man has come among us! Come now, lord Marlin, give me your hand and let us seal this bargain.'

They shook hands, and then Marlin stepped back and saluted to acknowledge that Chesterman was the senior lord in the enterprise.

Chesterman nodded in return and then turned towards one of his men:

'Bustop!' he called and a tall, square-chested warrior stepped forward:

'My lord?'

'Take Lonsdale and Puma with you and get ahead to the meeting. Tell my lord Celsius that we are coming now for a full council,' he paused, 'a full council of war.'

The warrior grinned and showed his sharpened teeth. 'My lord!' he replied, saluted and with Lonsdale and Puma hurried away up the street.

By the evening of that day, plans for the campaign were in place and the preparations had already begun. Riders had been sent out to every corner of the Stain kingdom with strict instructions for a 'kingdom muster' to be held at Brokinburgh in ten days time. That meant that every able-bodied man bearing arms was to come to the capital with five day's rations and any weapons he could carry. Only those of less than sixteen years age, or older than forty were exempt, and told to stay at home and protect their farms and villages as best they could.

Within Brokinburgh itself the blacksmiths, engineers and technical armourers were already busy, firing up their forges, powering up their lathes, and taking down their specialist tools from the wall racks. Steam pumps and fixed engines of all kinds whirred and clattered into life. Some were powered by evil smelling fuel, but mostly they were driven by electricity from the half-ruined hydro-electric power-plant at the head of the great lake just north of the city. Soon, slab-sided wagons and plane-carts were bringing in extra supplies of coal and wood from outlying storage centres and timber yards. They would be used to power the steam generators and pumps for the engineering works.

As the sun passed noon-point on the following day, the streets of the stain-city rang to the sound of a thousand metal-presses and automated hammers. And three days later even that sound was muffled by the din and clatter of closely guarded convoys of country wagons piled high with supplies and provisions requisitioned for the campaign. Every gate was opened wide, and every roadway was crowded with folk streaming towards Brokinburgh. Some rode horses, some brought wagons and hand-carts. There were plane-carts everywhere. But many of the new arrivals simply walked. And as they came, there were no shouts of greeting nor the joyful answers and war-whoops usually heard when the muster gathered. Instead there was a low murmur that hung in the dust over the shuffling crowds, and the occasional whistle or crack of a whip as a wagon-drover steered his team of oxen towards the gates. And all this was nearly drowned out by the harsh sound of iron-rimmed wagon wheels as they screeched, slewed, bumped and rattled over the loose paving stones of the city streets. Only a few wagons had rubber tyres.

Above the teeming quarters and squares of the city itself, loomed the towering mass of the warlord fortress and its two main wing-spread

'Boieng' craft watch towers. Each tower glowed and pulsed with light from the main generator of the hydro-dam, while from entry ports in the upper parts of the wagon stacked walls, huge cables ran down to the city below. These cables carried power that in turn lit the main streets, as well as the guard posts that were placed at regular intervals along those streets. There was also a network of smaller cables running off a number of local generators and providing power for various workshops and armouries scattered throughout the Burgh. This meant that craftsmen and assembly workers as well as technicians could work both day and night, and there was not an hour when the factories fell silent.

For nine days the city prepared for war. On the tenth day, the main muster was called by Celsius, the regional commander of Brokinburgh. It was to be held outside the city walls on the great plain that stretched away to the north and west. There were stain-folk from every part of the kingdom. Those who had come some days earlier had put up tents and simple shelters on the edge of the muster area. Others who had only arrived the night before, had slept in the open around their camp fires, wrapped in their cloaks and keeping warm as best they could against the season's chill. And even on the morning of the muster-day itself there were still folk arriving. These latecomers came mainly from the north where the country was more difficult to cross, and the settlements were more scattered. But they came nonetheless. Some carried spears, others carried clubs. Many carried bows. Their elders and captains carried the 'fire-sticks' and 'thunder rods' of the olden days, and wore helmets – some rusted, some bronzed, some reinforced plastic – that denoted their rank.

And everywhere there were banners and battle-standards, each one showing the status and honour of a particular tribe, or clan, or family. There was no room inside Brokinburgh itself for these newcomers but they were welcomed anyway. On the orders of Chesterman, with the agreement of Celsius, market stalls and cooking fires had been set up all around the muster area, and market folk did a busy trade selling food, drink and warm clothing to their brethren from the outer lands. Some of the blacksmiths and metal workers of Brokinburgh who had finished their tasks for the chief technical armourer also came, setting up their forges and presses outside the gates, connecting the power cables and repairing or up-rating any weapons that were brought to them.

The warlords, including the Big Five, were everywhere on this muster day. They moved around the encampments finding their own folk, and taking a tally of those who had not yet arrived or would not be coming. With them went the provender clerks and supply-sergeants, checking what each man had brought to the muster, and what else he might need. Even Marlin sought out the men who had been conscripted from his own stadium fortress. There were only about twenty of them, but they were all well equipped, and came smartly to attention when Marlin approached. He felt proud of them, and hoped that perhaps word would filter back to Chesterman that lord Marlin's men, though few in number, looked like warriors worthy of this great enterprise.

'We came last night, my lord,' said Marlin's captain, saluting as his master arrived. 'As you instructed, we have left twenty-five men to hold the fort until we return.'

Marlin returned his salute, wondering how many of these, his men, would return. Perhaps none at all..

'Celsius, the chief warlord of Brokinburgh has called for a full parade on the third hour past noon,' he said. Take your banner and markers to the third sector of the front line. I will meet you there.'

The captain nodded. 'The messenger who came to the fort, said that we are going to advance against the Fence, my lord.'

Marlin smiled. 'More than that, captain. We are going to cross the Fence and advance against Serenity itself.' He paused. 'This is our moment. This is the day we claim blood for blood, and the day that we honour the memory of those we have lost, and those we have left behind.'

The captain saluted and turned to his men. 'Ye hear that, lads? The battle we all hoped for is now upon us.'

The soldiers knew better than to break ranks, or call out in reply. They held their line, but each man, almost as though he had heard a parade ground order, snapped his weapon to 'present', then raised his right boot and brought it down sharply. The resultant sound echoed across the line of tents nearby and made men on all sides stop and look around.

Again Marlin smiled. He was proud of these men. They had arrived at his stadium one by one, all those years ago. They had come as refugees and outcasts of Serenity: beaten men with nothing to offer Marlin except anger and a powerless despair. But he had taken them in along with all the others who came his way. He equipped them, and slowly turned them into a fighting force that, unbeknown to Marlin, was recognised and feared across the outlands.

'Stand easy, men,' he said, 'and get yourselves a meal before the parade. We march tomorrow.'

CHAPTER #7

THE BATTLE AT THE FENCE

Anna Seka could not remember when she had last seen such a beautiful sky. It was of the purest blue, untouched by clouds, and shimmering like white fire where the distant mountains pushed up against it like the broken teeth of a giant dragon. She leaned back against the railing of the barracks training-ground and looked up and across to the steep terraces of buildings that led to the commissariat. Her step-sister was somewhere there in that forbidding place, held in a prison capsule deep below the gleaming corridors and double-doored rooms of the central offices: deep below in the sunless gloom of the prison.

Anna knew that Talessa would almost certainly never see the sky again. That was the law. For Talessa, daughter of Akton was a stainer, one of the forgotten people. That was what the law said, and that is what the teachers of the law taught. Even when she was a child at school, Anna remembered that every day lessons began and ended with a recitation of the basic laws of Serenity, and a pledge of allegiance to the king.

So she knew, as every citizen of Serenity knew, that Talessa, daughter of Akton, would never see the sky again. Unless, as rarely happened and only at the mercy of the king, her capsule was raised to the surface and she was banished forever to the outlands far beyond the borders of the Serene kingdom. That was the most that anyone could hope for.

For a time she watched the coloured banners of Litra, Glamtech and Rebuild streaming out in the breeze that swirled about the towers of the commissariat. Then she turned to gaze across the training-ground to where a number of new recruits were learning to ride horses. The cavalry was an important part of the particular regiment she had been assigned to, and no one could hope to stay as a member of it, if they could not master basic horsemanship. Her step-sister Talessa was a skilled rider, and had been ever since Anna could remember. In fact it was Talessa who had taught Anna herself to ride. The young scout shook her head at the memory. All that time ago, her step-sister had been so patient with her, so gentle and so kind. Hours they had spent together with their horses in the public training arena next to the great park. How many times had Anna fallen from the saddle, or nearly so, and not once had her sister shown the least irritation or impatience. Always, she had helped her up with a smile, dusted her down and encouraged her back into the saddle once more.

'The more bruises you suffer the more experience you gain, the more experience you gain, the better the rider you will become!' Talessa used to say as she urged her on.

And then at last there came a day when Anna could gallop the length of the arena without faltering, and then turn her horse, stallion or mare, at the last moment, and gallop back. She could also leap the low hurdles placed there to test proficiency and then wave and smile to the cheers and laughter of her step sister and friends who came to watch.

'One day,' Talessa had said to her as they made their way back on a lazy summer afternoon in July towards the stables, 'One day we will ride together to the edge of the kingdom, and all who see us will think us to be warrior-princesses sent by the king on some great and mysterious mission.'

Anna remembered that day so clearly, and how she had laughed and said:

'Do you really think so, Talle?'

'I know so, little sister,' Talessa had replied, as she tapped her on the shoulder with her riding crop.

And now, years later Anna-Seka frowned as the horse-sergeant in charge of the drill she was watching, bellowed at the recruits, and made them start all over again. That was nothing unusual.

'Poor Talessa,' she whispered to herself, 'you will never ride again, nor see a horse, nor reach out and touch one.'

There was someone at her shoulder. She turned. It was her commanding officer.

'Day dreaming, soldier?' he asked and smiled, giving the hand gesture that denoted a smile when a mask was worn.

Anna straightened, saluted and smiled back. She liked this commander of her new regiment. He was an older man, quieter, proud of his family and understanding of his recruits.

'I was watching the training, sir,' she replied. 'It reminds me of my earlier days at the College.'

'Ah, yes. You're a scout, are you not? And a lone scout too. Trained by lord Hartley, I see from your records.'

'Yes, sir. He taught me a lot. I could not have survived without him.'

The commander nodded. 'Well, we could do with him here in the city right now. The trouble is he hasn't been seen for some days. I don't suppose . . .'

Anna shook her head. 'It must be two weeks at least since I saw him last, my lord. He informed me of my posting to this regiment and then left without telling me where he was headed.'

The commander smiled again. 'But if you had to make a guess?'

'Well, sir, I would say he was headed back to the outlands and the northern borders.'

'That is certainly my guess,' replied the commander, 'and it's also the considered opinion of the security services, as well as the High Dean of the College of Scouts.'

'But we do not know for sure?'

'Precisely. All we know for sure is that he has disappeared, and that if he did cross the border into the outlands, he is now overdue.'

'Overdue for what, sir?' asked Anna.

'Oh,' the commander waved a hand, 'overdue for one of those endless conferences and meetings that the commissariat love to insist on calling.' He paused. 'There's quite a flap on, y'know. Intelligence, and that sort of thing. We have received reports from both Rebuild and Triple S sources that confirm our suspicions that something untoward is happening,' he shrugged, 'something blowing in the wind north of the borders.'

'Trouble, my lord?'

The commander shrugged. 'Could be, but I'm hoping not. At least our watch towers report nothing, and nor do our Fence patrols. If there is something brewing, it must be miles north of the Great Border Gates.'

'Then that's where lord Hartley will have gone,' replied Anna-Seka with that direct simplicity that Hartley himself so respected.

The commander looked at the young scout in front of him. Now he saw why Hartley had chosen her, and why he had made special mention of her qualities in his transfer report. He turned to look at the recruits who were just finishing their training for the afternoon. How soon, he wondered, before they would have to be sent into action?

'I must go now, sir,' Anna saluted, 'I am on duty at the barracks in half an hour.'

Returning the salute, the commander hesitated and then spoke. 'I was sorry to hear about your sister,' he said.

'Thank you, my lord.'

'It's a terrible thing.'

Anna nodded, suddenly eager to leave. 'Yes, my lord. For all of the family, and especially for my sister.'

Again, the commander held his gaze. 'Her young man has also gone north to the borders,' he said. 'Barvarik, is that not his name?'

'It is my lord.'

A trumpet sounded from the barracks gate. The commander lifted his head to the sound. 'Barvarik is a good man, from a good family,' he went on. 'He is a credit to his regiment.' He paused. 'But I do not believe that any amount of fighting on the borders will distract his heart from what he has left behind here in Serenity.'

Anna did not know what to say. She had never even heard her father talk in such a way, let alone the senior officer of a principal regiment in the imperial army, and a man she scarcely knew. 'He will do his duty, my lord,' she replied, stumbling over the words.

The commander sighed. 'Aye, he will do his duty,' he shrugged again, 'as we all must.' The trumpet sounded again, and he nodded. 'Now, away with you, soldier. Away to that duty of yours before the sergeant major comes at the double, roaring like a bull to know what has kept you.'

They both smiled. Anna-Seka saluted once more and left.

The commander watched her go. 'So young, so beautiful, so loyal,' he said to himself, 'and so unknowing.' He sighed, shook his head and set off for his office. He could take off his mask there. Of course there were papers to sign and orders to issue before the evening watch sounded. And if what he feared came to pass, there would also be orders in the morning for a regimental march to the northern borders.

As he reached his office in the centre of the barracks, something quite different was happening far away to the north of Serenity, and high on the ramparts of the Fence itself: a young captain of a border-force patrol was standing on watch, waiting. He had just taken position on the top step of an observation post and was looking towards the third quadrant of the outlands. It was Barvarik, and throughout much of that day he had led his men and their war-horses along the Fence-line near the Great Gates in a long, gruelling patrol. Only once had they stopped to rest the horses and take food and water. And now, at last, with the evening watch less than two hours away, he had led them to this observation post and told them to make camp for the night. They had responded gratefully, but without the usual muttering and murmuring expected from conscripts. They were good men, and whoever had chosen their horses had also chosen well: broad-chested, tireless beasts with keen eyes and a steady spirit.

Having taken early watch, he mounted the observation post and shifted the wall-mounted scope towards true-north. Adjusting the settings, he peered through it. The far off hills leapt into view, their rocky flanks etched out by the setting sun, and the arrow-straight road of the imperial highway disappearing into the narrow valleys that flanked it. There was nothing. He looked again. Again, there was nothing. It had been like that all day, and yet . . . Barvarik swung the scope further to the east: a river several miles away gleamed gold as it wound its way across the deserted plains. Frowning, he stood up, blinked and rubbed his eyes. There was nothing, nothing at all, and that was what bothered him. It wasn't what he wanted to see.

Usually, there was some sign of life: perhaps no more than a distant mule-driver with a weary train of mules, or a farmer trudging home from his fields. On earlier patrols from earlier years, they would often spot small groups of outlanders going in and out of woodlands with axes over their shoulders and baskets under their arms, or a shepherd driving his little flock down some grassy slope towards shelter and the hope of better pasture. Or, as sometimes happened, he would see distant goose-girls gathering their geese by a distant stream. Always, or nearly always there was something to see.

But for the past couple of days there had been nothing, and it had troubled him. He had reported his concerns to his senior officer at the border-post, but the man had merely paused in signing off another requisition form, sighed and looked up at Barvarik.

'If it's all quiet out there, that's all I need to know, captain,' he had said. 'Don't worry about what you can't see, worry about what you can.' He reached for another form. 'When you see something worth reporting, then come and tell me.'

And so that is how it was. Nothing had changed. And there was still nothing to see.

'Where are the outlanders?' Barvarik muttered to himself as he made his way down the steps. 'Where have they gone?'

A hundred miles further north, if the wall scope could have seen that far, Barvarik would have had his answer. In the shadow of the walls of the great city called Burgh or Brokinburgh, a great army was making ready to march: in the morning.

The power cables of Brokinburgh had done their work. The workshops and forges, lathes and presses of that city had forged, updated and repaired ten times a thousand weapons. Every sergeant-of-the-line now carried a 'thunder-rod', a shaft of metal with a wooden handle and several small cables charged with an electrical pulse. It was a deadly short range weapon. The warlords made sure that their swords and war-clubs were also fully charged. And more than this, the kitchens of the meeting hall and its surrounding mansions had been busy preparing food that could be easily carried as rations by troops on the march.

But perhaps the most impressive of all were the war-wagons. These were four-wheeled, high sided carts drawn by teams of oxen or bullocks. Each cart was reinforced with armoured beams and had a fire-step running both left and right as well as to the rear. At the front where the driver sat, was a raised platform protected by iron shutters, and provided with arrow slits from which bowmen either side of the driver could shoot. But what made these carts stand out above the army Chesterman had assembled, were the iron towers mounted on plated cross beams in the mid-section of each war-wagon. Cables stretching down from them to battery points enabled the infantry to recharge their 'thunder rods' even in the midst of battle.

Every time Marlin saw one of these carts, he wondered at them, and the skill that had gone into their construction. It seemed as if every kind of wreckage from earlier times and forgotten conflicts had been used to put them together. But on this day he was even more impressed, not so much by the construction of the carts, but by the sheer number of them. In such a short space of time the artisans and craftsmen of Brokingburgh had managed to produce from the heaps of debris and metal scrap at least forty wagons. And what's more the stewards and commissioners of the high council had succeeded in finding enough animals to haul, and enough harnesses to yoke and draw these carts.

But most impressive of all were the chariots of the warlords. While not as big as the war-wagons, or as heavily armed, they nevertheless were constructed in such a way as to strike fear in the heart of any opponent who saw them. Flying machines called 'MIGS' or 'Boeings' from the ancient times, before the Great Burning, had been used to construct these chariots in much the same way as the remains of ancient buildings and machinery were also scavenged to construct the gateways and towers of the city of Brokinburgh.

But there was no chariot for Marlin. As evening drew on, he found himself sitting by the camp fire with the rest of his men after the final parade had ended. They had been dismissed from the parade ground only when the last of the war-wagons had rumbled by to their assembly position for tomorrow's march.

'It's a lucky man gets to ride in one of those, my lord,' said one of the men and Marlin turned and smiled. It was Martin-Doc, a veteran in his service, and one of the first recruits to his cause.

'Aye, but not for the likes of us, I'm afraid Martin-Doc,' answered the king's brother. 'Each wagon is assigned a squad of warriors from the high council garrison. They're specialists y'know, trained to fight from war-wagons, and better equipped than most of us.'

Martin-Doc shrugged, chewed on a chicken bone and then threw it into the fire:

'Well, at least we'll be able to keep up with them. I plan to find myself one and make sure I walk right close to it.'

Marlin laughed. 'Stick with me lad, and I'll see you safely through this little expedition.'

'Well, my lord, you'll have the thanks of my wife at least if that is what happens.' The man's smile faded for an instant. 'Not that I've seen her or the little ones for more than three years now.'

'They are in Serenity?'

'They are, my lord. I was declared a stainer over three years ago, spent some time in prison, and then was deported with a work-detail to a settlement near the imperial highway. They needed road builders.'

'They?'

'Rebuild, my lord. Their leaders wanted to extend the highway deeper into the outlands, but they were short of workers. We were told that many had perished in that harsh winter you might remember, the one that saw half the kingdom almost buried under snow drifts and blizzards.'

'I remember.' Marlin shook his head. 'I didn't think that even the likes of Rebuild would carry on with engineering works in such conditions.'

Martin-Doc grimaced. 'Why shouldn't they, my lord? If you are a stainer they see less worth in you than they would in a dog. I worked on that highway for six months and I saw more men and women die of ill treatment and starvation than I saw folk perish because of weather conditions.'

For a long time Marlin gazed into the fire. 'I see now why you came to me. I thought you were just a ragtag farm labourer who had seen an opportunity to slip across the Fence and make your escape. You never said.'

'I was grateful that you never asked me, my lord. I feared that if I told you I had fled from a road gang, you might think me some sort of criminal who had escaped from a penal battalion.'

'It's true I never like to ask,' Marlin replied, 'Each man's story is his own, but if you had told me I would still have taken you in.'

There were some grunts of approval from the other men sat around the fire. One of them stood up. 'Do you think, my lord,' he asked, 'we will, all of us here, be allowed to march together tomorrow, and fight together when the time comes?'

Marlin thought for a moment and then replied;

'We will march together, that is certain, but when we approach the enemy and lord Chesterman orders us into battle formation, we will probably go where we are sent.'

'Probably, my lord?'

Marlin grinned. 'Don't worry, Samsung, I will make sure my banner is held high. If any of you should happen to lose your way in the confusion, you will know where to find me.'

Samsung returned the grin. 'Then all is well, my lord,' he said.

In the morning, as promised, the army marched. Women folk and children came to the gates and walls to wave them off, and there was a guard of honour for Chesterman. He rode his plane-winged chariot, with its polished tubular aluminium frame, through the main gateway and onto the parade ground. And he did not waste time with speeches. Standing tall in the chariot's cockpit, he simply saluted the army, pointed south, and nodded to his driver who with a flick of the reins stirred his oxen into action.

The army moved like a dark tide, lifting itself against the icy fields and pushing out from the city and across the southern plains. It did not follow the road, but marched on a broad front, that only narrowed for forests and rocky outcrops. And always it kept its banners dipped towards the border hills that lay like a distant cloak of faded blue beneath the wintry skies.

The light infantry went first, advancing on foot in a loose scattered formation to clear the way ahead and check for hostile scouts or border-force patrols. Then came the heavy infantry, marching together in close ranked cohorts of leather and steel, their serried weapons glinting in the pale light, and their polished helmets catching the sun whenever it appeared between the scudding clouds. Each cohort carried a banner which flapped bravely in the chill breeze that swept across the plain from the north, and each company had a sergeant with a 'thunder rod' and a captain with a trumpet in his belt.

After the heavy infantry came the war-wagons in three great divisions, and behind them another troop of heavy infantry and a battalion of engineers. To the right and left of the war wagons, the chariots of the warlords kept pace with the army: all except for the plane-chariot or MIG of Chesterman. He rode at the front of the foremost cohort of heavy infantry. Next to him, marching with a measured step to keep pace with the chariot, were Marlin's men, with their own captain at their head.

Marlin had almost expected to have been forgotten in the frantic preparations for the march, but before dawn that morning he had been woken by a message from headquarters that he was to present himself with his men, to the front and centre of the army when the trumpets sounded 'parade'.

And so, after a hasty breakfast he had reported as ordered. Chesterman, helmeted, was already there, with Celsius alongside him, and he greeted Marlin with that characteristic nod for which he was known. Then he gestured to him, indicating where he should draw up his men, and without saying anything turned to talk to another captain who had just come up with a message from another division.

And that was all. When the army marched, Marlin found himself marching alongside Chesterman's chariot, with the rest of the army streaming out on either side and behind him.

They made good progress. There were storm clouds building up at their backs, to the north, but the way ahead was clear, and there was not the least sign that they had been spotted or were even expected.

The army made camp on the evening of the first day near a lake that lay to the west of their chosen route. It was partly frozen, and the ice was thick enough for pickets to be placed on the lake to warn the army of any approach by enemy scouts. By order of Chesterman, no fires were lit. And so they ate a cold supper, endured a freezing, sleepless night and rose at first light.

They broke camp and set off without breakfast, but stopped just before the forenoon watch, and rested along a patch of deserted downland that looked towards the border. As the sun set that evening, they had their first faint sighting of the distant towers of the great gates, almost lost against the horizon. At last Chesterman ordered that camp fires could be lit. 'Now is the time we let them know we are here,' he said to Marlin as he walked by on his way to a meeting with his warlords. 'We are too close now to be stopped before we reach the Fence, so we may as well let them know what they are in for.'

He laughed as he left, and left Marlin wondering at Chesterman's nerve as a commander: to light fires now was either foolishness, or a bold show of confidence in sight of the enemy.

But his men did not complain. They lit fires and roasted meat, then ate, drank and rested in the warmth of the firelight.

Twenty five miles away to the south, Barvarik was on duty at the border outpost. He had just taken over from his sergeant, and was beginning a watch that would take him to the third hour of the evening. If there was nothing to report by morning, he had orders to move on from this particular outpost, and begin a patrol to the east where small numbers of wild folk had been sighted in groups that could indicate raiding parties.

The skies above the outpost were clear, although there was a promise of rain from the north. The stars were already appearing in bright, friendly clusters and a new moon was just cresting into view. Climbing to the top step of the observation tower, he gazed northwards. There was nothing, just shadow and a great stillness.

With a grunt of annoyance, he told himself that however much he knew that it was a waste of time, the regimental watch-manual was explicit that the far scope must always be used at least three times during any hour long period of observation. Wearily he swung the 'scope around to the north west, leaned forward and put it to his eyes. Slowly, he moved it from left to right, muttering as he ticked off the vectors. 'Just as I thought,' he muttered to himself. Then he moved the scope back from left to right, careful not to hurry the process so that he could tell his commander that all had been done according to regulation.

He had just reached the midpoint of the scan when something caught his eye. It was very faint, and indistinct but it was something he had not expected to see: a pinpoint of light.

Adjusting the focus on the scope, he stared for a long time at the light. It was not moving. And then to his surprise he noticed something he had missed on the first sweep: there were other faint points of light, set further back and in some sort of line. Very slowly he tracked across with the far scope: there were more lights, just as faint and indistinct as the first, but definitely there.

'Watch fires!' he whispered to himself, and began to count: five, ten, twenty, fifty, a hundred and more still. He straightened, and looked into the darkness: they were not watch-fires he could see, they were camp fires. And that was not a hunting party he had spotted: that was an army.

Quickly leaning over the guard-rail, he called down to his sergeant:

'Light the beacon! Turn on the signal beams! They are coming, sergeant. They are coming.'

'Where away, my lord?' answered the sergeant, looking up at Barvarik in surprise.

'To the north and north west. Camp fires, and more than a hundred of them.'

The sergeant hurried away, Barvarik heard some shouted orders, and moments later the beacon on the rampart flickered into life. It was soon blazing, and it was not long before other beacons mounted on the Fence about a mile each side of the border post were lit in reply. There was a pause and then whole sections of the wall between the beacons were suddenly illuminated in green and gold.

Barvarik turned and looked directly south of his position. Again, a mile distant and almost lost in the darkness, yet another beacon blazed, and another stretch of wall lit up. He nodded with satisfaction. It would not be long before Serenity itself received, as the beacons were lit, word of what he had just seen.

There was the sound of boots on the steps below, and the sergeant appeared, breathless and carrying his double-pulse cross bow.

He saluted. 'The beacon is lit, sir, and the men have stood to arms,' he said, gasping over the words.

Barvarik smiled grimly. 'That is good, but I doubt if it will come to fighting until morning.' He paused and instinctively loosened his sword in its scabbard. 'But there's no harm in being ready. We'll wait for an hour, then if those fires haven't moved, you can stand the men down.'

'Except for the watch, my lord.'

'Aye, except for the watch, and double the guard on that observation post by the stable. I don't want any outlander scouts sneaking in close while we are busy staring at their camp fires.'

The sergeant nodded and rubbed his beard. When on duty at the Fence, few men wore masks. Barvarik looked at the sergeant's pale blue eyes. He was a veteran, and bore the scars of many years service on the borders. The sergeant had only recently transferred to Barvarik's regiment, but he was already proving himself to be valuable. Barvarik liked his steadiness, and his quick thinking.

'Do you have family?' Barvarik asked him suddenly.

The sergeant nodded again. 'Yes, my lord. A bonny wife and two daughters. We have a house in Lower Town near aquaduct C.'

'Well, all going to plan, we will stop this army before it gets anywhere near the walls of Serenity.'

The sergeant gazed northward into the darkness. 'If they march at dawn, my lord, they will be here by sunset tomorrow.'

'That they will,' agreed Barvarik, 'but if those beacons do their job we will have more than enough troops here by morning to meet them.' He turned and looked towards the other observation post. 'Keep the beacon burning, sergeant. We want those outlanders to know that we've spotted them.'

The sergeant saluted and disappeared down the steps, leaving Barvarik to return to his watch. He reached again for the farscope, swung it into position and peered once again through the eye-piece. Now he knew what he was looking for: the distant fires sprang into sharp focus, and he wondered why it had taken him so long to see them at the first. There were no longer a mere hundred or so fires. Now there seemed to be thousands: it was as if more and more were being lit even as he watched.

With a sigh, he stood back from the 'scope, and scratched the back of his neck. 'This is no raid,' he said to himself. 'This is an invasion.'

Far to the north, Marlin threw another branch on the fire, leaned back and watched the sparks whirl upwards into the night. The smell of roasting meat and wood smoke filled his nostrils. He smiled. As long as it didn't rain, he might even get some sleep and wake refreshed for the march to the Fence on the morrow. As if to answer his thoughts, there came a far-off rumble of thunder and the breeze from the north quickened.

One of his men stood and looked back the way they had come. 'Three hours away at least, my lord,' he said. 'We'll be dry enough until then.'

'Well, I'll make the most of it then,' replied Marlin. He wrapped himself in his cloak, settled down just a bit nearer to the fire, and was soon asleep.

The storm struck the army some time before dawn. There was lightning, and there was rain, swift and drenching blown across the backs of sleeping men on strong winds, but it past quickly enough. Within an hour the worst of the storm had passed, and the men took their rest again where they could find it, lying between the muddy puddles of rainwater, or beneath the war-wagons and the winged chariots.

At last the camp awoke shrouded in morning mist and the smoke from cooking fires. Trumpets rang out among the wagons and open bivouacs. Slowly the men emerged, shaking out their sodden cloaks, and stamping their feet to bring some warmth to frozen feet. Officers moved among the huddled groups of infantry, giving the orders for the day, and checking that all their men had survived the night along with their equipment. An hour later all was ready for the first march of the day. Chesterman's own banner-bearer marched to the front of the army, a single trumpet sounded and the advance began.

As they splashed their way out of the camp site and onto the open heath-land, Marlin shouted for his sergeant to take up a position on the right flank of their detachment.

'I will hold the left flank!' he called out. 'Make sure that Pentax keeps to the centre. We don't want to be wandering off now.'

The sergeant waved and shifted to the right, his thunder-rod catching the early morning sun which had appeared through a break in the clouds on the eastern horizon. Marlin nodded to himself. Already his men were setting an example for discipline and efficiency in this army. With any luck he would see most of them safely home, though there was no telling how long that would take. He glanced over his shoulder as he heard the first of the war-wagons lurch into action behind him. Their iron towers swayed back and forth making the electrical cables flap against their stanchions but nobody seemed bothered: Chesterman had trained his drivers and engineers well. They sat easily on top of the driving platforms whistling to the oxen and calling out a warning to any of the infantry that strayed too close. Everyone knew how dangerous these tower-weapons were, and how vital they would be in the coming battle. Chesterman clearly had confidence in his war wagons, but he also appreciated that they had to be handled with skill and determination. For this reason he had spared no expense in their construction and in the training of their crews. It was also said among the militias that it was Chesterman who had developed the 'power-sword', a weapon that carried in its blade an electrical charge almost equal to that found in a 'thunder-rod'.

Although Marlin had not dared to ask Chesterman if it was a power-sword that had proved to be the vital difference between himself and Hartley in the recent fight in the safe house at Brokinburgh, he guessed that it was probably so. Instinctively, he put his hand on the hilt of his own sword. This was a sword given to him by his father when he was just a lad, and he had kept it at his side ever since. All its power lay in the quality of its blade, nothing else, but it was a formidable weapon nonetheless. If not today, surely tomorrow it would prove its mettle against the blades of the swordsmen of Serenity: his own people.

Lifting his head, he stared south towards the Fence, faintly visible against the pale horizon. 'At least another twenty miles before the fighting starts,' he muttered to himself, and spat neatly into the heather.

As it was, over twenty miles away Barvarik stood on the ramparts of the border post, his captain at his side and a trumpeter next to him. He had taken a brief rest during the night, but was now back on duty, trying to calculate when the Stainer army would arrive at the Fence Line. He was also waiting to see whether they would swing east and south to strike the defences where he now stood, or instead head directly for the great gates of the main defences. It scarcely mattered. There would be a fight, a fierce one, and it would need both courage and commitment to see it through no matter where the blow fell. Already Barvarik had given instructions that the horses were to be taken to the relative safety of the stables, but that they were to be saddled, harnessed and ready to advance against the outlander army, if it broke through at this sector of the border.

At least, Bavarik admitted to himself, the defenders had to acknowledge one piece of good fortune: whoever was leading the invading army had decided against a night march, and instead had camped for the night about twenty miles north of the the Fence itself. Had the army arrived during the night whole sections of the Fence would have been desperately under manned and especially vulnerable to attack.

Turning, Barvarik looked towards the open ground immediately south of the wall and about a bowshot from the outpost: it was covered with lines of tents around which men were moving, carrying equipment and bringing supplies and provisions to those soldiers who were already hurrying to the ramparts. Three regiments from Rebuild had arrived in the hour before dawn, and there was word that another two were on the way to this sector, and should arrive by the noon watch.

The young nobleman switched his attention once more to the northern horizon. Scattered clouds and haze made it difficult to see clearly beyond several miles, but he knew that the stainer force had almost certainly set off by now, and with no one to oppose them, they would probably arrive at the border by late afternoon.

A soldier came up the steps and saluted. Barvarik returned his salute. 'What is it?' he asked.

'We have a report from a sector two miles east of here, my lord.'

'Yes?'

The soldier swallowed hard. 'Wild folk, my lord. In significant numbers. They are assembling on a ridge just north of the Fence.'

Barvarik grunted. 'They have come to watch the fun, perhaps.'

For a moment the soldier hesitated, then he replied. 'The scout who brought the report in, says that they were beating war drums, and had dragged launching machines to a firing position about fifty metres from the wall.'

Barvarik stared. 'Impossible,' he said. 'They do not have the technology to do such a thing.'

The soldier risked a shrug. 'My lord, it seems that they do.'

Three days march away, beyond the second quadrant, in the city of Serenity itself, there was a sense of unease and fear that had settled over both the Upper and Lower Town. Not only had the wave of unexplained and frightening poisonings continued, but rumours had drifted in of a threat to the northern borders and the increasing presence of raiders from the outlands communities.

At first the imperial authorities had denied the stories, and even forbade citizens to talk of them, but it soon became apparent that few people within the city walls were inclined to accept the hastily written and broadcast communiqués from the commissariat and imperial chancellery.

Everyone was aware that beacons had been sighted the previous night, and that moreover regiments had been seen marching through the gates and along the main road north towards the borders.

Anna Seka had been placed on 'city patrol' with her regiment. A curfew had been imposed after several key members of the imperial council fell victim to the staining, and the king had ordered that anyone breaking the curfew was to be either shot on sight or placed in indefinite custody without trial. This meant that scouts and soldiers like Anna had to move through the deserted streets in companies of no less than five, and crossbows were to be carried in addition to the usual side arms.

Anna hated this work and scarcely understood why it had to be carried out. But orders were orders, as her commanding officer had said, and this was no time to be challenging the authority of the king and the commissariat. On the rare occasion that she was allowed home from the barracks, Anna tried to talk the situation through with her parents. Her father remained tight lipped about the orders coming out of the imperial council, but was clearly worried. Her mother, on the other hand talked freely about what she had heard in the street markets and cafes of Silver Street. 'They have closed the schools,' she said, 'and no children are allowed in the parks or play areas. There is talk that the poorer quarters of Lower Town are harbouring stain-folk, and that there is one precinct that is close to revolt.'

'What do you think, papa?' Anna asked her father at lunch.

Her father looked up from his plate, frowned and then sat back. 'I cannot speak to such a question as if I were your chancellor,' he said quietly, 'but I can tell you this as your father: rumour is the child of panic, and although your mother is as honest as the day is long, I wish she would not be so trusting of the gossip she hears on Silver Street.' As he spoke, he reached out, smiled and took his wife's hand. 'Forgive me, my dear,' he said.

Anna's mother arched her eyebrows, but nonetheless returned her husband's smile. 'Your father is right of course, Anna,' she murmured, 'but some of the gossip that I have heard was from the lips of the chief secretary of a senior commissariat official.' She paused. 'It seemed to me less like rumour, and more like useful fact.'

'So we cannot be sure,' Anna added quickly, 'but I know that our regiment has been placed on full alert, and one of the captains told me that we should make ready for a posting to the northern borders.'

Her father nodded slowly, clasped his hands together and brought them slowly to his chin in that way he had when he was deep in thought. 'Strange times,' he said quietly after a while, 'but still no reason to keep us from so excellent a lunch. Eat well, my daughter. You will need to keep your strength for the days ahead.'

'As will Talessa,' replied Anna, hating herself for saying such a thing.

But her father merely smiled sadly, while her mother lowered her head, then looking up, gazed out of the window as if distracted by something. 'We all miss her terribly,' she whispered.

Not long after lunch, Anna farewelled her parents and left, promising to return when next she got a leave-pass. She was due back at the barracks later that afternoon, but had just enough time to go by the first court chateau where Barvarik's family lived. Although she feared it was a slim chance, she hoped that they might have some news of Talessa via their son, or perhaps even some information from the commissariat.

They were both at home, sitting in the inner conservatory when Anna was announced by the door keeper, one of the servants. There was a moment's confusion when they thought that she herself had arrived with news from the prison, but once that moment had passed, they invited her to sit with them and take tea.

'I cannot stay long,' said Anna as she sat down on a reclining chair next to the garden pool. 'I have just been to see my mother and father, and wondered if by any chance . . .'

'No my dear,' Barvarik's mother interrupted gently. 'We have heard nothing for some time. I know our son has approached the commissariat on at least one occasion, and we were also told that your father had petitioned the king for clemency, but all without success.'

Anna nodded. 'We will not give up hope, my lady. I am also convinced that Barvarik will not let the matter rest until justice is done.'

Barvarik's father gave a slight smile and a shake of the head. 'Oh, justice will be done, Anna whether we like it or not, but I fear it will be the justice of the commissariat, and nothing more.'

There was a fountain playing in the centre of the pool with tropical birds bathing in it. Anna noticed how the sunlight caught the droplets of water, making them shimmer. Rain birds danced around the pool. It seemed so peaceful. 'Barvarik will return soon?' she asked.

'There is no way of knowing,' replied Barvarik's father. 'His posting is meant to be a temporary assignment, but things change so rapidly these days, and until the poisonings stop all military forces have been placed on high alert.' He smiled again. 'I can tell you that much, Anna, but I would be surprised if you had not already received such orders yourself.'

Anna nodded. 'All official leave has been cancelled, but from today our commanding officer is allowing half day passes as long as we stay within the city.'

A maid came into the garden to ask if the visitor would be staying for tea, but Anna stood, and bowed. 'I must take my leave,' she said. 'My parents send their love and greetings, and they have promised to meet up with you when time allows.'

'Go well, daughter of Akton,' replied Barvarik's father getting to his feet and farewelling Anna in the way of the old custom. 'We will be writing to our son in the next couple of days, and will let him know that you came to see us.'

With another brief bow, Anna left the garden, and followed the maid through the series of hallways and precincts to the front gates. The requested shuttle glided her along the connecting bridge to the city. Moments later she found herself out in the street once more. Although there were still two hours at least before the curfew, and the sun still shone brightly, it was strangely quiet. There was almost no one about, and even those that were in the street hurried by with heads bowed and masks almost hidden beneath hoods and scarves.

Setting off for the barracks, she noticed as she came down the escalators from the interchange of the great tower, that storm clouds were building up on the horizon far to the north. Distant flashes of lightning flickered over the hills, but it was too far to hear the thunder. What other troubles were they facing along the borders and the Fence? she wondered to herself.

If Anna had been able to go to the top-most viewing stand of the royal tower high above the city, and look through the wall-mounted far-scope, fixed on a permanent mounting, she would have been able to see the answer to her question:

Columns of smoke were rising up from several points along the Fence, and the great gates of the imperial highway appeared to be ablaze. The army from the outlands had arrived.

DEFENCE

Barvarik was exhausted. The lead elements of a stainer attack force had appeared over a low ridge about a mile away from the outpost about two hours after the noon watch had sounded. At first they seemed to be no more than a reconnaissance force in strength, but as they streamed down the forward slope and fanned out into line of attack, a substantial force of heavy infantry had appeared from behind them. And then, even as Barvarik and the other captains ordered their men to the ramparts, the swaying towers of the war-wagons crested the ridge and rumbled forward.

What surprised Barvarik was the speed and extent of their advance. Although his outpost was some distance from the Great Gates, and not considered to be a key point in the defence line of the Fence, the stainers had clearly committed a large number of troops to an assault on the position he now held. Swinging the far-scope from left to right, Barvarik searched in vain for an obvious flank to this attack: the line of stainers seemed endless, and without any sign of a gap which a sally-force from his regiment might have been able to exploit.

Someone came up alongside him. He turned. It was the commander.

Barvarik straightened and saluted. 'They look to try and break through here, sir. We will need the crossbowmen.'

The commander, an older man with a pepper-grey beard, nodded. 'Our crossbowmen should do some damage, but I see those fellows have got scaling ladders and grappling hooks. They mean to have us if they can.'

Barvarik glanced along the ramparts. The reserve regiments were still hurrying into position, and several squads of crossbowmen were already on the firing steps of the wall, and atop to watch-towers to the east. 'We can make things hot for their infantry, sir, but I don't know about those war-wagons. Although I heard about them in training-school, I haven't yet got to see one in action.'

The commander shrugged. 'Well, you won't have long to wait, captain. Whoever is in charge of that lot out there seems keen to hit us with everything he's got before we can get ourselves properly organised.'

He leaned forward and peered through the far-scope. 'Who taught them to drill like that? Those are Serenity formations: cohorts of twenty men across by ten deep, and three paces between them. And look how they have set their skirmishers to the front, and their heavies to the second division.' He straightened. 'Rather beautiful, don't you think?'

Barvarik stared at the commander. A stainer army described as beautiful? He had never thought to hear that from the lips of any senior officer. Throughout his training in officer school, Barvarik had been constantly assured that stainer armies were at best loosely organised crowds of part-time fighting men, and at worst barely controlled mobs of barbarian mercenaries.

Still, he had to admit that the commander was right: this was like no other outlander force he had ever heard about or come across himself.

There was a sudden cry to his left. 'Ware, front! Incoming!'

He looked. An arc of fire and trailing smoke had risen from one of the enemy war wagons. The fire climbed into the sky to a great height, slowly curved over and began to drop towards the Fence in a blazing ball of light. Men scattered in all directions, each one looking for shelter and protection on the narrow wall-walk, or in the lee of the lower defences. The projectile fell with a strange, high pitched whistling sound which to a rose to a deafening scream as it plunged to earth near where Barvarik was standing. He just had time to hurl himself to one side before there was a terrifying crash and great chunks of masonry and pieces of timber erupted skywards in a cloud of smoke and sparks. For a moment they hung there as if suspended high above the ground, and then fell like rain on the heads of the stunned defenders.

Barvarik himself was narrowly missed by a piece of rock bigger than a horse's head, and he stared as it struck a paving slab, broke it into pieces and then skittered off into the confusion of smoke and hurrying shadows. He staggered to his feet in time to see two more fireballs fired from the war-wagons. They also rose high against the sky and settled to a fiery arc, almost merging in their course as they struck an observation post five hundred paces from where Barvarik now stood. When the smoke cleared the observation post had gone, and the nearby officers were trying to rally soldiers back to their positions on the wall.

There followed a sustained bombardment that threatened to clear some sections of the wall of all of its defenders, and even brought down parts of the Fence for about a hundred yards either side of where Barvarik now crouched.

When the bombardment eased, he stood up, took a trumpet from the body of a fallen infantryman, and sounded it. Even as the echo faded, another trumpet sounded, and then another from further along the ramparts.

Barvarik grimaced, and wiped his hand across his brow. It was impossible to tell how many defenders had been killed or wounded, but at least there would be someone to offer token resistance when the outlander hordes struck the wall. At last the enemy infantry had come within range, and to Barvarik's relief the crossbowmen from regiments brought up from Serenity began to shoot directly into the enemy ranks. At the same time the ballistas and mangonels that had survived the stainer bombardment began their own barrage. There had not been time to manhandle the catapults up onto the walls, so these engines of war were now firing blind from the open ground immediately behind the ramparts. But that was better than nothing, and so many attackers were now closing in on the wall that the catapults once fired could scarcely miss.

Ducking instinctively as he felt the breath of a ballista ball pass over his head, Barvarik crouched lower and pulled his helmet across his brow. It was good not to have to wear a mask, but although this gave him better vision, it meant that he was more vulnerable to the arrows and slingshots that the first wave of stainers seemed to be using.

The sergeant was suddenly at his side again. There was a bloody gash on his cheek, and his helmet had gone, but he was smiling. 'We are holding, sir,' he said. 'The lads along to the right of us have been in the thick of it, but they are standing firm.'

'Casualties?'

The sergeant nodded, and winced as another ballista bolt skimmed upwards and over the wall. 'More than we would like, sir, but the guards regiment near the far observation post has promised us reserves once they have seen off that attack by the wild folk.'

Barvarik grunted. He had forgotten about the wild folk. It would be a bitter irony if they managed to tip the balance in this battle. 'Thank you, sergeant,' he said. 'Get down to that ballista battery, and tell them to lift their range. Those bolts are getting too close for comfort.'

The sergeant grinned, gave a half salute and disappeared down the steps. Barvarik never saw him again.

To the north of The Fence by three hundred paces, Marlin, among the advancing cohorts of stainer infantry, led his men towards the heart of the fighting.

'Steady lads!' he shouted as arrows whipped and whined among them. 'Keep those shields up and your heads down!' He glanced at the front ranks and the forest of scaling ladders. 'And if you love life, hold to the drums and stick together!'

A stone from a mangonel narrowly missed them and plunged into the ranks behind. They quickened their pace and the drums took up the beat. Ahead, Marlin could make out the section of wall they had been assigned to attack. To his right, some five hundred paces away he could just make out the towering shadows of the Great Gates, already wreathed in smoke, with flames flickering out of the darkness. But to his front, the wall, though lower, was being fiercely contested, and the ramparts were crowded with defenders. He bit his lip. He would know some of those men. They would be fighting under banners that had been familiar to him during his years of military service: banners that he had been proud to serve under, and one in particular that he once called his own. He could even see it now, there right in front of him, almost lost in the smoke, but distinctive with its crimson field and depiction of a mailed fist. It was a king's regiment, and part of the royal guard, but what was it doing here so far from Serenity? Was the imperial army already so badly stretched that it was sending elite guards' regiments to the front line?

He scarcely had time to shake his head at the thought before a ballista bolt crashed into the party of men in front of him. They had been carrying a scaling ladder, and pieces of its wooden rungs fell like a bloody rain not seven paces from his next step.

Hesitating, he swung the line of march to avoid the fallen men, and then straightened again as they cleared the wounded and the dead.

'Up lads!' he shouted again, drew his sword and pointed it at the ramparts. 'Take the first ladder you find. and a month's pay to every man who makes it to the top of the wall.'

Marlin smiled to hear them cheer, and they all rushed forward. He was vaguely aware of two men falling to his left, and one to his right, then all at once in the midst of the confusion there was a ladder directly in front of him. It had been driven hard against the wall and the iron hooks at its top had gripped the stone battlement. Three or four men lay sprawled at its base, but the way was clear. Shortening the grip on his sword, he sprang to the ladder and began to climb.

CHAPTER #8
THE WESTERN PINNACLE

The king had summoned Akton, Shadwatch, and senior officials of Litra and the Commissariat to a meeting on top of one of the platforms that flanked the western pinnacle. It was the first time he had ever done such a thing, but he was convinced of the rightness of his choice. The balcony of the pinnacle platform was just as safe as any meeting hall in the city, and from there he and the others could see not only over the city walls, but also beyond to the lands that stretched away to the northern borders. And it was about these lands that he was now most concerned. Last night the beacons from the north had burned green. It was three days since the initial beacons had been sighted, and reserves had been rushed to the border. But now the beacons burned green, and that could only mean one thing: The Fence had been breached at one or more points, and the enemy had therefore managed to cross the border.

Even as he sent word for the meeting to be held at the western pinnacle, a messenger had entered at the gates of lower town. He entered breathless and stained with the dust and blood of battle. His horse was winded, and his sword broken and useless in its scabbard. A Triple S unit instantly met him and hurried him to the king's location. When he arrived, the king looked up from the papers spread on the table in front of him. Then as the messenger advanced towards him, he got to his feet: there would be no time nor need for formalities. 'You have news, soldier?' he asked.

The messenger knelt quickly and got to his feet, still breathing hard from the ride. 'My lord king,' he said, 'two days ago the borders were breached by a stainer army,' he paused, 'outlanders.'

'Where?'

'At the Great Gates, my lord, and at two points to the east in the second quadrant.'

The king studied him intently. What was left of his uniform bore the flashes of a guards' regiment. He was young, but clearly already a veteran: his weather-tanned skin, and the clear look in his eye despite his exhaustion told the king that much.

'You fought, soldier?'

'We all fought my lord, but many of us will fight no more.'

The king glanced at a servant, standing to one side of the table: 'You will escort this soldier to the imperial barracks. See that he gets food and drink, then escort him to the pinnacle.'

'The pinnacle, my lord?'

'Aye, the west pinnacle. I will meet you there within the hour on the balcony.'

The servant bowed, the soldier saluted and they both left.

With a sigh, the king now turned to his secretary who was sitting open-mouthed at the end of the table, a pen poised in his hand. 'Up now, Altoff! Gather up those papers and your wits. We are due to meet members of the high council, and I would not have them waiting.'

A short while later the meeting was convened. The messenger had not yet arrived, but the king gave Akton and the others the news they had guessed at since the beacons had been sighted.

'We as yet have no details,' said the king, 'but it seems clear enough to me that we have suffered a significant defeat, and casualties are likely to be high.'

'It would be better if we had at least some good news to give to our citizens,' said Akton. 'There has been a mood of panic in the streets since those beacons were sighted.'

The king nodded. 'Well at least we can tell them the truth of it, and that should stop any other rumours.'

'Or give wings to such rumours, my lord,' muttered Shadwatch.

The Glambot type II, known as Teevey Blue Ray that often accompanied Shadwatch, was hovering at a discreet distance. Suddenly, but not unexpectedly, they were all aware of strange and ancient music coming from the Glambot. It was, of course, yet another of Glamtech's whimsical inventions, or more specifically Shadwatch's. What they could now hear was one of the randomly selected tunes and audio quotes drawn from the Glambot's vast library of long forgotten films or videos. These were weird, disconnected echoes from another era and Shadwatch, for reasons known only to himself, had loaded them via Glamgel circuitry onto his robotic friend some years ago.

Few people questioned Shadwatch about his Glambot, but they quietly marvelled at its technical brilliance and scientific eccentricity. It was as if Glamgel could accomplish almost anything if applied in the right way. Some said in private that it was just another Glamtech exercise devoted to its own propaganda and self promotion, but no one seemed inclined to challenge Shadwatch about this most recent and openly eccentric 'toy'.

Even the king, normally a stickler for custom and correct form, chose to ignore the presence of this floating machine that seemed to have no other purpose than to remind everyone of the lost world of what was once called warner brothers, streaming, youtube or cinemascope: a technical but popular oddity that had disappeared with the Great Burning. And that was many, many years ago.

Perhaps the thing that genuinely annoyed the king about Teevey, but he never openly admitted it, was that somehow Shadwatch had programmed this Glambot to broadcast spoken phrases and sentences as well as theme tunes from the seemingly endless selection of films or movies on its hard drive. What was noted, however, was that whenever Shadwatch was on official business within the city, his Glambot, Teevey Blue Ray, was always with him. Its Glamgel battery hummed softly as it drifted apparently aimlessly around or through whatever room, corridor or high lane it found itself in.

One of the officials, an elderly academic from Litra frowned, choosing to give Teevey a sideways glance. 'Do we release our reserve regiments for the front?' she asked quietly.

The musical excerpt from a movie called 'Casablanca' played on.

'That is perhaps our first decision,' replied the king, 'and the messenger may have additional information to help us. If our forces have been broken and scattered along the Fence, there is little point in sending any more men up there, but if there has been an orderly and controlled withdrawal, we can perhaps move to support it.'

'And so delay the inevitable,' Akton added.

'The inevitable, lord chancellor?'

'Play it, Sam, play: As Time Goes By.' A woman's voice drifted from the Glambot.

Akton gave a slight inclination of his mask. 'Yes, my lord king. The siege of Serenity. That would appear to be now inevitable.'

The king was about to reply, when suddenly the messenger and his escort appeared on the balcony. Unusually, the king waved him forward without ceremony. 'Welcome, soldier,' he said. 'Describe to myself and to these ladies and gentlemen here exactly what news you bring from the borders.'

The messenger came forward, bowed and spoke:

'Well, my lord king, the border is indeed breached. The Great Gates have fallen and two other observation posts to the east were overrun near the River of the Lost. My regiment was stationed at the Gates. It was a dawn attack. We were ready and waiting but they came at us in such strength and with engines of war we had never seen before.'

'Explain,' interrupted the academic from Litra.

The tune from the film 'Titanic' floated across the room, and Teevey Blue Ray drifted above their heads. The messenger, as he was advised to, ignored the Glambot and nodded. 'Normally we would have expected an assault from local raiding parties, some mounted, some on foot and all armed with little more than javelins and crossbows. But these folk came at us several divisions strong, at least fifteen thousand, and they came in good order. It was almost as if we were fighting against ourselves: their regimental formations were just like ours, and deployed to attack just as we would have done. They advanced in order of skirmishers, light infantry, and then heavy infantry.'

'And the war-engines?'

'Women and children, first,' the Glambot crackled and circled away.

Again the messenger ignored the Teevey Blue Ray and nodded: 'Nothing like I've ever seen before, my lady. They had huge wooden carts, reinforced with iron plates and surmounted by iron towers with strange cables. Our arrows were of no use against them, and even our ballistas could not stop them.'

'You speak of towers?'

'I do, my lady. As they advanced, these towers were able to hurl firebolts at us.'

The official from the commissariat snorted. 'Talk sense man! No outlander army would be capable of such a thing.'

The messenger was still without his mask which he had not worn since the fighting. He frowned and his frown was obvious. 'I know what I saw, my lord. Three men in my section on the walls were killed outright by a single blast from one of these towers. Although no damage was done to the ramparts or the actual defences, we had little defence against the power that came from these towers. Our reinforced leather shields helped against the smaller bolts, and we were able to slow the attack for a time with catapults and fire arrows, but once their infantry reached our walls, it was clear we could not hold for long.'

'I don't understand,' interrupted the king. 'Our troops are more than a match for any stainers. We all know that.'

It took the messenger some time to answer. He looked down at his boots for a moment, swallowed hard and then looked up. 'My king, you would have been proud of the way we fought. There was not a regiment that did not uphold the honour of Serenity. Every man sold his life dearly. As the outlanders swarmed over the walls we met them, sword to sword and shield to shield.'

'But . . ?' the king raised his eyebrows, and his mask glowed.

'But their infantry were also armed with weapons the like of which we had never seen before.'

'Thunder rods?' asked the Litra academic quietly.

The messenger glanced at her with a look of surprise. 'You have heard of them, my lady? Is that what they are called?'

The official smiled and in turn looked at Shadwatch. 'Have we not worked on such a weapon ourselves, my lord Shadwatch,' she asked with a slight smile.

'We have lady Larissa, but as yet our experiments have not borne fruit.' He paused, and glanced at his Glambot, which had disappeared for a moment but now entered the room from the far side. 'One of our patrols captured such a weapon last year. It was badly damaged, but we hoped to understand and copy its construction. As yet . . .' he spread his hands, 'we continue to work on the problem.'

The king grunted. 'It seems my lord Shadwatch that your efforts may have come too late. From what this soldier here says, our forces on the border have been defeated by technologies superior to our own.'

For a time no one spoke. As if drawn by a single thought, they all now turned and looked out across the balcony and towards the northern hills. Almost lost in the far haze, they could make out a dark and slowly rising line of smoke. The land was burning.

The music from an ancient movie once called 'Back to the Future' rose for just a moment and then faded discreetly.

At last the king shrugged, walked away for a moment as if he were leaving, then turned. 'They will be here by the end of the week,' he said.

'My lord king,' said Akton quickly, 'if our forces regroup, they could yet hold their advance. I can order up the last of the guards' regiments and seven squadrons of cavalry.'

'For what purpose, chancellor?' The king shook his head. 'If we could not hold the Fence and the Great Gates, we can certainly not hold the lands between the borders and Serenity.'

'There is always Rebuild,' replied Akton. 'They have Arx, they have Cornus, and their own civic guard.' He paused. 'And Arx has sun-reflector rays.'

'My lord,' the messenger broke in, 'as I rode south from the battle, I passed a Rebuild city a mile or so west of my path. It was ablaze.'

'Impossible!' Akton almost shouted.

'I know what I saw, my lord.' The messenger looked at the king who smiled sadly and gestured for him to continue. 'When my commander ordered me to return to Serenity,' he went on, 'he told me not to divert for any reason. It was already suspected that another stainer force had broken through the Fence west of the Great Gates, and was threatening to outflank and then surround any reserve forces coming up the main highway from the city.'

'You had a good horse then?' asked Akton.

'The best, my lord, and a companion from my youth. He carried me like the north wind, but even then I barely escaped the outlanders' advance. Twice their scouts mounted on those moor ponies they favour came within a bowshot of me, and twice I had to ride hard into woodland to escape them. There were even raiding parties of wildfolk roaming freely south of the Fence."

The official from the Commissariat now spoke. 'It seems as if we are all but overrun,' she said. 'If what this fellow says is true, the lead elements of the Stainer army will be here in a few days.'

'I guess you guys aren't ready for that yet, but your parents are gonna love it!' Teevey whirled softly above their heads as 'Back to the Future' played.

The king glared at the Glambot which was now hovering above the doorway. 'That is true, lady Follicia,' he said at last, 'there is always a chance they will pause to sack the cities and settlements of Rebuild, but I somehow doubt it. Serenity is the prize they seek.'

'Then we shall have to deny them that prize,' Shadwatch put in. 'With your permission, my lord, I will mobilise the Glamtech defence-programme. I have already alerted my people to such a possibility.'

The king frowned. 'The entire programme, you mean?'

Shadwatch hesitated. 'That is a decision for the king and the king alone,' he said quietly.

There was a silence. The messenger sensed that it was his moment to leave. He bowed saluted and turned away. Seconds later he had disappeared with a servant who guided him back through the double doors, and down the elevator of the pinnacle.

'Gentlemen, ladies: this way please.' The king led them to the far end of the balcony. From there they could see over the great sweep of the city with its buildings, parks, arcades and avenues. Beyond the walls the shining highway that led to the north, and another broad road that led across the open countryside to the east and then branched away to the coast.

'This is our land,' he said, 'and I am your king. It is my duty to defend it no matter what the cost.'

No one replied, but both Shadwatch and the academic from Litra nodded, so the king continued. 'We have failed to stop the enemy at the borders, and it is almost certain that key cities of Rebuild have also fallen, so this city and its port are all that remains.'

'Apart from The Island,' put in Akton.

The king shrugged. 'If Serenity falls, The Island will be taken, and with the Island captured our fleet will be scattered, that much is guaranteed.' He looked away towards the north and the distant clouds of smoke. 'No, this is where we make our stand, and this is where we show these stainers how implacable a foe we really are.'

'You have a plan, my lord?' asked Akton, keenly aware of Shadwatch's sudden look of alarm.

'A plan?' The king laughed and clapped his hands. 'Why, bless you, no, chancellor! I leave planning to my generals and their captains of arms.' He paused and behind his mask his eyes narrowed. 'And I have the Glamtech defence programme. But even more than this, I have the determination that we will meet the Stainer army with a challenge that they will struggle to oppose.'

'Go on, my lord,' said Akton quietly.

Again the king stared out across the city. 'We will let them know via our semaphore towers that if so much as a single stainer soldier sets foot in this our city, we will kill all the prisoners held in the imperial precinct.' He glanced at Akton, 'Every one of the prisoners, stainer or unstained, without exception.'

The chancellor's mask glowed, but he did not move, nor did he speak. It was Shadwatch who replied for all of them:

'My lord king, we do not have a law that would allow for such a thing. What you propose,' he hesitated, 'the high council would never agree to it.'

The king sighed. 'There is a law that allows it,' he replied. 'It is the law that is sealed by the oath that you made to your king: an oath and a promise to follow him who leads,' he paused, 'and decrees: the king.'

'And he who decrees must be obeyed,' added the lady Follicia quietly.

'Just so, just so,' said the king. 'As the constitution allows, and as my duty requires, the king's will is to be the law, and at the same time to enforce it.'

There followed a long silence. It was Akton who spoke at last:

'My daughter, sire,' he said, his voice breaking. 'You are saying that her life is forfeit?'

The king nodded. 'That is so,' he answered. 'From the moment that she was declared to be a stainer, she ceased at law to be your daughter, and all her rights and privileges as a citizen of Serenity became null and void.'

'This is madness, my lord!' said Shadwatch suddenly, and as he spoke the Glambot, with lights flashing, whirled away and disappeared.

'Agreed!' said the king raising his voice, and staring after the Glambot. 'But it is the madness of necessity in mad times. We are about to be overwhelmed, to be scattered and destroyed or at best enslaved. We must give this stainer horde an ultimatum that might make it pause, reconsider and perhaps even withdraw for a time.'

'And if the outlander army does not pause?' replied Shadwatch. 'If it breaks our gates and crosses the walls into our streets, how much mercy will it show to our people, if we have slaughtered all the prisoners within the precinct?'

'Then we will make an end worthy of our people, and worthy of the matchless beauty of our city.' The king forced a smile.

Shadwatch shook his head, turned away momentarily, and then turned again to face the king. 'I am bound by my oath to follow you, sire,' he said, his voice strong and level, 'and I will not break that oath, but neither will I stain the blade of my sword with the blood of any of our prisoners.'

The king walked up to Shadwatch, stared hard at him and spoke:

'I will keep you out of it, lord Shadwatch. Your sword will not be required, but your signature on the decree in council will be.'

Shadwatch did not reply. He stepped back, bowed to the king, and made as if to leave. But the king held up his hand. 'Stay awhile, my lord,' he said, 'we have not yet finished.'

Shadwatch gave a slight frown, but inclined his head. He moved several paces and sat down on a bench near the door.

The others remained standing where they were. Akton's head was lowered, but the lady Follicia of the Commissariat and Larissa of Litra looked straight ahead, past the king and towards the high towers that marked the northern most gates of the city. A flock of white doves wheeled across the rooftops, and then rose skywards until they were lost against the clouds.

'We are agreed, then?' said the king after a while.

'We have little choice in the matter, sire,' replied Akton, his voice giving nothing away.

For just a moment the king studied Akton, then he walked up to him and put a hand on his shoulder. 'Do not worry old friend,' he said quietly. 'It may not come to this. If those stainers have an ounce of common sense in their souls, they will surely listen to reason.'

The chancellor nodded sadly. 'That may be, sire, but is there not a chance they may scatter reason to the wind and make an assault on the city nonetheless?'

'All life is ruled by chance, Akton, is that not so?'

'I leave such thoughts to the wisdom of the king,' replied the chancellor. 'Let the king's will be done, and we will see what the days may bring.'

The king smiled. Although he himself was wearing a mask, he suddenly wished that his chief adviser had followed Shadwatch's lead, and broken with protocol. A man with a mask could so easily hide his thoughts. Shadwatch was, however easy to read, and the officials from Litra and the Commissariat would be unswerving in their loyalty, but as for the chancellor he would always be his own man, and keep his own counsel.

He turned and looked once more towards the borderlands. How long would they burn like this? How many good men had he already lost? How big was the army coming against him, and who was leading it?'

As if Shadwatch could read his thoughts, the head of Glamtech got slowly to his feet and came and stood beside the king. He too stared across the city to the far horizon. 'We will make them suffer for what they have done, my lord king,' he said. 'The walls of Serenity are high and well defended. Any stainer who makes it onto the ramparts of the city will have to climb over the dead bodies of his comrades first.'

The king glanced at him. 'You believe that, lord Shadwatch?'

The head of Glamtech smiled sadly. 'In these days, my lord king, belief and hope are horns on the same ox.'

The king nodded. 'Then let us hope,' he said, 'and do our duty when we see where duty lies.' He bowed to Larissa and Follicia, saluted Akton and Shadwatch, then left.

'He is a great king,' said Follicia as she watched him go.

'I am not sure what makes a king great,' replied Shadwatch, 'but our king has more steel in his soul than I am accustomed to seeing in other men. As for wisdom . . .' he bowed, then shrugged, 'I must away. Our research technicians want to see me in the main laboratory.'

He clicked his fingers, Teevey Blue-Ray glided into view, and together they left, the faint strains of 'The Dambusters', another ancient theme tune, following them along the corridor.

Follicia followed shortly after, leaving the lady Larissa and Akton alone on the balcony.

'What do you think, my lord?' asked the Litra official after a while.

Akton removed his mask, and smiled. 'Now you can see exactly what I think, my lady,' he said.

She nodded. 'I see nothing but sorrow, my lord,' she paused, 'and I hear nothing but that absurd toy lord Shadwatch insists on carrying about with him.'

The chancellor smiled sadly. 'Just so: nothing but sorrow. This king of ours would bring our city down in a welter of blood and senseless slaughter, and yet he calls it duty.'

'In any other company, those words might be seen as treason, my lord chancellor.'

Akton looked at the woman in front of him, mysterious in her unseen beauty:

'Are you married, my lady? Do you have a family?'

Larissa nodded again. 'My lord, you know my state. I am married with three children.'

'And so you understand my words, and therefore perhaps you can forgive my treason?'

The official gave a short laugh. 'I may understand them, my lord, but I do not hear treason spoken of here. All I hear is the voice of sorrow.'

Akton hesitated. 'You are wise beyond your years my lady. So tell me, what's to do?'

'Beyond our duty, my lord?'

'Aye, beyond our duty. What does your heart tell you, lady Larissa?'

Larissa looked around, but they were still alone, except for a guard standing at the far end of the tower balcony.

'I doubt if we can hold the city,' she said, lowering her voice, 'but we can hold The Island.'

'You speak of the fleet?'

'Yes, I do. Our finest regiments may have been defeated on the northern borders, but we still have the royal fleet, and its harbour at Portus-Portus. If Litra, Glamtech and the chancellery work together we can organise an evacuation from the city to The Island.'

Akton shook his head, more in bewilderment than denial. 'Are you so sure that Serenity will fall?'

Larissa sighed. 'There is never certainty in situations such as these, but if what we hear is true, the stainer army is using a technology we scorned to adopt in earlier years. Our fear of the war-making skills of our ancestors has made us fatally vulnerable to the very folk that we despise.'

'Electricity?' Akton asked.

'Yes, electricity, and all that goes with it. Any Glamtech technician will tell you that we know enough to be able to launch ourselves into the heavens, or swim beneath the seas, but we have rejected such science as corrupt and ancient. Our mistake has become the stainers' opportunity.' The Litra official glanced in the direction of the guard, and went on:

'Their thunder-rods, and lightning bolt towers are superior to any weapons we have.'

It was Larissa's sudden, deft and graceful movement to remove her mask that took Akton by surprise. For a moment he ducked his head and looked away, then turned again to face this woman he so admired: her ebony black eyes and shining copper-skin belied the silver greyness of her hair. The faint smile on her lips told Akton that here was a woman that was confident of her beauty, and not afraid to reveal it.

'We have our archers, our javelin men, and our cavalry,' Akton said slowly.

'Do we? And if we do, how many of them still remain fit for duty?'

'Time will tell, my lady.'

The lady Larissa's eyes flashed. 'We do not have time, my lord. The stainer army will be here in a matter of days. See now!' She pointed at the far horizon and its thickening band of black smoke. 'They come on apace, lord chancellor. Even as we speak the darkness grows.'

Akton grunted, and leaned on the rail of the balcony. Far below he could make out people moving about in the streets and broadways of the Upper Town. It seemed unhurried, and at peace, but he knew that that was an illusion.

'My step-daughter is in a civic guards regiment,' he said quietly. 'She sent word to me this morning that they are posted to defend one of the outer watch-towers a mile north of the main gates.'

Larissa stared. 'Whose piece of madness was that order?'

Akton shrugged. 'It was from the king, and what my step-daughter does not know is that it was I who had to sign off on the instruction before it was sent to the commander of Anna's regiment.' He hesitated. 'There was no alternative. There was a royal seal.'

'I am sorry.'

'Thank you.' Akton looked away for just a moment. 'I have not yet told my wife. I would appreciate it if you would not . . .'

'Of course.' The councillor from Litra gestured towards the guard, who came to attention and hurried forward.

'My lady?' he asked.

'I must leave now. You will escort the chancellor and myself to the base of the tower and then direct us through security. Understood?'

The guard saluted. 'It will be done, my lady.' He looked at Akton. 'The king told me to accompany you to royal reception area, court-number two, my lord. He did not say why.'

The chancellor shrugged as he put his mask back on. 'It matters not, soldier. See the lady Larissa safely through security, and then take me by the most efficient route to the reception area.'

A short while later Akton found himself waiting on a bench outside a pair of imposing, gold-gilt doors inscribed with a large numeral-two in the old-school style. He was happy to wait. He knew why the king wanted to see him again. He wanted of course to test his chancellor's loyalty to both the crown and the high council. On the other hand, in times such as these Akton doubted that even this king would throw him into prison or deliver him to the interrogators of the Triple S.

As he waited, gazing vaguely at the doors and a painted mural of a royal procession, partly obscured by an out of date poster for a Frozen Bride auction, he thought of his daughters: first he thought about Talessa, and then his mind turned to Anna-Seka. What would happen to them? Was he about to lose them both? If that did not break his heart, it would surely break that of his wife.

He shook his head. How could this happen? How did the council so massively miscalculate the power of the outlanders, and the folly of this king? Surely the signs were there. Surely the security services would have detected the rising level of threat, and if not the security services, then surely Hartley himself would have spotted it.

Again he shook his head: where was Hartley? Where was that man? If there was ever a moment when that ever-present official of the college of scouts was most needed, then this was it.

He stood up, walked to the door and ran his hands over its ornately carved surface. If the outlanders had captured Hartley, surely the city officials would have had word by now, or at least the imperial general staff. If he was dead – how could that be? – the warlords leading the outlander cause would have been quick to trumpet the news the length and breadth of the outlands. But the security services had heard nothing, nor had the college of scouts. Besides that, there were no useful reports concerning Hartley's disappearance from any of the regimental outposts and patrols. Semaphore messages, and heliograph messages were coming in frequently from military detachments up to three day's march north of the city, but there was nothing in those messages to give any clue about the scouting noble's whereabouts.

With a shrug, Akton returned to his bench and sat down. For a few days now, he had half expected to suddenly see Hartley appear in the palace. He could see him now: a little the worse for wear after several days in the saddle, but grinning at everyone's look of surprise, and then without any hesitation, giving orders right and left for the defence of the city.

But Hartley had not returned, and with every day that passed his return seemed less likely. Akton gave a shake of his head, and frowned. Just when Hartley was needed so much, he was nowhere to be found. Was that not typical of the man?

Looking across to the other tower, the chancellor tried to dismiss the thought. After all, he had to admit to himself, his anger at Hartley's disappearance was solely for one reason: if lord Hartley had been here in the city, he would never have allowed Anna Seka to be sent on such a madcap, foolhardy mission to help defend an outlying defence point. The king's order would have meant nothing to Hartley. He would have quietly countermanded it, arranged for a better solution, and when the time was right simply given the royal household all the credit for its success.

Smiling despite himself, Akton got wearily to his feet. The doors swung open and with a deferential bow, a servant ushered him into the presence of the king.

THE CROSSING

Barvarik stooped, hands on knees, head down and breathing hard. He had come some distance already and the day was not yet done. But there was something else he must do before there could be any thought of rest. He straightened and looked around. They had reached a river bank. There were about fifty men under his command, perhaps more, scattered about him. They were all that remained of the regiment: all that he had managed to lead away from the fighting, even as the the Fence was breached and the stainer troops had poured across the ramparts and through two sets of gates left and right of his position.

He had earlier received orders that the walls were to be defended to the last man, and that retreat was not an option, but he had ignored such madness. Whoever had sent the order was clearly no soldier, nor one worthy of any respect. So instead he had ordered his trumpeter to sound the 'rally and reform', then shouted for the survivors to gather up such wounded as they could find. Then he had put them all into a fighting formation with crossbowmen at the front, then spearmen in the next rank and swordsmen on the flanks. Somehow they had managed to do all of that in the confusion and fury of the fighting, and at last he had managed to lead them clear.

They were all exhausted: a number were wounded, some badly. There were others who would not be leaving the field of battle at all. They were the fallen, and they were for the crows, or the faint hope that the victorious outlanders might give them a decent burial.

The regiment was defeated, but it was not scattered, and Barvarik drove them on. He knew that none of them would be safe until they had reached the Crossing. This was a narrow bridge that spanned a fast flowing river not far from the great Rebuild city of Arx. If they reached this bridge before nightfall, there was a chance they would find it still open, and perhaps even held by a guards unit sent from Arx itself. That's if the defenders at Arx were alive to what had happened. Once across the river, Barvarik hoped his men could at least rest, prepare a defence point, and hold open a way of escape for any other survivors of the attack on the Fence.

And so, Barvarik's regiment had reached the river. He was sure that this was the place he was looking for, but to his surprise there was no sign of the bridge in the gathering gloom.

Scanning the bank to the right and left, he paused and waved a corporal across.

The man came up to him and saluted: 'Sir?'

'Malthus, you were born in this area weren't you? Where is the Arx Crossing?'

The corporal managed a grin. 'Well, it ain't here sir, and that's plain enough.' He turned and stared back the way they had come, and then looked across the river as it flowed west. At last he pointed. 'That way, sir. Less than a mile I'm thinking. If we just follow the bank and cut around that bluff to our right, I'm sure we'll catch sight of Arx. Its beacons will be lit.'

Barvarik nodded. He liked Malthus, and his steadiness. If they both lived long enough to make it to Arx, he would raise him to sergeant. 'Right,' he said. 'No sense waiting here to be picked off by stainer patrols. Get the men on their feet, corporal: we push on until we find that bridge.'

They set off, Malthus now taking the lead, and Barvarik following with the rest of the regiment. The evening drew on, and dark shadows obscured the way ahead. It did not look hopeful, but no sooner had they rounded the bluff, than they saw in the middle distance, and bright against the skyline: the beacons of Arx.

Barvarik almost cried out with relief, but thought it best to simply slap the corporal on the shoulder, and mutter, 'Well done, soldier. By the look of it, we're nearly there.'

Malthus grunted. 'Not quite, sir, but near enough. It's the size of Arx that makes it look closer than it is. Still, the bridge t'aint far off.'

When they finally reached the bridge, they could just make out two shadowy figures standing at the far end. Barvarik called out to them, giving his regimental number, and signalling for his men to make ready their crossbows.

There was a pause, and then someone lit a glow-stick at the far end of the bridge. It cast a steady green-white light for half its length. A voice from out of the gloom called for Barvarik to come forward on his own, without weapons. With a nod, he sheathed his sword and obeyed the order. When he was at the centre point of the bridge, he saw a soldier advancing slowly towards him, a shield across one shoulder, and a spear held at the hip. The man was dressed in the leather embossed tunic of a Rebuild militiaman, and his helmet carried the crest of one of the pioneer regiments.

With a weary smile, Barvarik stopped and raised his hand. 'Peace,' he said. 'We have come from the Fence.'

The soldier, a younger man but taller than Barvarik and broad in the chest, came up to him and smiled nervously:

'What are you doing here, sir?' he asked, glancing beyond Barvarik to where the others were waiting.

'Our position at the Fence has been overrun,' Barvarik replied. 'We fought our way clear, but our regiment has lost many men.' He paused. 'We have wounded, as well.'

Without taking his eyes off Barvarik, the man whistled back over his shoulder, and seconds later another man appeared, armed with a multiple crossbow. Then the soldier nodded:

'We heard there was trouble. Our watch towers have seen smoke and fire along the road to the north. The commander at Arx sent us here to hold the bridge, and report back at the first sign of trouble.' Again, he looked along the length of the bridge. 'How do we know you are not outlanders?'

Barvarik grunted. 'If we were outlanders, you wouldn't be alive now to ask me that question. They are well trained and well armed and they came at us with weapons that can kill a man at fifty paces, and knock down a whole file at less than thirty.'

There was a short silence. The soldier glanced at his companion, who had raised his crossbow. 'They don't look like stainers, even in this light,' he said quietly to him, 'and they are certainly not wild folk.'

The crossbowman nodded. 'We should let them cross. If the outlanders have broken through, they will be here soon enough.'

A short while later they had crossed the bridge, and were all gathered about a fire, hastily lit by one of the guards.

'When the tower guards in the city see the fire,' the first soldier said to Barvarik, 'they will send cavalry down here quick-smart. Mark my words.'

Barvarik stared towards the beacons of Arx. He could just make out the high walls and soaring towers of that famous Rebuild city. 'That's good,' he replied, 'but you're going to need more than cavalry to stop this stainer attack. It's not a raiding party, or a group of commando-scouts. This is an army, and a big one at that.'

The soldier shrugged. 'We saw the glow on the horizon late in the day. There's no good in such a thing or the seeing of it, but our city will hold. Arx is built for just such a time. It's not all glitz and glamour like Serenity, y'know. There's no army I know of can cross our walls or breach our gates. And our forests are grown for times such as these, ready to be set ablaze by our sun-refractor batteries. They can burn an army as easily as a toddler can burn ants with a piece of glass,' he hesitated, 'when it's clear daylight.'

'We'll see,' said Barvarik with a smile, 'but I thank you for being here.' He looked towards the far side of the bridge and the woods that lay beyond. 'By my reckoning, the first of the stainers should be upon us pretty soon.' Glancing at the two guards, he nodded. 'Are you two with us? I wouldn't blame you if you decided to head back to the safety of that city of yours.'

The first soldier gave a short laugh. 'Well, if you're mad enough to stay and fight, we're mad enough to stay with ye.' He slapped his companion on the shoulder. 'Besides, Marcus here, and my very self were given orders to stay right here until morning, so I guess it's a case of you joining us, and not us joining you.' He laughed again, and gestured towards the rest of the regiment who were lying around the fire. 'Those fellows of yours look like they've still got a bit of fight left in them, but if I were you I'd shift your wounded back to those rocks over there. It's more sheltered, and warm enough too. If the cavalry arrives in time, I can arrange to get the badly wounded back to the city.'

'Thank you.' Barvarik waved one of his men across. It was Malthus. He came up to them, nodded to the soldiers and saluted:

'Sir?'

'Malthus. Organise a screen defence at the head of the bridge on the far side, with crossbows, pulse-bows if you have them, and spears. Then I want a squad about half way along its length. Crossbows only. Lastly, get the wounded back to those rocks, and then set up two flanks either side of the bridge. They'll also act as a reserve.'

Malthus nodded. 'And where will you be, sir?'

Barvarik smiled. 'Everywhere, Malthus. I'll be everywhere, but I want you with me all the time. On my right hand. Understood?'

'Understood,sir.' Malthus saluted again, turned and hurried away.

'That's a good man,' said the first soldier.

'Aye,' replied Barvarik. 'And he left a few good mates behind him at the Fence; men we could scarce afford to lose.' He paused. "If this is to be our last battle, I think I should at least give you my name and then you can give me yours.' He held out his hand:

'I am Barvarik of Serenity.'

The soldier smiled, and took his hand. 'And I am Ajax of Arx.'

A horn, harsh and bright, sounded in the woods about half a mile away.

'They're here,' said Barvarik. 'Where's that cavalry of yours?'

'Late as usual,' grinned Ajax, 'but they'll be here, isn't that right, Marcus?'

The Rebuild guard with the multi-crossbow nodded nervously. 'If I go down to the river bank,' he said, 'and hide up in those bushes, I might be able to bring a few of them outlanders down before they reach the middle of the bridge.'

Ajax of Arx grunted. 'Well, all right then, but just give them one volley and then get out of there. I don't want to be telling your Verita that she's now a widow.'

The outlander horn sounded again, and those soldiers of the regiment that had not yet stood, now picked up their weapons and scrambled to their feet. Less than three minutes later, they were all in position, with Malthus giving the last of the orders. It was not a moment too soon. Even as the screen defence reached the head of the bridge, the advance infantry of the outlander force appeared at the edge of the woods. Without pausing, they gave a shout and rushed towards the bridge.

Barvarik, standing with Malthus and the squad of eight men who he had positioned about half way along the bridge-walk, heard the crossbows sing, and watched as the steel-tipped shafts winged their way towards the attackers in the gathering gloom: men staggered and fell, others ducked their heads and came on. Another volley sang among them, and more stainers were struck. But it was not enough, and Barvarik saw at once that these men who now advanced against them were both determined and disciplined. He watched as the outlanders lowered their shields, raised their weapons and charged towards the bridge.

The defenders at the head of the bridge loosed one more volley, then fell back to the midpoint of the bridge where Barvarik, Malthus and the rest of the squad were waiting. Without waiting for orders, even as they arrived, the spearmen turned and knelt, lifting their spears to guard, while the others quickly reloaded their crossbows.

'Good lads!' said Barvarik. 'We'll tickle them as they come, and make them sorry they thought to cross the river here.'

Someone laughed, someone swore, but the rest just nodded and stared at the swarming mass of infantry that now poured in even greater numbers out of the woods and began to surge towards the bridge.

For a fleeting moment Barvarik thought of Talessa, lost somewhere in that prison cell in the heart of the commissariat, then all was swept away in the fury of the attack.

LEVEL 4 BASEMENT

Talessa leaned over the metal bench and rubbed her eyes: dust, sweat and stinging eyes. So much dust. She rubbed her eyes again and looked about. Good. The supervisor had not seen her. Not yet, anyway.

She sighed and reached for the assembly-tool. It was clammy to the touch, and slick with oil. For a moment she hesitated, listening to the whirr of the machinery, and the muffled sounds of workers moving about her.

'Number 78, is there a problem?

Talessa turned and saw the white-coated supervisor staring down at her through the grey slits of his prison orderly mask. He wore Section 8 epaulettes and a gold Triple S pin on his collar.

'No problem, sir. No problem,' she said quickly. Lowering her head, she bent over the line of tech-boxes moving slowly past on the conveyor. Grasping one, she slid it onto the bench, flipped open the inspection cover and began to extract the old components.

'Anything,' she told herself, 'anything is better than being stuck in the capsule.'

She lifted the last of the cross-valves clear of the box, checked the wiring and then slid the new Glamtech board into place, aware that the supervisor was still watching her. She picked up her soldering iron and completed the refit.

Moments later, the conveyor hummed, and the bench trembled slightly as yet another tech-box slid away into the darkness towards the inspection and test zone.

Pausing only to mark the box serial number on her worksheet, Talessa reached for the next box.

She had completed another five boxes before the supervisor at last gave a grunt, rapped the back of her work-stool with his baton, and moved away down the assembly line.

'Are ye all right, lassie?'

Talessa, her eyes now red and streaming, turned to the voice. She saw an older woman, with graying hair and a kindly smile, standing beside her. The woman was wearing a grade three prison smock, and carried a tray piled high with spare parts from the Stores Section.

'Are ye all right, lassie?' she repeated. 'You look as though you need a cup of water.'

Talessa managed to smile in return. 'I need a long, cool lemonade and a hot shower,' she whispered, 'but I don't think there's one coming.'

They both laughed, that dry, cracked laugh of the capsule-folk, and the laugh of all those who dwelt deep beneath Serenity, far below the lowest level of the Commissariat.

The woman reached into the pocket of her smock and drew out a small leather bottle.

'Here,' she said, glancing around. 'Take a swig of that and hide the rest under yer bench for later. Don't worry, that fool of a supervisor is busy making someone else's life unpleasant. He won't see ye, if you're quick about it. Drink now. It'll do ye a power of good.'

Nodding gratefully, Talessa took the bottle and drank. She felt a warm glow straight away, and yet at the same time a strange coolness filled her senses.

'What is that?'

'Never you mind, lassie. It's just something I found in the Glamtech stores up on the next level. The less I tell ye the better, and the less ye know, the longer ye'll live, if ye get my drift.'

Talessa nodded again, and slid the bottle under the bench. 'Thank you,' she said quietly, and paused. 'I suppose it's best if you don't tell me your name?'

'And neither you, yorn,' replied the woman in the old dialect of Lower Town.

They both looked away for a moment. Another tech-box slid from the conveyor to the bench.

'Have you been a long time?' Talessa asked as she picked the box up and opened it.

The woman shrugged. 'Long enough to lose my looks, and long enough to forget what it was I left behind me.'

'Forget everything?' asked Talessa.

The woman nodded. 'Aye, forget it all: those who loved ye and those who did not.' She hesitated and glanced around. 'It's what they want here: to make a place of forgetting, and to leave us in it.' She shrugged again. 'I must get on.'

Talessa finished the box while the woman moved away and emptied her tray at the neighbouring work stations. But then, after a while, she came back and pretended to check a component that didn't need checking at all. She looked down at Talessa and smiled sadly. 'Such beautiful hands,' she said. 'Hands that once only knew fine things, and all that was soft against the skin.'

Talessa did not reply, but bowed her head, brushed away a tear and kept working.

'Ye'll get used to it after a while, lassie,' the woman said quietly.

Talessa did not look up, but reached for another box. 'I hate the dust, the blinding light when you step out of the capsule-cell, and the heat,' she shook her head, 'and this conveyor. It never stops.'

'Ach, ye won't notice it, my bonny one, when ye stop expecting anything else.'

'That will never be,' said Talessa quickly, and again she looked along the line towards where the supervisor was standing, his back still turned to them.

It was the woman's turn to fall silent. She sighed, turned one of the new components over in her hand, studied it for a moment then dropped it back into the tray.

'We must never lose hope,' said Talessa suddenly, giving the wiring flex on the tech-box a twist and pushing it into its coded slot.

The woman sighed. 'Ye have spirit, lassie, I'll say that for ye, but don't hope for things that can never be.'

'What do you mean?'

'I mean that we are here until the day we die, and not before. As far as the world above our heads is concerned we are dead already. Buried, forgotten, listed on records that no one ever reads.'

She paused, then went on. 'All we can hope for is enough rations to keep us working, and enough sleep at night to keep us awake in the day.'

Talessa reached for the bottle, took another drink and nodded gratefully. 'I am hoping for something else,' she replied. 'And that is what keeps me at this bench, still breathing and alive.'

Waiting until the supervisor had moved even further down the line, the woman gently put her hand on Talessa's shoulder:

'Is there someone up there ye are waiting for? Someone who will come one day and take ye home?'

Talessa closed her eyes. 'Perhaps,' she whispered.

'Well, I'm thinkin' he'll be a fine young fellow, and just as fair and beautiful as ye are,' laughed the woman, then suddenly put her finger to her lips. 'Hush now! Here's that oaf coming again. He'll want to see if you've been doing what ye should.'

Moments later a klaxon sounded, and then from somewhere in the shadows a loudspeaker gave a metallic click:

'All workers to their transport bays now...All workers, now.'

Almost as one, the capsule-folk stood, placed their assembly-tools on the benches with a harsh clatter and turning, shuffled away towards the bays. Groups of commissariat guards appeared silently, and moved among the workers, checking that they had taken nothing with them, and pushing the slower prisoners forward.

Talessa found herself beside the woman, who seemed to have a status separate to the rest of the workers, and was not ordered to silence when she leaned over to speak to Talessa.

'It's canteen day, tomorrow. We should eat together.' She paused and glanced around. 'They make the light here so bright for a reason ye know. They want to half blind you every time you step out of your capsule for a work detail. Its to control you' She paused again. 'Squeeze your eyes up tight. Open them ever so slowly. It helps, you know,'

Talessa looked across at her. She longed to know her name, but feared to ask. Still, she already counted her as a friend, perhaps one she could trust. Of course she could also be an agent of the Triple S, sent among the workers to listen for any talk of sedition or escape. But what did that matter? At last she had someone she could talk to, someone who would remind her of who she herself was, and perhaps someone who might help her never to forget Barvarik. Barvarik! His name filled her head. She wanted to shout the name out loud, but instead her lips moved softly and there was no sound, not even a whisper.

'Ye are missing yer man, lassie?'

Talessa look startled. 'You heard me, just now?'

'I see the tear,' replied the woman gently. 'That's all. Now wipe yer cheek, lassie and we'll talk tomorrow.'

As the supervisor drifted towards them once more, the woman melted away, and was soon lost in the crowd of stoop-shouldered workers.

And even as they approached the transport bays and their waiting capsules, the bright Glamtech lights began to fade and heavy, livid-green colours lit the walls.

WATCH-POST

Anna-Seka was not sorry that she had been posted outside the city. It somehow made her feel free again, and at least she was doing something that would take her mind off all that was happening inside Serenity itself.

She had arrived at the watch-post late in the day, but there had been time to stow her kit in the barracks room, take a meal with the rest of the garrison in the cramped but warm kitchen block and then report for her first duty on the walls. There was no doubt that they had, all of them, been assigned to this place with little hope of survival. But she had laughed with the others when the senior sergeant told them that they would all be receiving a bonus in pay for this mission because no one at headquarters expected them to be around to pick it up.

'And don't wear your masks, lads and lassies,' he had added. 'The scars of battle are marks of honour, not marks of shame.' He smiled. 'Besides, you will see all the better.'

'So we can see what it is that killed us!' someone called out, and they laughed again.

Anna's evening duty was nearly over when the post commander came to find her on the walls. He acknowledged her salute and then turned his attention to the stretch of road that headed away from their position and towards the low tree-covered hills of the northern sector. The last light of day lit their western slopes and made them seem much closer than they really were.

'That's where they'll come at us,' the commander said quietly, 'and by the look of those smoke clouds they are only two days away at most.'

'They will probably send their scouts in first, sir,' Anna replied carefully. 'At least that is what we were taught at the college.'

'The college?'

'Yes, sir. The college of scouts. Lord Hartley trained the group I was in.'

The commander glanced at the young woman. 'I did not know,' he said. 'I thought you were all regimental infantry.'

Anna smiled. 'We are sir, except for me. I have been seconded to the regiment.'

With a shake of the head, the commander turned his attention to the hills once more. 'Strange times, soldier,' he said. 'Everything is upside down these days. What with the poisonings, the rumours of spies in the city, and now a stainer attack on the the Fence.'

'And my lord Hartley posted as missing, sir.'

The commander nodded. 'I had heard,' he said. He reached for the far-scope which was standing on its wall-mount nearby. 'Let's have a closer look,' he muttered, put the scope to his eyes, and swung it to the east. For a long while he said nothing, then at last he straightened, stood back and pointed to a promontory to the north-east about half a mile away:

'Do you see that, soldier?'

'I do sir.'

'Would you say that that is a good spot for a scout of Serenity to take position?'

Anna frowned. 'It has the advantage of a good line of sight, sir, but . . .'

'Yes?'

'It is perhaps too obvious a position, sir. Any stainer scouts coming from the north will spot it straight away and move to check it.'

It was the commander's turn to frown. 'I see,' he said slowly. Then he looked at Anna. 'Where would you suggest I might send a scout?'

Anna-Seka studied the ground in front of the watch-post. The road, flanked by low scrub and open heather, headed straight like a lime-white arrow into the gathering darkness.

'The ground is exposed sir, but if I was on my own I would make a hide just ten paces off the road in that dip with the gorse bushes and the two boulders. Do you see it, sir?'

The commander followed the line of Anna's extended arm. He squinted into the gloom. 'I can't see it.'

'Exactly, sir. It looks to be no more than a continuation of the heather that slopes down from the edge of the road, but if you look closely . . .'

She offered him the far-scope. Peering through it, the commander cursed softly:

'Yes! I see it now.' He smiled at Anna. 'You know what comes next, don't you?'

'Yes, sir.'

'Tell me, soldier.'

'You want me to take up position at that point, tomorrow morning at the latest.'

The commander nodded. 'Lord Hartley trained you well. If and when he returns I will let him know exactly how well.'

The following day, at the second hour before the noon watch, Anna-Seka took up her position near the two boulders and in among the gorse. She had water and rations for two days, a multi-bow for extra defence and a helio-mirror to signal back to the watch-post. Her orders were clear, but not encouraging. She was to signal back to the post the moment she saw any movement from the north, and then relay information concerning numbers and speed of advance, once that became obvious. After that she was to lay low until a squad was sent out from the watch post to bring her back.

There seemed little prospect of her survival in such an isolated position, but then it was almost certain that the watch-post itself would be overwhelmed if the stainers arrived in any numbers above brigade strength. And so she resigned herself to the inevitable fact that this appeared to be her last and only battle.

As she crouched beneath the spreading gorse and peered through the thorns at the heather-covered plain that led to the northern hills, she wondered how long it would be until the invading army arrived. Surely it would not come today, she told herself, but then if their scouts had horses they might perhaps cover the ground more rapidly and arrive before nightfall. Of course it was hard to tell exactly when anyone would arrive. The Fence had been breached, but the smoke clouds on the horizon, and the way that they had spread so steadily and faded to an ugly stain told a story: the breach cannot have been less than three days ago, and perhaps as much as a week.

As it happened, the enemy scouts were closer than Anna or any of the defenders had at first thought. And if she had not thought to stand to stretch her limbs for a moment, before settling down for the last watch of the day, she would not have noticed them. Her eye, so well schooled by Hartley, had picked up that faint, far-off movement, almost hidden against the heather by the shadows of drifting clouds. In that instant, her senses told her that what she had noticed was not a trick of the eye. Nor was it some stray animal, nor the branch of a tree stirring in the wind. It was a human, and one that was moving straight towards where she now stood.

'When you see movement,' Hartley used to say to her on their training missions, 'then the most important thing is not to move on your part. Stay still, even if you are standing upright and in full view.

More scouts are betrayed by the way that they move, than by the way that they stand.'

And so she stood, motionless, upright, eyes fixed on the place where she had just now seen the movement. There was nothing. She waited. Still nothing. She waited again. Then, at last when she was about to tell herself that she had in fact seen nothing, the far off speck of humanity moved again. And with it, several others emerged from a dark-faced patch of woodland, almost concealed by a fold in the heathland, and began to head across the open ground towards the edge of the northern highway: they were horsemen.

THE MARCH TO THE BRIDGE

Marlin could not believe how well things had gone. In a single day and night his detachment had managed to breach the Fence suffering only minor casualties. It was true however that the outlander infantry that had gone in ahead of them had suffered terrible losses on that first assault. But once they had gained the walls, and another party had forced its way through a sally-gate, it wasn't long before they sent the defenders streaming back towards the open country that lay beyond the Fence and marked the way south.

How many men had he lost? Not many, but enough, as his sergeant had said to him. 'Why is it, sir,' he had said to Marlin as they leaned on their bloodied weapons and watched the enemy retreat, 'Why is it that we always lose the best of our men whenever we win a fight?'

Marlin had not replied. He was too weary to think of an answer, and besides his mind was fixed on the idea that they might not even have time for supper before Chesterman ordered up the pursuit. A defeated enemy could be vulnerable in a headlong retreat, but they were also very dangerous. If the border defenders were falling back in good order, and discovered good ground where they could turn and make a stand, then there would be trouble, and no easy victory.

'Despair in battle makes cowards and heroes in equal measure,' his old regimental instructor used to say. 'When you are chasing a defeated enemy, keep a sword at their back, but never get too close. They can turn and tear you like a wild bear.'

And so Marlin and his men had followed, with empty bellies, pursuing the retreating remnants of Serenity's border force. Even in the half light of the dying day, they saw that their route was marked with the huddled bodies of the dead and wounded. The command of 'No prisoners!' had filtered down to Marlin's men from Chesterman himself, but they chose to ignore it. Marlin had no stomach for such an order and he was heartened to see that none of his men were inclined to slaughter a wounded and helpless opponent. Once that day, he even saw a soldier he knew turn aside to help a dying infantryman, and offer him a drink from his water bottle.

Later, when he asked the man about it, he had merely shrugged: 'He was wearing the shoulder flashes of my father's regiment,' he said simply. 'I couldn't pass him by.'

They advanced steadily, with the sun setting on their right hand, and lengthening shadows slowly obscuring the way ahead across the great plain. Soon they had come to an ancient woodland. They entered cautiously, grateful for a squad of outlander storm-troopers on their right flank, and a party of militia with thunder-rods and pulse-bows just behind them. As it turned out they reached the other side of the wood just as the day sank into evening. Immediately they saw in front of them a river and a bridge.

Marlin now shook his head at the memory of it all. What he saw in front of him was what he had feared. The bridge was defended. A regiment from the broken border force had decided to turn and fight and make a stand. They had chosen their ground and chosen it well. Marlin was unable to make out their regimental banner in the evening light, but he could tell by the way that they formed rank that they were a Guards Regiment. Even as he stared at them, old memories flooded back, and for an instant he felt himself to be once more the king's brother and a citizen of Serenity.

While he hesitated to order an attack, the outlander forces on his flank and behind him were not so uncertain. They surged forward around Marlin's men, shields locked and banners raised. Then, with a blast of horns and a great shout, they rushed forward to attack the bridge.

They paid a terrible price.

Marlin watched as a storm of pulse-arrows and crossbow bolts struck the leading ranks of outlanders, throwing them into confusion. But only for a moment. They reformed, shouted again and went on. He could not help but admire their determination as they pushed on through another volley of arrows, advancing over the bodies of their comrades and forcing the defenders to retreat to the centre of the bridge.

Someone slapped him on the shoulder and he turned to find himself looking into the helmeted gaze of a stainer warlord:

'Lord Marlin, why do you wait here?' the warlord asked, and as he spoke he gestured with his thunder-rod towards the bridge:

'That's where the battle lies, my lord Marlin. There is your enemy!'

Marlin nodded, then shouted to his men. 'Up lads! There is work to do! Follow me, but keep your shields high.' Without waiting to see if they would spring to the order, Marlin raised his sword and began to run towards the bridge.

Although he ran, there was nothing hot-blooded in his charge: no battle madness, no thirst for revenge, just a deep sadness that it had all come to this. If this fight was to go well, he would be killing men he once counted as friends and brothers. If it went against him, he would die at the hands of men who had once taken the same oath of loyalty to Serenity, the oath he himself had sworn all those years ago. Curse his brother! Curse this king for bringing him and his family down and sending him and others to this place of slaughter. His hate was for his brother, not for those his brother ruled.

Waving his sword, he quickened his pace, and then gasped as an arrow whined past his cheek and struck the man behind him. Another shaft buried itself to its fletchings in the turf just in front of him. He stumbled. It was well that he did. A third arrow skidded off his helmet and disappeared into the darkness with a metallic screech.

Someone cried out, and fell against him, but he staggered on and at last reached the bridge. It was already a mass of fighting men, striking at each other and driving forward with shield and spear. A single glance back over his shoulder told Marlin that most of his men were still with him, but even more outlanders were pouring out of the woods, now almost hidden by the dark.

It was a stubborn defence and well organised, but Marlin sensed that it could not hold for much longer. The group defending the centre of the bridge were well supported by flanking fire coming in from the opposite bank. There were either more crossbowmen than he could see, or at least one of them had a multi-bow. He ducked as another arrow hissed over his head. Then he picked up a fallen shield just in time to feel a crossbow bolt thud into its leather facing, jarring his shoulder.

Turning, he shouted at his men: 'We can't stay here! We'll work our way along the bank and see if there's another crossing point.' He crouched, then waved them forward. 'Get moving now, at the double-quick!'

It was only as he came away from the bridge, and looked back to see how the fighting was going, that he saw someone he knew. It was someone among the defenders on the Serenity side of the fight, and he recognised him instantly: Barvarik, a lord of the Upper Town, the first court and a warrior he had trained alongside briefly during his own military service. Barvarik! He almost called out the name as he stared, but had the presence of mind to crouch even lower as another brace of arrows came his way.

Swinging his shield onto his back, he began to run after his men. 'Barvarik,' he muttered to himself. A good man. What was he doing here? Was the city already so stretched of resources that they were sending their finest soldiers to defend the northern borders? Where was Rebuild and their militia? Where were the border cavalry, and the regiments and divisions of the north? Surely they had not been broken and scattered already?

Catching up with his men, Marlin led them into the shelter of some river-willows, and turned yet again to see if the outlander force had broken through at the bridge.

They had not. The defenders were still holding out, although they surely must have been tiring. From where he now stood, Marlin could not see exactly how many soldiers were under Barvarik's command, but they were giving a good account of themselves. He shook his head. Such men did not deserve to die but they were surely doomed, especially if the stainers brought still more troops to this fight.

CHAPTER #9
THE BRIDGE

On the bridge, Barvarik was preparing to pull his men back. They had done well, far beyond what he had expected of them, but they had paid a price. The wounded were propped against the dead, and the living were forced to lower their shields to protect those who were wounded. Gasping with exhaustion, they loosed their crossbows at point blank, and struck at the attackers with their chipped and broken weapons.

Taking Malthus by the shoulder he pulled him back. 'Get out of there, man! I'll hold the gap. You take the first squad back to the river bank, I'll follow with the others.'

The corporal, bloodied from a cut across his brow, grimaced, but then nodded. Turning he slapped several of the other defenders on their shoulders and shouted at them to retreat.

It was not easily done. As the outlanders saw the line in front of them weaken, they pushed forward, urging each other on. If it wasn't for a sudden, sharp volley from the multi-bow carried by Marcus, the militiaman of Arx, all might have been lost. At least three stainers were struck death-blows and another couple wounded. For a moment the charge faltered, and in that moment, Malthus escaped with his men. Barvarik, with Ajax now at his side and two of the reserve squad close behind, stepped into the breach.

The sword he carried was known as a weapon of renown. It was made of the finest steel of Serenity, carefully worked by a master sword smith, and tempered and edged by another craftsman skilled in the ancient arts. Endless care had gone into the three year process that had produced such an instrument of war. And Barvarik had been well-schooled in its use. Over hours of relentless training, he had toiled and toiled until he and this sword became as one. For Barvarik it seemed as though the sword had a spirit of its own, a spirit that guided his hand, strengthened his arm, and moved with perfect balance when he stuck at an opponent, or moved to parry a blow.

Today, that sword had been tested as never before. Not only because of the determination and skill of many of the stainer warriors who came against Barvarik, but also because of the fearsome weapons some of them carried. The thunder-rods were most to be feared. Not only could they deliver an electrical pulse that could knock a man senseless and even stop his heart, utmost care had to be taken to avoid contact with any part of their metallic surface. Barvarik and his men had learned to strike hard at the faces of their attackers, to throw them off balance, and then strike again before they could recover. At the same time they had to be aware of other stainers attacking them from either side.

'Every man fights for his brother!' Barvarik had shouted more than once. His men knew what that meant: in the battle line, it was best to strike at the attacker immediately to your right, and leave the attacker in front of you to your brother-soldier at your left hand. That took trust and self-belief. Not every man could manage such a thing, but it was with grim satisfaction that Barvarik saw that on this day, and in this fight, his men all fought in that very way.

Now, as the first squad fell back and reformed at the far end of the bridge, Barvarik, Malthus, Ajax and the remaining men of the regiment held the line, but barely. But it could not last. Slowly they inched their way back, shields lapped, helmets lowered and weapons braced for the charge that they knew must be coming.

From further down the river on the opposite bank, Marlin watched, strangely fascinated. He saw an outlander captain, standing on the bridge amid the wounded and dead, call his men to order, reform ranks and order the attack that must surely sweep the last of the defenders away and into the river.

But even as they moved, Marlin heard something that he had not anticipated, though later he told himself that he was a fool not to have thought of it. It was the sound of a cavalry horn, a sound that he well knew: the high, piercing note of the horn carried by the buglers of the militia cavalry regiments of Rebuild.

ENCOUNTER

A nna was watching events unfold at a different place and time. What she saw was nonetheless an equal threat to Serenity. From her scout's hide north of the watch-post she could see horsemen approaching, and from the way that they rode, they were not friends of Serenity.

Taking her tiny heliograph, she unwrapped it quickly and signalled back to the watch-post: 'Riders approaching from the north. Must presume hostile.'

An answer, in code, flickered back almost immediately: 'Understood, maintain position.'

Anna shrugged. She had expected nothing less. Perhaps a part of her hoped that she might have been ordered back to the relative if temporary safety of the watch-post, but she knew that the officer of the watch had little choice but to countermand any such order. He would surely be waiting until she sent another message confirming numbers, distance and direction of travel. Then and only then could he possibly bring her in.

Turning again to the north, she noticed that at least two of the riders seemed to have disappeared, but the others were pressing on towards her. She reached for her multi-bow, carefully cocked it, and slid an extra two crossbow bolts into its magazine. If she was lucky she might be able to bring down a couple of the riders before the others got to her, then it would be all over. For her, at least.

'How long do I have?' she muttered to herself as she knelt among the gorse bushes, and leaned forward trying to keep the riders in view. They were about a mile away, perhaps less, and coming at the same steady pace they had shown when they first appeared. For a moment she again lost sight of them as they dropped behind a rising scarp. When they came into view once more, she saw at once that they had veered away and were now heading north east of where she had taken up position. It seemed to a stroke of unimaginable luck. What had drawn them to move away from their line of travel? Surely the watch-post must have been so obvious to anyone approaching across that heath land from the north. Perhaps they had spotted another patrol, either hostile or friendly and were moving to investigate it.

She shook her head as she took the heliograph once more and quickly signalled the news. There was a pause, longer this time than the first, and then came the reply:

'Received. Maintain your position.'

Rising slowly to a crouch, and then standing, Anna scanned the heath land both to the north and the north-east. One by one the riders disappeared behind a distant stand of pine trees. There was nothing else to be seen: no one. It was as if those riders had never existed. She gave a half laugh, tapped the bow against her thigh, and then stepped clear of the gorse. It was good to be in the open again, and she knew that she was still almost completely hidden to all but a practised eye. She would not risk a fire, not yet at least, but at least she could enjoy some sort of supper. Only a short while before she had been almost resigned to the idea that there was little prospect of her ever eating another meal, and yet here she was now blessing her luck, and looking forward to some rations.

A short while later, the birds were singing as the evening shadows gathered among the scattered patches of scrub and low-growing trees. It was peaceful, and Anna hummed a childhood song to herself as she prepared her narrow meal of corn biscuits, cheese and dried berries. Soon enough she ate, and as she ate she glanced around, instinctively scanning the ground all about her. She had water enough for this meal and perhaps breakfast, but she would need to find a stream or spring in the morning. Surely there was one nearby. The birdsong told her that.

The birdsong? She inclined her head, pausing as she drank and switching her gaze to a group of laurel trees. Moments ago she had heard night-larks calling from their branches. Suddenly, they were silent. What could that mean?

In that moment, Anna did not see the shadow that rose behind her. Nor did she see the uplifted war-club.

AN ALTERNATE PLAN

Akton had just come away from yet another meeting with the king, and his inner circle of advisers. He was worried. Of course, as his wife said, he worried all the time, but in these past few days he was more than usually anxious and 'pressed out of sorts' as he used to say. Things were clearly going badly on the northern borders, the poisonings continued in the city, although they had lessened a little with increased security, and nearly all the reserve regiments had been committed to duties outside Serenity itself. What's more, except for Arx, virtually all contact had been lost with Rebuild and its supply cities. Rumours drifted in that the northern defences had been significantly breached, and that an outlander army of great size was heading south. The few messages that had come in by cavalry courier and the signals delivered by heliograph told the same story, but it was one that the king seemed unwilling to accept. His reluctance to act seemed to strengthen within him, despite the urgings of his council members, most notably Shadwatch and Akton.

What they strove to get the king to recognise was this: clearly there had been a catastrophic defeat on the northern borders, and even the reserve regiments had failed to stop the advance of the invading stainer hordes. It was not known if Arx, the main supply city had fallen, but there were strong rumours that at least three other supply centres including Cornus had been captured by the invaders. And there was still no sign of Hartley.

The king's strategy, expressed with much shouting and waving of arms, was to concentrate the last of the Guards regiments north of Serenity, and hope to draw the stainer army on to a decisive battle on open ground some twenty miles north of the city gates.

In vain Akton had urged the king to think again. 'If we lose such a battle,' he said, not fearing to raise his voice, 'then all is lost. Our strength lies in the defences of Serenity itself, but if we do not have enough soldiers to defend the walls and gate towers, then any resistance to a determined attack will be in vain.'

The king had scoffed. 'You have forgotten that you yourself were once a soldier, chancellor. These stainers are nothing but a rampaging mob of outlanders. If we meet them on our own ground with our seasoned professionals and our Glamtech technology then victory is assured. They will scatter before us like chaff in the wind, and we will slaughter them in the open fields before they can get back to the outlands.'

'That is not what we hear in the most recent reports, my king,' interrupted Shadwatch quietly. 'The stainers appear to be well organised, highly trained and equipped with a generation of weapons we have not encountered before.'

The faint whirr of the Glambot cut through the awkward silence. No one moved, nor even glanced to see from where the Glamtech robot might suddenly appear.

The king stared at Shadwatch, but said nothing, so the man of Glamtech continued: 'What we do have, my lord is a battle fleet. We also have the military installations at Portus-Portus.'

'So?' The king frowned, unseen behind his mask.

'My lord king, if we have Portus-Portus and the battle fleet, we have a route to The Island.'

'The Island? If ever there was a lost land, it is that place.' The king grunted, then turned to Akton. 'Lord chancellor, it sounds as if the our lord of Glamtech is planning his escape. What is your opinion,' he paused, 'of this cut-and-run strategy?'

Akton hesitated and chose his words carefully. 'My lord king, I believe that our colleague here is suggesting that if we mobilise the fleet, we might achieve three advantages in this campaign.'

'Go on.' The king leant forward, hands clasped and eyes fixed on his chancellor, and his mask glowing faintly.

'Well, my lord, at present our navy is the one and only clear tactical advantage we have over the outlanders. As you know they are almost entirely deficient in that area, and rely exclusively on their land forces. For this reason, we can as lord Shadwatch says, secure the sea routes to The Island, protect the western coastline of the kingdom, and if I may venture, my lord, we can even use our marines with their ship-board catapults, landing assault craft and war engines to open a second front in this conflict.'

For just a moment the king appeared interested, almost animated by what Akton had said. He nodded, and even smiled within his mask. 'The marines! Yes, I had forgotten about the marines. If as you say we control the coastline beyond Portus-Portus, then we can come up on the stainers' flank from the seaward side.' He clapped his hands. 'We could land in force, form the marines into assault teams and push on towards the northern borders.'

'I agree, my lord,' said Akton quickly, 'but as Shadwatch here indicates, our priority would be to make sure that the way through to The Island is safe, and that we can evacuate as many of the citizens as possible before the siege of Serenity begins.'

Akton regretted that he had spoken these last words. Even as he finished speaking he saw the king's expression change and his mask redden.

'Evacuation? Siege?' The king raised his voice. 'What are you saying man? We have not been defeated.' He slapped the table with his open palm. 'We have not yet begun to fight!'

'My lord . . .' Akton began, but he stopped speaking as the king got to his feet, walked over to the window of the council room, looked out over the city, and then came back and stared at Akton:

'You have grown soft in your old age, Akton. I thought I could rely on you to show some mettle, some sinew in these days of trial.' He shook his head. 'But what do I get but mealy-mouthed whimperings about evacuating the city, and preparing for a siege.'

'Surely, sire,' replied Akton quietly, 'surely it makes sense to get all the old folk, women and children out of the city and to a place of safety before the battle comes to our gates. And what's more, the poisonings continue apace. Have we not, all of us, seen close friends and family members struck down and then interned because they suddenly become stained.'

'I agree with the chancellor, my lord king,' put in Shadwatch. All at once the Glambot was beside him. 'The men will fight better without the worry of having to protect family and loved ones. Besides, the less people there are in the city, the easier it is to organise a defence and allocate rations and resources. It may also give us a better opportunity to identify some of these poisoners.'

The king shot a look at Shadwatch. 'I see that this spirit of defeatism has spread even to you, lord Shadwatch. Do you not believe that we can meet these stainer rogues in open combat on ground of our own choosing, and utterly overthrow them?'

For a time Shadwatch did not reply. He studied his clasped hands for a moment, glanced at Akton and then spoke:

'My king, there was a time when I would have been utterly convinced of our ability to overcome any force come against us, either outlander or wildfolk.' He spread his hands. 'But if even half of what we hear from the northern borders is true, then we have been outmatched and out-fought by an invading army that has breached our first lines of defence – defences that we believed to be impregnable. And not only that, this so-called mob of stainers has defeated all the counter-attacks launched from the south and other thrusts initiated by our reserve forces.'

'You believe all these rumours and panicked messages, then?'

Shadwatch shook his head. 'Not all the rumours, my lord, but I search in vain for any reports, reliable or otherwise, that say we have made any progress at all in this campaign.'

The king grunted once more. He admired Akton for his statecraft, but he did not value him for his military skill. On the other hand he respected Shadwatch, not just for his skill in the normal operations of Glamtech, but for his almost unfailing ability to interpret warcraft, and the subtleties of any armed conflict. And it was Shadwatch who had persuaded the king that the poisonings were part of an orchestrated attack, and not a merely chance outbreak of the disease. But there was a darkness in him that the king could not read, a little shadow in his glance that few could see.'

And so he nodded, sat down slowly and rested his hands on the table. 'Gentlemen,' he said after a time, 'I see it is now fallen upon me to do my duty as a king,' he paused, 'and as a man of war.'

'My lord?' Shadwatch looked genuinely puzzled. 'To infinity and beyond,' intoned the Glambot, and the ancient tune of 'You've got a friend in me,' crackled away quietly.

The king smiled. 'In two days time I shall take over direct control of all imperial forces both inside and outside of the city. That will include the fleet at Portus-Portus. I will convene a full meeting of the council tomorrow and make the formal announcement. That should give you, as well as Litra and the commissariat time to make the necessary arrangements. Rebuild will have to look after itself, but since it has proved incapable of giving us useful or meaningful reports from the northern borders, we have to assume they are somehow cut off from normal lines of communication.'

'You mean to lead the armies personally?' asked Akton, his voice betraying his unease.

The king shrugged. 'I do. Since, it seems that everyone else has shown themselves incapable of such a task, it is clear that I must do it myself.'

Akton was about to reply, but he caught an anxious look from Shadwatch and so reluctantly held his peace. Instead, he stood, saluted and left the council chamber with Shadwatch following close behind.

The other advisers who had hardly spoken throughout the meeting, remained behind with the king. That in itself was not a good sign.

Moments later, Akton had found himself walking alone through the royal precinct past the doors of the empty throne room not sure where he was going, and his mind full of the prospect that the king was about to lead his kingdom to unutterable and irredeemable defeat. He could not help but think of his wondering days all those years ago, north of the Fence. There was a wild freedom in those Lands.

There were hurried steps behind him. He turned. It was Shadwatch.

'Ah,' said Shadwatch coming up to him, Teevey-BlueRay hard on his heels. 'I am glad I caught you. You wandered off down a side corridor, and by the time I had passed through security, you were nowhere to be seen.'

Akton took off his mask, and smiled. 'I was on a path to nowhere,' he said.

'Much like our lord the king,' replied Shadwatch.

'You think so?'

Shadwatch looked around. They were alone. 'My lord Akton,' he whispered, 'I am convinced of it. He is most certainly on a path to defeat. You heard him back there. He has convinced himself that he is some sort of king out of a fairy tale, springing onto a horse waving his sword and leading his people to a glorious victory against barbarian hordes. And more than that, he is prepared to put some of his own citizenry to death just to make a madcap point to the warlord who is leading the stainer army.' He paused and then went on: 'We must assume that that warlord is Chesterman of the motorcycle.'

Akton stared at the young man. He could not disagree with what he had just said, but it was treason to openly admit it. 'What's to do, then?' he asked lowering his voice.

Shadwatch shrugged. 'We must take matters into our own hands,' he replied.

Akton could scarcely believe what he had just heard. For a moment his jaw dropped, his eyes widened and he struggled to think of anything to say. Two heavily booted guards came down the corridor followed by

Graders. That at least gave Akton time to gather his thoughts. Waiting until they had passed, Akton took Shadwatch gently by the shoulder and led him to an alcove where there was a polished glass bench. They sat down.

Leaning forward, the chancellor gazed at the tiled floor in front of him. 'What you have just said is pure rebellion,' he muttered.

Shadwatch shook his head. 'It is rebellion against a tyrant-fool perhaps, but not against the citizens of Serenity,' he replied. 'If we just sit on our hands and give this king his head, he will lead us all to certain destruction.'

Akton now knew he had a clear choice. Either take this conversation one step further, or he simply walk away, report the conversation to the commissariat and have Shadwatch arrested for treason. The first choice was dangerous and against all his instincts, the other was safe, loyal and praiseworthy but would almost certainly guarantee the destruction of Serenity. He turned to Shadwatch, and took a deep breath: 'What do you propose?' he asked.

'Only this,' said Shadwatch quickly, his voice already betraying the relief he felt at the chancellor's question. 'We, that is to say you and I, go ahead without council clearance or royal decree and arrange for the evacuation of the elder folk to The Island via Portus-Portus.'

'But the king will hear of it!'

'Not if the order for the evacuation is done under the royal seal, and counter-signed by the commissariat,' he smiled at Akton's look of surprise. 'Glamtech is well used to reproducing such documents, and I have friends in the commissariat who will not question any documents I put across their desks.'

Akton nodded slowly. 'I see. So what you are saying is that no one will think to tell the king about something that they believe he has apparently ordered himself?'

'Precisely, but it will be a narrow window. Eventually, the truth of it will leak out, but before it does I am confident that I can lay as confusing a trail of responsibility as you could ever imagine in these corridors of Serenity.' He paused again, stood for a moment and checked to see that no one else was nearby, then sat down.

'Once that part of the evacuation is underway, and the fleet is mobilised, we can then put in motion the evacuation of all women and children, the sick too, and the wounded.'

Akton sat back, shook his head and sighed. 'That is a mighty enterprise,' he whispered.

'Aye, and it comes with every kind of danger, but I do believe it to be necessary,' answered Shadwatch. 'With the imperial fleet in command of the northern waters, The Island will be secure from invasion, and what troops we have left can prepare for the siege that is coming, without the interference of the king.'

Again Akton stared. 'And how do you propose to achieve that?'

'Ah, that is where you come in my friend. As chancellor you will have to convene, order and organise all supplies with the help of senior officers of the city regiments, as well as the militia of Lower Town. The king can hustle and bustle all he likes, but he won't be leading his army beyond the gates and walls of Serenity until each regiment is properly equipped and supplied.' He paused. 'And you can do it my lord, at your very own pace.'

Akton grimaced. 'That's very neat,' he said.

'I have thought about it for some time,' replied Shadwatch. 'You might say that I've seen this coming.' He shrugged. ' I'm not sure it was ever that clear to me until the beginning of this year, but it's become obvious these past few days. We all know our duty. It's just a pity that our king seems to have forgotten his.'

'And yet, he is still our king.'

Shadwatch nodded. 'He is, and for that reason, and that alone I am content to leave him where he is, living up there in that dome of his.' He paused again. 'But I won't have him drag this kingdom down just to suit his own twisted view of the world.'

Akton studied the young head of Glamtech. He knew that Shadwatch was something of a maverick, a shadowy figure in the corridors of power, but he was not expecting to hear all this even from him. It was treason, open treason but in a deep and disturbing way it made sense, and it had more than logic behind it. In short, it sounded the right thing to do.

He glanced along the corridor: 'So we organise an evacuation of the city right under the king's nose and hope to get away with it?'

'We do, and the heavens help us,' replied Shadwatch himself looking down the corridor once more. 'I will also tell the king that we have mobilised part of the fleet at Portus-Portus and that we have sent a force of marines up the coast to land north-west of the city and from there advance inland in support of Arx, and perhaps take the stainer army on its flank.'

Akton breathed deeply. 'Well, that will at least provide us with some cover for our main plan.' He studied his mask which he still held in his hands. 'And it's no bad thing to use the marines. They will be eager to go into action, and their assault craft and mobile batteries of ballistas are very effective.'

At that moment they both heard voices coming towards them. Shadwatch stood quickly. 'I must be going. Meet me at the Glamtech reception area this evening when the first night watch is called. I will give you an update.' He hesitated. 'You are with me on this, lord Akton, or have I just betrayed myself?'

Akton smiled and put his mask on. 'I am with you, lord Shadwatch. I am not entirely sure why, but I am.' He held out his hand and Shadwatch took it:

'Good!' the younger man said. 'Go well, and take care.' He headed away, shadowed by his singular invention, and the faint strains of a long forgotten video called 'The Eye of the Tiger'.

RETREAT TO ARX

Barvarik gave a gasp of relief. The Arxian cavalry had come just in time. Even as Barvarik led his men to the end of the bridge, and the stainers poured after them, the horsemen of Arx had thundered into the clearing beyond the bridge, reined in and let fly with a volley of sling- javelins and crossbow bolts.

It was night time, but in the moonlight Barvarik saw a whole rank of stainers, swept by spears and bolts, topple forward, some pitching into the water, others falling onto the bridge itself. He smiled with grim satisfaction, but then ducked as a flight of arrows fired by the outlander support troops whined about their heads and disappeared into the darkness. There was no time to consider options. The captain of the cavalry galloped up to Barvarik, and swung from the saddle.

'Are you the senior officer here?' he shouted as the sound of the advancing outlanders surged about them.

'I am,' replied Barvarik, 'and we are glad to see you!'

'Save your thanks for later, captain,' replied the officer, glancing at Barvarik's badge of rank. 'We have orders to get you back to Arx as soon as possible.'

'Can we hold the bridge?' asked Barvarik.

The officer shook his head. 'No longer defensible. There have been breakthroughs by stainer detachments at several points east of this position. We need to move before we are outflanked.'

As if to emphasise the point, a catapult stone whined between them, bounced into the turf a few paces away and smashed the trunk of a young sapling at the edge of the clearing.

With a hurried salute, Barvarik nodded and drew his men back from their defensive positions on and near the bridge. Their shields were raised and spears thrust forward as they moved away from the bridge in huddled ranks. Several crossbowmen who had come from Arx, dismounted and crept forward to the edge of the river and began digging in. Even without being ordered, they used their broad-bladed daggers to dig through the turf and make firing pits. They were not much more than a mile from Arx and the safety of its gates, but not once did they look back over their shoulders.

'Get along with you! shouted the captain, when he saw that Barvarik's men were now formed into a defensive line, and had taken position to face the enemy. 'Go now! We need you to be out of here! He turned away to reform his cavalry.

Barvarik nodded once more, shouted to his men and began to lead them further away from the bridge and towards Arx. Arrows, throwing stones and strange streaming balls of fire fell among them as they retreated. Some men fell, and of these a few were left where they lay. The others, wounded but still living, were picked up by their comrades and carried to safety. As they reached the shelter of the tree line, Barvarik waved his battered regiment through and then turned to look towards the bridge they had just left. In the light of the moon, weapons and armour gleamed as the cavalry from Arx charged and counter-charged the steady advance of the stainer infantry. He also noticed the soft orange glow of thunder-rods among the attackers, and behind them on the far side of the bridge, the pulsing glimmer that flickered across the face of a war-wagon drawn up in front of the woods. Surely, the cavalry could not stand against such an engine of battle. Even as he watched he saw the wagon lurch, and two fire balls arced into the night sky. Together they rose high above the approaches to the bridge and then descended on the cavalry like two comets, crashing earthward from space. From where he was standing, he heard cries of alarm as the Arx cavalry scattered as the fire balls burst among them.

Malthus was suddenly by Barvarik's side. 'We cannot wait here and watch!' he shouted. We must go back. We must help them!'

Barvarik hesitated. It was madness, but it was the only thing to do: they must go back. But even as he turned to shout the order, something happened that neither of them had expected: a shadow, like some giant's hand moved across the face of the moon. A chill breeze swept across the river from the north, and a storm broke about their heads.

There was a flash of lightning, a roll of thunder and sheets of stabbing rain scythed down on the heads of the fighting men. Both sides paused and then fell back, the infantry struggling to keep their footing on the bridge, and the horses rearing up and skittering to right and left. There came another reverberating clap of thunder, and night turned to day before the outlander war wagon was plunged into sudden darkness. It's power-tower, briefly silhouetted, swayed, flickered and then disappeared in a flash of smoke and sparks: a lightning bolt had struck it.

'Now!' shouted Barvarik, his ears still ringing from the thunder. He led a group of men back towards the bridge, but saw to his relief that the Arx captain had seized the opportunity to order his men to get back to the tree line. Those that had survived the fire balls, brought their horses under control and galloped towards Barvarik. As they approached, turning in the saddle to fire their crossbows one last time, he noticed that Ajax was with them. He was holding onto the stirrup of one horse, running alongside, and shouting as he ran.

Ajax was even grinning as he came up to Barvarik, let go the stirrup and slithered to a halt.

'What say you?' he laughed. 'Was that not a blessing from heaven? I thought we were dead men for sure, and then that lightning bolt put the very devil among them!' He laughed again. 'Come on! The captain has told me to escort you to Arx. They will cover our retreat from the tree line, but I do not think there will be any more fighting this night. Look at that storm, will ye! See how she howls!' He wiped his face and streaming hair. Then he pointed towards a track way leading through the woods towards the west. 'See there? That's our way. I will lead, your men will follow, and Marcus, see he comes now, will take the rear.'

Too exhausted to argue, Barvarik smiled wearily and ordered his men to do as Ajax said. Picking up a wounded man who had slumped to the ground with an arrow still fixed in his shoulder, Barvarik slung him across his back, ignoring the man's groans and set off into the woods.

As Marcus, the guardsman from Arx followed, he noticed Malthus who had hung back to make sure that no survivors had been left behind in the dark. Coming up to him, he gestured towards Barvarik:

'That young captain of yours is as strong as an ox,' he said and instinctively turned to cover their retreat.

Malthus nodded as he eased his own shield across his back. 'He is that,' he replied. 'He might look like a stripling, but he can lift a man twice his size.' He paused. 'He's got spirit too,' he said. 'We hardly know the man, but we'd follow him to hell and back, we would.'

Marcus grunted. 'Ye may have to,' he said, 'Those stainers won't let the matter rest here. Their blood is up. They may have done their fighting for this night, but they'll be hard on our heels come morning, and that's for sure.' He stared into the blackness and spat. 'Let's be gone,' he said.

Walking alongside one another, and almost in step, they followed the rest of the regiment, soon found the trackway and headed towards Arx.

It wasn't far. In a while they saw the lights of the center towerr of the city, and not long afterwards a patrol came out to meet them and escort them in.

They had just cleared the tunnel gates and were entering the vast comlpex of the peripheral precinct, when the cavalry that had fought for them at the bridge came clattering in behind them. Their captain, a bloody bandage around his scalp, and his dented helmet hanging from the saddle, reined in and dismounted.

'That's good!' he shouted to Barvarik, who was lowering the wounded man to the ground. 'Leave that fellow there. Our medics will look after him and the rest of your men. Come with me, now. The high council of this fair city is waiting to see both of us.' He smiled. 'They will be hoping for good news, but I fear there's not much of that about at the moment.'

Barvarik came up to the captain and smiled back. 'The news is good enough for me and those of my men who made it,' he replied. 'Thanks to you, captain.'

The man shrugged. 'We fought well enough, and saved our skins,' he replied and led Barvarik across corridors and up broad metal staircases that led to the council chamber.

It was a formal, unhurried meeting. But as was traditional for a Rebuild council meeting in time of war, no masks were worn. Both men gave their report to the council, and both were thanked. Then the chief Rebuilder stood up. 'Tomorrow,' he said, 'we expect to be under attack from reinforcements coming in support of this same outlander force that challenged you at the crossing.' He paused to allow the secretary to catch up. 'But we do not expect that these attackers will be able to breach the walls of Arx. We have our refractor and sun-beam systems in place, and as long as the weather holds, those systems at least guarantee an effective defence during the day. Moreover, our patrols tell us that the lands to the west of here are still untouched, and that the great forest that lies to the south, and the river that runs to the north is preventing them from encircling the city in significant numbers.'

'The way to Portus-Portus is open, then?' asked Barvarik.

The Rebuilder nodded. 'It is, and we are determined to keep it so. You are not the only survivors of the battle at the Fence to make their way here, captain. They will prove useful, I'm sure, in the coming siege. Although you are now cut off from Serenity, I am sure you will want to help in the defence of this city.'

'To what end, my lord?'

The Rebuilder nodded. 'A good question. Yes, we know we can stop these stainers from smashing their way into our city, but in the end they can starve us out, if they have a mind to. We do not have sufficient troops to launch a counter-attack, nor do we have sufficient supplies to hold out for more than a month.'

Barvarik thought for a moment. 'You are proposing establishing contact with Portus-Portus before Arx is cut off, and perhaps even organising an evacuation of non-combatants.'

The Rebuilder smiled and turned to his fellow-councillors: 'See my ladies and gentlemen, we have here a warrior who can think beyond the length of his sword, or the breadth of his shield.' Then he turned again to Barvarik. 'What you say is true. In fact we have already sent a cavalry patrol to Portus-Portus with an appeal for assistance.'

Barvarik saluted and stepped back. 'Then that is good, my lord,' he said. 'My men will support your cause as if they were sons of Arx already.'

The Rebuilder gave a slight frown. 'And yourself, captain? You did not include yourself in your answer. Will you be as loyal to Arx they are?'

With a shake of his head, Barvarik replied. 'My lord, my duty lies in the heart of Serenity. I must return to that city post haste, and I must report to my commanding officer. Above all, I must return to my own people.' He pointed to the crown on his sleeve. 'As a captain of a household guards regiment, I am bound to defend the city, the people and the king himself above all else, and besides that . . .'

The lord of Rebuild raised his hand. 'Besides, you say? What else draws you away from your obligations here?'

For the first time Barvarik lowered his head, then he looked up: 'My lord, someone very dear to me in Serenity waits for my return, trusting that I will keep my promise to come as soon as I am able.'

'And you cannot wait?'

'I may be too late already, my lord, but I need to know.'

For a long time the Rebuilder lord did not answer. At last he turned and had a whispered conversation with one of the councillors, an older woman of remarkable beauty. Then he straightened.

'It seems that my fellow councillor, whose opinion I rate above all others, agrees with your request: that you return to Serenity as soon as possible.'

Barvarik looked relieved. 'My lord, I thank you. If you could perhaps provide me with a horse, I will set off for Serenity early tomorrow morning.'

'What's that you say?' Rebuilder chuckled. 'A horse and a rider in open and dangerous country like this, and stainer scouts no doubt pushing in from every sector to the east and south? You would not get beyond ten miles.'

'That may be so, my lord,' Barvarik frowned, 'but I must at least try.'

'To what end?' asked the lady councillor who had earlier spoken with the Rebuilder lord. 'Your bravery guarantees almost certain death. It would accomplish nothing beyond sorrow.' She spread her hands. 'Young captain, there is a better way, perhaps not so suited to a warrior of your particular skills, but one far more likely to succeed.'

'My lady?'

The councillor smiled. 'Arx, as you know is a supply city.'

'It is, my lady.'

'And how do you suppose that we send such supplies to the city of Serenity?'

Barvarik thought for a moment, then his eyes widened:

'The supply capsules! You mean to use those as transport? But surely . . .'

The councillor tossed her head and gave a light laugh. 'The capsules are indeed designed to transport specialist supplies but they are also used routinely and discreetly to ferry our agents to and from Serenity.' She paused, and glanced at the other councillors. 'We like to keep a cautious eye on the corridors of power within the great city. It amuses us that we are seen as somehow cut off and detached from all the goings-on within the imperial precinct.' She turned to the chief Rebuilder. 'Is that not so, my lord?'

'It is my lady, and I see that you trust this young man greatly in that you have revealed this to him.'

The councillor nodded. 'I do trust him, my lord. He has offered his regiment to us in the service of Arx, and has freely confessed before this council that there are some things that are higher than even duty or his oath of service.' She looked at Barvarik:

'Is that not so, captain?'

Barvarik reddened, and for a moment struggled to reply. He was weary. It had been an exhausting, broken day and he had lost good men. All he wanted now was a drink of fresh water, and a corner to lie down and sleep.

'My lady,' he said after a while, 'I will not disappoint your trust in me, and in turn I will trust you,' he paused, 'and your supply capsules.' He bowed, hoping that at last the meeting might be coming to an end.

It did. Barvarik was dismissed with instructions to report to the transport bay in the morning. He was also told to pick up a dispatch from the communications office before he left, and make sure that it was given to the Rebuild liaison chief in the commissariat of Serenity.

Ajax was waiting outside the council chamber to escort him to the main barracks where quarters had been provided for both him and his men.

'Well, I see you're still in one piece, captain,' said the Arx guardsman with a grin. 'I was half thinking they might clap you in irons for causing such a fuss at the bridge backaways.'

Barvarik shrugged. 'Perhaps they should have, but they have instead decided to send me off to Serenity in one of those supply capsules you folk are so fond of using.'

Ajax gave a low whistle. 'Now, there's a surprise. They must trust you.' He led Barvarik through the vast complex of the inner citadel until they came out onto an open courtyard, lit by floodlights. In the middle distance he could see a building Barvarik took to be the barracks block. Next to it was an even bigger structure again with high towers and a massive pitched roof.

'That's transport-command,' said Ajax. 'I'll get you there after breakfast tomorrow. We'll go via the communications office. No one gets anywhere near the transport bay until they are given a day pass from that lot.' He laughed. 'The office will know you're coming.'

When Barvarik awoke the following morning, the clear blue skies and bright sunshine told him nothing of the threat that lay outside the gates of the city. Nor did it lessen the sudden memory of the fight at the bridge, and the men he had left behind. He took breakfast, spoke to what was left of the regiment and placed Malthus in command as acting senior sergeant. After a brief farewell he left with Ajax for the transport bay.

At breakfast he had promised his regiment that he would try to return to Arx as soon as his mission was accomplished. He had no idea when that might be, and they did not ask.

'We won't let you down, sir,' Malthus had said, and Barvarik had returned his salute. 'And nor will I let the regiment down,' he had replied, as he turned away. A short time later, with Ajax at his side, he found himself in the transport bay.

The supply capsule was a type E/Mark 3. It was designed to take larger components and technical equipment. As such, it was relatively roomy and well padded, with two vents on the side, and a clear plastic inspection window at the front.

The Rebuild transport foreman, with Ajax watching on, showed him how to enter the capsule, lie down on his stomach, grasp the two bracing bars and then ease himself forward, so that he could see out of the capsule in the direction of travel.

'The Mark 3 propulsion system is a combination of compressed air and power pulses,' said the foreman and then he grinned:

'No brakes, no steering, and no hope! Just hang on and pray that the engineers at Serenity are expecting you.'

Barvarik thought for a moment:

'So, I won't just get arrested for appearing in the middle of a commissariat loading bay?'

With a shake of his head, the foreman glanced at the control panel. 'Don't worry, captain. The loading bay folk at Serenity are our folk, every one of them. Glamtech is on the next level up, and they never bother us, and nor do those lay-a-bouts in the commissariat bloc. If you survive the journey, you'll be safe enough in the loading bay.' He grinned again. 'Just show the capsule team your pass and dispatch wallet, and they'll wave you through, no questions asked.'

'Thank you.'

'Hah! Don't thank me, captain! When you take off in a minute, you'll be cursing whoever it was persuaded you to take this ride.' He winked at Ajax. 'It wasn't you was it, soldier?'

Ajax laughed. 'No, the young fool volunteered. Can you believe that?' Then he leaned forward and tapped Barvarik on the shoulder as the hatch was about to be closed:

'I'll keep an eye on your men, both fit, and wounded,' he said. 'They'll be as good as gold.'

Barvarik nodded his thanks, the warning klaxon sounded and the hatch clicked shut. There was a short pause, and then the capsule whirred into life. Then came another pause as it lifted slightly off the launch-rails, and with a sudden hiss of compressed air, it shot forward and into the supply tunnel.

A HOSTAGE

When Anna woke up, at first she was aware of only two things: a bright light that made her clench her eyes tight, and a deep throbbing pain at the back of her skull. She must have moaned, and tried to roll over because suddenly someone was at her side, leaning over her and whispering:

'She's awake! The lassie is alive! There's a mercy.'

The voice boomed in her head, and yet was strangely muffled but she seemed to recognise it, and yet could not.

Slowly she opened her eyes. The voice was now a shadow:

'Are you all right?' the shadow asked.

'Where am I?' Every word she spoke echoed in her head. She tried to sit up, but a hand gently held her down.

'Rest easy. You've taken a heavy blow to the head, but the bleeding has stopped, and our surgeon says your skull is not broken.'

Anna lay back and stared. Slowly her eyes stopped hurting, and the throbbing eased slightly. 'Where am I?' she repeated, her voice dry and cracked.

'You're safe. No one will harm you.'

At last Anna recognised the voice. 'Leviss,' she whispered.

Someone chuckled. 'Aye, it's me, and it's lucky you are that I was the one who found you first.'

'Not that lucky,' someone else spoke and then laughed. 'You almost brained the lassie.'

A cup of something warm and sweet was pressed to her lips. She drank. It tasted good.

'More,' she said.

'Later,' said Leviss. 'The surgeon says you are not to drink more than half a cup until he checks on you again.' The young outlander scout who had been sitting on a bench just behind Anna, came and knelt beside her. 'There's a little more colour in your cheeks,' he said. 'When I first picked you up, I thought I'd killed you.'

Anna smiled up at the lad. 'You hit me then?'

'Aye, I did, but it was by mistake, and a glancing blow. Came upon you all of a sudden I did, and moved to strike before you could turn. I couldn't believe it was you, at first. What are the odds against that?'

Slowly the words formed in Anna's mind, and slowly she spoke them. 'I remember now, or at least I think I do. It was evening. I was in my hide. There was a sound. I think there was a sound.'

Almost awkwardly, Leviss put his hand on hers. 'You must rest now, Anna. No more talking. But just this: if it wasn't that you turned your head ever so slightly as I brought my club down, I would never have known it was you. It was so dark, ye see. I pulled the blow, and twisted the club away at the last, but it struck you just a tad.' He gave her hand a little squeeze. 'Thought I'd killed you, I did.' He shook his head. 'I said that, didn't I? But I did, I really did.'

Anna closed her eyes. Suddenly she felt very tired. 'All's well,' she whispered and slept.

When she awoke, to her relief the pain in her head had gone. She sat up and looked around. It was a room lost in shadow, but she could just make out the shape of someone sitting in one corner near what seemed to be a doorway. Even as she looked, the figure stood and came towards her. She recognised Leviss again.

'You are still here,' Anna said.

He grunted. 'I never left,' he replied. 'We've been worried about you.' Pulling a bench towards the bed, he sat down. 'That surgeon is a magic man,' he said. 'You look so much better.'

'I feel it.' Anna sighed. 'Tell me where I am. Please.'

Leviss glanced towards the door, and then turned to Anna again. 'You are in the watch-post,' he said. 'Your watch post. We took it yesterday. It was a sharp fight, but we took it, and your friends took to their heels and escaped towards the city.' He shrugged. 'Officially, you are now a prisoner of lord Chesterman's army.'

'An unofficially?'

Leviss smiled. 'Unofficially, you are in my care, and that of my father. Nike too.'

'You are all here?'

'Aye, we are, and all conscripted into this great army of liberation. We stuck together, of course we did. My father wasn't going to have some stainer townsman from Brokinburgh shouting at us, and giving orders no one understands.' He grinned. 'It was pure luck that put us in a scouting party sent to investigate the very watch post you were assigned.'

Anna-Seka thought for a moment. 'So what becomes of me?'

Leviss shrugged. 'Well, you rest up for now, and while ye can. One of the captains told me that we will probably get orders to join the main advance in the next couple of days. You can see it, y'know. The city, I mean. You can see it from the observation tower on top of the barracks.'

'I know.'

'Of course, ye do.' Leviss smiled. 'Stupid of me.'

Anna smiled back. 'Not at all. Although the city is quite close, there are hills enough to hide it, and it's only the gap made by the imperial highway that allows you to see it from here.' She paused. 'You are going to attack the city, then?'

Leviss gave a short laugh. 'Well, that's why we're here, t'aint it? My father says that this time lord Chesterman's blood is really up, and besides he has the king's brother with him.'

'Lord Marlin? I never knew.'

'It's not every one that does, but us scouts got to meet him when he came by our camp fire a couple of evenings ago. Chesterman was with him too, and the meanest escort of ruffians yer ever likely to meet either side of the border.'

'His own men?'

'All sorts, Anna. Not a lovely bunch, I can tell ye, but all outlanders, every last one of 'em, and good fighting men too.' He hesitated. 'I heard tell that some of them once served in household regiments of the king himself.'

Anna nodded, and lay back. She was feeling better, but was still very weak. The room spun for just a moment, and then settled. 'I think I need to sleep,' she said.

'There's a truth.' Leviss put his hand on hers She felt the gentle strength of it. 'Sleep now. You are safe. No one is going to harm ye now. Promise.'

But Anna did not reply. She was already asleep.

CHAPTER #10
OVERRIDE

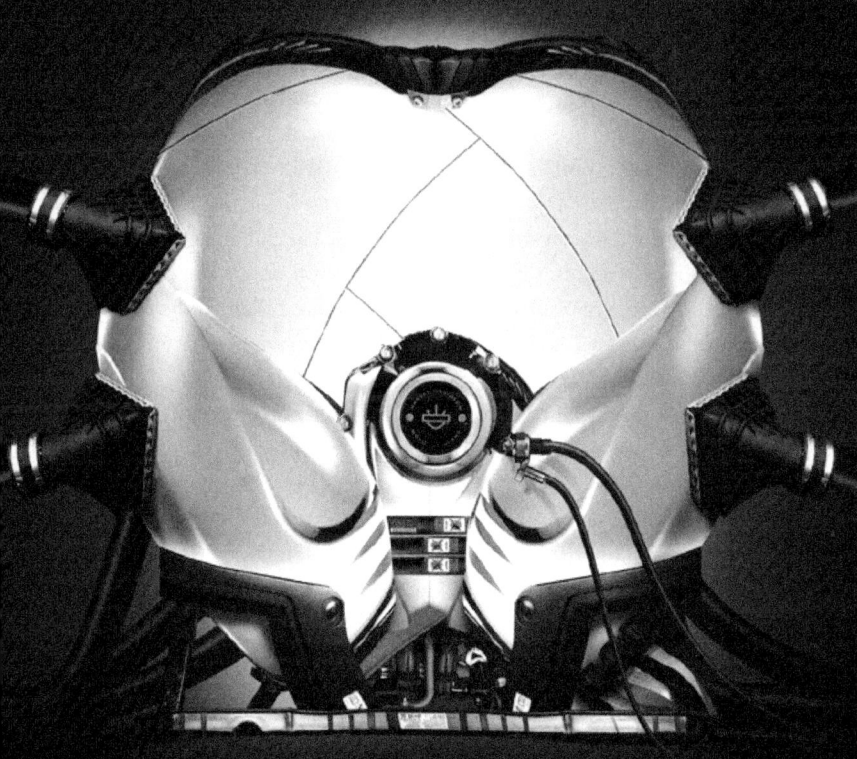

Shadwatch stood next to Akton, and looked out over the city. The streets were busy, but not with the normal traffic of the day. Instead, groups of soldiers and civic workers moved to and fro among wagons, supply carts and engines of war. Banners had been set up on the rooftops of every corner building to mark out the zones of different regiments, and smoke hung over the squares and towers where fires had been lit to prepare the 'flame-stones' of the catapults and ballista batteries.

'I see your preparations are underway,' Shadwatch said quietly. 'Have you been keeping the king informed?'

'All that the king needs to know, he has heard,' replied the chancellor. He paused. 'The evacuation is also underway.'

Shadwatch nodded. 'I signed the counter-order this morning for my Glamtech colleague in Portus-Portus. And yesterday, I received word that the fleet was mobilised, and all shore-leave for the marines had been cancelled.'

'That is good.' Akton stared for a moment. He had been distracted by a flash of light coming from something afar off on the imperial highway north of the city. 'One of our watch-posts has fallen, and a cavalry patrol of the Imperial Light Horse report troop movements on a wide front less than five miles from the city.'

'Time to evacuate the prisoners, then?' Shadwatch turned and looked along the wall-walk. There was no one about. His Glambot, Teevey, hovered discreetly about twenty paces away, its Glamgel battery recently charged, and signalling with a gently pulsing blue light.

'It is time, but I still have no idea how you plan to do it, my lord.'

Shadwatch shrugged. 'It is all a question of DNA and the Gene Pool,' he replied. 'That has been the centre of our research for years.'

'Ah, I think I see,' said Akton. 'Is it not true that we have a security and identification system that is based on our knowledge of DNA signatures?'

'Broadly speaking, yes.' Shadwatch shrugged. 'Some of the science is beyond me, but I understand the basic mechanics, and how they have been applied to our passport system and identity screening procedures. As always, Glamgel research has allowed us several unexpected breakthroughs.'

They both paused as they watched a giant crane swing a ballista from one tower to another, and then lower it onto its battle-platform.

'So what you are saying,' said Akton after a while, 'is that you can override or interfere with the prison security system by meddling with the DNA recognition system?'

Again, Shadwatch shrugged, and this time gave a faint smile. 'Yes, that's about the shape of it. My technicians have applied all the necessary subtleties. All I need to do is press a switch.'

'And?'

'And every prisoner-capsule in every wing of the prison will be raised to the commissariat reception level, scanned for a clearance pass, and then lowered to the transport and dispatch bay.'

'Where your people will be waiting?'

Shadwatch grunted. 'And a good number of yours also, my lord Akton, I am hoping. Did I not receive your coded message assuring me of armed chancellery personnel on standby for duty in the transport bay.'

Akton nodded. There was that distant flash of light again, only this time it was closer. 'Just give me your estimated time, and they will be there.'

'And all sworn to secrecy?'

'Every man and woman,' replied Akton. 'They are all highly trained, but more importantly, most of them have relatives who are now inmates of the commissariat prison.' He paused. 'They know the risks, but they also know the stakes are high. They will make sure that the prison-capsules are opened, and that the prisoners are released without objection.'

'Perfect.' Shadwatch leaned on the balustrade of the wall-walk and looked out over the ocean. He swung his head in the opposite direction, paced to the other side and looked towards the twin towers of the main gates. 'Do you think we can hold on long enough to allow the prisoners and any others to escape?'

Akton frowned. 'We have an even chance, my lord. So much can go wrong, but on the other hand there is a cunning simplicity to your plan that gives me enough confidence to throw my weight behind it.'

'And if we fail?'

'Then we all go down together,' replied Akton, 'We will be executed by a royal warrant enforced by imperial guards, or put to the sword by a mob of outlanders.' He sighed. 'In the end I do not see much of a difference.'

The head of Glamtech did not shift his gaze. 'It seems I am in danger of doing something noble,' he muttered. 'It is a very strange feeling, and one I am not entirely comfortable with.' He paused, and they were both quietly aware of the Glambot drifting above the wall-walk to a dialogue which naturally Akton did not recognise, but Shadwatch knew as 'Gladiator.' He waited for the programmed quote, but nothing happened, and the music played on. 'Do you think perhaps I have had an attack of sentiment?' he asked.

'It's called doing the right thing, lord Shadwatch,' said lord Akton after a time as he gazed at the Glambot, still unable to fathom its real purpose. 'It may make you a sworn enemy of the king, but at least you will have the satisfaction of knowing what mercy tastes like, and how setting the innocent free is infinitely preferable to condemning them.'

'Hmmph!' Shadwatch straightened. 'You sound like one of those old magistrates from Litra.' He gave a slight shake of his head. 'But what you say tells me that you are least committed to our cause.'

A guard came up onto the wall-walk, and Shadwatch moved his hand to the hilt of his sword. 'It's beginning to get crowded here. Come with me now to my laboratory. I want to show you something remarkable that we have developed as a result of our research into DNA and gene-science.'

'I am due at an inspection meeting for the ministry of supply. Will this detour to a Glamtech laboratory be useful.'

'Very.' Shadwatch spread his hands. 'It may even give you cause to hope.'

'To hope?'

'Yes, to hope that this present state of affairs may yet turn out better than any of us would dare to dream.'

Akton had never heard the head of Glamtech talk in this way before. He stared at him, not understanding what he had just heard, and struggling to believe that the words did not conceal some deeper stratagem.

Yet again, Akton had put aside his mask and Shadwatch saw the doubt in Akton's eyes.

He smiled and put his hand on the chancellor's shoulder. 'Do not worry, my lord. I have not lost my wits nor my edge. Of course I see an advantage for myself in this present state of affairs, and yes, even opportunity.' He looked towards the guard who had taken his post about twenty yards away further along the wall, then continued:

'I am loyal to Serenity, as I know you are, and would do nothing deliberate to bring harm upon its citizens,' he hesitated, 'but as we have agreed our loyalty to the king has become somewhat compromised.' He paused. 'Action has to be taken, and that is precisely what we are doing.'

Akton nodded. 'Then take me to the laboratory,' he said, ignoring the Teevey as he crackled away: 'A man's gotta do what a man's gotta do.'

THE SIEGE

M arlin stood beside Chesterman on the tower of the watch-post which had just been captured. They were looking towards Serenity.

'You see, sire?' said Marlin pointing. 'The imperial highway leads directly to the main gates. If we carry the gates, the city is ours.'

Chesterman did not take his eyes off the distant glow of the walls and spires. 'You sound very confident of that, lord Marlin. Even from here, those gates or what we can see of them, will be difficult to capture, and even I know that Serenity has more than one line of defence.'

Marlin nodded. 'That is true, sire but I was born in that city, grew up in it, walked its streets, and got to see it with a soldier's eye.'

'And?'

'There are multiple lines of defence, lord Chesterman, but they all depend on the gate walls remaining barred and bolted. If the gates and gate-towers fall, there is a clear line of advance through the heart of Lower Town to the inner gates that guard the walls of upper town.

'And the hotplate? What of that?'

Marlin shrugged. 'It is a problem, I admit, but our war-wagons offer some protection, and if we can bring a section of the wall down, the rubble alone should neutralise it.'

'Go on.' Chesterman glanced back over his shoulder at the lines of infantry forming into marching order on the open ground around the watch-post.

Marlin smiled. 'Once we get inside the outer defences, the situation will swing to our favour. My brother the king ordered several pleasure-domes to be built to mark the boundary between upper and Lower Town, and placed parkland in between. Those buildings, raised to honour the king, look down on the gates of the upper city. They are in themselves not defensible, but they have broad platform roofs ideal for our engines of war.'

Chesterman nodded slowly. 'You are not the first in our company who has noticed this, lord Marlin, but you are the first to suggest that we carry the city by a concentrated frontal assault on its strongest point of defence.' He gestured towards the army that was gathering below. 'Such an attack will cost us dearly,' we have to deal with the hot-plate. I am not sure that the war-wagons can endure the heat of such a defence-system.'

Marlin thought hard. He was worried that Chesterman for all his military skill, might be tempted to divide his forces in order to storm the city, and so weaken the assault, and make his army vulnerable to a counter-attack.

'Let me lead the assault, my lord,' he said. 'I and my men will go against the outer gates as the lead battalion. If there is a price to paid in blood, it is our blood which will be spilt first.'

For a moment, Chesterman was taken aback. He had not expected that response from the king's brother. He did not doubt his courage, but he had thought him more careful with his own safety.

'You would do that, to prove your argument?' he asked quietly.

Marlin gave a slight inclination of his head. 'I would, my lord. And I would feel all the more confident if you promise to give us the necessary support. Back us up with your fighting towers, war-wagons and siege engines, and I will lead the assault.'

'Come with me.' Chesterman turned suddenly, and walked towards the tower steps. Marlin followed, and together they made their way down into the barracks area of the watch-post. There was an outlander scout lounging against the doorpost of the guard-house. Chesterman waved him across. The man came and saluted:

'Sir?'

'Bepsi-Loca, isn't it?'

The man smiled. 'You have a good memory for names and faces, my lord.'

Chesterman shrugged. 'That young scout you captured a couple of days ago. Is she still alive?'

Bepsi-Loca nodded. 'Yes, my lord. She is still a bit groggy. When we caught her, my lad gave her a clip across the skull, but the surgeon has done his work well. She lives.'

'That's good.' Chesterman grunted. 'My intelligence officer will need to interrogate her before I order the main advance on the city.'

Bepsi-Loca nodded. 'You might have to wait a bit longer, sire. Unless of course, you don't care if she survives the interrogation or not.'

Chesterman rubbed his chin and looked at Marlin. 'What is your counsel, lord Marlin?'

'We should not delay the advance, my lord. We have the advantage. But to interrogate the scout when she is still weak will only hasten her passing. They are trained not to give information, y'know.'

'I know it.' Chesterman nodded. 'Well all right, we'll do without her.' He paused. 'But bring her along anyway. She might prove useful later on once we get a good look at the defences.'

Bepsi-Loca nodded. 'Although she wears the uniform of a city regiment, her identity disc shows that she is no ordinary scout: she is a member of the College of Scouts.'

'Is that so? They tell me that the College Scouts are the best that Serenity has to offer. She is a prize indeed, and one worth holding onto.'

'Oh, we won't be letting her go, sir.' Bepsi-Loca smiled. 'Where we go, she will go. I've told my men as much already.'

Chesterman nodded, half turned away, and then turned back again to the stainer scout. 'In the morning, I want your men to push out to the right flank, beyond our light cavalry, head south for no more than a mile, and then set up an observation post. You think you can do that?'

Bepsi-Loca smiled as he saluted. 'It's as good as done already sire. We will send up a flare-rocket when we have taken position.'

'Good!' Chesterman glanced at Marlin. 'Let's have a look at your men, lord Marlin. I want to know for sure that they are equipped for the assault.'

Bepsi-Loca watched as the two warlords walked through the barrack-gates and headed towards the open ground where the army was assembling:

'Equipped for the assault, eh? Well, that sounds like trouble, right enough. Am I glad I won't be part of that? You bet your life, I am,' he muttered to himself, and looked towards the city. 'Just stay out of trouble, Master Loca,' he said and spat languidly at his feet. 'That's what's to do, and I'll be doing it for me and mine and that poor, wee lassie.' He smiled. 'What a stroke of luck, being ordered out to the right flank just as those two fine gentlemen over there are cooking up some kind of grand attack.'

He saw Nike coming out of the barracks and waved to her. 'Away here, lass! We've orders, we have, and as sweet a set as you're ever like to get in this here army.'

Smiling, Nike came across. She was wearing a leather breastplate she had picked up on the battlefield, and her hair was tied back in a 'fighting-knot'.

'How sweet is sweet, father? I hear a rumour that we are to join an assault on the city in the next couple of days, and there's little sweetness in that idea.'

'Ha!' Bepsi-Loca laughed and clapped his daughter on the shoulder. 'We've only been posted by lord Chesterman himself to an observation post on the right flank. A nice quiet spot'll be, and well away from the action.'

Nike frowned. 'Is Anna coming with us, then?'

'Aye, lass, she is,' her father grinned and glanced towards the half-ruined barracks office where the intelligence commandos had set up a headquarters. 'But there was a moment I thought she was going to be handed over to those fellows over there.'

Nike turned and looked towards the barracks herself. 'She wouldn't last a day in their hands, papa.'

Bepsi-Loca nodded. 'Don't I know it!' He shrugged. 'No matter, lord Chesterman decided against it, anyway. Young Anna-Seka is still with us, and I aim to keep it that way.'

Nike nodded. 'That's good then. I'll let Leviss know. I never seen him worry about anyone so much as he worries about our Anna.' She gave a short laugh. 'Near finished her, he did, with that club of his.'

Bepsi-Loca was distracted by a war-wagon which was being dragged into position just inside the barracks square. A pulse shot from its fighting tower had knocked a hole in the watch-post wall during the fighting, and now the wagon was crossing the breach it had made. An extra team of oxen strained to bring the wagon safely over the rubble.

'They won't find it so easy to hammer down the walls of the city,' he said quietly to Nike. 'An engineer was telling me that they estimate the outer walls to be twenty-five feet thick at the base, and reinforced with steel rods every five paces.'

'I never knew that.'

'Neither did I, not until yesterday. And Serenity also has heavy wall-mounted catapults and ballistas. Not like the mobile ballistas we came up against at the Fence. And there's the hot-plate, too.'

'That's too much information, papa. If what you say is true, losses will be heavy among our people.'

Bepsi-Loca looked away. 'Well, it can't be helped, daughter mine. There's nothing holding our lord Chesterman back, and there's not one of the warlords leading this here army that ain't convinced they can break into the city like a young calf walking through wet grass.' He frowned for a moment and scratched the back of his head. 'I know our leader is a great general, there's no arguing against that, but I worry that he is not as careful with the lives of his people as he could be.'

Nike glanced at her father. She had not heard him talk like that before, not during this campaign anyway. 'Hush, papa,' she said. 'Anyone could be listening.'

Bepsi-Loca gave the slightest of nods. 'Good advice,' he said quietly. 'I'll hold my peace until we all get back safe and sound to our kindred and home.'

'Where maman waits.'

'Aye, your mother, bless her and the elder folk. It will be a good day when we see them again.'

As Nike left to see how Anna was doing, and to tell Leviss the news, an officer came out of the barracks block and walked towards her father. He had a dispatch in his hand and he seemed to be in a hurry.

'What now?' Nike muttered under her breath as she walked through the shadowed doorway and along the narrow corridor to the room where Anna-Seka lay.

The war-wagon shook, its iron tower swayed for a moment, and with a roar like thunder a pulse of blinding white light leapt from the transmitter-dish atop the tower and soared in a gleaming arc towards the city.

It was not alone. Almost simultaneously another twenty war wagons lurched and fired their thunder or pulse bolts. The roar of the first wagon was almost lost in the deafening chorus from the other war engines when they joined in. And besides this, the air was filled with sound of the catapults and ballistas as their cables and knotted ropes were released under tension, counter-weights crashed against the heavy timber stay-beams, and giant rocks, and iron balls, glowing red hot sang into the air.

Officers shouted, 'Reload! Reload!', men cursed and groaned as they re-charged the war-engines, and horses snorted and stamped the turf, sensing the coming of the order that would send them against the enemy.

Standing alongside his men just ahead of a war-wagon, Marlin shook his head in disbelief at the noise and fury of the artillery barrage that thundered against the gates of Serenity.

'They'll never survive that,' he said to himself. He lifted his head to watch the cloud of missiles gather over the city and then descend in a series of shuddering explosions that almost obscured the towers and ramparts of the main gates.

He was surprised to hear someone answer despite the roaring of the engines, and turned to see a veteran captain who was standing alongside him.

'Looks pretty, don't it?' said the veteran with a grin, 'but wait a moment and ye'll see that the folks holding those gates and walls will have something to say to us, as well.'

He had only just finished speaking, when there was a rippling glow of light along the soaring walls of Serenity and the war engines of the city replied with their own barrage. The ballistas and catapults of Serenity were at full strength.

As he watched, Marlin had the strangest feeling: his own city was sending against him a message of death and destruction. Rough hewn rocks, smooth polished iron balls, and bolts of flame whirled skywards, hovered for just an instant and then swept down and towards him.

'Cover!' someone yelled, and men scattered to left and right, diving under wagons, tumbling into ditches and crouching behind their shields.

Marlin, however, did not move. Fascinated, he watched the barrage as it plunged against the outlander army.

'Get down, you damned fool!' There was a hand on his shoulder and he found himself flung into a trench behind a low stone wall. Even as he hit the ground, he felt the air tremble. A rock hissed by his head and thudded against the turf before leaping up and crashing against a war-wagon, ripping it apart in a cloud of splinters and twisted metal.

Scarcely believing himself to be still alive, Marlin gasped and looked around. Chesterman, his motorcycle helmet still firmly on his head, was staring back at him.

'You might not care either way,' he said to Marlin, 'But I would very much like you to stay in one piece at least for today.'

They both flinched and ducked as two more missiles swept over them. Marlin, aware that he himself was now shaking, forced a smile. 'Thank you, my lord,' he said, 'I did not expect . . .'

'Hah! You are surprised that they would shoot at you, the king's brother? Hah! I thought as much. It's strange what battle does to a man, my lord Marlin. It makes him think that he alone is somehow the centre of it all, and that without him nothing else can be.'

Marlin nodded. More ballista bolts and iron balls were falling, but the outlander batteries had also roared back into life. 'Thank you, my lord Chesterman,' he repeated, 'A moment of madness, that is all.'

Chesterman nodded, stood for a moment and looked around. 'Madness is sometimes useful,' he said. 'We have suffered some damage,' he went on, 'but not as much as I feared. Those Serenity gunners are firing long, but we need to move quickly before they shorten their range, and knock a hole through our centre.'

Marlin nodded. He was impressed by this warlord, who was always so calm no matter what the crisis or moment of confusion that came against him. If anyone could breach those walls, it would be him.

'I will order my men into position,' he said quietly to Chesterman, and began to move away.

'Thank you, lord Marlin,' Chesterman replied, 'but keep your head down, and do not go beyond that forward entrenchment until I give the word.' He said something else, but his words were lost in the sound of a volley of pulse rockets fired from a nearby battery. Even as Marlin hurried towards his men, more ballista stones were falling, tearing up the turf, smashing war-engines and hurling men to the ground.

Chesterman watched him go. He did not entirely trust Marlin, but he liked him. The man had the kind of instinctive courage that was not reckless: it was simply unselfish and somehow kind: too kind. This king's brother would never make a leader – there was not enough cruelty in his soul – but he would be a useful tool as long as he survived.

Barvarik opened his eyes. Where was he? He could not tell. He must have passed out at some stage. Yes, he remembered now: as the capsule had rushed along the tunnel deep underground somewhere between Arx and Serenity, it had suddenly dipped, accelerated, and risen violently. Then it dipped again and finally spun for a few seconds before levelling out and losing speed.

And then he had felt himself rock forward as though a huge weight was pushing him from behind, and in an instant all had become darkness.

As so he woke, shook his head and looked around. He seemed to be in some kind of holding bay. The hatch of his capsule had opened, either by impact against the buffers he could just make out, or by some automatic release device. It was difficult to tell. The lighting, a form of glow- tech, was in evidence along the walls but it was poor light and flickered uncertainly.

What's more, as far as he could tell there was no one about. He had expected a team of Litra workers to be on hand, or even just a lone duty officer, but there was no one.

Carefully, painfully, he eased himself back and stood up. He could see more clearly now, and his head was no longer ringing. At the end of the bay there was an open door, and from along the darkened corridor he could hear the faint sound of voices. Moments later, just faintly, there was a distant metallic echo as if some kind of equipment was being shifted. As his eyes adjusted to the gloom, he made out, on one of the walls near the capsule, in large letters neatly painted in the military style: 718 Q. 'Well, that's something,' he said to himself as he glanced down and saw the same letters on the side of his capsule, 'I'm meant to be here.'

Stepping out of the capsule, still a little unsteady on his feet, he reached for his sword which had been stowed next to him, and checked that he had the dispatch and pass the Litra official had given to him back in Arx.

Slowly he headed towards the door, uncertain what to do, but keen to make contact with someone from Litra before he bumped into a guards patrol from commissariat security. He was nearly at the doorway when another door to his right he had not noticed swung open, and a mechanic in the blue overalls of the general maintenance department appeared. They both stopped and stared at one another.

The mechanic spoke first:

'718Q?' he asked, his hand sliding to the personal protection baton in his belt.

Barvarik nodded. 'From Arx,' he replied. 'I'm from Arx. I was told you would be expecting me.'

'We were,' said the mechanic, looking slightly relieved, 'but when we didn't get a confirmation signal, and no one replied to our counter-message, we assumed that the operation was off, for some reason.' He smiled slightly. 'My boss is going to be very put out.'

Barvarik frowned. 'How so?'

'Well,' the mechanic shrugged, came forward, leaned over the capsule and flicked a switch. The hatch closed, the motor whirred and it slid backwards before disappearing down the tunnel. He straightened. 'Well, it's like this: we got your signal just over three days ago, and replied to it after the standard wait for confirmation.'

Barvarik's eyes widened. 'Three days? That's not possible. I can't have been here for three days.'

The mechanic laughed. 'It's not only possible, lad, it's the only explanation. This here bay, the one you've landed up in, is the one assigned by Litra for special-only cargoes and shipments. It's not used for the normal shifting of supplies and standard equipment or tools.' He tapped his forehead. 'Top secret,' he said and winked. 'This here is our top secret bay. No one has been near this place for at least a week.'

'But that door is open, and I can hear voices.'

'Can ye now?' The mechanic paused, and put his head on one side. 'Well, I guess ye can. That will be our security and systems team. There's a bit of a flap on, ye see. Something has gone wrong with our locking and unlocking procedures.'

'Wrong?'

'Yes, wrong. All the doors and gates are opening for no reason on this level. What's more, the factory and prison entrances and exits on the levels above are doing the very same thing.' He laughed again. 'It's mad here,' he said, 'and it must be bedlam upstairs.' He cupped his hand to one ear. 'Yep! That's security and systems all right. They'll be along here soon doing a check and scratching their heads no doubt.'

'And if they find me here?'

'They'll be as surprised as me, lad, but I'll look after you. Have you got your pass? Yes, that's right. Give it to me, and hold onto that dispatch you're carrying.' He glanced at the pass. 'Good! It says for Litra eyes only. That tells me exactly who you are meant to be seeing. Come on!'

Barvarik followed the mechanic to the door, not sure if he should trust him, but resigned to the thought that he didn't have much choice. 'How can I have been here for three days?' he muttered, half to himself.

'Oh, that's easy,' replied the mechanic, tossing the remark over his shoulder. 'Those capsules can play the very divvil with ye. They often go faster than they are meant to, and anyone inside can end up pretty scrambled for a few days.' He paused, and they began to walk down the corridor. 'But count yourself lucky,' he went on, 'sometimes we lift poor fellows out of them capsules, and they are all in pieces. It's not a pretty sight.' He paused again, shone his torch on an inspection panel, and grunted. 'Most of the time, ye are safe enough in that particular mark of capsule, but they are a bit old the 718's are, and it's not unusual for special guests such as yourself to take a day or so to recover.' He stopped at another inspection panel. 'I guess they warned ye.'

The voices were getting louder, and torch beams flickered along the walls.

'Right ho!' said the mechanic. 'Leave this to me.' He put his fingers to his lips and gave a whistle. At once the voices fell silent, and the torch beams converged on the mechanic, and then onto Barvarik. There was a pause and an armed security officer came forward. He nodded to the mechanic, and then stared at Barvarik:

'Who are you?' he asked.

'I am Barvarik, a soldier of this city, but I have come from Arx with a dispatch.'

'Have you, now?' The officer kept his gaze fixed on Barvarik. 'Well, give me the dispatch, and we will escort you to Interrogation.'

Glancing at the flashes on the man's shoulder, Barvarik saw that he outranked the man, but only just. He gave a weary salute and then shook his head. 'That is not possible, lieutenant,' he replied. 'I am instructed by the commander at Arx to hand this directly to the senior officer of Litra Transport Command. I have a pass.' He looked at the mechanic, who grinned and showed the pass to the lieutenant.'

The lieutenant studied the pass for longer than he needed to, then scowled. 'You Litra people are all the same,' he said. 'You think you own the place. You think that a grubby little pass stamped by some grubby little clerk in a supply city is enough to let you walk through Commissariat Security whenever you like.'

Barvarik frowned, and rested his hand on the hilt of his sword. 'I am a captain of a Household Guards regiment. I have been sent with my regiment to defend the northern borders while you skulk here in some hideaway-posting, pretending to be useful in a pit you call the Commissariat. Good men have been lost defending the likes of you.'

The officer went pale and looked back over his shoulder at the men standing behind him. But Barvarik was not finished:

'In one week, we have fought at least three separate actions against a stainer army bigger than anything that has ever come against the kingdom. I lost men, brave men, trusted men. Everyone one of them was a better man than you. Now get out of my way, or I'll shorten you by a head, and file a report with the king that shows you were guilty of dereliction of duty and deserved to die.'

He stepped forward. That was enough to make the officer flinch, and take half a step backwards.

'Thank you,' said Barvarik crisply, and brushed against the man with his shoulder as he went by. Someone laughed as the officer stumbled, and that was all that was needed. With the mechanic by his side, Barvarik continued down the corridor. 'Don't look back,' he muttered to the mechanic. 'We don't want them following us, do we?'

The mechanic chuckled. 'You've made my day, cap'n,' he said. 'Can't wait to tell the wife when I get off shift. We've all been hoping someone would put those security fellows in their place.'

'Just get me to the office, and my job is done here,' replied Barvarik, 'but I'm obliged to you for what you've done already.'

They reached the end of the corridor, climbed a metal staircase and came out on a platform with a glass-partitioned office at one end. As they approached the entrance to the office, Barvarik tapped the mechanic on his shoulder:

'What's happening above ground?' he asked.

The mechanic stopped. 'You mean in the city?' He sighed. 'It's all a bit of a mess, but we are holding. There's a stainer army at the gates, and doing its best to get in, but the officers in the commissariat and Litra are telling us that everything is under control.' He winked. 'We've also been told that the king keeps to his palace, and shows no sign coming down into the city. Is that a good sign, do ye think?'

Barvarik shrugged. 'It might be, but what's this about all the doors opening on every level? The prisoners . . .'

'Hah! That's a hornet's nest I am staying well away from!' The mechanic laughed. 'The second my shift here is finished, I'm away home to my wife and family. Those security types from the commissariat can sort the prison levels out.'

The mechanic went to the door of the office, rapped twice on the glass pane and led Barvarik inside.

There was a Litra official seated at a desk that was partly covered by untidy piles of paper and stacked files. He looked up as they came in.

'Gentlemen,' he said softly, 'what problem do you bring me now?'

The mechanic managed a salute:

'I found the captain here in loading bay 78Q. He's from Arx, and he has a pass to prove it.'

'Bay 78Q? That doesn't make sense. We had no confirmed order for a delivery from Arx to that bay.'

'Well, he's here sir, as you can rightly see, but maybe he should be speaking for himself.' He gave a short laugh, saluted again and stepped back.

The official, an older man and balding, nodded and looked at Barvarik with interest verging on boredom:

'I see you have a dispatch for me, captain.'

Barvarik glanced at the code on the dispatch bag. It matched the code on the desk-plate in front of him. He nodded and handed it over.

'Thank you, captain,' said the official. 'That is all. I will ask my mechanic here to take you to the medical bay and then see you safely to the exit floor. I presume you are not returning to Arx.'

'Not yet, sir. I have one or two matters to attend to here first, and I should also report to my regimental headquarters.'

The balding official smiled. 'You'll be lucky to find anyone at headquarters,' he replied. 'All the Guards and Household regiments that have not already been sent to the northern front, have been placed on full alert defending the walls and gates.'

'I see,' Barvarik hesitated. 'Then it seems as if time runs hard against me.' He saluted. 'I will leave now, sir.'

The official returned his salute with a weary gesture. 'I wish you well, captain.' He smiled once more and began to open the dispatch bag. 'I wonder what parcel of joy we have here.' He looked up expecting a reply, but Barvarik had already gone and the mechanic with him.

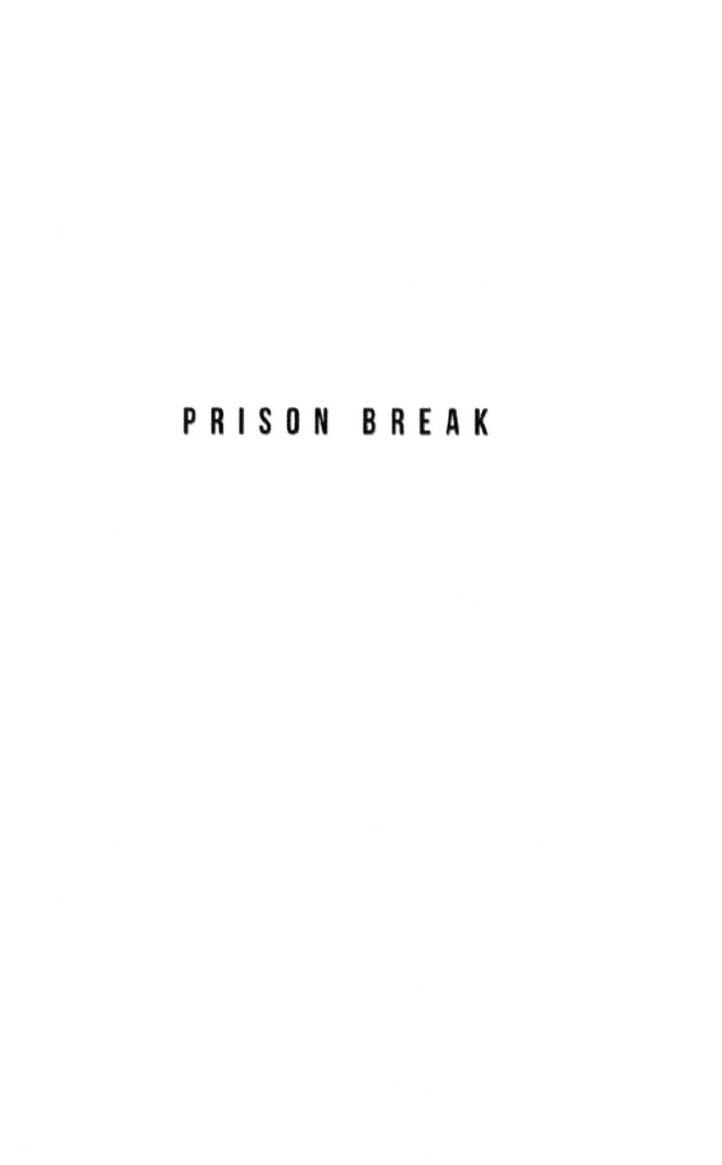

PRISON BREAK

Even as Barvarik was waking up in loading bay 78Q, Shadwatch and Akton were making their way down to the prison-reception level from the upper security zone of the commissariat. Earlier that morning they had both been summoned to an emergency council meeting with the king. It had not gone well. Both men had been accused by the king of holding back information, and making key decisions regarding the defence of Serenity without royal approval. Of course they had denied that they were trying to mislead the king, and assured him that the seriousness of the situation at the outer walls and gates had meant that decisions had to be made quickly and without normal protocols.

But the king, suddenly tiring of their excuses, had merely waved his hand. 'Enough!' he had said. 'I am the king and it is my task to defend this city. The task is my responsibility not yours. My responsibility!' He glared at the two men. 'Do you understand?'

'My lord,' they had both replied, and bowed.

'Then stop treating me like a child who cannot even wipe his nose, and start treating me as your lord and king.' At this point the king had stood, and taken up his staff of office.

'Do I make myself clear?' he had said, his voice falling away to a hoarse whisper.

Neither Shadwatch nor Akton had replied.

'Do I make myself clear?' the king repeated, and with a shout brought the staff crashing down onto the conference table.

Neither Akton nor Shadwatch flinched, but the other council members sat back, and two of them put their hands to their masks in token of submission.

At last Shadwatch spoke. 'My lord, both the chancellor and myself have only one concern, and that is the safety and prosperity of Serenity.'

The king's eyes shining behind his mask, had narrowed. 'That's two concerns, Shadwatch, not one. Do you include me in both of them?'

'That goes without saying my lord king,' Shadwatch had replied, hoping that the king had not noticed the slight tremor in his voice. 'But we must both ask to be excused from this meeting. I have just received word that there has been a major security lapse at the commissariat building effecting the Glamtech, Supply and Prison levels.'

'What kind of security lapse?'

'That is what we aim to find out, my lord,' answered Shadwatch quickly, 'and then we will of course report back to you.'

For some time the king did not reply. He had stared at the two men as if there was no one else in the room. The awkward silence was only faintly broken by the distant sound of the fighting at the main gates. At last the king had shaken his head. 'Get out!' he said and waved them away.

'That was close,' whispered Shadwatch as they left, and he gave a low whistle as both he and Akton approached another security check and yet another lifting bay.

'Too close,' whispered Akton, 'If Serenity survives this siege, I doubt that we will survive the king's temper.'

Shadwatch smiled. 'Cheer up, old friend,' he said. 'This game is not yet over, and we have much that we can do.'

Teevey floated out of the shadows and almost up to Shadwatch's shoulder. The Glambot's display screen flicked on and 'Chariots of Fire' echoed across the open area in front of the security bay.

They cleared the security check without difficulty. The guards were clearly distracted by problems on the lower levels. Not only had there been an unusual delivery of prisoner capsules to the transport bay, but during the process every door and entranceway on every level had swung open. And now all the exit-gates were now proving difficult to close.

'Trouble?' Shadwatch asked a security guard as they passed yet another checkpoint. 'Is there trouble?'

The guard nodded. 'It's all chaos on the next level down, sir. Every prison capsule has either emptied out, or been sent to the transport bay for Portus-Portus. It doesn't make sense.'

Shadwatch risked a wink at Akton, but did not reply to the guard beyond a casual salute. Moments later they had taken a swift-lift to the main level of the prison block, and found themselves walking out and onto the open balcony where capsules were lifted by crane to the floors that soared above their heads, or descended further and deeper into the shadowy world known as basement five.

The guards were armed, and clearly nervous. They hurried back and forth shouting orders or calling out according to their rank, in reply. Some of them were escorting prisoners who had already been recaptured. They mostly ignored Shadwatch and Akton, apart from a cursory glance, and it was only one of their number who chose to challenge the two men.

He was a senior officer of the commissariat security cohort, and as he approached them, Akton saw at once that he was both angry at what had happened, and fearful of the consequences.

'You, there!' he shouted, choosing to disregard their obvious badges of rank, 'this is a high alert zone. Leave now, or I will have you placed under arrest.'

Shadwatch fixed him with a cool, searching eye. 'A colonel of security, I see,' he said. 'It is a pity that you will not be holding that rank by the end of this day's watch,' he paused, 'and you will be lucky not to be under arrest yourself.'

The officer stopped and stared as if he had been slapped. He knew that Shadwatch was of Glamtech, but it was only when Shadwatch spoke that he seemed suddenly to recognise him for who he was. His lack of mask should have given it away.

He saluted hurriedly. 'My lord, forgive me. I did not expect to see you down here.'

'Then you need to open your eyes, soldier.' Shadwatch did not alter his tone. 'Glamtech has automatic security clearance to every level of the commissariat.' He raised his voice slightly. 'Or were you not aware of that?'

'Of course, my lord. Of course.' The guard-officer stuttered to his reply. 'My men will escort you to wherever you wish to go.'

'That will not be necessary, colonel,' replied Shadwatch, smiling inwardly to see the man's look of relief that his rank was still his own. 'I can see that you are busy enough at the moment.'

They walked to the edge of the balcony and looked down into the shaft. There was certainly more activity than usual. Akton frowned. 'It looks as though at least part of your stratagem has worked, my lord,' he said under his breath, 'but it is a pity that every door in the complex was opened at the same time.'

Shadwatch nodded and clasped his hands as he leaned on the railing and glanced fleetingly at another capsule descending from the security clearance level and being lowered towards the basement. Had he looked more closely, he might have recognised the huddled figure of a woman crouched in the corner of the capsule, and all at once looking up at him. It was Talessa.

'Yes, I agree,' he said slowly and turned away from the railing, even as Talessa waved desperately in his direction. 'That was not meant to happen, lord Akton, and it will certainly delay things.'

'It was a problem with the DNA signature on your coding system?'

'Almost certainly.' The head of Glamtech frowned. 'It's more difficult and complex than we anticipated. At first we thought that if we could develop a reliable serum or at least an anti-dote to deal with staining, we could use the same chemical imprint to modify or mimic the DNA security process.' He straightened: '"Two birds with one stone", as the old saying goes.'

Akton nodded. 'But it did not quite work out that way.'

'Well, it worked,' Shadwatch shrugged, 'but as often happens, it also came with certain side effects.'

'And one of these side effects has de-stabilised the entire commissariat security system.'

Shadwatch chuckled. 'Yes, it has, has it not? A charming little scene of chaos wouldn't you agree?' He hesitated. 'This is without doubt something to put into my back pocket for later, but at the moment it is, I admit, a little inconvenient.'

Akton thought for a while. 'How many of the prisoners do you think might have escaped to Portus-Portus?'

'That's what we are about to find out, my friend.' Shadwatch turned and looked towards where the guard-officer was still issuing instructions as men hurried about him. 'Some will have certainly got away by now,' he replied. 'There was a very useful delay between the shifting of prison capsules to the transport bay, and the sudden unlocking and override of the main security systems. If my initial calculations are correct, about fifty capsules out of two hundred would have been given full security clearance before the first alarms went off on the dispatch levels.'

'And the others?'

Again, Shadwatch shrugged. 'Who knows? I see that the capsules are still rising and falling between the upper and lower levels, and no one seems inclined or able to try and stop them.' He gazed at a capsule as it slowly drifted by with its prisoner still inside. 'Let's get down to the transport bay now.'

Several minutes later they stepped out of a swift-lift and found themselves in the transport bay for Portus-Portus. It was strangely quiet. There were officials about, some armed, but they seemed untroubled or alarmed by the events taking place above their heads.

'Those officials are my people,' said Shadwatch. 'It's good to see they have not yet been disturbed by commissariat security.'

A young woman in a Glamtech uniform and carrying a pulse gun came up to Shadwatch and saluted:

'All quiet here, sir,' she said. ''We have managed to get a good number of the prisoners away already. Most came via the capsules, others came down the main stairs. They said the cell doors and security doors had suddenly opened.'

'How many?' asked Shadwatch.

'In total, sir? I'm not entirely sure, but the captain over there said at least a hundred prisoners had made it through to Portus-Portus.'

'Good.' Shadwatch turned to Akton. 'I guess you are concerned for your daughter.'

Akton nodded. 'Is there any way of finding out at this stage?'

The young woman bowed to Akton. 'I will check, my lord chancellor. What is your daughter's name?'

'Talessa,' he replied, and smiled. 'I would be obliged to you, soldier,' he said.

With a salute the young woman turned and made her way towards the captain.

'Everything seems under control down here,' said Shadwatch, 'but there's none of us can stay in this place much longer. Once the commissariat guards drop to what's going on, they'll be here in a flash,' he smiled, 'and there will be the very devil to pay.'

Akton was watching the captain: he listened to the young woman, nodded in their direction and began to check the paperwork on his clipboard.

There was a pause. 'Could we not wait for just a couple of minutes?' Akton asked Shadwatch, but even as he asked, he saw the captain frown, look up from his clipboard and give a shake of his head.

'No need,' Talessa's father said quietly. 'My daughter is not on the list. Let's be gone.'

'I am sorry,' muttered Shadwatch. 'We could wait if you wish.'

Akton shook his head. 'That won't be necessary. If Talessa is not here by now, she will have taken another route. I know her well: she thinks clearly, makes swift decisions and then acts. Always.'

'Then fortune be with her,' said Shadwatch. 'Wait here while I tell the captain to shut down this part of the operation. I think it's best if you and I now return to the Glamtech laboratory and the Gene Pool. I want to see how many batches of the serum my people have managed to prepare. Then we need to talk about distribution.'

The chancellor of Serenity hesitated. How much deeper would he sink into this conspiracy? The sabotage of the commissariat, and this plot to release a supposed serum to combat the stain: how much more would this young Glamtech rebel require of him before he, Akton, a lord of Court 2, cried enough?

Slowly he lifted his head. 'I am with you,' he said. 'Lead, and I will follow.'

Neither man was wearing a mask. They both held each other's gaze for just a moment. Then Shadwatch inclined his head. 'My lord,' he muttered, turned and went towards the captain, with Teevey at his heels.

UNCERTAIN ALLIANCE

It was Barvarik who saw them first. Both men were coming up an emergency staircase from a lower level, and they were clearly in a hurry. He met them at the top of the stairs.

'My lords,' he said, and held up his hand with the salute of a Household Guards officer.

They both stopped. 'Captain Barvarik,' said Shadwatch. 'What are you doing here? Were you not seconded to the border defence force?'

Barvarik explained.

Shadwatch shrugged. 'But here? Surely your place is on the walls. The outlanders are at the gates.'

'Captain Barvarik has come for my daughter,' interrupted Akton. 'Is that not so, captain?'

Barvarik nodded. 'I thought to come to the prison, though I had no idea how I might set her free.'

'You would break the law?' asked Shadwatch, his voice level.

'It is a law which is broken already,' replied Bavarik, glancing around. 'I see no justice in that law.' He looked at Akton. 'Do you not agree, my lord?'

Akton sighed. 'The law is the law,' he said quietly, 'but it was made for the people, was it not? And the people were not made for the law.' He hesitated. 'We are poisoned from within, and attacked from without, but when we look to our king, all he offers us is meaningless sacrifice.'

'Just so,' said Shadwatch, 'but we cannot stand here debating the finer points of our treason.' He looked at Barvarik. 'Captain,' he said, 'Many of the prisoners were released this morning, and shortly afterwards there was a major security breach.'

'So Talessa is set free?'

Shadwatch grunted. 'She is missing. That is all we know.'

'Then I must look for her,' said Barvarik as he turned away.

But Akton took him by the shoulder. 'No,' he said quietly. 'If you are caught by commissariat security wandering around down here, you will be hung for desertion. Every soldier of the household guards is posted to the defence of the walls.'

'But I have a pass.'

Akton shook his head. 'I doubt if you would get a chance to show it. Those commies as folks call them, are on edge and afraid for their own skins. They smell defeat in the smoke from the city gates, and this prison break has made things so much worse.'

Barvarik drew his sword. 'I will take them on as they come. If they lay a hand on me . . .'

Again Akton shook his head. 'Barvarik, you are as a son to me, and Talessa is more dear to me than life itself, but if you go off on your own, you won't last five minutes. They'll cut you down as soon as they look at you.'

'That's right,' Shadwatch broke in. He looked along the corridor. 'We need to leave. We need to leave now!'

There was a brief pause, and then the sound of shouting from somewhere along the corridor, and a sudden clash of steel.

'All right,' said Barvarik, 'I am with you.'

With Akton at his side, he followed Shadwatch who led them across the open landing towards a high tiled wall, faced at intervals with polished metal plates. There seemed to be no way out, and Barvarik was about to say something when Shadwatch suddenly snapped his fingers. The rivets on one of the metal plates flashed twice, and a section of the wall slid open, revealing a dimly lit passage.

'Quick!' said Shadwatch. 'There is not much time.'

Moments later they found themselves inside and the door slid shut behind them.

'That was neat,' muttered Akton.

Shadwatch smiled. 'A small benefit,' he replied. 'As a Glamtech official I was ordered to oversee the commissariat security systems.' He looked around for his Glambot. 'Those commies may be as cunning as street dogs and twice as ruthless, but they haven't got half a brain between them when it comes to understanding the systems we installed for their security network.' He pointed into the gloom. 'We follow this passage for a little while and then up an airlift I have had installed.'

'It leads to the outside?' asked Barvarik.

'No, my friend. It leads to one of Glamtech's research laboratories.'

'But Talessa!'

'Your lady will have gone to ground somewhere, I'm sure of it. Our best chance of surviving ourselves and finding her as well, is to go this way.'

'To the laboratory?'

'Just so. Come on!'

CHAPTER #11
THE STORMING OF THE CITY

Anna Seka was standing alongside Leviss watching the main army of the outlands as it fought to secure the approaches to the gates of Serenity.

Much of their view was obscured by smoke and flame, but they could see the bright pulses of light through the thick clouds as the pulse-towers fired volley after volley against the gates and walls. They could also make out the great orange balls of shimmering fire when the bombard and ballista batteries of Serenity directed their missiles against the oncoming phalanxes of stainer troops, and the war engines they were dragging forward.

At least one of the gate towers had been badly damaged, and another was on fire, but that had not stopped the defenders from crowding the ramparts and pouring fire down on the heads of the enemy. The hot plate was partially weakened by the heaps of rubble strewn across it, but where it was active it forced the attackers to crowd together as they advanced against the walls. This made them an easy target for the snipers and sharp shooters of the Serenity defence forces.

'Have you ever seen the like of it?' said Leviss, raising his voice above the roar of battle.

Anna-Seka nodded and brushed her face, but said nothing. Leviss looked at her. 'I am sorry,' he said quietly. 'Of course, it is your home.' He paused. 'At least you are safe here.'

'I should be in there,' Anna replied. 'With my people.'

It was Leviss's turn not to reply. He glanced to the right to where his father, Nike and several of the others had taken up a forward observation post. They had been signalling information as best they could to the control-division just behind the outlander forces, and had received regular replies, but it was still difficult to tell how well the battle was going.

'I don't think we'll be going anywhere in a hurry,' said Leviss after a while. 'That last reply from Control confirmed that we hold our position.'

Anna looked at Leviss and couldn't help but smile. 'You sound like a soldier,' she said.

Leviss shrugged. 'I pick it up as I go along,' he said. 'My father always used to say, try and sound as if you know what you're doing, even if you've got no idea at all.'

They both laughed for just a moment, and then Anna frowned.

'Many people will die today,' she said. 'It all seems so pointless.'

A bombard roared from somewhere behind the ramparts of the city and almost instantly a flaming missile appeared, soaring over the walls, climbing through the ash-black smoke and then curving slowly over to burst in a cascade of fiery shrapnel above the heads of a stainer attack-battalion. Men fell. Others staggered on. A few ran for cover.

Even as Anna and Leviss watched the dust settle over the devastated battalion, the outlander batteries replied. It seemed as if every pulse-tower on every wagon that was still in action fired, along with every ballista that carried solid shot and explosive. A curtain of projectiles hissed through the air and fell against the walls and gates.

The effect was immediate.

As masonry shattered, steel beams, suddenly glowing red hot, were wrenched clear of their mountings and flung skywards. Whole sections of rampart caved in and crashed into the outer ditch, carrying defenders with them. A single tower overlooking the main gates suddenly exploded as its stores of ammunition caught fire, and huge chunks of concrete reared up, and then plunged down into the rubble-filled ditch.

Almost without thinking, Leviss took Anna's hand. 'We make war against ourselves,' he said, his voice dry and cracked. 'Are we not cousins, after all? Are we not the same people: yes, brothers and sisters under our stains and beneath our masks?'

Anna stared at him. There was a deep strength in what he had just said, and yet she could scarcely understand it. 'But Serenity,' she said. 'If only you knew what a wonderful place it is.'

'As wonderful as the hills and valleys of our home?' he asked, and flinched as another explosion lit the sky, and a black shower of shattered and scorched stonework fell across the distant ramparts.

Anna did not reply. Her eyes were fixed on the gates. All but the roofs and upper battlements of the top towers were obscured by smoke, but on one rooftop a banner still flew. It was the banner of her regiment of scouts: lord Hartley's regiment. Somewhere in that smoke and flame, her friends were now fighting and dying. They would not surrender. She knew that. They had taken an oath, all of them, to defend the city with their own lives and not to count the cost.

It was as if Leviss guessed her thoughts. 'There is nothing you can do,' he said. 'Fortune has brought you here.'

'Has it?' Anna did not take her eyes off the banner.

Leviss shrugged. 'We have your promise, your parole. You gave it to the captain did you not? You will not attempt to escape as long as you are in our care.'

With the slightest of nods, Anna turned away. 'You are right,' she said. 'I have given my word, but I do not think I would have given it so willingly, if I thought I would have to watch this.'

The last of what she said was almost lost in the deep whooshing sound of the stainer catapults and several large boulders hurtled towards the city. But even as they crashed against the walls a battery of Serenity bombards replied. For one mad moment the sky above both defenders and attackers was filled with whirling projectiles and flaming missiles. Some even collided, disintegrating in flashes of dazzling brightness, but most continued on their path, plunging against their targets and adding to the destruction on both sides.

Bepsi-Loca appeared. 'We've just received word of a general advance,' he shouted. 'If you see a green flag, it means we shift our position and approach the walls. If the flag is red, we hold the line.'

'It will be good to move,' said Leviss. 'We have been here long enough.'

Leviss's uncle smiled sadly. 'Try telling that to your sister over there. She has seen enough death for one day, and sees no reason to add to it.'

Leviss shrugged. 'We came to fight, didn't we? Then that's what we should be doing.'

Bepsi-Loca frowned. 'We are not here to fight,' he replied. 'We are here to survive. That's why I led you to this place.' He pointed towards the walls, almost lost in the smoke. 'Anna will tell you that the people we fight are not so different to us.'

'I know it, uncle.' Leviss nodded. 'Did I not just say, Anna?'

Anna nodded. 'Then why do you want to fight?'

Leviss looked at the strangely beautiful woman in front of him, smiled, and then glanced at his father. 'How can I go home knowing that at the time of greatest danger, I was nowhere to be seen?' He hung his head. 'That I hid.'

Bepsi-Loca shook his head. 'You're a young fool. Listen to me, you're not hiding, you're staying out of trouble. Staying out of that madness over there.' He paused. 'And what's more, if you stay here you're just giving yourself half a chance to get home safely.' He took his crossbow from his belt strap, reached for a bolt and slid it into the arming channel. 'Besides, it's almost certain we'll be called to the advance sooner or later, then we'll have to go whether we like it or not.'

He slapped his nephew on the shoulder. 'Look after Anna. Keep her safe, and there's an even chance you'll both come through this alive.'

Someone called out. They all looked. It was Nike and she was waving them across.

'She's just got the signal,' muttered Bepsi-Loca. 'Come on!'

TO THE TOWER

Marlin and Chesterman were making their way along a side street that ran close to the inner security wall of Lower Town. They were inside the city. Outside, beyond the gates and towers, the battle still raged, but they had entered the city by themselves, slipping through an unmanned sally-port and passing unseen into Lower Town.

Marlin was impressed. Not long ago, agents of Chesterman operating within the city, had signalled to the warlord from a high observation tower on the inner security wall. Chesterman had replied, then set off with Marlin, leaving instructions to his senior staff officers about how and when the main gates might be captured.

They had skirted the right flank of the stainer army, then approached a section of the outer wall almost lost in the shadow of a defence tower which had as yet not been fired on. Hiding in some scrub and thorn bushes about five hundred paces from the central advance of the outlanders, Chesterman had outlined his plan to Marlin:

'As you can see,' he said, 'we cannot get near to the wall or gates with our infantry until we have dealt with the hot-plate. My people on the inside should be attending to it now, as well as finding us a safe entry point into the city.

Marlin stared at the structure known as the hot-plate. It was a well known component of Serenity's defence, and there were few who dared to put it to the test. Made of super-strengthened steel, it extended about ten metres from the base of the outer wall. It was heated, not permanently but whenever hostile forces approached. The temperatures achieved by the hot-plate were so high that anyone unprotected coming within a metre of its surface would be instantly killed. To touch its surface was to be instantly vaporized. The means to produce such heat were a closely guarded Glamtech secret, and those entrusted with its operation were drawn from the highest levels of the SSS, and Commissariat security.

'Your people must be remarkable agents,' said Marlin to Chesterman as they waited. 'How did they manage to penetrate the ministry of security and defence?'

Chesterman smiled. 'By being on the inside already,' he replied. 'At least three of them have been embedded in high security units for the past five years. All of them are loyal citizens with impeccable service records.'

A short time later, a figure dressed in the uniform of the commissariat appeared on the walls. She raised her hand once, paused and then turned away.

'That's our signal!' Chesterman had said, getting to his feet and running towards the hot-plate. Marlin had followed, keeping a couple of paces behind in case the plate was still live.

He need not have worried. Once the plate was turned off, heat loss was unseen but remarkably rapid. Chesterman hit the plate at full stride and sprinted towards the wall. Almost immediately a sally-port door opened directly in front of him, and he disappeared inside with Marlin hard on his heels.

The door had shut behind them, the interior lights had come on automatically, and they found themselves in a deserted attack-chamber.

And so, alone they had entered the city.

'Perfect,' muttered Chesterman as they emerged into the open and entered a small market square. Two armed guards were coming towards them.

'More of your people, I hope,' replied Marlin, reaching for his sword.

'Of course,' smiled Chesterman, 'and if I am right they will have the daily password to enter Upper Town.'

Marlin shook his head. 'But the security barriers are all palm-protected,' he said. 'The password will not be sufficient.'

Again Chesterman smiled. 'All taken care of,' he said. 'I am most fortunate to have a contact in Glamtech.'

It was almost as Chesterman had predicted. Escorted by the two guards they passed unchallenged through the streets of Lower Town, which were themselves almost deserted apart from one or two folk hurrying to the civic shelters, or evacuation points, and the occasional detachments of infantry marching at the double-quick to the walls.

But when they came to the gates of Upper Town, they immediately saw a stronger military presence. Among the security personnel were household guards, each carrying a Glamtech side-arm, as well as the usual fighting-sword.

Chesterman swore under his breath.

'A problem?' asked Marlin.

'Could be,' replied Chesterman, adjusting his helmet. 'I only expected to see my men on the gates, but at least three of those guards are unknown to me.'

'We could try the porter-gate,' suggested Marlin. 'It's further round, but as I remember only lightly guarded. There's enough of us to bluff our way though, I'm sure of it.'

Chesterman shook his head. 'We can't leave off now. See, we've been noticed already. That captain there, he's pointing us out. If we try to move away now, they will come after us, for sure.' He swore again. 'There's nothing for it. We will have to take them ourselves, and leave not a one alive.'

Marlin stared, first at the guards by the gate and then at Chesterman. 'But they are my people,' he said.

Chesterman grunted. 'So what of that?' he said. 'You have been willing enough to kill your own people outside the city. What is different now?'

Both men had been walking slowly towards the gates, but Marlin now stopped.

'That was in battle,' he said. 'Eye to eye and man to man. This . . .' he gestured towards the gates. 'This is slaughter. I am the brother of a king, and a king of Serenity, too. I am not born to the likes of this.'

'Hah!' Chesterman put his hand on the hilt of his sword. 'Then, we are dead men,' he said. 'Come, let us at least die with some scrap of honour, and not be hung in a cage from the walls by that brother of yours.'

But even as he spoke, they both noticed two of the security guards leave the gates and come hurrying towards them, their sidearms raised in salute. As they came up to Chesterman, they lowered their weapons.

'It is all right, sir,' one of the guards said, and he gave a sign to Chesterman that Marlin took to be a recognition signal. 'We have just explained to the captain that you are here on a mission from the borders, and that the king is expecting you.' He hesitated. 'We are ordered to escort you, as far as we are able, to the king.' He winked. 'The necessary papers were prepared as you instructed. They bear the stamp of the SSS.'

Chesterman nodded. 'You have done well. I assume that you have not revealed anything to that captain.'

The guard shook his head. 'He asked for your name of course, my lord, and noted that you had a stainer warlord's helmet, but I told him that you were under a regimental battle-oath, and could neither remove your helmet nor reveal your name until the stainer army had been defeated.'

Chesterman smiled. 'That's quick thinking, soldier. I am in your debt. Take us to the captain.'

With the guards leading the way, they came up to the gates.

The captain saluted them. They saw at once that he was a veteran: tall, bearded, and with several campaign flashes on his leather tunic. His deep, dark eyes took them in at a glance, and Marlin noticed that this officer had already noticed the mud on their boots, and their non-regulation tunics. He had also picked up that they carried expensive side-arms. The captain smiled.

'I would ask what regiment you are from, but I do not expect an answer,' he said, his voice measured and level.

Chesterman saluted and snapped to attention. 'We are both from a regiment of the imperial border force,' he said, his voice obscured by the helmet-speaker. 'We can reveal no more than that, until our mission is done.' He paused. 'But I can tell you that we both bear a rank equal to yours.'

The captain stared at Chesterman. For a moment Marlin thought he was going to deny them a security pass, and he tightened the grip on his own sword. But the moment passed, the captain sucked his teeth, frowned and then turned to one of his men. 'Ho there, Cedric, you are duty corporal today. Come here and be quick about it. You are to escort these gentlemen into Upper Town, and from there to the imperial precinct and the entrance court 2. No further, understand? I will give you the passwords for the day.' He paused and watched as both Chesterman and Marlin completed the security checks, and successfully passed through the palm-print machine. Then he called another man forward.

'Aleph!'

'Sir!'

'You are to go with these officers and corporal Cedric. Make sure that they reach the imperial precinct in one piece, escort them into the inner court and ask at the Commissariat office for the whereabouts of the king.'

The captain caught Marlin's puzzled look and smiled. 'Security has tightened around here these past days,' he said. 'Aleph is the company ensign. Only he of all the men under my command can escort visitors or emissaries into the royal apartments and the audience chamber of the king. Is that not so, Aleph?'

The soldier bowed, but did not reply. Then he gestured to Chesterman and Marlin before leading them through the open gates and into the broad open square that stood at the head of the great avenue.

Marlin took a deep breath. How many years had it been since he had last seen this magnificent sight? And yet all was strangely quiet, if also strangely familiar. He was aware of the distant roar of battle behind him, as the storm-battalions of the stainer army threw themselves against the main gates, but here, in Upper Town, all was weirdly peaceful.

'Where is everyone?' he asked.

One of the guards gave a short laugh. 'The household regiments are either defending the palace or fighting on the walls,' he replied. 'The wealthy folk and the families of the nobles have retreated to their own houses and gardens. They have bolted and barred their doors, armed their servants and set a watch at their windows and balconies.' He shrugged as they walked. 'Apart from the odd commissariat street patrol, we are alone.'

The two soldiers, the corporal Cedric and the ensign Aleph, were soon walking further ahead, talking quietly. Only occasionally did they glance back over their shoulders to check on the progress of Chesterman and Marlin .

The imperial precinct and the palace loomed ahead of them. Its curving buttresses and polished walls reached skywards, and the vast central column that held the royal apartments seemed impossibly high and impregnable. Marlin knew that the last of the security checks and perhaps the greatest challenge would be at the base of the central column which guarded the lift shaft and direct access to the uppermost section of the palace. He took another deep breath. How casually in years past he had approached this edifice, confident that everyone knew the king's brother, and would step aside at first recognition. But now he had to hide himself beneath his close fitting helmet and behind his half-mask. If Chesterman's extraordinary penetration of the SSS security systems failed this last test, then he above all would suffer the ignominy of arrest and almost certain execution.

'Courage, my friend,' whispered Chesterman. 'We have come this far, and there is little that can stop us now.'

A PARTING
OF THE WAYS

Akton gazed at the rows of test tubes, specimen jars, computech-screens, mixing jars and other paraphernalia of the Glamtech laboratory. Shadwatch, with Barvarik at his side was talking to him, but he scarcely heard him: the young head of Glamtech was saying something about the Gene Pool and the serum, and a possible plan, but Akton's mind was elsewhere: the chancellor was thinking about his daughter and his step-daughter, as well as his wife and the rest of his family. He was also thinking about the defence of the city: of the peril at the gates, of the mysterious poisonings, the palace conspiracies, the madness of the king and the desperate efforts of a few officials to save any innocent citizens of Serenity.

'My lord!'

Akton looked up. Shadwatch was staring at him. He stumbled to a reply:

'My lord Shadwatch. Forgive me, my mind was elsewhere.'

The young Glamtech prince smiled. 'I understand,' he said. 'You have seen and heard much this day, and precious little of it is good news.' He paused. 'I was just explaining to you and Barvarik that I believe we are close to a serum to finish once and for all this curse of staining.'

'Close, my lord?'

Shadwatch nodded. 'Yes, close, but not yet close enough. I will need at least two more days and a healthy dose of luck if we are to achieve the result I am looking for.'

Akton frowned and slowly nodded. 'My lord,' he said carefully, 'I must leave you now.'

'Your family?'

Akton's eyes widened slightly. Shadwatch's ability to read people never ceased to surprise him. 'Yes, my lord. Precisely. I must return to my family home, and see who waits there.' He hesitated. 'If there is anyone.'

Shadwatch shrugged. 'I understand. Of course, you must go. The evacuation proceeds at pace even as we speak, while many other folks are fleeing to the shelters, or bolting their doors. Your family is important.'

'Hah!' Akton tried to smile. 'There is not a family in this city which is not important to me, but I admit none are as important as the one that bears my name.' He glanced at Barvarik and then turned again to

Shadwatch:

'And what of your family, my lord?'

Shadwatch spread his hands. 'This is my family,' he replied. 'All you see here, within these walls: this is my family, my first love. I will stay here in the laboratory, and I will stay here as long as it takes to prepare the final adjustments to the Gene Pool solution and the serum.' He paused. 'You of course are free to go, and good fortune speed you.'

Akton had reached the door, and was about to open it, when he turned:

'Barvarik,' he said. 'What of you?'

The young warrior inclined his head. 'My lord, I will follow soon. There is still much that I must do, but first I will stay awhile with my lord Shadwatch.'

'You have an interest, perhaps in this plan?'

Barvarik shook his head. 'It is not an interest, my lord Akton, but a necessity.'

The chancellor nodded. 'I understand,' he said quietly. 'But promise me this, if you find Talessa . . .'

'I will send word, my lord, as I trust you will also send the same to me.'

Barvarik raised his hand in salute. Akton bowed, turned and was gone.

At the same time, almost as if he was waiting for Akton to leave, Teevey rose uncertainly with is screen flickering from between a stand of laboratory jars and a printing desk. He rose to the muffled sound of 'Raiders of the Lost Ark.'

Neither Barvarik nor Shadwatch seemed to notice or even hear him.

'All right, then,' said Shadwatch briskly. 'We do not have much time. See on that bench over there? Yes? Good. That is where I will be working. All is prepared. All is ready, but I must now bring it together for a final testing. Up to now it has been guesswork with trial and error.' He sighed. 'But now I am ready to put that guesswork into action.'

'How can I help?'

Shadwatch smiled. 'With the experiment? You cannot, my friend, but nevertheless you can be of great assistance.'

Barvarik frowned. 'I do not understand.'

Moving across to the bench, Shadwatch pushed some papers to one side, leaned forward and picked up a test tube. He studied it. 'It is simple. You will keep me alive for as long as it takes me to do what must be done.'

Barvarik looked around. 'We are expecting trouble?'

'Of course. There are many beyond that door who wish to see me dead, and Glamtech broken.' He paused. 'I have enemies.'

Barvarik drew his sword and stepped towards the door. 'Then they will have to come through me first,' he said.

Shadwatch chuckled, held the test tube up to the light and shook it gently. 'I was hoping you might say that.'

The laboratory clock struck the hour, and both men glanced at it. 'Let's be busy,' said Shadwatch.

THE BALCONY

The king rested his hands on the balcony rail, and looked directly down through the reinforced glass floor beneath his feet so that he could see the city far below. He saw skeins of thick, black smoke rising up from the outer walls, and drifting over the enclosure walls of Lower Town. Flames flickered through the distant gloom, and the towers of the main gates were only just visible. The sounds of battle rolled across the ramparts and into the deserted streets. Well, those streets far below him were almost deserted. He tapped the tip of his boot twice and the view zoomed. He looked more closely. There were groups of soldiers hurrying back and forth, and there, close by the college of scouts, a bombard was being wheeled into position.

He grunted. 'They fight,' he muttered. 'That is good.'

No long before he had been in the pleasure gardens of the royal quarter, a place so cut off from the rest of the city, that there were even those who served in the palace itself who had never seen beyond the high, bronze-faced doors of the gardens. It was peaceful in those gardens. The king liked it, and increasingly stayed within its spacious precinct. He had had special apartments built into the walls which surrounded the pools and flower beds of that precinct. A law passed by the high council forbade anyone but members of the royal family and their servants from entering the innermost courts of the royal gardens. It was a law that was scarcely needed. Hardly anyone, even in the courts of Upper Town, had heard of the royal gardens, and fewer still knew the whereabouts of the royal apartments. They probably were aware of the great elevator in the heart of the imperial sector, but had no idea what lay beyond its upper platform.

And yet, on this day, the king had left this sanctuary, and made his way to the viewing balcony where he now stood. He had thought to ease his mind by coming to the balcony with its glass floor. After all it was the duty of a king to understand how his kingdom fared. It was the king's father who had taught him this, and it was the memory of his father's ice cool gaze and humourless voice that drove him to be where he at now last stood.

Well, he decided, he would not stay long. He had already seen enough, and he felt he could easily guess the rest. When he returned to the gardens, he promised himself that he would take a short stroll along the winding path to the flower-conservatory. He had not been there for at least three days. It was time to see it again. The flowers eased his mind.

Someone unexpectedly appeared at his side. He turned. It was his secretary, and with him Larissa, the head of Litra.

'My lady,' he said quietly. 'What brings you here?'

'My lord, you sent for me.'

'I did? Why yes, I forget.' He smiled. 'Tell me why I sent for you.'

'I have news, my lord. From the gates, from the civic shelters and from Portus-Portus itself.'

'Good news, I hope. I cannot abide bad news on such a day as this. Tell me good news.'

The lady Larissa held out a single sheet of paper. It had the crest of the Commissariat on it. 'From the lady Follicia,' she said carefully.

'Read it to me,' said the king, turning away and looking down at the city once more.

Pursing her lips, Larissa gave a slight shake of the head and began to read:

'My lord king, the security of the Commissariat has been compromised for a short period of time. Some prisoners escaped. Most were recaptured. However, we believe that the lapse in security was not an accident, and that elements of hostile forces within the city are aiding their escape.'

'Glamtech!' hissed the king.

'We are not sure my lord, but the report also says that an evacuation of the city has begun in certain quarters, and many citizens have already made their way to Portus-Portus.'

The king gripped the balcony until his knuckles whitened. 'Who ordered the evacuation?'

For a time, the lady Larissa did not answer. She studied the paper, and then lifted her head. 'It was your signature and seal on the evacuation order, my king.'

'The devil it was!' the king shouted, so that the guards standing at the far end of the balcony started and took a step forward. 'I gave no such order! The only order I gave was for the immediate execution of all prisoners if the stainer army should cross our walls.'

'Then someone sanctioned the order on your behalf, your majesty.'

'Glamtech! Shadwatch!' The king clenched his teeth. 'I'll have his head! And that of Akton too! Just see if I don't! Vipers! Traitors!'

'My lord king, we cannot be sure. But there is more news. It concerns Arx.'

The king went pale. 'It has not fallen?'

Larissa shook her head. 'No, my lord. Arx still stands, and bravely too.'

'I knew it!' The king clapped his hands together. 'The people of Arx have always been loyal, and made of better stuff than the cringing malcontents I have gathered around myself in this city.' He took a pace to his right, turned and came back and looked down towards the gates. 'Serenity is a city of poisoners, plotters and scoundrels. If Arx were here, this would not have happened. If Arx were here not one stainer would have dared to approach our gates.'

The lady Larissa gave a slight cough. 'My lord, Arx has stood because marines from the fleet at Portus-Portus made a successful landing west of Arx and marched to its aid. When the outlanders heard of their coming, they withdrew their forces.'

'Hah! You believe that?'

'It is in the document my lord.'

'A commissariat document.'

'Just so, my lord, and from the lady Follicia.'

For a moment the king stared. 'It is just like the Commissariat to try and claim credit for a victory hundreds of miles from here. Was it not the Commissariat that ordered the marines to sail up the coast?'

Larissa frowned. Her mask glowed faintly. 'My lord, was it not yourself who gave the order for the fleet to sail from Portus-Portus? And now . . .'

'Enough! Enough!' The king waved his hand angrily. 'Arx stands because it is loyal and brave. That is all. Do you understand? That is all.'

When Larissa did not answer, the king took a step towards her. 'Do you understand?' he repeated.

The head of Litra bowed. 'My lord king, I understand perfectly.'

'Well, then,' the king held out his hand. 'Give me the document, woman! I will read it for myself.'

Reaching forward, he snatched it from Larissa's hand, and began to study it. For a long time he said nothing, his head bent and his brow furrowed. At last he straightened. 'This is an important document,' he said slowly. 'It shows me the true extent of the treachery in this idle and corrupt city: prison breaks, evacuations, lapses in security, false rumours, stories of defeatism and . . .' he stabbed at the paper with his finger, 'still the poisonings go on, and no arrests.' He looked up. 'No arrests! Is that not the mark of a conspiracy, a co-ordinated conspiracy?'

'My lord, the Commissariat and the SSS are patrolling constantly, and interviewing suspects, even while the fighting continues at the gates.'

'And with what result, my lady? With what result? Tell me!'

Again Larissa's mask glowed. 'None, my lord king,' she whispered, 'none as yet.'

'Pah!' The king tore the document and threw it down. 'Useless! Useless!'

Larissa stepped back and bowed again. 'If my lord allows,' she said quietly, 'I will return to my duties.'

'What?' The king now looked out over the ocean. 'Yes, go! Go! And if you come across the head of Commissariat wherever she may be hiding, send her to me at once.'

'My lord.' The lady Larissa turned and headed towards the balcony door.

'Wait!'

She turned. 'There is something else?'

'There is! I will send one of my guards with you. On your way to Litra, you are to go via the personnel section of Security. Internal personnel. Understood?'

'My lord.'

'Ask there for the whereabouts of lord Shadwatch and my chancellor. The main security scanners should be sufficient to pick them up. I want a full squad, an armed escort, to find them and bring them directly to the gates of the royal precinct.'

'And should I return with them, my lord king?'

The king smiled. 'Only if you no longer value your safety,' he said. 'They will not come without a fight. They are both outlander at heart. No, get you gone! Return to Litra. Do what you must do, and do it well.' He paused. 'For your king, and your king alone.'

Again, Larissa's mask glowed. 'As you speak, so I obey,' she replied, and left, with the guard close by her.

Snapping his fingers, the king spoke to his secretary. 'Resend my communiqué to the commander of the main gates,' he said.

'And to which particular communiqué do you refer?' answered the secretary, glancing down at his dispatch-pad.

The king ground his teeth. How was it that this simpleton from Lower Town whom he had raised to the level of imperial secretary, saw fit to speak to his king without giving due title or even the slightest hint of respect? But he said nothing. He liked the man for his sheer nerve, as well as his skill with letters. And besides, he found his veiled insolence even slightly amusing.

'The communiqué concerning the execution of all prisoners if the stainer army crosses our walls,' said the king.

The secretary gave the hint of a sigh. 'That communiqué to which you refer, my lord, has been sent three times, along with the reminder that its contents should also be signalled to the outlander army as well.'

'And you have received a reply?'

'Not as yet, my lord.' The secretary raised his dispatch pad and studied it. 'However, I can confirm that it has been received and acknowledged by the commander's regimental headquarters.'

'But without confirmation and reply from the commander himself?'

The secretary nodded. 'So it would seem.'

There was a low rumble from across the city, and the balcony gave a slight tremor. Both men looked in time to see a plume of smoke and fire rise up from just beyond the gates.

'Ahah!' the king grunted. 'It seems as if one of our war engines has scored a direct hit.'

'One war engine does not make a battle, sire, and one lucky shot hardly makes a difference.'

The king glared. 'Well, it made a difference to more than a few of those fellows down there,' he replied. He slapped his chest. 'And it has made a difference to me. I shall declare that lucky shot as you call it, a taste of better news to come, and retire to my apartments.'

The secretary did not reply, but sighed again, typed something on his dispatch-pad, and straightened, returning to the formal pose of an imperial official: shoulders back, head erect and eyes fixed on nothing in particular.

With a shrug, the king drew his cloak across his shoulders and left.

The secretary watched him leave. 'There goes our kingdom,' he muttered. 'Gone to ruin, and led by a fool who is little more than a hermit.' He glanced around quickly to make sure that no one had heard him. The guards remained at their posts, motionless, staring along the length of the balcony. They had not followed the king. He would be escorted by other guards of the household regiment. Only when he reached the doors of the royal precinct and gardens would they leave him. Everything would be done perfectly, everything would be completed with a snap-salute and a presentation of arms. All according to tradition and custom, and all in the same old style. And not a hint of chaos and impending disaster.

The secretary shook his head wearily. Up here in the palace, almost lost in the clouds, it was as if nothing had changed, and nothing was happening. There was no sense that a vast army of outlanders was at the very gates, shaking the streets of the city and covering the rooftops of Lower Town with smoke and ash and fire. And more than this, there was no clue, here in the heart of the palace, that every corridor and every reception area of Upper Town was whispering of conspiracy and yet another random poisoning. Yes, there was no doubting that they were ruled by a hermit-king.

He shook his head again. 'Madness,' he whispered. 'Nothing but madness.'

THE GATES

Meanwhile the battle for the gates and towers of the outer walls raged on. The catapults, ballistas and pulse-towers of the stainer army fired salvo after salvo against the defenders who crowded the ramparts and crouched in trenches and earthworks behind the main wall. One of the towers was so badly damaged, it could only be defended on two sides, and its facing casements were themselves so battered that they threatened to topple inwards at any point. The other tower was largely intact, but its roof had been set on fire, and the regiment that held it was in danger of being overwhelmed by the flames.

Three of Serenity's largest bombards had been put out of action by direct hits, but there were still at least half a dozen smaller batteries that had survived the storm of artillery fire, and were launching volley after volley against the attackers. Their crews, all members of the city militia, loaded, laid and fired their projectiles without pause and without complaint. They were mostly stripped to the waist, and barefoot but still they sweated freely in the intense heat, and were only sustained by teams of waterboys who ran between the batteries with buckets of water hung from yokes across their shoulders.

The hot plate which had gone down for a short while, was back on line and making short work of any attacking infantry or engineers that strayed too close to its glowing surface.

Squadrons of archers and crossbowmen from every Lower Town regiment, lined the ramparts, shooting down on the heads of the stainer infantry as best they could through the thick and acrid smoke. But they themselves suffered a heavy cost from the return fire of outlander marksmen, especially those who were armed with the deadly long range pulse-guns and thunder rods.

As yet the household guards and elite regiments of Upper Town had been largely held back in reserve. Some platoons and companies had been released to support the defenders along the broken and blasted ramparts, but the senior commander ordered that the greater part of these regiments be lined along the support wall that ran parallel to the great outer wall. They stood in ordered ranks, shoulder to shoulder, silent, grim-faced, watching the battle ahead of them. It was a battle that they knew would soon come against them and test their mettle. Every man and every woman wore a sword on their left hip, and their sidearms on their right. Officers wore breast-plates of armoured plastic, the other ranks wore mail shirts of tempered steel, and face-guards of plexi-glass, while the regimental banner bearers were dressed in ceremonial battle dress, with a fighting-shield of flexi-plastic strapped to their backs. Every tenth warrior carrier a fire-launcher, and every tenth officer wore the regimental honour-badge on a golden chain around his or her neck.

The roar of battle was so loud and so intense that even orders shouted by officers could scarcely be heard, so commands were given by signal bearers and technicians from the Royal Engineers. There had been no let up for days, and even at night the fire from both sides scarcely slackened. The faces and forms of the defenders were weirdly lit by flickering shadows and bursts of dazzling light, while the smell of brimstone filled the air and mixed with the sickly-sweet stench of blood and burnt flesh. The medics were everywhere, dragging the dead and wounded from the smoking rubble and setting up casualty clearing stations less than a hundred paces from the front line. Many of these medics had fallen during the fighting, but always they were replaced by willing volunteers, who stepped forward, retrieved the white smocks, often bloodied, from the fallen and took their place immediately.

It was all this that drew Akton to the gates. He had hurried home, farewelled his wife and household and then, assured that they were being escorted to the dispatch-station for Portus-Portus, set off through the streets towards the main gates.

His rank gave him swift passage. Almost everyone in Serenity knew the chancellor and knew his mask. And all who saw him on that day, nodded, smiled wearily and stepped aside to let him pass. The soldiers saluted. The citizens bowed. A young girl pressed some flowers into his hand. He scarcely noticed: his mind was set on reaching the walls, his heart was fixed on his family. He knew nothing else beyond duty, a desperate need to get to where the fire was at its hottest, and a desperate sorrow for a great city so lightly deserted by its king.

At last he came upon a senior officer who was bringing up some reserves from the college of scouts. The officer led him to the area commander, standing by a bombard and surrounded by his aides. The commander, his face smeared and blackened by ash and gun powder, looked at Akton, frowned and then nodded.

'At last the palace has seen fit to send someone,' he said, but without a trace of resentment. He wiped his sweat-stained brow. 'It's hot and bloody work,' he added, raising his voice.

Akton grimaced. 'We are holding?' he shouted.

The commander shrugged. 'The hotplate has been restored,' he said, using a sudden pause to explain. 'It was sabotaged earlier on, and that caused us some grief, but our engineers have restored it, and three saboteurs were caught and executed.' He took a deep breath. 'As long as the plate holds, their infantry cannot get at us.'

'And the gates?'

The commander looked weary and drawn beneath the stubble of his unshaven jaw. In common with most of his officers, he had discarded his mask while the fighting continued. He nodded. 'The gates have been damaged, but they are holding. When the hotplate went down, several stainer battalions rushed the gates with rams and blasting equipment. We were hard pressed to drive them off. I lost good men.' He paused. 'Many good men.'

'But you held.'

'Aye, chancellor. We held, but if our engineers had not restored the plate in time, I would not be standing here talking to ye now.' He took a written order from a nearby officer, scanned it, nodded and handed it back. 'Another hour, and they would have broken through,' he went on.

Akton looked at the gates and towers, or what was left of them, and what was visible through the smoke. 'You have done well, commander,' he said. 'Your king is proud of you and your soldiers.'

'Is he now?' the commander muttered as he watched a team of engineers rush forward with beams, sandbags and siege-hammers to strengthen a section of the wall which had been cracked. 'I wish his majesty would come down here and tell us himself.' He paused. 'No disrespect to you, chancellor, no disrespect at all. You are welcome here, but keep your head down. I don't want to be sending news back to the palace that lord Akton got himself killed for nothing.'

Akton smiled. 'I'll stay behind these mantlets and earthworks you have constructed, commander.' He hesitated and then smiled again. 'But because we are in a war zone here, I want you to treat me as no more than one of your junior officers. Give me an order and I will obey it.'

The commander studied the man in front of him. 'Spoken like a young lieutenant, fresh out of officer training school,' he said, 'and ye know, I think ye might even mean it.'

A flaming projectile from a stainer catapult whooshed over their heads and crashed onto the roof of a warehouse a hundred paces behind them. There was the blast of a whistle and shouts as a fire fighting team hurried to put out the flames.

'I do mean it, commander,' said Akton, 'but tell me this: if the hotplate holds I cannot see how the stainers can possibly get in. Anyone who touches it will be vaporized immediately.'

'Anyone, but not anything,' replied the commander. 'I have reports from our observation towers that the stainers are constructing some kind of siege engine behind their front lines.'

'An engine?'

'Aye, an engine that looks like a giant ramp mounted on rollers. Its dimensions approximate the width of the hotplate where it guards the approaches to the gates.'

'And you think it will work?'

The commander wiped his brow yet again. 'We have to assume that it might. We will bring all our firepower to bear on it as they bring their engine up, but I believe they have more than enough covering fire to match us.'

As if to emphasise the commander's words, there was all at once a tearing sound followed by a rumbling roar from beyond the walls as a battery of pulse-rockets was fired from the forward positions of the enemy line. Akton instinctively crouched and then looked up to see blazing contrails of purple and red smoke soar above him. The rockets just cleared the topmost ramparts, swept several defenders away, and then plunged onto the houses of Lower Town with a series of deafening explosions.

The commander put out a hand to steady Akton, and then turned and stared at the whirling cloud of dust and debris that marked the site of the impact.

'They are lifting their range,' he said grimly. 'That is not war; that is murder.'

Akton nodded. 'Then it is well that an evacuation is already underway. Those who have not gone to the civic shelters are now being transported to the docks at Portus-Portus.'

The commander looked surprised. 'At this very moment? If they are caught in the open, it will be a slaughter.'

'We are doing what we can, commander. Our best people from Litra and the interior ministry have been assigned to the task.'

There was yet another roar as the artillery from Serenity fired a counter-salvo. The commander waited for the echoes to subside. The acrid smell of sulphur filled the air. 'I did not expect the king to show such mercy,' he said bitterly.

Akton looked steadily into the eyes of the soldier opposite him: 'The king did not give such a command, my lord. I did.'

There was a silence, and yet not a silence. With the noise of battle still raging about them, the two men were empty of words to say, and yet both were filled with thoughts, despairing and confused.

At last the commander spoke. 'There is a fine line between treason and patriotism,' he said, raising his voice against the battle. 'I think you may have crossed it.'

'Then so be it, replied Akton, not sure if what he was saying could be heard. 'If it is treason to protect the people, then treason is exactly what I am guilty of.'

All at once, there was a shout of alarm as a section of the wall on the western flank of one of the gate towers gave way, and came crashing down in a shower of masonry and twisted metal. The commander stared, shook his head as if to clear it, and glanced at the chancellor. 'I must see to our defence,' he said. 'You may stay here, or you may leave. I am for the walls.'

As he turned to leave, Akton caught him by the arm. 'My lord,' he said, 'give me leave to come with you. Better to be here than trapped within the corridors of the palace.'

His face streaked with sweat and dust, the commander smiled. 'You are welcome,' he said. 'Can you still remember how to use a pulse-launcher, or perhaps a pulsar-club?'

Akton smiled. 'Not my weapons of choice,' he said, 'but in my younger days I trained with the pulsar-club, and achieved class 2 status with the pulse-launcher.'

'Good enough for me!' said the commander. He pulled his pulse-gun from its holster and gestured to one of his aides to bring up a launcher with the support equipment. 'Follow me!' he shouted to Akton, and headed for the walls.

THE FLEET SAILS

The dockside at Portus-Portus was more crowded than it had ever been before. At least that was the opinion of the harbour master, and no one had served longer on these docks than he himself. He was proud of that, but this was not a day for pride.

He adjusted his mask, tugged at his cap and looked at the ships in front of him. They were, all three of them, moored alongside quay number five, and they were but a small part of the fleet that was now making ready to sail. Most of the fleet were transport ships, their sails already set to the expected southerly breeze, and their long, sleek hulls settling low in the water as the long queues of escaping citizens filed up the gang planks and onto the crowded decks. There was no sense of panic – the harbour master was grateful for that – but there was a sense of urgency. And mixed in with the urgency, he could see by the stoop of their shoulders, and the slow shuffle of those that carried burdens, there was a deep weariness. It was almost exhaustion. These people had come in desperate haste from the city, and there were still more to come.

He paused and watched briefly as they streamed down Serenity's landscaped cliffside that connected the city to Portus-Portus, filling the many stairways and pulley-lifts of the Cascading Gardens like ants.

Now the harbour master glanced at his inventory sheet. He hoped there were enough ships to accommodate this exodus. He feared that there were not, but he calmed himself with the thought that every mariner captain had strict instructions to return to port from across the Narrow Seas once they had offloaded their passengers and cargo at The Island.

A shipping clerk came up alongside him and saluted.

His boss returned the salute with dull resignation:

'What is it Cyrillus? Have I not told you not to salute me? Save your salutes for commissariat officers.'

The clerk smiled. 'Some good news at last, sir. Five battle cruisers from the fleet that transported the marines further up the coast are now on their way back. They should be here by late tomorrow.'

The harbour master nodded. 'That is good news. How many times have I asked the Commissariat to requisition an escort flotilla for these transports?'

'Four times, sir,' answered the clerk with crisp satisfaction, and held out an order sheet stamped with the crest of the Naval Signals division. 'At least the Navy is taking these stories of pirates in the channel seriously.' He paused. 'And they should know.'

The harbour master shrugged. 'We all should know,' he answered, 'but it's really a question of what we choose to believe. Did I not send a pictogram of a wrecked pirate vessel washed up on these shores after last week's storm?'

'You did sir, and I sent it to all the relevant departments myself.'

'Without reply?'

'Without reply, sir. But I suspect they have their hands full at the moment,' he paused, 'with other distractions.'

'Other distractions,' repeated the harbour master, muttering as he stared again at the fleet. 'Other distractions: I suppose that is the best way to describe it, though there is a particular distraction that I fear Serenity may not survive.'

The clerk frowned. 'The siege, my lord?'

'Aye, the siege,' replied the harbour master, ignoring the unnecessary title. 'The enemy is at the very gates of Serenity. Outlanders have broken through our northern border defences, and are now sweeping unopposed through the kingdom. Only Arx has stood, and that is only because of our brave marines and it's sunbeams.'

For a moment the clerk did not reply. He had a brother in a city regiment defending the gates, and a sister who was a serving officer with the marines somewhere near Arx.

'We will stand, my lord,' he said quietly.

'Aye, we will stand,' replied the harbour master wearily. 'But at what cost?'

The clerk looked away down the dockside. Another contingent of refugees had emerged from the loading bays near the transport shuttles. The dockside was getting crowded again. 'I should return to my duties at Dispersal, my lord,' he said.

The harbour master grunted. 'Go, then. And, oh, Cyrillus?'

'Sir?'

'Well done.'

'Thank you, sir.' The clerk saluted again and hurried away.

Watching him disappear among the groups of hurrying figures, the harbour master sighed and looked again at his clip board: there was a signal from the security office of the Commissariat, and another from the Triple S, both ordering a halt to the evacuation until all passes had been checked. Both signals bore the 'most urgent' code, but he was happy to ignore them. After all, he had also received signals from the Chancellery and Glamtech ordering the evacuation to proceed without delay. 'No passes will be checked, in order to speed the process', was the specific instruction from the Chancellery, and it bore the seal of lord Akton. That was good enough for the harbour master, and besides he could not see any point in obstructing the evacuation of civilians from a war zone. His own military training told him that much.

He flicked the orders over and stared at the latest sheet listing the names of evacuees. That was all that was required, and that would certainly be enough.

A horn sounded. It was a ship's horn. He looked to see a ship pull away from the dockside, and glide smoothly away and across the harbour, keeping to the marked channel that led to the 'heads' and the open sea beyond. It was a beautiful sight, and one the harbour master had never tired of in more peaceful times. Even on days such as this: 'mad days!' as his wife described them, there was something inspiring in the sight of a ship leaving port. And yes, there was beauty.

Another horn sounded, this time it was the strident blast of a battle cruiser, and he turned to look. The harbour master saw the heavy, squat shape of the cruiser, slip its moorings and set off in the wake of the transport vessel. Despite its rough-cut design, the harbour master nodded approvingly as he watched the cruiser cut effortlessly through the water and begin to close the distance between itself and the other ship.

'It will be a reckless pirate that tries to challenge those fellows,' muttered the harbour master and he smiled.

Then all at once there was someone at his side. He started, turned and looked down. A young woman, eyes wide, was looking up at him.

'Yes, miss?' he asked, only mildly surprised that she was not wearing a mask.

The woman, unmasked, was dressed in a simple smock, with a rough hooded cloak about her shoulders. When she spoke, he knew at once that she was not from Lower Town. Her accent gave her away as nobility, probably of the second court.

'My lord,' she said, clasping her hands together to stop them from shaking, 'I have come from the city.'

'Have you come or were you sent, miss?'

For just a moment the woman looked confused. 'I came of my own accord,' she said. 'I was told that I might find help here,' she paused, 'that I might . . .'

'Find passage to The Island?'

He saw a look of fear in her eyes, and smiled to dispel it:

'It's all right, miss. You are safe here, but will be safer yet on the The Island. All I need is your name.'

She gave it, but he noticed that she stumbled on the patronymic. He smiled again, and gave a shrug:

'That's a fine name,' he said. 'You are from Upper Town?'

'I am my lord, or rather, court 2. Is that perhaps a problem?'

'Why no, and why should it be?' He held up is hand. 'No, do not bother to answer such a question. I can see that you are weary from your journey.' He scribbled something down on a pad clipped to the side of his clip board, tore the paper along its perforations and handed it to her:

'Take this to that clerk over there. See: the one with the red cap and the embarkation-mask? He will show you where to go, and if he is as civil as I have trained him to be, he will also show you to a place where you can sit and rest awhile. Your ship will leave within the hour. It's further along the dock, just next to the transport freighter bound for Arx.'

The young woman nodded gratefully. 'Thank you, my lord,' she said, 'I am in your debt.' Then she glanced nervously over her shoulder as if expecting to see someone.

'Do not worry, miss. I told you, you are safe here. My men will see that you come to no harm.'

The young woman replied with an inclination of her head and the slight and graceful bob that is only seen among the families of the courts or palace precinct, and then she was gone.

'Mad days,' said the harbour master to himself, as he entered her name on his inventory list. Another ship's horn sounded, another cable was slipped and the man watched with a weary smile as yet one more transport headed gracefully into the channel.

CHAPTER #12
THE FIGHT AT GLAMTECH

Shadwatch had almost finished. The last test tube had been tested, the last result recorded and the first specimen jar sealed with the colour-coded seal Glamtech used to indicate 'success'.

He straightened up with a sigh and was about to say something to Barvarik, when there was a sudden and furious banging at the door. Both men stood back, and Barvarik drew his sword:

'We have company,' he said.

Shadwatch looked around. 'The best thing Glamtech ever did was to put automatic locks on the laboratory doors,' he said, 'but the worst thing they did was to have only one door for every laboratory.'

Barvarik stared. 'There is no alternative exit?'

Shadwatch shrugged, as the pounding on the door increased. 'Cost cutting, I'm afraid,' he said. 'No emergency exits: just one way in or out.'

'Will the door hold then?'

Moving to the far end of the bench where it overlooked the Gene Pool, Shadwatch called back over his shoulder. 'Whoever that is at the door, even if it's just some lab rat who has forgotten his key code, we could stay in here all week if we liked. The only exception is, as I fear it may be, a search-squad from the Triple S. Doors and locks are no barrier to them and they will be in here very much sooner.' He scooped up a rack of serum phials, and tossed it across to Barvarik. 'Fill these as quickly as you can, while I get some samples from the Gene Pool.'

'But the door!' shouted Barvarik.

With a laugh, Shadwatch knelt down by the pool. 'Don't worry, soldier! You'll know exactly what to do when it opens.'

Less than two minutes later, with the sound of tearing metal the door flew back, and hung drunkenly on one hinge. Six officers dressed in the black combat uniforms of the Triple S, and carrying riot clubs burst into the laboratory. Seeing Shadwatch and Barvarik, they did not pause but rushed at them, clubs raised.

Barvarik reacted as though he were all at once in a battle, and back on the bridge at Arx facing the outlander attack. He raised his sword and cut once, twice, three times, not moving to parry but swaying to one side with each cut, letting his opponent over reach, and striking him as he stumbled.

The first three men fell without a cry. Two collapsed at his feet, the third crashed back against his comrades, blood streaming from a wound to his chest.

Stepping back, Barvarik now raised his sword to guard, and waited for the survivors of the search squad to come at him. He could hear Shadwatch behind him, gathering up the serum, and he could hear the heavy breathing of the men in front of him. Otherwise, the room was silent.

At last one of the officers spoke. He had a captain's rank on his shoulder flashes, and he also had a badge indicating service in the house-hold guards: a professional, and not one likely to make the same mistake as his fellows.

'We have been sent by the king,' he said, his voice strong and clear. 'You are to accompany us to the court of the inner chamber where you will be questioned on a charge of treason . . . ,' he paused, 'and murder.'

Barvarik replied, unable to keep his voice from shaking. 'You could have at least asked,' he said. 'Your eagerness has cost three men their lives.'

The captain removed his mask. He was an older man, with a close cropped, greying beard, and grey flecked eyes, common to many folk in Serenity. Barvarik noted the quiet strength in those eyes, and felt a twinge of regret that he was now faced by a man who once he might have counted as a friend.

'Your resistance has added to your troubles,' said the captain. 'Lay down your sword now, and I will see that you and lord Shadwatch are treated with honour.'

Barvarik glanced back over his shoulder: Shadwatch was still gathering the serum and specimen jars.

'Now is not the time for me to lay down my sword, captain. I do not have a quarrel with you or your men, but it seems I do have a quarrel with the king. Let us pass.'

When the captain moved, he moved with a speed that even took Barvarik by surprise. He covered the ground between himself and Barvarik in less time than it took the young warrior to bring his sword up and against the upraised club. But in that hairbreadth moment, Barvarik was able to fling himself forward, so that he moved under and inside the captain's attack.

Both men collided. The impetus of the captain's sudden charge carried the moment, and both men toppled backwards.

As he fell, Barvarik felt himself crash against the low bench still stacked with serum jars. There was a sound of breaking glass, and then the bench gave way.

With the captain now holding him by one shoulder, Barvarik stumbled, slipped sideways and then plunged down into the Gene Pool.

There was little more that Barvarik remembered. When he came to his senses sometime later, he was lying beside the pool, his head throbbing.

Shadwatch was saying something, kneeling next to Barvarik and lifting him up slowly. The words came to him out of a blur of pain and confusion:

'Barvarik! Are you all right? Barvarik!'

He opened his eyes wide and looked around. 'What happened?'

Shadwatch smiled. 'Not much, my friend, but enough. You and the captain over there fell against the bench and then down into the Gene Pool. I managed to get you out before you drowned, but I was too late to save that fellow,' he pointed at the captain, still floating face down in the pool. 'We will now be executed for sure, if they catch up with us.' He propped Barvarik against what was left of the bench and checked his wounds. 'What's more, you nearly bled to death. I'm not sure how I managed to stop the bleeding, but I've patched you up as best I can.' Looking around, Shadwatch nodded. 'We've got to get out of here, before the others get back.'

'The others?'

Shadwatch smiled again. 'You are a mess aren't ye? The other two commies: remember? They lost interest once they saw their officer go to the bottom of the pool, and left me standing here with a stun-club.' He gestured towards the doorway. 'They took off like marsh rabbits, but I'm guessing the moment they can find some help . . .'

'We need to leave.' Barvarik started to get to his feet. His chest hurt and his lower back, but at least he could stand. The room was swaying.

'Are you all right?'

Barvarik tried to smile. 'I've been better.'

'Let's get you out of here.' Shadwatch grinned. 'Think of your girl. That will keep you on your feet.'

Teevey, who had been hiding somewhere beneath a lab-bench, emerged to the heavy rhythmical beat of 'O Brother, Where Art Thou?' He drifted alongside his master: 'We're in a tight spot, we're in a tight spot.'

They moved towards the door. Shadwatch had a satchel slung over one shoulder, and with the other he was supporting Barvarik. They had just set off along the corridor when Barvarik suddenly groaned. 'My sword,' he said. 'I have left my sword. We must go back.'

'And what's this, then?' replied Shadwatch tapping his right hip. Barvarik glanced down, and smiled despite his pain. The hilt and scabbard of his sword was showing just beneath Shadwatch's vest:

'Thank you,' he said.

'You'll thank me by walking faster,' said Shadwatch. 'I can hear somebody coming along the back corridor, and there's more than one of them.'

How Barvarik made it along that stretch of corridor, down a flight of steps and through a panelled door he had no idea, but he knew that without Shadwatch half carrying him, it would have been unlikely, if not impossible.

He leant against a wall, breathing hard while Shadwatch looked in his satchel for the DNA override card that would get them through the next door. His head hurt, he was sweating despite being soaked through, and a dull stain was spreading through the padded dressing Shadwatch had strapped to his chest.

'How much further?' he asked.

Shadwatch looked up, and smiled. He had found the override card. 'Not far,' he said. 'Once we get through that door up ahead, it's a pace or two to the Senior Glamtech transport unit for court one. There won't be any TripleS types there.' He looked at Barvarik's wound. 'That's an interesting colour,' he said, 'but it could be worse.'

'Aye, it could be,' croaked Barvarik, risking a smile. 'When your blood stops flowing, that means you're dead. Isn't that it?'

'Hah! Come on you idler! A few scratches and you start to think you're for the city morgue.' He put his arm around Barvarik's shoulder. 'One last effort, my friend, and we'll have you away from this place.'

They reached the door, Shadwatch used his pass and the door swung open. There were guards on the other side, but they were dressed in Glamtech uniforms, and both men stepped aside when they saw their senior officer, with the Glambot floating along behind him.

But it was Barvarik that mostly drew their attention. It was clear that he was wounded and that he had been in a fight. At the same time, they could see from his demeanour, even wounded that he was a citizen of court one. His shoulder flashes told them that he was of an elite regiment.

'A casualty, sir?' asked one of the guards.

Shadwatch nodded. 'There's been fighting further back. This fellow got himself injured defending one of our labs. He has been given a battle-pass for Portus-Portus.'

The guard, a senior sergeant, nodded and then turned to the other guard:

'Corporal!' he said crisply. 'You will accompany lord Shadwatch and this wounded man. Leave your pulse-gun with me. You can lend your shoulder to one of our heroes.'

The corporal hesitated, then saluted and unslung his pulse-gun. 'That's a transport pass for court one I will be needing, sir,' he said as he moved to take Barvarik's weight against his shoulder.

'I'll get you a return pass issued at the Portus docks,' said Shadwatch quickly. 'Come on! We don't have much time. I want this man here on a hospital ship as soon as possible.'

And so they set off again, Barvarik still limping but grateful for the unexpected strength of the corporal. As his head began to clear, he also noticed that Shadwatch had not come unscathed through the fight at the laboratory. The young Glamtech lord's shirt was torn at the sleeve, and he was bleeding through a hastily tied field-dressing.

'You're hurt,' he mumbled to Shadwatch as they neared the transport unit.

'You noticed?' Shadwatch chuckled. 'Those last two guards didn't exactly leave straight away. I had to persuade them.'

Barvarik took a deep breath. His chest no longer hurt. 'I never took you for a fighter,' he said. 'Just a rival.'

'I'm neither,' said Shadwatch. 'Not now anyway.' He paused. 'Not anymore. But like you I was born and brought up in court one. The day I turned sixteen I was sent by my father to do my military training.'

'With a Guards Regiment?'

Shadwatch shook his head. 'My father was a man of the people. He was raised in the poorer quarters of Lower Town. He sent me to do my service with the citizen militia. That sort of thing teaches you your roots. He said as much when he waved me off at the gates to the barracks.' Shadwatch paused. 'I'm not sure it did,' he said slowly, 'but I know I will never forget that day.'

'And Talessa ?'

Shadwatch smiled wearily. 'I see where her heart lies. And that is enough'

They soon arrived at the connection bay. It was almost deserted but there were a few guards standing about, for the most part looking bored and listless. An officer standing by a transport shuttle near the main gantry looked up and waved them across.

'You're the first to come our way on this watch,' he said as he checked Shadwatch's palm-screening, and glanced at the override pass. Is there trouble in the other courts?'

'Some,' replied Shadwatch, 'but most of the fighting is at the main gates.' Have no other evacuees come besides us?'

The officer shook his head. 'We are stuck here the back door,' he said and grinned. 'All the fuss is going on over there in transport bays one to five. They are pouring through, or at least that's what we hear. I'm getting some confusing signals though.'

'Confusing?'

'Aye, my lord. For every Glamtech or Litra signal I get confirming the evacuation, I get one from the Commissariat telling me to action all delay and arrest procedures.'

Shadwatch held his expression. 'That sounds like the Commissariat,' he said. 'They are always slow on the uptake, and question absolutely everything until the king himself appears and shouts at them.'

The officer grinned. 'That's about the strength of it, my lord. Long live Glamtech, eh?' He stamped the pass, and ordered a guard to make the shuttle ready. 'It's a four-seater,' he said, 'so you can all get aboard. Mind you get a return pass for any of you that's coming back this way.'

Shadwatch nodded. 'Thank you officer.' He paused. 'I suggest you seal the doors we just came through. There are saboteurs on the loose somewhere between here and Glamtech. The SSS are tracking them down as we speak, but it would be a shame if they slipped through our fingers by using this transport bay.'

The officer saluted. 'It will be done, my lord. No one else will get through.'

And so Shadwatch, Barvarik and the guard came to Portus-Portus. It only took a moment for Shadwatch to arrange a return-pass for the guard which would take him back to his unit. They thanked him, and he left.

Escorted by a shipping clerk, the two men made their way down to the main dock. Barvarik was walking freely now, and no longer needed a shoulder to lean on. Shadwatch, who knew the severity of the young warrior's wounds, was surprised. He kept staring at him as they walked together, and shook his head more than once. 'Remarkable,' he said at last.

'My lord?'

Shadwatch stopped. He did not reply. They were nearly at the dockside. There was a hospital ship and a merchantman drawn up alongside the quay with a battle cruiser anchored some distance away in the channel. Safety was within reach. He signed for the clerk to wait for them, and turned to Barvarik:

'Less than an hour ago, I dragged you half dead out of that Gene Pool. Somehow I patched up your wounds and got you on your feet.'

'You did my lord, and for that I am grateful.' Barvarik, only half aware, was scanning the crowd. He was desperate for a glimpse of Talessa.

'Yes, yes, but listen!' Shadwatch went on, 'you were seriously injured. It was almost miraculous that I got you to walk at all, let alone managing to bring you the distance that I did.'

Barvarik looked puzzled. 'That may be so, my lord, but perhaps I was not so badly injured as you at first feared.' Again, Barvarik looked around. There were so many people, but no sign of Talessa.

Shadwatch shook his head. 'You were dying on your feet, man! I'm no surgeon, but I know enough about war wounds to see when they are little short of fatal.'

Barvarik did not know what to say. He looked at the shipping clerk who shrugged and lowered his head. Then he turned and looked back the way they had come from the arrivals bay. The crowd was a sea of faces but there was no sign of the face he most wanted to see.

'We should be getting on board,' he said.

'Aye, we should.' Shadwatch nodded. He gestured to the clerk, who bowed and began to lead them towards the hospital ship. There was already a queue for the merchantman, but the gangplank for the hospital ship was still clear. A ship's officer was standing at the quayside, waiting to check the evacuees and their papers. This would be their last challenge.

A TROUBLED APPROACH

Leviss crouched beside Anna-Seka, and looked cautiously over the heap of rubble. They had been sheltering behind it for some time and were still waiting for the order to advance. Nike was to Anna's right, and Bepsi-Loca was a little further away sitting in the lee of a wrecked catapult. There were others nearby, all stainer militia as well as a detachment of Burgh city-engineers and a group of miners.

Keeping to their orders, they still held the right flank, some distance from the gates, but were now much closer to the walls and hotplate. If they could not clearly see the battle that was raging for the gates, they could certainly hear it: the thunder of artillery from both sides and the almost constant sound of explosions and detonations as flaming projectiles, solid shot, and pulse-volleys struck their targets. Anna had wrapped a scarf across her mouth and nose to keep from choking on the acrid dust, but her eyes were stinging, and her ears rang with the noise of the constant barrage.

'How much longer, do you think?' she shouted to Leviss during a momentary lull.

Leviss grinned. 'No telling,' he said, 'but I'm happy enough to be here. If we can make it to nightfall, there's even half a chance we might survive till morning.' He pointed towards a war-engine being brought up by some engineers towards the front line. 'See that?' he shouted. 'I see what they're trying to do. They are going to push that thing onto the hotplate, and get right up to the gates.'

Nike leaned across to Anna, cupped her hands and shouted into Anna's ear:

'Stay with us, Anna! No heroics!'

Anna pulled her scarf down, smiled and nodded. 'Where ever you go, I go,' she shouted back, and coughed.

'That's it, Anna. You're more friend, than prisoner.' Nike said something else, but Anna did not hear. Her words were carried away in a sudden blast as a wall-mounted catapult-battery turned its fire against their position.

For a moment the air was filled with bits of shattered masonry and clumps of turf. They all flung themselves down, and put their hands to their heads. A dense cloud of smoke and dust reared up in front of them and spilled across their position. For a time all was darkness and confusion, and then the air about them slowly cleared. The brief silence was broken by the groans of the wounded and dying. At least one squad had taken a direct hit.

Bepsi-Loca bent-low, sprinted across to Anna and his two adopted children, and threw himself down beside them.

'Are you all right?' he asked, but didn't wait for an answer. 'We need to get out of here. We've been spotted, and that's for sure.'

'But our orders were to hold this position,' said Nike uncertainly, staring up at the battery which was being swung to one side as it was reloaded.

'Our orders were not to get ourselves killed!' Nike's uncle pointed up at the walls. 'Our artillery will try and give us cover, but there's not an officer would expect us to stay here now.'

'Where to?' Leviss asked, wiping the dust and dirt from his face.

Bepsi-Loca thought for a moment. 'We'll go in a-ways, closer to the gates.'

'Closer, uncle? That's madness!'

The outlander scout shook his head. 'See that ditch there and the wreck in front of it? It's perfect.' He smiled, and slapped Leviss on the shoulder. 'Let's go, my lad!'

Leviss looked at Anna who nodded. He smiled and got to his feet. 'Well, here goes nothing,' he said, offering his hand to her and then hauling her to her feet.

They set off together, running in the familiar half-crouch, weaving and dodging to make it harder for the snipers on the walls to track them.

Anna dared not look back to see if the others were following. All that she knew was that she and Leviss were running together, eyes fixed on the ditch ahead. She tried to ignore the zifft and wooft of crossbow bolts and leaden ballista balls as they flew about their heads, or ploughed into the ground in front of their feet. There was part of Anna-Seka that just wanted to keep on running. And running. And running until she reached the gates, crossed the barricades and fell into the arms of her own people. Perhaps her own family. But instead into the madness, she ran, stride for stride with Leviss waiting every moment for the arrow that must surely strike her, or the ballista bolt that would sweep them both away.

Twice Anna almost stumbled, and twice Leviss swerved to reach out and steady her. She shouted at him to keep his distance. She was instantly afraid that even more snipers would see them together, and pick them out as an easy target. At last the ditch came within a spear's cast, and the wreck of the battle wagon loomed in front of them, its jet-fighter's wing jutting from the rubble.

It was then that a crossbow bolt struck Leviss high on his back, almost lifting him off his feet and pitching him forward.

He sprawled face down in the mud and lay still. With a cry Anna turned back for him, and scrambled to where he was lying motionless, the bolt still quivering in his back.

'Leviss!' Anna was unaware of the arrows that flickered around her, and thudded into the squared timbers of the broken battle-wagon. She took hold of Leviss and began to drag him towards the ditch. A ballista bolt screeched against some twisted aluminium sheeting and hummed past her shoulder. Suddenly she heard a voice:

'Run!'

She stared. Leviss had opened his eyes. 'Run!' he said again, gasping to catch his breath. 'Run, Anna!

Then as she hesitated, she took a blow on her back. It was Bepsi-Loca. 'Leave him! Run!'

Releasing her grip on Leviss and stumbling awkwardly, Anna sobbed as she ran. At last she fell into the ditch with Bepsi-Loca and Nike hard on her heels. Gulping in the ash-filled air, she lay at the bottom of the ditch. 'He's alive and you left him! You left him!' she at last blurted out. 'Your own kin, you left your kin.'

'Aye, my uncle left his nephew and I left my brother too,' said Nike. 'If we hadn't we'd all of us be dead by now.'

'But Leviss?'

Nike shrugged. 'Oh, he's all right, isn't he papa?'

Nike's uncle leant against the wall of the ditch and looked up at the sky, almost lost in clouds of smoke and swirling dust. 'As long as he stays right where he is, until we call him in, he'll be just fine,' replied Bepsi-Loca.

Anna shook her head. 'I don't understand.'

Bepsi-Loca chuckled. 'And you a scout from Serenity itself? Well, there's a thing, lassie. Didn't ye see where that bolt struck our boy?'

'I did. It was clean between his shoulders.'

'Aye, where his baldric crosses from one shoulder to his hip.' The stainer scout took his water bottle from his belt, drank and then passed it to Anna. 'It's good thick leather we use in a baldric like that. Given to him by me, it was.' He grinned. 'I promised his mother I'd look after him, and I reckon I have. Mind you, he's a lucky one is our Leviss.

Three inches lower and we would have lost him, and that's for sure.' He took the bottle back from Anna and passed it to his daughter. 'If he's got the good sense to play dead for a while longer, we can get him back here in one piece, with nothing to show for his adventure but a champion bruise on his spine.'

Anna-Seka wiped her eyes. 'I thought he . . .'

Bepsi-Loca smiled. 'You're a good lassie, Anna-Seka. I saw what ye did, and I know why ye did it.'

Anna blinked. 'I didn't think,' she whispered. 'He was there. He fell. That is all.'

'Good enough for me,' chuckled Bepsi-Loca. 'It was like you were one of us. Now keep that pretty head of yours down. There's no mercy in those kindred of yours who keep the walls. They are shooting at anything that moves, alive or dying.'

Nike settled herself beside Anna and turned to look back at her brother, who was lying perfectly still about twenty paces away.

'It will be nightfall soon,' she said, 'and darker sooner than later with all this dust that's hanging about. If Leviss has any sense at all, he won't be moving until then.'

And so they waited. The battle raged about them: war engines were wheeled into position. Some were toppled and set ablaze by the defenders, while others were slowly heaved by outlanders onto the hotplate. Infantry and engineers crowded onto each engine, careful to avoid the super-heated plates and hiding as best they could from the constant barrage of projectiles that fell about their heads from the ramparts. Those that were struck and knocked from the war-engines were instantly vaporized, disappearing with a terrifying flash of light.

The wheels of the engines themselves glowed with heat, and the sub-frames of pressed aluminium alloy smoked and sparked as the intensity of the hotplate increased but not one of them burst into flames. As the evening drew on, the battlefield descended into drifting shadows made strangely beautiful by bursts of light: orange, yellow and fiery red. Men became huddled shapes moving suddenly and uncertainly amid the wreckage of war. But with every explosion or thunderous volley, soldiers and their weapons were thrown into dazzling relief for a flickering instant, making the darkness even deeper.

Despite her exhaustion, Anna found that she could not rest. As long as Leviss was alone out there in the wasteland of the battlefield, she stayed wide awake, starting into the darkness and watching for him.

Her heart turned on that single thought: that while she wanted more than anything to be reunited with her family, she could not bear to leave Leviss out there alone on the battlefield.

Although Bepsi-Loca had signalled their change of position to the forward headquarters of outlander-command, he had received no further orders apart from a brief acknowledgement and the coded command: 'hold until relieved.'

They seemed to have been forgotten, and it was well that they had been. Towards the end of the third hour of the evening watch, Leviss made it back to them.

He came like a night-hawk, slipping silently through the shadows, unseen despite the glare from a dozen fires along the ramparts and from beacons among the ragged lines of the attacking army. It was Anna who saw him first. She gasped with relief and stood, forgetting how easily she could now be seen, silhouetted by the flames of a burning plane-wagon behind her. But even if she had been spotted by a ballista team on the ramparts, or a crossbowman in an observation tower, they would not have had time to bring their weapons to bear.

Leviss ran to her, took her in both arms, and swept her to the ground. 'Down, you fool!' he said, then rolled over onto his back and laughed. Eyes wide with surprise, Anna started to get to her feet, but suddenly stopped as a ballista bolt hissed over her head and smashed into the wagon sending a cloud of sparks whirling skywards. Ducking down again, she grinned at Leviss.

'Thanks,' she said.

'Hah!' Leviss sat up, and nodded to his father and sister. 'The thanks is mine to give, I'm thinking. When you came back for me . . .' he shrugged, 'it made me think.' Reaching around, he pulled the arrow, now bent, from his baldric and tossed it into the darkness. 'I was winded, but I knew I wasn't dead. Lucky, I am,' he said and smiled, 'it's the lucky one I am today.'

'You are that, and right enough,' said Bepsi-Loca, sitting down beside his nephew. 'We thought we'd lost ye.'

Leviss glanced up at the walls. 'It's not over yet, uncle,' he replied. 'If they send us in against the gates, there's a fair few of us won't be going home.'

'Well, I don't think they'll do anything now, not until the morning anyway,' said Bepsi-Loca. 'The artillery will keep a good hot fire as long as they can, that's for sure, but it would be madness to try and carry the gates in this mess and murk.' He leaned back and looked towards the gates. 'I see they are pulling the war-engines back off the hotplate. That's good. There's no thought of an assault now until dawn, mark my words.'

Nike crawled across to her brother, and gave him a playful tap on the cheek. 'It's good to see you in one piece, brother. Now apologise to our Anna for knocking her off her feet just now.' She tapped him again. 'No manners, no manners at all!'

They all laughed, confident that they could not be heard above the roar of the artillery. Then without another word, they all settled down to sleep as best they could until the morning. And tomorrow, and only tomorrow they would have to think of an assault on the gates.

CHAPTER #13

IN SEARCH OF THE KING

Chesterman and Marlin were making their way along a deserted corridor. They had been escorted to the commissariat checkpoint, where once more their security status had been checked and verified. But an audience with the king had been refused, and their escort, including the ensign had been sent back to the original checkpoint. Chesterman and Marlin had been directed to a visitors' hostel, and told to wait there until morning.

They had not waited. As soon as they saw an opportunity, both men had left the hostel unseen, and disappeared into the outer corridors of the tower base. There was no one about. For a time they wandered about, strangely disoriented by the maze of corridors, ante rooms, deserted reception areas and open leisure areas. For Marlin it was as though he had entered into a world he had never known, much less simply forgotten. Perhaps, he told himself, his brother had been more than usually ambitious with his building programme during Marlin's long exile. All he knew was that the king's apartments lay far above from where they now stood, and that somehow they must find the elevator that would take them there.

At last, they heard footsteps coming towards them from afar off. The echo of the footfalls made it difficult to place exactly where they were coming from, but Chesterman suddenly pointed to a narrow, ill-lit passage that intersected the main corridor.

'Those are military boots we can hear,' he said. 'We should not be found here by any armed patrols.'

Marlin shrugged. 'We have passed through several security checkpoints,' he said. 'If we keep our cool and stick to our story . . .'

'But surely, they will suspect something.'

The footsteps were getting nearer.

'Remember,' said Marlin quickly. 'I grew up in this place. Anyone who has penetrated this far without being challenged will be seen as only one of two things,' he smiled, 'official or lost.'

Chesterman did not have a chance to reply. A soldier in full imperial uniform, with a king's glow-pike across his shoulder appeared from the passage way, took two paces into the main corridor and stopped. Swinging his pike to present and guard, he waited while three other soldiers appeared behind him and halted.

Marlin stepped forward. 'King's business,' he said, holding up his hand with an open palm. It was the old informal salute only shared between members of household regiments. 'We have been sent from the main gates to report to the king on the state of the fighting.'

The soldier, a sergeant-major with the greying hair of a veteran, stared hard at Marlin for a moment. 'The king sent for you?'

Marlin shook his head. 'No, sergeant-major. The commander sent us. The situation at the gates is critical. He did not wish to send a message to the palace via the usual means. He believes that our security has been compromised. He has sent us instead.'

The sergeant-major did not relax his gaze. 'You mean that Alexus Regius of the First Defence Corps sent you?'

Again Marlin shook his head. 'Not Alexus Regiius, sergeant-major, but Priam Secundus: he commands the Third Corps, and therefore the main gates. He sent us,' he paused, 'and with orders not to delay or to be delayed.'

The veteran sergeant visibly relaxed. There was even a faint smile behind his mask. 'You have passed through security, then?'

'Naturally.' Marlin's clipped and assured manner surprised even Chesterman who had determined to stand quite still and say nothing, but instinctively, his mind played, ready to leap and use the shadowy walls of the narrow passageway to bring them all down in a few steps.

'We were sent to a hostel as part of normal procedure,' Marlin continued, 'but I decided that our orders must have priority over procedure.' He returned the sergeant-major's guessed slight smile. 'And so you find us here.'

'You are lost then, captain?' The sergeant lowered his glow-pike and Chesterman's mind eased.

'Somewhat, but I hope only temporarily. Can you show us through this court to the royal precinct and apartments, or at least the elevator that can transport us there.?'

The sergeant-major's level stare returned. 'No one disturbs the king once he has retired,' he said. 'No one.'

'And if the king was to awake in the morning to find that the city had fallen while he slept?' Marlin raised his voice so that his words echoed along the corridor.

'You are telling me that the situation is that serious?'

'I am telling you nothing, sergeant-major, nothing officially until I have spoken directly to the king. But you should know this: the commander Priam Secundus can only retrieve the current situation at the gates with a tactic requiring a particular use of certain weaponry. However, by agreed decree in council he cannot initiate that tactic until the king himself has officially endorsed it with signed and sealed orders.'

If the sergeant-major was not convinced, Chesterman certainly was. His opinion of Marlin's quick-thinking ability under pressure had increased significantly.

At last the sergeant-major nodded. 'As you know the king has at least a dozen different apartments where he might choose to be sleeping. They are all within the royal gardens. We will take you there.'

And so most of the guard-patrol led, and Marlin with Chesterman close behind followed. Both men noticed straight away that one of the guards hung back, keeping a discreet distance behind them.

'They are well trained,' whispered Marlin. 'Did you notice that there was no order, but one of them broke away as if it were standard security procedure.'

Chesterman gave a slight nod: 'I did notice. It's clear we cannot mess with these fellows. They know their trade,' he replied, keeping his voice low. 'This is going to need careful handling.'

They walked on for some time, found the elevator which was pass-protected, and a short while later found themselves gliding upwards to what seemed to be an impossible height. It was well that this pinnacle was called 'the cloud piercer'. At last they slowed and came to a halt. The doors of the elevator slid open: they had come to the main entrance of the royal precinct.

It had a tall, pillared entranceway, elaborately decorated, with two high doors of brass, faced with a plexi-glass screen, from which could be perceived the huge domed grounds.

Automatic-guards scanned their palms and passes. The doors swung open.

'Wait here,' said the sergeant-major, waving them towards a long marble bench under a spreading vine. 'There are three apartments on this side of the precinct. I will check them, and then if necessary we will carry on.'

He began to move away, then suddenly stopped and turned around. 'Don't move from this place,' he said. 'Your security status depends on always being accompanied by at least two guardsmen.' He signed to two of his men who saluted and took station at either end of the bench. Then he turned away again and disappeared along a winding path, overhung with foliage of every shade of green. Fronds of scented flowers, cascading in petal-showers of light blue and purest white spilled over and through the foliage. It was still, and peaceful. The silence was only broken by the sound of a nearby waterfall, and the faint and fading footfall of the imperial guards. Above their heads flamingos flew high under the great dome of panelled glass that shimmered against the night sky, reflecting back the light from the myriad glow-lamps and torches that lined the paths and patios of the garden.

Chesterman adjusted the speaker-phone on his motorcycle helmet. 'I was hoping that security would be next to nothing in the royal precinct,' he said. 'I'm not sure how we are going to handle this.'

Marlin nodded. 'It must be the fighting that has heightened security. Or my brother has become more nervous in these past years.'

Chesterman glanced towards the guards to check that they were out of earshot. 'Whether we meet him on his own, or without an escort, we will have to take our chances. Are you with me in this?'

Marlin nodded. 'I'm not going back now. We've come too far and it has cost me too much. Besides, my brother has a price to pay, and I will make sure he pays it.'

'Then all is well,' whispered Chesterman. 'But promise me this: when we meet the king, wait for my lead. 'You may speak, and say whatever is on your heart, but when I move, move with me. If we hesitate, we are lost.'

Marlin risked a bitter smile, all but obscured by his helmet. 'I will tell him what he most fears to hear. That is all I ask.'

Chesterman leaned forward, picked up a leaf, studied it for a moment, then crushed it between his fingers. 'You know, I almost feel sorry for your brother.' He paused. 'But almost is a world away from pity.'

Marlin grunted. 'We are not there yet, my lord. There is much that can yet go wrong, and so much that needs to go right.'

There was a sound from along the path ahead of them. The foliage stirred and the sergeant-major appeared. They stood up as he came up to them:

'You're in luck,' he said. 'It was the first apartment we checked, and the king was there, and not yet asleep. It took a bit to persuade his personal attendant to disturb him, but when I gave the message that you had come from the gates with news,' he smiled, 'that did the trick. He wants to see you both straightaway.'

'Good,' said Marlin. 'Is there anything we should know?'

'You mean, protocol? Nothing that you won't be already aware of,' the officer hesitated, 'except that it will be an exclusive and private audience.'

Marlin tried to show no reaction. 'That is unusual.'

'Not these days,' muttered the officer. 'Our lord the king seems to think there are spies everywhere. He wants even the least communication to be for his eyes only.'

'Then that is well. Will you wait to escort us back to the gates?'

'I will. I will be waiting here with my men. The attendant has been dismissed to his own quarters already. You will be totally on your own.' He smiled again. 'Don't get lost.'

TEAR

Barvarik and Shadwatch were nearly on board. The last security check had been cleared, and they were both at the top of the gang plank. They paused for a stretcher party to bring a wounded soldier onto the safety of the deck.

'You know,' said Shadwatch quietly, 'I think you are more than a walking miracle, Barvarik.'

Barvarik stared at him. 'What do you mean?'

'The more I think about it, the more I know I'm right: the only reason you are alive and standing in front of me now is down to just two things: the serum and the Gene Pool.'

Barvarik was puzzled. He didn't reply, so Shadwatch went on:

'Listen! You fell against that rack of serum tubes in the laboratory, cut yourself badly and then fell into the pool.'

'I know that. So, what?'

Shadwatch smiled. 'So, what? So this, my friend: you must have picked up a dose of anti-stain serum in your bloodstream, and along with that went a dose of DNA. I know it sounds crazy, but it's the only rational explanation. Somehow you received a magic dose, which dramatically heightened your immunity, accelerated your self-healing process and allowed you not only to survive, but to pretty much recover in a matter of hours.'

The stretcher party was on board. The queue began to shuffle forward again. Barvarik shook his head uncertainly. 'That does sound crazy,' he muttered, 'but I admit this: I'm a little surprised that I have begun to feel better so soon.' He chuckled. 'And maybe it means that I can't pick up the staining-disease?'

'It's more than maybe,' replied Shadwatch, glancing back towards the dock. 'The serum is designed to attack the stain by dramatically boosting the immune system.' He tapped Barvarik on the shoulder. 'You, soldier, are a walking laboratory, and at this moment probably the most important person in all of Serenity and the kingdom.'

There was too much noise around them, as the ship's crew made ready to cast off, for their conversation to be heard, and the sick and wounded who were already crowding the deck showed little or no interest in the Glamtech official and imperial warrior who were about to step aboard.

A ship's officer steadied Barvarik as he stepped down onto the deck: 'Welcome aboard, sir,' he said, glancing casually at the pass.

'Thank you, officer,' replied Barvarik. 'My companion is also injured. I suspect his need is greater than mine.' And then, he turned and looked for one last time along the dock. In that instant a woman, standing on her own, caught his eye. She was some distance away and wearing a cloak that was hooded, perhaps to conceal a stain. As he looked, she turned. He saw the way her hair fell across her cheek, and the curve of her face, and he knew her in an instant:

'Talessa!' He shouted and his voice echoed across the dock.

She looked in his direction and stared in disbelief.

But there was no time for anything else. No sooner had Barvarik called out than there was a sudden burst of shouting from the far side of the dock and landing bay. Instinctively, everyone else turned.

They saw in the distance a party of men in commissariat uniforms, carrying clubs and pulse-guns. They had appeared on the dock and were pushing their way through the crowd, calling out orders and threats as they came. One of them, wearing the gold arm bands of a senior intelligence officer, was pointing up at the hospital ship that Barvarik and Shadwatch had just boarded.

'Trouble,' muttered Shadwatch, and put his hand on Barvarik's arm:

'Go and get your girl,' he added, 'and get back here. Quick as you can.'

Barvarik nodded, and began to head down the gangplank, but the ship's officer called him back:

'You'll never make it!' he shouted. 'Those commissariat bully boys mean business. If you get in their way, they'll finish you, for sure.'

'I'll take my chances!' Barvarik shouted back and as he went, he saw that Talessa had started to run towards him.

But at the same time further along the dock, the harbour master came hurrying up to the commissariat squad. He looked angry but saluted and started to say something. But he had only uttered a few words before one of the squad lifted his club and brought it down sharply on the harbour master's shoulder. The man collapsed immediately. Someone screamed, the crowd scattered, and some cursed as they ran, while others ducked their heads and stumbled away.

'Hell's teeth!' shouted the ship's officer, 'they might get away with that in town,' he drew his side-arm, 'but they won't get away with that here.'

He began to set off down the gang plank after Barvarik, and called back to Shadwatch. 'Stay here. This is our fight.'

Several crew members followed him, seizing batons from a deck-rack as they ran and swarmed down the gang plank.

Shadwatch shook his head, as he watched Barvarik and the others. 'The man's a fool,' he said to himself. 'He's almost recovered, but not enough to mix it with that lot down there.' He drew his own sword from his side, and grinned. 'Well, here goes!' he muttered, 'I've enough fight in me for both of us.'

Teevey Blue Ray appeared as if from nowhere, the opening sequence from 'Apocalypse Now', playing on his display and blasting out of his speakers, as he tried to follow his master.

Pushing past some walking-wounded who were still trying to come on board, Shadwatch hurried down the gang plank. Straightaway, he saw that there was no doubt that the commissariat squad were looking for him. Shoulder to shoulder, and with weapons drawn they were hurrying towards the hospital ship. And when their lead-officer caught sight of Shadwatch and Barvarik, he shouted something, and waved his men forward.

By the time Shadwatch reached the dockside the fighting had already begun. Soon, two men were down, one from each side, and several were grappling with opponents, while the rest were using their weapons at close-quarters.

It must have been five seasons at least since Shadwatch had completed his military service, but his training instincts had not deserted him. With his sword held at low guard, and his left arm across his chest, he ran at full stride into the melee. His wound pained him, but he was scarcely aware of it, and tensed himself for the collision.

The man ahead of him raised his pulse-gun and levelled it. There was a flash of light, and a blast of white-hot air as the pulse-ball hissed over Shadwatch's shoulder and exploded against a dock-stanchion. Momentarily deafened, and dazzled by the light, Shadwatch thrust his sword forward, and somehow kept his balance. He struck someone – he was not sure who – and heard him cough and choke as he toppled to one side and disappeared into the brawl.

There was a scream of rage from directly in front of him, and he thrust again with his sword. He heard a clash of steel, and instantly felt the parry of a war-club as it blocked his sword, and almost tore it from his hand. Staggering sideways, he ducked as he had always been taught by his weapons-trainer. The war-club missed his head by a hairsbreadth, and he felt its passing.

Again he struck, but this time his vision had cleared and he saw the trooper in front of him. The man had twisted neatly to keep his footing, and was swinging the club back towards him in a low arc. For just a brief moment that passed almost in slow motion, Shadwatch felt both admiration for his attacker, and a pang of sorrow that one of them would now almost certainly die. He moved inside the blow, and struck hard. The blade of his sword took the man at his neck, cutting through his leather collar and penetrating muscle, sinew and bone.

With a look of surprise, the trooper fell. Catching his breath, Shadwatch stumbled forward over the body, and came up against the commissariat officer, who immediately raised his side-arm and fired. Shadwatch felt himself lifted off his feet and hurled backwards. The projectile had hammered against his chest, breaking ribs and tearing his shoulder muscles, so that he dropped his sword as he came down hard on the dockside paving. He groaned, lifted his one good arm to cover his face, and waited for the death blow.

Someone stepped over him. He heard a clash of blades. And then another, and another even further away before a strange voice cried out. All else was lost in the roar of battle. As he slowly slipped into unconsciousness, he was aware of arms lifting him, and a blurred sensation of being carried backwards. Then, nothing.

Barvarik glanced down at his friend as he stepped over him. He knew that he had been scarcely in time to save Shadwatch, but the battle still raged, a battle that had to be fought and there, yes, on the other side of the dock he could still see Talessa. At last it seemed that she had broken free of the confusion, and was running towards him. She ran with one arm outstretched, head back, gasping with the effort, and eyes wide with hope and joy.

Knocking one man down with the hilt of his sword, and driving his shoulder hard against another, he too ran, his gaze now fixed on Talessa and heedless of the fighting around him. She was closer, so much closer already. Surely! But there was little more than forty paces between Barvarik and Talessa, when all at once there was a flash of light and with it came a searing explosion which swept across the dockside. It enveloped all in its path, a cloud of dense, dark acrid smoke and debris swirling over and around the crowd that was trapped between the warehouses and the mooring posts where the ships were waiting.

Barvarik, thrown back by the shock wave, had only a mere glimpse of Talessa's last despairing effort to reach him before she disappeared into the fury of the blast. Her hands were spread, as if trying in that moment to reach hold of him, and her mouth was open in a silent cry.

He staggered back, and collapsed onto one knee, hardly aware of the stonework and timber shards that fell like rain around him. His ears rang with the echoing roar of the detonating munitions, and then after a pause came the muffled groans and sobs of the countless wounded and dying that now lay across the dock. He gazed, half-stunned, into the madness.

Someone took him by the shoulder. 'My lord!'

He turned. A young sailor, bruised and bloodied with a club in his hand, was staring up at him. 'My lord! You must come now!'

'But . . .' he gestured vaguely in the direction where he had last seen Talessa, where there was now nothing but drifting smoke and a tangle of torn and twisted bodies, some partly buried under rubble.

'There's no-one over there left alive, my lord. No one. We must look to the living. The ship is casting off now. We cannot wait.'

'I will stay here,' muttered Barvarik, his mind overwhelmed and confused by what he had just seen.

The sailor straightened wearily: 'Then more of us will die here my lord. We cannot leave you now. We are in your debt after what you have just done here.'

Barvarik shook his head. 'I cannot go.'

He was all at once painfully aware that he could hardly stand. His limbs shook. He swayed, and felt sick. Then as if from nowhere, he was aware of people either side of him and strong, gentle arms folding about his shoulders and leading him back towards the ship. The dockside melted away.

When Shadwatch awoke, his body heavy with pain, he found himself in a ward-bed on the hospital ship. Everything was white: a bright light made him screw up his eyes. He groaned. At once a figure appeared and leaned over him. It was a woman. She had the mask and gown of a surgeon. Her gloved hand rested gently on his hand which was clenched. 'Rest easy now,' she said. 'You have been badly hurt.'

He tried to speak, but the words wouldn't come. Her hand squeezed his. 'Rest,' she said. 'Your friend brought you here. There was fighting, but you are safe now.'

After a while, Shadwatch was aware of the room rocking slowly from side to side. He tried to speak again, but again there were no words.

'Yes,' the surgeon said, as if she understood him, 'We are at sea at last and on our way to The Island.' Lifting his wrist, she checked his pulse, then turned and spoke to someone else. Shadwatch took that someone to be a nurse, but he couldn't quite tell. Everything was fading again. The room slowly filled with shadows and swirled above him. He slept.

Barvarik was sitting wearily on a bench near Shadwatch's bed. He stood. 'How is he?' he asked the surgeon as she began to move towards another bed and another casualty.

'Your friend is dying,' she replied.

THE FIGHT FOR THE GATES

It was still dark when the war-horns sounded. Anna-Seka awoke cramped and cold in the little hollow where she had slept during the night. The cloak she had wrapped herself in was covered in dew, but the moisture hadn't penetrated and she herself had kept dry, even if she was chilled by the still, damp air. The first faint promise of dawn lit the eastern horizon with a familiar sword blade-blue, and from somewhere she could hear the distant call of a lark. Then the war-horns sounded again, and all else was forgotten. She shook Nike by the shoulder to waken her, and got unsteadily to her feet, confident that the fading shadows of the night were enough to shield her from the eyes of any watchers on the walls.

All about her, the rest of the encampment was stirring, with the usual coughing and clearing of throats, and then, after a moment's pause, the short, sharp barks of the sergeants and provost-marshals. The army had slept where it had stood in the last hour of fighting the day before. Men had simply thrown themselves down in the nearest sheltered spot, ate what rations they had, then curled up and gone to sleep. Some, caught in the open, had used the bodies of their comrades as a shelter, huddling against them, and in some cases pulling the arms of the dead across back or shoulder to shield themselves against a sniper's arrow or pulse-gun.

Someone called her name softly and she turned to see Leviss emerge from the darkness, like a miner coming up out of a pit.

She waved. 'You slept?'

He grunted. 'Some,' he muttered. 'The cold kept me awake, and I kept hearing sounds as though raiders had come out from the city and were crawling towards us.'

'Rats,' said Anna and shuddered.

Leviss stood, grinned and stifled a yawn. 'Most likely,' he said, 'but when you're lying awake at night staring up at the stars, your mind makes up strange tales.' He pointed towards the gates, all but hidden in shadow and a rising mist. 'There's our job for the day, I'm thinking. And here's Uncle Bepsi coming too. He's gone and got our orders already.' Leviss stared towards his uncle for a moment. 'He's not in a hurry, anyway. That's for good or ill, and nothing in between.'

Nike got to her feet, looked up at the walls, and shook her cloak out. 'Let's be gone from this place,' she said. 'If we are here when the sun comes up, those batteries on the walls will make short work of us.'

They began to walk towards Bepsi-Loca, stepping over and around the dead, and crouching in that instinctive way soldiers have when trying not to be an obvious target.

Bepsi-Loca met them with a whispered greeting: 'Good to see you all survived the night,' he said, then frowned. 'No time for breakfast, I'm afraid. We're going in on empty bellies.'

'Going in?' Nike looked puzzled.

'Aye, lass. The senior sergeant over there says we're no longer needed for scouting duties. Headquarters is sending us in with the first wave.'

'That's nice of them,' muttered Leviss. 'In over the hotplate and smack up against the barricades.'

His uncle nodded. 'Looks like it,' he said. 'We'll follow the big engines – the ones they are bringing up now. See, they've got jet-wings as well, and that will give us some extra shelter. We've been assigned war-wagon number 35. You can't miss it.'

'Ah, my lucky number!' laughed Leviss.

'Is it?' asked Anna softly.

The lad turned and put his hand on her shoulder. 'I certainly hope so, Anna. I certainly hope so.' Then he smiled, and gave her shoulder a squeeze. 'Stick close by me. Remember? Where I go you go, but always have my back between yourself and the enemy.'

'All this effort for a prisoner,' said Bepsi-Loca, and he chuckled. 'We must like ye, lassie.'

Again the war-horns sounded. Dawn was lifting on the far horizon, and the shadows were falling back. Whole ranks of men and women now shuffled into line, weapons held at the ready, and war-shields raised. The giant siege engines rolled forward, flattening the ground in front of them, and moments later the first one was heaved up onto the hotplate. Its front wheels sparked and hissed as clouds of steam billowed up and around the strengthened bodywork of wood, steel, aluminum and leather. Almost instantly the lower carriage of the engine began to glow red, and the spokes of the wheels went white with heat. But the super-structure, though smouldering did not burst into flame.

From all sides came a great cheer, and the outlander attack formations, realising that the war-engine was not going to be destroyed by the heat of the plate, surged forward.

It was now that the defenders on the battered walls and towers of

Serenity, reacted: there was a single trumpet note blasted through multiple speakers, and immediately all the batteries and bombards fired at once and together. It was a deafening roar. Instinctively Anna put her hands to her ears and half turned away. There was a hand on her arm:

'Come on lassie! It's our turn now. Come on!'

She looked to see Leviss staring at her. His smile had faded, but there was a purpose in his eyes that she had never seen before.

'Come on!' He shouted again, and they both began to run towards the gates.

Arrows flicked and hissed about them. They scrambled into a low ditch that ran parallel to the walls, and crouching low hurried with the others towards the next of the war engines to approach the hotplate with another war wagon close behind it, both with broad, swept-back wings of painted aluminium. Even as they approached it, a fireball struck the wagon, shattering its frontal guard-plates and sending a wall of flame sweeping through its interior. Men scattered in every direction, some ablaze already, and others holding up their hands to shield their faces from the heat.

But the war engine that followed, though hit repeatedly by ballista bolts and flaming projectiles, kept lumbering forward, towards the hotplate where the first wagon had come to a halt. About two squads of infantry had already clambered aboard. Most of them were armed with pulse-guns and crossbows, and were now directing return fire towards the defenders on the walls.

A thick pall of smoke, carrying the sickly sweet smell of burning flesh drifted over Anna and Leviss as they neared the hotplate and gates. Anna glanced back over her shoulder once again. Nike and Bepsi-Loca were close behind, grimacing as a hail of bolts and ballista shot rattled over their heads, and then both nodding almost in unison as if to say, 'Keep on!'

She tapped Leviss on the shoulder. 'That second war wagon!' she shouted. 'See it? Just beyond that group of spearmen. We should head there.'

Another fireball screeched overhead and plunged into a squadron of horse-archers. Leviss blinked, hesitated for a moment and then shook his head.

'No,' he said. 'That city tower-battery has got their range. We should go to ground here and wait for the next war engine.'

As he finished speaking, a third fireball burst just short of the war wagon Anna had noticed, sending a column of turf and stone whirling skywards, and flinging gouts of flame among the spearmen. When the smoke cleared there were not many standing. But to Anna's surprise the surviving spearmen held their position, weapons held upright as if they were on parade. 'Just like a Guards Regiment,' she muttered to herself. She looked back towards Bepsi-Loca who shrugged, and waved them all down. Then he crawled towards them, with dust and grit from more explosions falling across his face and back.

As he came up to them, and scrambled into the ditch where they had taken shelter, he got to his knees and looked to the gates. 'No point dying too easily,' he said, and lay down again. 'But we can't stay here, neither. The moment that war engine on the hotplate makes a dent in those gates, we make a run for it. Understand?'

Nike frowned. 'But we can't go near the plate on foot. We'd be fried.'

'Aye, we would!' shouted Bepsi-Loca, raising his voice above a volley and counter-volley of bombards. 'But more engines and wagons are coming up soon. One of them is bound to make it onto the plate.'

'Then we run?'

Bepsi smiled at his daughter and ruffled her hair. 'Aye, lassie, and we run like the very devil. Are ye up for that?'

Nike managed a grin. 'Aye, uncle, but it's not the running that worries me, it's the arriving.'

'Ha!' He laughed and rolled onto his back as another shower of earth and stones swept across them. 'Leave that to your wits, lassie-mine. The second you see the barricades and the enemy in front of you, you'll know what to do.' He paused. 'Trust me.'

No one else spoke. Anna lay prone in the ditch, her hands clenching the turf as the roar of battle swept back and forth. Was this her last day?

As if he understood her thoughts, Leviss rested a hand on her shoulder. 'I'll get you through,' he said, 'just see if I don't.'

She tried to smile. 'But what am I to do?' she said, raising her voice and hoping he could hear. 'I cannot fight my own people.'

Leviss thought for a moment. 'You'll know what to do, Anna,' he said. 'Just stay alive. That's all that matters.'

There was a pause in the cannonade. The sound of shot and shell rolled away in a series of fading echoes as the battlefield fell silent.

'There's a piece of luck,' said Bepsi-Loca. 'Both sides reloading and bringing up more ammunition, I'm thinking.' Pushing himself up cautiously on his elbows, he peered at up at the walls, and then looked back towards the main body of the stainer army which was drawn up about half a kilometre away.

'They're bringing up more engines and war wagons,' he said, 'though I don't know how they spare the men to do it. That's difficult ground they are coming across. They'll take a good thrashing if they don't make the plate at the double quick.'

War horns sounded, and several trumpets answered from the ramparts and towers of Serenity, but as yet not a single bombard, catapult or ballista renewed their barrage. Even the bowmen and stone slingers had taken a rest, slumping down behind the battlements, or crouching in the ditch.

Standing up, Bepsi-Loca shifted his buckler to cover his neck and shoulder against arrows from the ramparts. 'There's a war wagon coming almost directly at us,' he said. 'It looks as though it's going to try a crossing on this flank.' Reaching down he helped Nike to her feet, and nodded to Anna and Leviss: 'We'll run back to it now and the moment you can, scramble aboard.'

It didn't take them long to cover the ground between themselves and the wagon which was rumbling steady forward. Without waiting to be asked, they grabbed hold of the boarding-ropes and hauled themselves up and over the bulkheads of the war-wagon.

A captain-of-arms spotted them immediately, and waved them across. They pushed their way through the heavily armed militia and civic-soldiers, and coming up to the captain, gave a hasty salute.

'Scouts?' he asked, glancing at their weapons.

'Aye, sir,' replied Bepsi-Loca. 'We've been holding to that right flank, but when the wall-batteries picked up our range, we thought it best to find a war wagon.'

The captain nodded, and looked at Anna-Seka. 'You're not one of us,' he said.

'I am now,' answered Anna without a pause. 'I was captured a few miles north of here, and my command post was wiped out.'

The captain glanced at Bepsi-Loca, who shrugged. 'She's technically our prisoner, sir,' he said. 'I have her papers.' Reaching into his tunic, he handed them across. 'But I reckon she's become one of us over the past few days.'

Staring at the papers for a moment, the captain looked up. 'Well, all right,' he said. 'She's your responsibility and not mine. And when the fighting starts, we'll not be showing her any special protection. None at all.'

Bepsi-Loca saluted. 'None expected, sir. Actually, she has proved herself useful since we have come up hard against those walls.'

The captain grunted, gazed at Anna for just a moment, and then handed the papers back. 'Take station by that ballista over there. We lost half the crew in the last barrage. You can take over where they left off.' He hesitated. 'You do know how to operate a ballista?'

Bepsi-Loca grinned. 'My son and I built one just last year for our war lord, and that daughter of mine over there is better than any of us at laying and sighting both light and heavy ballistae.'

'Good!' The captain grunted again. 'Well, get ye moving! Those fellows on the ramparts will be giving us full measure any minute now. They've already stalled that war engine we managed to get onto the hotplate.'

By the time they arrived at the ballista platform, orders were being shouted by artillery-sergeants, and crew were hurrying to their positions. At the same time the heavy calibre pulse-guns at the front of the wagon were being swung into firing position.

As Anna clambered up onto the platform, she noticed that the planking was slick with blood. Broken equipment and bits of torn clothing had been pushed aside one corner of the mounting plate. She shuddered.

'Men have died here,' she whispered as she helped Nike wind the left hand windlass back and fix it into the launch setting.

'And will you fight against your own people?' said Nike, with a glance towards the ramparts.

Anna frowned. 'I have people on both sides of those walls, some happy to be citizens and some not.' she replied, leaning hard on the handle of the windlass until she heard the ratchet click.

'Family, then?' Nike waved to Leviss to bring across a ballista bolt.

'Aye, family,' answered Anna with a shrug, but her hands were trembling. 'In the end we fight to survive. We fight to see another day. We fight for each other.'

'And hope to see those we love in that same day,' muttered Nike.

They both looked at each other and smiled sadly. 'You are family now, Anna,' said Nike softly. She reached for the arming-bar, and swung it to the left, so that the head of the ballista swung round to face the ramparts.

As she did so, Leviss came up with a ballista bolt cradled in his arms, and without pausing slid it into the firing channel. 'We have at least a dozen more of these brutes,' he said. 'I found them in an ammunition locker. Here's hoping we get to fire them off before one of those batteries on the walls finds our range.'

The war-wagon rumbled on beneath their feet as they approached the ditch. It would have to turn soon to come up against the hotplate. Then they would be almost flank on to the ramparts and exposed to the full firepower of the defenders. It was going to be a dangerous manoeuvre, and they knew that their only hope lay in the distraction of other engines and war wagons as they also headed for the gates. Although the war-wagons carried pulse-guns and ballistas, they were nowhere near the calibre of the artillery that the soldiers and engineers of Serenity could bring to bear. Chesterman and his warlords had made sure that all of the heavy calibre bombards and mortars the outlander army possessed had been manhandled towards the support line and dragged into position. But there were fewer of them now than there had been at the beginning of the day's fighting, and they were dug in well back from the forward positions that the war-wagons now contested.

Bepsi-Loca hurried up to where they were waiting, a medium range fire-bolt resting over his shoulder:

'The fun will start soon,' he said, but there was no laughter in his voice. 'When the rampart-guns fire, take cover behind those bulkheads. I'll tell ye when to return shot.'

No sooner had he spoken than a flare-rocket arced into the sky high above the city walls, and burst in a shower of blue and white sparks. 'Get down!' he shouted, and they all hurled themselves against the nearest bulkhead.

A storm of lead shot and flaming ballista-balls swept over the war-wagon, which rocked with each impact. Then a shower of wooden splinters scythed across the open deck, knocking men down, and flinging some up and over the bulkheads. One of the pulse-guns at the head of the wagon reared up and then disintegrated as it was struck by battery fire. Its crew were hurled in every direction, and the wooden planking burst into flames. As soldiers, both men and women, ran to clear the wreckage, others helped the wounded away and cleared the dead as best they could before the next volley struck.

Anna saw one militia man run forward with a blanket to beat out the flames. An arrow struck him in the chest, and he staggered sideways, falling to his knees as someone else picked up the blanket and rushed at the fire.

A hand slapped across her cheek. It was Bepsi-Loca. 'No time!' he shouted. 'Aim at the ramparts! Aim high! Shoot now, shoot!'

Almost without thinking, Anna-Seka reacted to her academy training and the long and tiresome days she had spent being instructed in catapults and the ordnance of war engines. With Nike crouching alongside the firing panel and adjusting the sighting mirror, Anna spun the ranging wheel until the angles of shot and deflection intersected.

'Ready!' she called, and stepped back, holding the lanyard in her right fist.

Nike nodded, bit her lip as she focussed on the target and then suddenly pushed the firing-switch.

There was a pause, the lanyard pulled, the mechanism released and immediately the ballista whooshed into life. As the launch-arms thrust forward, the main-frame jerked and the ballista-bolt left its channel in a steel-blue blur of tempered metal.

'Shot away!' shouted Nike straightening, then without pausing shouted: 'Loaders!

Leviss and his father had loaded the next bolt even before the first one had reached its target. Anna just had time to glance up as the ballista bolt they had launched skimmed the top of the ramparts and smashed into a wall-mounted battery at a range of about five hundred paces. It toppled from view, its support-legs rearing skywards, and one of the gun-crew falling, arms spread, down the face of the wall.

'Shot!' said Bepsi-Loca. 'Shot!' He pointed wildly. 'Now, let's see if we can't hit that pulse-gun three degrees to the left. See it?'

Nike shook her head. 'Uncle, we can't. It has an armour-plate shield. Too strong!'

They all ducked as another storm of shot swept across the wagon, but this time the wall-batteries had fired high. To their relief all the bolts, projectiles and flame-balls did no more than clip a few stanchions and railing bars as they ploughed on and over the wagon, plunging into the infantry about fifty yards further back.

With a high-pitched laugh, Bepsi-Loca hit the ballista-frame with the flat of his hand:

'Ah, did ye see that? Either they forgot to lower their sights, or we've managed to get under their guns.' He laughed again. 'Come on lassies! We may not be able to pierce that armour, but we can make that battery of theirs rattle like a tin-can. Up, now! Up!'

They fired again. And again. The war wagon lurched to the left, shook and then rumbled on, smoke now pouring from its wheels and plated underside as it reached the edge of the hotplate. Fire-arrows snaked out of the smoke and dust clouds, striking men down at random, or thudding into woodwork and leather facings. Operating from deep within Serenity's defences, the crews of howitzer-mortars hurled solid shot as well as the feared glass-bombs which shattered on impact and spread flaming liquid in every direction. To those on the war-wagon who were still alive, it seemed as if they were headed inexorably towards a shimmering wall of flame and dense, acrid smoke, out of which projectiles of every type hissed and howled towards them.

It was cold comfort for them to know that their own artillery was hurling a similar barrage about the heads of the defenders on the ramparts and towers of the city.

Heaving the ballista around, Anna and Nike brought it to bear on the armour-plated pulse-gun for a final shot before they reached the gates. It was a good shot, but not a lucky one. It hit the armoured mantlet of the pulse gun, and then skidded off, whining harmlessly into the ruins of a battered warehouse inside the city by less than a hundred paces beyond the outer wall.

'Prepare to ram!' shouted the captain.

Its generator screaming, the war-wagon gathered pace, straightened slightly to bring it into line with a massive war engine that had appeared on its left flank, and rushed at the gates. Its wheels were now glowing white-hot, and sparks whirled up from the axles and suspension, but despite the increasing heat, and ever thickening clouds of smoke, it held its course.

'Hold on to something, and keep your heads down!' shouted Bepsi-Loca, and an instant later there was a shuddering roar as the extended ram of the war-wagon cannoned into the gates.

That alone would not have been enough to threaten the walls, but even as the ram struck, the war-engine hurled its great bulk at the point of fissure that had started to grow. And even as its leaden snout struck home, the stainer engineers fired all of their forward artillery.

The sound was so deafening that for a moment Anna lost all sense of where she was and what was happening. The world seemed to spin around her head, and the air was filled with glowing embers, metallic splinters of armour plate and pieces of jagged masonry. Letting go of the bulkhead, she collapsed onto the decking, and put her hands to her ears. Nike fell half across her, blood already streaming from a scalp wound, and Leviss was driven hard against the main support of the ballista. Bepsi-Loca had disappeared somewhere in the confusion of smoke and flame.

But the wall held. Both the war wagon and the engine of war pulled back, and prepared to attack again.

On the other side of the gates, the defenders were also making ready. Huge timber supports had been dragged into position by teams of engineers, while squads of soldiers hurried back and forth with sandbags, packing them against the gates. Still others repaired cracks in the masonry as best they could, forcing quick-dry cement and fixing foam into the gaps, and driving steel stakes against the foundation stones.

A few paces further back a city regiment was drawn up, pulse-guns held at the ready, and the regimental trumpeter waiting for the order to sound the advance.

Lord Akton was standing among them. He was trembling inwardly at the thought of the fight that must surely come when the stainers finally broke through, but he could not imagine himself to be in a better place. 'Here,' he muttered to himself, 'is a place where I can truly serve the king's people.' No one overheard him, nor would they have cared if they had happened to overhear him. All eyes were on the wall of the main gates, and even the commander who had just come to where Akton was now standing, had no more time for words, or clever speeches. What was needed now was a steady hand, a cool head and more luck than any of them could reasonably expect or deserve.

The commander breathed deeply. The gates shook to another blow and clouds of dust fell in curtains from the ramparts above.

'Hot work, my lord,' he shouted to Akton.

The chancellor smiled wearily, and leaned on the corner of a broken wall. 'Will it hold do you think?' he asked.

'Who knows.' The commander shrugged. 'But we will be ready for them if they come our way. Won't we lads?'

The soldiers raised a ragged cheer. 'We are ready, sire,' said a colour-sergeant. 'We'll make the king proud of this regiment, no matter what the cost.'

'You'll do, lads,' shouted the commander. 'But get ye into the shelter of that rubble over there. No sense in standing out here in the open any longer than we have to. There's more excitement coming our way, and sooner than we would like.'

Even as he finished speaking the air was split by the screeching roar of incoming fire-bolts, and as they came the city ballista batteries replied.

CHAPTER #14

A BROTHER AND A KING

Several hours earlier, high atop the living quarters in the heart of the royal precinct, Marlin and Chesterman had confronted the king.

When they entered the royal apartments, he was still awake, alone as usual on a garden terrace, and staring up at the vast canopy of steel and glass that sheltered the precinct from the weather, whatever the season. He glanced at the two men as they came towards him. For a moment, he hesitated, then shrugged and looked away.

'Such a sky,' he said quietly. 'So many stars, so clear and bright.' He paused. 'And so very peaceful. So very still.'

Marlin removed his helmet. 'Unlike our city, your majesty,' he replied.

The king nodded slowly and turned. 'Ah, brother,' he said, without a trace of surprise. 'I thought it was you. It is your stride, you see. The way you walk. Too much time in the army, I fear. Too much of the parade ground.' He shook his head. 'All that spit and polish.'

'It has served me well,' answered Marlin. 'Perhaps you would have been better served if you had spent more effort . . .'

The king smiled as he raised his hand. 'More effort at playing toy soldiers, brother? No, I think not. I spend my days tracking down traitors and discovering all manner of plots and conspiracies.' He looked narrowly at Chesterman, still hidden by his motorcycle helmet. 'I commend you gentlemen for daring to penetrate my security, and for managing to get this far. It is a pity that you will, both of you, be dead before the next hour strikes.' He smiled again. 'You have been expected of course. And observed. Throughout this evening, I have received reports of your progress. Even now, my bodyguards and imperial protection squad watch your every move. They are close by of course. A snap of the fingers away.'

For a moment Marlin looked confused. 'But that's impossible,' he said.

'Hah!' The king shook his head. 'This entire city, this kingdom you so happily betrayed, it is impossible. Look now! What do you see? Is it not magnificent? Is it not beyond the petty dreams of ordinary men?'

'It is doomed,' replied Chesterman, his voice distorted by the speaker-foil in his closed helmet, 'as are you, and that lying tongue of yours.'

The king's eyes widened. For a moment he said nothing. When at last he spoke, it was a single word:

'I see before me a stainer scoundrel from the outlands. That helmet you wear gives you away. My people tell me your name is Chesterman,' he said and his voice shook.

'That is my name,' replied Chesterman, 'and as you have your warlords, so I have mine. And as you have your city, so I have mine also.' He gestured towards Marlin. 'Your brother has been of great assistance to me over these past years.'

Marlin did not reply, but kept staring, his hand resting on his sword, and his helmet now hanging from the strap on his hip. It was the king who spoke again:

'How can this be, brother?' said the king suddenly. 'You are a defender of Serenity, a noble of royal blood, and one who has sworn an oath to defend Serenity and the kingdom.'

'Aye,' replied Marlin. 'And that has not changed. I am a defender of the city and the kingdom, but not a defender of its rogue king.'

Straightening, the king raised his voice. 'You are right. I am the king. Serenity is the king, and the king is Serenity.'

'Hah! By my faith you are not a true king!' Marlin spat the words. 'You are a wretch and always have been. You destroyed my family and exiled or murdered the queen, my wife. You ground every royal principle beneath the sole of your boot, and called it justice.'

'I did not!'

'Liar!' replied Marlin shaking with anger. 'You condemned my wife and children who trusted you, even loved you and loved me as I loved them. You were without pity to either myself or them because they fell under the curse of the stain. Despite all my pleas, as brother to brother, blood to blood, you treated my family as common criminals. And more than this, all who have ever opposed you, you have crushed without mercy. And all those who fell beneath the stain, you have imprisoned, executed or driven into exile.' He paused, struggling to catch his breath. 'Nor did it did move you to mercy when I too fled to escape the terror of your rule.'

The king grunted. 'I always worked within the law,' he answered. His hand moved to the hilt of his dagger, and he glanced around as if expecting to see the arrival of the security services.

'Within the law?' Marlin took a step towards his brother. 'You ignored the law of the high council, and wrote laws of your own when any whim took your fancy. The blood of my family is on your hands, and I have come to avenge them, wherever they are, or wherever they might lie.' As he spoke, his sword slid from its scabbard, and he raised it. 'Say your prayers, brother.'

Stepping back quickly, almost cat-like in his movement, the king drew both dagger and sword in a single practised movement. He had never shown much interest in military affairs, but there was not a day went by that he did not practise the art of swordsmanship with the imperial arms-master. His skill was as renowned in the palace as was his temper.

'If you want my blood then come and claim it, but know this,' said the king, 'I gave sentence against your wife and family, but I did not carry it out. What happened to them is unknown to me.' He paused. 'Nor do I care.'

'Tell me what you know,' said Marlin, his sword still raised, 'and I will make your ending swift.'

It was Chesterman who now interrupted. 'We do not have time for this,' he said, drawing his own sword and switching it on, so that the blade glowed. 'Nor am I interested in the details of this man's treachery. You may want blood, lord Marlin, but what I require is a simple surrender, and a simple execution, no more. This brother of yours can seek mercy, and perhaps I will grant it, but he must abdicate before the people, and stand trial in the high court for his crimes against those same people. Then, if I am moved to mercy, his ending will be swift.'

'But you promised, my lord!' Marlin looked confused. 'You promised me my brother's head. At my hand.'

'Did I? Perhaps I did, but even I am inclined to mercy when I see this poor fellow before me. No, let him beg for such mercy, and then I'll have him put to shame and then death before the people. That is all.'

'I spit on your mercy!' shouted the king and as he shouted the doors to the apartment swung open, and the security team entered.

Levelling their weapons, they came forward and saluted. 'Sire,' said their leader, 'we have come as ordered.'

'Arrest these men,' said the king quietly, with a soft smile.

'That officer is not talking to you, my lord,' said Chesterman, 'he is addressing me.'

The king stared. 'What do you mean? What nonsense is this?'

'I mean,' replied Chesterman, 'that these men whom you supposed to be your servants, are in fact mine.' He turned to the leader of the security team. 'Stand your men down, colonel.'

The officer saluted and nodded to his men, who shouldered their weapons.

The king went pale. He trembled and clenched his fist. 'Betrayed at every hand,' he hissed, 'betrayed!'

'Accept your fate,' said Chesterman, his voice cool and level. 'Surrender your sword.'

'By the gods of Serenity and the courts of the kingdom, I will not!' cried the king, and he leapt at Marlin, his sword raised.

The two brothers met in a blur of steel. Blades clashed, and clashed again sending an echo through the open-roofed apartment. Both men stepped back and then closed once more: three cuts, three parries, and sparks flew from the blades. Chesterman with the security team at his back now stepped forward, but Marlin seeing him come, warned him back.

'No, my lord!' he shouted. 'The king is mine. I will not have him slaughtered like a pig at market. If he could not live like a king, he at least will die as one!'

Chesterman stepped to one side, and watched as the king and his brother came against each other. Again the blades struck sparks. Both men recoiled, recovered and attacked once more. This time Marlin cut high, and the king cut low. Both were killing strokes, and executed with skill, but it was Marlin's blade that was the fraction faster.

The king gave a cough as his brother's sword took him at the neck. The blade bit through the brass-studded leather collar that the king always wore as a guard against assassination, but on this occasion it was not enough to save him. Letting go of his own sword even as it swept down to take Marlin in the thigh, the king fell to his knees and slumped sideways to the floor. Instantly, blood pooled about him, and his breath came in a gasp. Marlin did not hesitate. He gave a cry, let go his own sword, and In a moment was by his brother's side, kneeling and cradling him in his arms.

With eyes wide, Marlin looked up at Chesterman: 'I have killed my brother,' he said, 'See! I have not killed a king. I have killed my brother.' Then he turned to the king, still holding him in his arms. 'Brother,' he whispered. 'Forgive me, brother.'

The king opened eyes, such eyes once renowned for their beauty once jet black, but even now fading against the smooth and whitening pallor of his face. 'Is this not a beautiful death?' he asked, his voice scarcely more than a guttural whisper. 'And all for beauty's sake.'

Marlin nodded, and brushed the matted hair from his brother's brow. 'How did it come to this?' he said, ignoring Chesterman's impatient sigh.

'Ah, my brother,' the king's eyes rolled back in his head for just a moment, and a trickle of blood appeared at the corner of his mouth. 'Why should I need to forgive you, my brother? You have set me free. You have set me free.' For a moment, he seemed to rally, looked at Marlin and gave a slight smile. 'My chancellor knows the fate of your wife and family. Ask Akton, he will know. He is an honourable man, he will . . .' His voice trailed away, his head rocked back, he choked, coughed blood and was gone.

For a few seconds Marlin held the king in his arms, and then he gently lowered him to the floor. Reaching down, he moved to close his brother's eyes but something made him hesitate. And although he lightly touched his brother's face, the eyes remained open.

Again he looked up at Chesterman, and the security men who stood silently around him. 'We cannot leave the king here,' he said.

'We must,' replied Chesterman. 'The dawn is upon us. Look!' he gestured towards the over-arching canopy of skylight. 'Not every man and woman in the palace is loyal to me. The duty officer and his patrol will be here directly. They always come at dawn. You know that. If we are found here now, all is lost.' Leaning down, he took Marlin by the shoulder.

'Up, man! Up now! We must to the spire. I must tell the people.'

'That the king is dead?'

'Aye, and that we have a new king.' Chesterman tapped the side of his helmet. 'Come now. You have your revenge. Come!'

Marlin slowly got to his feet. He gazed at the body of his brother. 'There lies the beauty of Serenity,' he said, 'and it was me who struck him down.'

'By all the gods!' hissed Chesterman. 'This is no time for pity and speeches. The man was a rogue and you know it. You have your brother's blood! Away now, or we too, all of us here, will be lying there in our own blood.'

Shaking his head, Marlin sheathed his sword. 'You go to the spire,' he muttered. 'Take those men with you. Put on the king's apparel. Take up his mask, if you need to. Do what you must. I will find Akton.'

For a moment Chesterman stared at Marlin, expressionless. Afar off, both men could hear the sound of booted feet coming along a corridor.

'All right, then,' said Chesterman suddenly. 'Find the chancellor. I have other people in this precinct. They will get me from this place to the capsule and the spire.' He paused, and gestured to the security men. 'Get moving,' he said, 'we have a long way to go.' He glanced at Marlin: 'Return to me if you are able.'

Without waiting for a reply, Chesterman turned and followed the others towards the main door of the apartment. The king's mask was hanging on a display stand to one side of the door. Lifting it clear in one easy movement, Chesterman pushed the door open and disappeared.

Marlin watched him go, then knelt by the body of the king. 'So long, my brother,' he muttered. 'My hate for you ran deep for all these years, but that river is now dry.' He stood. 'No more hate,' he muttered. The sound of boots was getting closer, 'Not hate, just sorrow.'

Looking around, he saw an open door and a side passage with a stairwell. He ran towards it.

THE WAY HOME

The surgeon had completed her rounds. On her way back to her cabin and the hope of a few snatched hours of rest, she stopped at Shadwatch's bedside. He was sleeping but the young warrior who had brought him onto the ship and into the ward was still sitting on the bench, waiting.

'How is he?' she asked.

'He breathes,' replied Barvarik, 'but he does not breathe well.'

The surgeon nodded, checked Shadwatch's pulse, and then put her hand on his brow. 'There is little we can do,' she said softly. 'That pulse-gun was fitted with cadmium pellets.'

'Poison?'

'Yes, and fast-acting. There is nothing that can arrest it. Your friend will be dead by morning.'

Shadwatch's eyes flickered and opened. 'So, I will not see The Island,' he said. 'That is a pity.'

With a glance of surprise, the surgeon nodded, and then smiled. 'You are stronger than I ever guessed,' she said. 'Are you not in pain?'

Shadwatch smiled back. 'My body is broken,' he replied. 'It has forgotten pain.'

He tried to sit up, but slumped back with a grimace. 'Where is Barvarik?'

'Here, my friend.' Barvarik came and stood by the bed. 'What can I do?'

Again Shadwatch grimaced. He was struggling to speak:

'Barvarik, listen to me. The serum. The Gene Pool. All that was in it. You have it, Barvarik. It's in your blood.'

'You mean?'

'Tell her, Barvarik, tell the doctor. You recovered because of that, and that alone.' His voice faded away, and he closed his eyes for a moment. When he opened them again, they were bloodshot. Sweat glistened on his forehead, and his limbs were trembling.

The surgeon rested her hand on his chest. 'Easy now,' she whispered. 'Rest easy.'

'No, no.' He choked on the words, speaking more slowly and catching his breath: 'You must understand, doctor. Please. My friend here has the answer to the stain, and the answer lies in the immune system, his immune system. That was the combination we were looking for. You understand? Freedom at last.' Exhausted, he groaned and sank into a deep sleep once more.

Frowning, and with a slight shake of the head, the surgeon stepped back from the bed and looked at Barvarik. 'You had better explain,' she said.

Quickly, Barvarik outlined the story of the fight in the laboratory, and their escape from Serenity and arrival at Portus-Portus. He described his own wounds, his recovery and the last desperate effort to board the hospital ship. He did not mention Talessa.

'And so here we are,' he said, coming back to himself, 'and here I am about to lose another friend.'

The surgeon looked intently at the young man in front of her. 'Well, I'm not sure your story makes sense, but I know that Shadwatch is the senior Glamtech official, and I see that you also wear the badge of an elite imperial regiment. Show me your wounds.'

She examined Barvarik, gave a shrug, looked away for a moment, and then turned again to him. 'Remarkable,' she said, 'truly remarkable.'

'Perhaps,' said Barvarik uncertainly, 'if what Shadwatch says is true, you could transfuse some of my blood to him.'

'Hah!' the surgeon shook her head. 'It's too late for that, and even if there was an opportunity, we would have to give him every ounce of blood you have, and then some. His whole system is saturated with cadmium, as well as internally scorched by the high-impact pulse he received.' She shook her head. 'No chance, I'm afraid.'

'But we could try. Surely.'

'I don't think you heard me,' replied the surgeon, picking up Shadwatch's notes from the end of the bed. 'He's a good man, no doubt about that, and a very brave one, but for all that he's a dead man already. He was dying from the moment that he took that shot from a pulse-gun. His internal organs have suffered critical damage. It's a miracle he was able to find the strength to tell us what he wanted us to hear just now.'

Barvarik stared, and for a while said nothing. The deck rocked gently as the ship changed course and turned against a rising swell. 'What's to do then?' he asked at last.

'For your friend? Very little. We can make him comfortable, and ease his pain. A heavy dose of sedatives, and then wait till morning, that's the plan.' She sighed. 'We've lost some good people already today, and we will be losing more no doubt. But . . .' she paused and brushed away a tear that took her by surprise, 'maybe there's some hope in what lord Shadwatch has told us. Maybe we have a chance here to make all of this sorry mess somehow worthwhile.' She paused. 'I'm not sure, not sure at all.'

A nurse came up to the surgeon, and handed her some notes. She scanned them quickly, signed the top copy and handed them back. 'Very good,' she said. 'Tell the rest of the staff to prepare for landfall in six hours. Last medication to be issued an hour before we dock.'

The nurse nodded and left. Teevey Blue Ray headed aimlessly towards the door, then turned and drifted back. The death song from 'Lord of the Rings' rose above the hum of the ward, and then faded away.

Below the ward deck, the wind generators of the main engine room throbbed and whirred, the sound rising and falling as the ship pitched and rolled in the ocean swell. But even through that gentle roar Barvarik could hear the gasps, sighs and muttered groans of the casualties. Men, women and children lay in carefully set rows across the ward, some in beds others on stretchers. Many were from the fighting in Serenity, while others were the survivors of the disorder that had broken out at the docks of Portus-Portus when the security forces of the commissariat had appeared and opened fire. Talessa was not among them.

There was a smell of blood mixed with disinfectant, sweat and dirt: a smell of the battlefield that Barvarik was all too familiar with. He blinked. His eyes stung and for the first time he noticed that he was sweating and yet trembling at the same time as he felt a sudden chill take hold.

Someone took his hand. It was the surgeon. 'You need to sleep,' she said, and gestured towards a canvas mattress that had been pushed against one of the steel bulkheads of the ward room wall. 'Lie down there. Sleep. I will wake you when we reach The Island.'

He shook his head. 'I will keep watch,' he replied. 'For my friend.' Then he paused. 'There was a girl, there on the docks. Did anyone see her?'

'A girl?'

'Yes, my girl. I had been looking for her, you see. And by chance I saw her on the docks just before the fighting started.' He shook his head. 'I couldn't get to her.'

'And you think that maybe she made it on board one of the ships?'

Barvarik looked at the doctor: 'It's what I'm hoping.'

'I'll check,' she said. 'A girl, you say.'

Barvarik nodded. 'Talessa is her name. She is from Upper Town.'

'You mean, Talessa, daughter of Akton, a citizen of the second court?'

'Yes. Will you check?'

The doctor now nodded. 'I will check.' She hesitated. 'Your Talessa: we heard that she had caught the stain, and had been imprisoned. A tragedy, and so unjust.'

Barvarik smiled wearily. 'Thank you.' He looked around. 'I will keep watch here.'

'No need,' she answered. 'Your friend has just passed.' She squeezed Barvarik's hand. 'The silver cord is loosed and the pitcher broken at the well. Isn't that what they used to say?'

Barvarik stared at the surgeon, struggling to understand that Shadwatch was suddenly not with them any more. How was it that the doctor knew that poem from the ancient book of books? And why did she quote it now? Was she really of that legendary priesthood, the priesthood that his grandparents used to talk about when the family were gathered about the fireside on a winter's evening?

'I know that poem,' he said quietly, after a while. 'My grandmother taught it to me years ago, but swore me to silence.' Part of his mind was filled with the realization that he had lost Talessa, and that Shadwatch was now dead. The other part clung to a memory of the ancient poem he had just heard.

The surgeon smiled. 'And now?' she said, 'Are you still sworn to silence? Now that your friend is dead?'

Barvarik looked to where Shadwatch lay still and pale, flawless beneath the glow of the hospital lamps. Then, still staring at the body, he spoke. He spoke almost without thinking, intoning the lines from the poem he had been learned all those years ago, and which just now the doctor had recited:

'Or the golden bowl be broken, or the wheel broken at the cistern. Then shall the dust return to the earth as it was, and the spirit shall return unto God Who gave it.'

'You have a good memory,' the surgeon smiled sadly. 'Your grandmother taught you well.'

He shrugged, all at once too weary to stand for any longer. 'We were told never to mention that poem outside our own homes. I kept my promise all these years,' he smiled sadly, 'but this was the day and the time to break it.'

'For your friend?'

He nodded. 'I need to rest,' he said. Then for the first time, he looked closely at the surgeon. So distracted had he been by Shadwatch's struggle to stay alive and his final surrender, that he had scarcely noticed the woman who gazed at him from behind her surgical mask. With her hair tucked neatly beneath her ward-cap, she had a youthful look to her, despite the greying hair and tired eyes. Her face was drawn, but not gaunt, and the cheekbones were high and graceful.. And those eyes, softly blue with flecks of green. 'I am sorry,' he said. 'I did not mean to stare.'

She smiled and lowered her mask. 'It is all right,' she said. 'I could sense that somehow you have only just noticed me. Your friend, of course. It is a time for sorrow.'

He shrugged. 'We are surrounded by sorrow in such times.'

'My name is Doctor Melchea,' she said, 'Sorrow comes with my trade, but every so often we find joy in it.'

'When someone recovers?'

She nodded. 'There is always hope,' she replied. 'And there are always those who recover. That is what keeps us going. Always and ever, among the wounded and dying, I find that there is one who has a spark of life that we can encourage.'

'It is a noble profession.' Barvarik knew that his voice sounded flat, wooden. But he was no longer sweating, and his chill had gone.

The doctor lowered her eyes and smiled again beneath her mask. 'My profession is a calling, given to me by my parents and their parents before them. We are a family of nurses and surgical folk, and a family of believers.'

'Believers?'

'Aye,' she glanced around the ward where white-coated nurses moved silently betweens the beds and stretchers. 'The book your grandmother taught you, and the one you were never to mention: for our family it has always been more than just a book. It is a code.'

Barvarik frowned. 'A secret code, I think.'

'In these dark days, that is safest. There was a time when the Book as we have always called it, could be read aloud in the streets and taught in the schools, but that time has long since passed.'

'That is safest,' muttered Barvarik, and he looked towards the entrance to the ward. Perhaps, Talessa had made it onto another boat.

'Safest but not best.' The doctor sighed and dropped her voice to a whisper as two nurses and an orderly came to take Shadwatch away. 'One day, things may yet change, and change for the better.'

They both watched as Shadwatch was carefully wrapped in a shroud, placed on a trolley and wheeled out of the ward, followed by Teevey.

'We will look after your friend,' said the doctor-surgeon. 'There is a graves-commission on The Island. They will give lord Shadwatch an honourable burial. Everything will be done as it should be, even in these times.'

'And I will be there,' said Barvarik quickly.

'That is indeed possible,' she replied, 'but first I would ask you to accompany me to the Health Ministry once we have made landfall. We need to do some tests, and establish if indeed as your friend said, you carry in your bloodstream the key to a successful anti-stain serum.'

'Surely that could wait?'

'Time is not on our side. Not everyone in Serenity approves of the evacuation of citizens to The Island. As you saw, the commissariat itself is not afraid to use force to try and disrupt the process, even though the process has the approval of the high council.'

'But not the approval of the king.' As Barvarik spoke, he sat down wearily on the mattress, and looked up at the doctor-surgeon. 'I think perhaps he would have us fight to the last man, woman and child rather than accept defeat.'

'You speak as though you expect the outlander army to carry the city.' For a moment she was distracted by another patient being brought into the ward. When she turned again to speak to Barvarik, he was already asleep.

With a slight smile, she took a blanket from a ward-trolley and put it carefully about his shoulders. 'Sleep on, young warrior,' she whispered. 'You have lost much today. You may yet gain something from tomorrow.'

The wind generators hummed, and the deck rocked gently as the ship settled to its course. Across the ward, ward-lamps flickered softly above the crowded beds, and threw shadows across the doctors and attendant nurses as they moved among the patients.

In five hours dawn would break on the eastern horizon. In six hours, all going well, the crewman posted to the look-out would sound the ship's klaxon as he caught sight of the harbour lights of Haven Reach, the main port of The Island.

DEATH AT THE GATES

The wall at the gate still held. Despite the repeated attacks of armoured wagons, war-engines and stainer infantry, the main defences of Serenity remained intact. Much of the upper wall-works, both ramparts and towers, had been reduced to ruins, half hidden by fire and smoke, but the wall-gate still held.

Engineers from Brokinburgh, ordered forward by stainer officers, had twice tried to mine the walls and pillars that framed the gates, but twice they had been hurled back by groups of defenders who had appeared from concealed sally ports. In the hand to hand fighting that took place, both sides suffered heavy casualties. But the outcome was the same: the engineers had been forced back, leaving their siege equipment battered and broken at the base of the walls. And even as stainer infantry armed with pulse-guns rushed forward to support the engineers, the surviving defenders melted away into the smoke and dust, vanishing through the sally ports as if they had never existed.

From where she crouched, next to Leviss in a drainage ditch, Anna-Seka watched the battle for the gates. She was horrified by the losses on both sides, but nevertheless strangely relieved that the gates had not yet been carried, and the walls not yet breached. Although more and more drawn to Leviss, Nike and Bepsi-Loca, she knew that she was first and last a child of Serenity. Her fear was that somehow in this fight, soldiers of Serenity would attack her outlander friends, here, now in front of the walls. She bit her lip. If that were to happen, she would have to decide who to protect, and against whom to raise her hand.

Again, it was Leviss who guessed her thoughts.

'Here!' he shouted in her ear. 'Take this!'

She looked down as something was pressed into her hand. It was a pulse-gun.

'I can't!' she shouted back.

'You must!' he replied and put his hands to his ears as a fire-ball exploded against a war-wagon not twenty-five paces from where they hid. A metal wing from its framework was hurled into the air, and fell like a fantastical shining leaf, into the rubble. As clouds of dust and debris settled about them, he moved even closer to Anna, reaching out to put his hand on hers. 'Use the gun to defend yourself,' he said. 'We will fight as we must, but if they break through, you will have no chance to explain who you are. They will shoot you down, as soon as look at you.' He looked at her, shook his head and grinned. 'I'll not let you die here, Anna. You were born to survive this day, and I was born to look after you.'

She looked at him through the dust, blinking as the grit blew against her face:

'Thank you,' she said, taking the pulse-gun and carefully testing the grip. Then she lifted it and rested the barrel across her breast.

An officer of the Brokinburgh corps of rangers appeared from somewhere behind them, and slid down into the ditch.

'What unit are you?' he asked, breathing hard..

'Thirty fifth, sir,' replied Bepsi-Loca. 'We pulled back from the hot-plate after the last attack, but are ready to go again.'

The officer squinted through the murk at the gates almost hidden by the wrecks of blazing war-wagons and a half-toppled siege engine. 'Good!' he said. 'Wait until the next battery of war-engines comes up, and get aboard any that come by your position. We are going to try and bring down the support-towers on both sides of the gates, and get in that way.' He glanced at Anna:

'What's your status, soldier?' he said.

Anna risked a salute. 'Border scout, sir,' she replied. 'Recently seconded to this unit.'

The officer stared at her for a moment, but her uniform, or what was left of it, was so bedraggled and dust-covered that he did not seem to notice the badges and shoulder flashes of the Serenity imperial force. 'Very good,' he muttered, and turned again to Bepsi-Loca:

'Wait until the next barrage is lifted, and then choose your moment.'

'Aye, sir,' Bepsi-Loca returned a salute crisp enough to make Nike and her brother grin. Then he pointed up at the walls:

'And if the towers are not brought down by the barrage?'

The officer shrugged. 'We go in anyway,' he answered, and with a last glance at Anna-Seka, he disappeared towards the centre of the line and another group of infantry.

'That was close,' laughed Nike. 'Those Burgh city rangers have a habit of shooting prisoners when the mood takes them.'

Leviss grunted. 'If he'd have tried, I'd have knocked his head off.'

'Ah, would ye now, my lad?' said Bepsi-Loca. 'Well, it's just as well that our Anna here had the good sense to save you the trouble.' Then he nodded towards where a formation of war-wagons was making its way towards the centre of the line. 'The heavies are on the move again,' he said. 'We won't have long to wait until our artillery picks up the pace.' He knelt down and checked his ammunition belt. 'Don't move till I move, but when I do, run like the very devil, and don't stop for anyone.' He looked at Leviss. 'No one, you understand, lad? No one.'

Leviss frowned, but slowly nodded. 'Don't worry, uncle,' he muttered, 'I'll run with my eyes shut.'

Moments later, all at once the air was split with the thunderous roar of every bombard battery still available to the outlander army. The pulse-weapons of the foremost war-wagons joined in, and a squadron of siege engines opened up with their catapults, fire-launchers and pulse-rockets.

Anna-Seka threw herself down and clung to some tree roots straggling across the bottom of the ditch. They trembled in her hands, and the walls of the ditch itself shook, sending clods of earth tumbling down onto her back. Her ears rang with the sound of the artillery, and although she was vaguely aware of Bepsi-Loca shouting something, she could not make out a single word he said.

A fire-shell burst almost directly over their heads, sending cascades of burning embers across the rubble, and down into the ditch where they were hiding. Beating the embers out with his gloved hands, Leviss grinned again and then hauled Anna up so that she found herself sitting with her back to the wall of the ditch.

'You can't stay here!' he shouted. 'Didn't ye hear my father? On his count, we run.'

Anna-Seka blinked. 'His count?' She mouthed the words in the deafening roar.

'Aye!' He nodded. 'The count of three, that's when we run. If ye can't hear him, just watch!' He laughed, and then winced as a pulse-rocket arced towards them from the remains of a defence tower, burst just beyond a fallen tree and sent a wave of hot air and dust across them.

'Too close! Too close!' he said, laughed again and slapped Anna on the shoulder. 'Are ye ready, lassie?'

She nodded. 'When you go, I go,' she said, and tried to smile.

'That's the spirit!' he shouted. 'Don't worry, I'll get ye through this.'

A counter-battery fired from somewhere behind the walls of the city. For a moment the smoke-filled air turned crimson, shot through with flashes of brilliant white light. The super-heated projectiles crested what was left of the city ramparts and then plunged in among the advancing war-wagons.

They watched as one explosion after another hurled war wagons skywards, or made them topple sideways. Three wagons were destroyed outright, another two lurched drunkenly out of formation and crashed against a reserve rank of siege engines. Yet another wagon which had just reached the hotplate, fell onto its side and disappeared in a curtain of flames.

'Now's our chance!' yelled Bepsi-Loca. 'Before they reload! We go now!' Forgetting to count, he sprang to his feet and began to run across the open ground towards the war wagons and siege engines.

Taking a deep breath, Anna-Seka scrambled to her feet, followed Leviss out of the ditch, and began to run. Nike was close behind her, carrying her own pulse-gun in both hands, and gasping as she ran.

A final salvo from the outlander support-artillery roared over their heads and thundered into the towers on either side of the main gate-wall.

Anna ran. She dared not look up, but even as she ran, she heard above the storm of shot and shell a strange and terrible sound. It was a deep harsh crackling sound combined with a weird, echoing rumble that seemed to go on and on.

'See now!' It was Nike who called out, and glancing back, Anna saw her pointing wildly towards the gates.

Both towers had collapsed, twisting and then buckling inwards as they broke up in a cloud of falling masonry, timberwork and dust. The full weight of the collapsed towers struck the wall, already weakened by earlier barrages of stainer artillery.

'They've gone! They've gone!' Nike's voice rose above the roar of battle, and mingled with the shouts and cheers of the infantry regiments that were hurrying forward to support the assault. The gates and towers had collapsed.

Almost instantly, they noticed that a significant amount of the rubble from the towers was now strewn across the hotplate, allowing the infantry to advance towards the breach without first clambering onto the war wagons. Horns sounded all along the line of advance, the banners of the stainer army dipped forward, and hundreds of soldiers rushed towards the broken gateway.

But what defenders there were, once they had recovered from the shock of seeing the gate towers come down, reacted quickly. The harsh bark of short-range catapults and ballistas rippled along the jagged ramparts, and pulses of white-fire zipped and whined out of the dust clouds, and into the ranks of the attackers.

Anna-Seka, Bepsi-Loca with Nike and Leviss ran towards the breach. Sniper-fire from concealed gun-ports in the walls kicked up the turf around them, and ricocheted off tree stumps and chunks of rubble. Once Anna was knocked off her feet by a near miss, and lay for a moment, gasping and struggling to catch her breath. Leviss reached down and lifted her up.

'Come on!' he said, 'There is death here. We must make the gates!'

His words were carried away by the whoosh of a ballista bolt as it sped by, missing his shoulder by a spear length and disappearing into the gloom. Anna did not reply, but snatched up her pulse-gun, shook her head, and stumbled on.

Reaching the rubble-covered hotplate, already strewn with the bodies of dead and wounded, they all saw, as the clouds of dust and smoke cleared for a moment, that not everything about the breach was to their advantage:

The towers had come down, breaking the gated wall, but they had also filled the breach with a giant mound of masonry, twisted steel work and split-broken concrete beams. It would not be easy to cross such an obstruction, even if there were no defenders left to challenge them.

But there were defenders, not a few, and they were ready to fight. They had gathered quickly along the top of the breach guarding a small replica reflector beam, and were waiting for the advance of the outlander infantry. The reflector flickered into life for just a moment. Beams of super-heated light swept across the far off open ground through opening, incinerating everything in their path. Then the sun fell behind a cloud, the dust thickened once more, and the reflectors were turned off.

'Are we really going up there?' asked Leviss, and he swallowed hard as he gazed at the mountain of rubble ahead of him.

'Well, we can't be hiding now,' replied his uncle. 'Where the others go, we must follow.' He laughed and spat the dust from his lips. 'Is that not the way of it?'

A fire-ball from a catapult somewhere behind the breach, rose above the wrecked gates, trembled for a moment and then plunged towards them.

'Down!' yelled Nike, and they all scrambled to find shelter. The fire-ball fell not twenty paces from where they had been standing, and sent a burst of flame and molten metal scything in every direction among the groups of attackers. Anna felt the searing heat of the explosion as she huddled between two massive blocks of stonework, and squeezed her eyes tight against the brilliance of the blast. When at last she looked up again, all around her was scorched and blackened. Even the rubble glowed, and smoked and sparked as the embers of the fire-ball slowly died.

To her relief, she saw the others emerge from out of the wreckage of tumbled stones. Both Leviss and Nike waved, and she raised her arm in reply.

'We move now!' shouted Bepsi-Loca. Climbing carefully across the rock-covered hotplate, and trying to ignore the pattering whine of enemy fire, they began to climb the breach.

To her left, about thirty paces distant, Anna could see that a whole regiment of stainer storm troopers was climbing with them, and that as they climbed covering fire from war wagons whooshed over their heads, and arced towards the defenders atop the breach.

She could not think, she dared not think, what she would do when she reached the top of the rubble and came face to face with her own people. Her only comfort was that she might be struck down before that happened, and no one would ever know the shame of her situation.

Again, it was Leviss who came to her in the midst of her confusion, and putting his hand on her back spoke to her as if he had always been her brother, and she had known nothing beyond a life in the outlands.

'I will get you through, Anna,' he said. 'Just stay close by me.'

And so they climbed.

And on the other side of the breach, Akton with the commander at his side, and a company of men gathered about them, waited to repel the attack.

Just below them, and twenty paces further back, a full regiment of reserves also waited. They had been brought up hastily from one of the military shelters, but they were untried recruits and the commander was reluctant to throw them into the first shock of battle. Especially this battle.

'We need to hold this breach,' he said to Akton, as he checked his weapon yet again, and glanced towards the smoking crest of the rubble. 'Our bombard crews are nearly out of ammunition, and we only have half a dozen ballistas left to cover what's left of the gateway precinct.'

Akton nodded. 'We still hold the walls,' he said.

'Aye, what's left of them, chancellor,' the commander replied, 'but I doubt if the enemy are going to be distracted by that. They will throw everything they have at the gates. Listen!'

From the far side of the breach, they heard a cheer, then the harsh rattle of war wagons as they ground their way up onto the smoking hotplate and then swung their ballistas and rocket launchers to the firing position.

'Up we go!' shouted the commander. He stood, blew his troop-whistle and then scrambled the last few yards to the top of the breach. With Akton following, his men leapt to their feet and surged forward, firing their pulse guns as they went.

They were met by a storm of projectiles: ballista bolts, fire-balls and solid shot from catapults. Several men went down straight away. Two were flung back several metres and vanished into the smoke and flames of the broken towers. Akton stepped over the body of a young soldier who had just been struck by a ballista-bolt, looked away and raised his pulse-club just as he reached the crest. All around him the surviving soldiers were standing on top of the rubble and pouring a relentless fire into the faces of the oncoming infantry.

To Akton it seemed impossible that anyone could stand upright and survive in that storm of fire, both from attacker and defender, and yet they stood. Men and women were falling on both sides, some wounded, some dead as they fell, but their places were always taken up instantly by another soldier, either outlander or citizen of Serenity. And as every soldier stepped into the gap left by his or her comrade, they raised their weapons and scarcely pausing to aim, fired.

The chancellor checked the setting on his pulse-club. It was set at twenty yards. He looked through the smoke and murk at a group of attackers coming towards him. They were at the most twenty five yards away, and no more than huddled shapes almost lost against the pile of rubble. But he thought he could see the nearest group: perhaps half a dozen but certainly three or four. The heap of stones and metal beams they were clambering across had brought them closer together than was wise, and he sensed that he could knock down at least two of them when they came within range.

Easing back the pulse-trigger, and raising the club-stock, he tried to ignore the hiss and snap of projectiles flashing by his head, and took aim. There were two women in his sights, he was sure of it. For a moment he hesitated. He had always hated the idea of women serving as front-line troops. Scouts, yes, like young Anna but not frontline of infantry troopers. It didn't seem right.

A ballista bolt struck a block of masonry in front of him and skidded away in a shower of sparks. It crashed into a two-man catapult that had just been hauled to the top of the breach, flung the machine to one side, and killed the two soldiers who were loading it.

Biting his lip, Akton frowned and took aim again.

Looking up the slope, Bepsi-Loca saw the silhouette of a soldier of Serenity standing on top of the breach. The man had a pulse-club and as Bepsi-Loca watched, the man turned the club-stock towards them and took aim. Kneeling quickly, the outlander scout raised his own weapon and fired twice.

The first pulse fell short, the second one struck the man on the shoulder and toppled him backwards and out of sight.

'One less to worry about!' shouted Bepsi-Loca, and turned to Anna, Nike and Leviss. 'Up now!' he said. 'There's no sense in staying here. Death loves a crowd!'

He leapt across a gap between two blocks of concrete, and with one hand grabbed hold of a piece of twisted reinforcing rod, hauling himself onto a broken slab of marble that had once faced the upper brickwork of a tower.

A shot rang out and the fire-slug of a sniper catapult hummed past Bepsi-Loca's ear. He shook his head and grinned at the others. 'See what I mean?' he said. 'Keep moving. Up now!'

The others followed, ducking and weaving as they crossed the rubble and worked their way up the slope. Anna-Seka found herself stepping over the bodies of the dead and wounded, noticing that as she climbed there were ever more bodies, and most were dead. Some of the dead were horribly torn, others looked as if they had simply tired of the climb, and had found a quiet place to lie down and sleep.

Once she knelt down beside a young soldier who had been hit in the legs by a pulse-bolt, and was lying between two pieces of masonry groaning and calling out for water.

She knew there was little that she could do, but she gave him her water bottle, and was about to help him drink from it, when Nike came up beside her:

'Leave him be, lass,' she whispered. 'You heard my father. If we stop here, we are dead for sure.' She took Anna by the arm. 'Leave him. The medics will pick him up, and do what they can for him. Come!'

A bombard shell burst high above them, and away to their left, spraying the slope with shrapnel.

With a nod, Anna pressed the bottle into the soldier's hands. She began to move up the slope again.

All across the breach stainer infantry pushed on towards the crest. Clouds of smoke from phosphorous grenades and fire-bolts swirled across the slope, concealing the advance, and then suddenly exposing it as blasts of hot air from the weapons of both attackers and defenders were fired in rolling volleys or haphazard single shots. Banners carried by both sides were torn to tatters by fusillade after fusillade, but they were still held aloft, and waved defiantly in the teeth of the battle. Every time a banner bearer fell, another soldier stepped into their place, and what was left of the banner would be raised again to a ripple of cheers and shouts.

It was clear that neither the siege engines or war wagons could ascend the steep slope of rubble, and although they were able to give covering fire to the attackers from their positions near the hotplate, the further the stainer infantry climbed up the slope, the less cover they had. On the other hand the defence-mortars and bombards the commander of the gates had set up in the chaotic but largely open area behind the gate-precinct were in the hands of skilled artillery men and engineers. Using maximum elevation, they launched their projectiles on an almost vertical trajectory, so that they arced across the walls and exploded over the heads of the enemy forces that were crowded into the breach.

Although the commander had only about three mortars and two batteries of bombards still in working order, and with the crews to work them, their punishing effect began to tell on the stainer assault.

Less than a dozen outlander infantry reached the top of the breach, and although they fought desperately, they were exhausted by their climb, and were soon overwhelmed and captured.

At last the war horns sounded through distant speakers, and what was left of the outlander assault force straggled to a halt, fired one last volley and then retreated back down the slope.

The defending regiments of the city, their numbers badly depleted by the fighting, did not try to take the initiative and charge after the retreating outlanders. They were too exhausted, and too few. On both sides, the artillery fell silent, the smoke slowly drifted away and a strange stillness settled over the battlefield and breach.

Anna and Leviss, along with Nike and Bepsi-Loca had found a place in the rubble to shelter. It was about half-way down the slope, out of sight and range of the weapons carried by the city militias and regiments. They were, all of them, tired thirsty and covered with the dust and sweat of battle. As scouts, Bepsi-Loca knew that they would be expected to occupy a forward position, and report back on any enemy movements. He knew that, but he hoped, along with the others, that the fighting was over for the day, and that they would be able to slip away under cover of darkness and find a place to camp and snatch some rest.

'Well, we're alive,' he said after a while, and grinned through the dirt and dust that caked his face.

'Aye, but only just,' replied Leviss slumping down with his back against a broken piece of concrete pillar. He looked at Nike. 'How are ye, sister?'

His sister, who was sitting down with her head between her knees, looked up wearily. 'How am I? Well, I'm thanking our mother's prayers that I'm still breathing,' she said. 'Do you think we'll have to go again soon? I'm not sure I could get up that slope again.'

Leviss shrugged. 'Who knows? What do ye think, Uncle?'

Bepsi-Loca did not reply. He was looking at Anna, who was lying on her back staring up at the sky. Her eyes were open, but it seemed as if she was seeing nothing.

At last he leaned forward. 'Are ye all right, lassie?'

Anna blinked, once, twice then slowly sat up. 'I was watching the clouds,' she said slowly. 'It helps.'

With a smile and a gentle nod, Bepsi-Loca sat back. 'You'll do me, lassie,' he said quietly. 'Rest on.' Then he turned to Leviss and Nike. 'If there's to be another attack before nightfall, they'll need to let us know soon.' He glanced across and then down the slope. 'There's no sign of movement among the officers, and no runners coming our way. I think we're safe enough for the moment.'

Shortly after Bepsi had spoken, there came the sound of trumpets, again through multi-speakers, not this time from just beyond the breach or behind the ramparts, but much further away. They were trumpets that were sounding from deep within the city, and from somewhere up high. Their call was clear and strong, and in perfect unison.

'There must be at least fifty of them, the trumpets I mean,' said Leviss scrambling to his feet and then crouching down again, as he realised he was exposed to sniper fire. 'What's it about?'

'It means that the Spire is been raised,' said Anna-Seka. 'It means that the king is about to speak.'

PART 1

SPECIAL THANKS

Beta reading & Feedback : Maryam Garbar, Cécile Okunola, Léo Artus, Sarah Sazzal, Allan Russel, Folks at writingforums.com **Early Promotion** : BiblioTheory, Beard of Darkness Book Reviews, David W Walters from fanfiaddict.com,

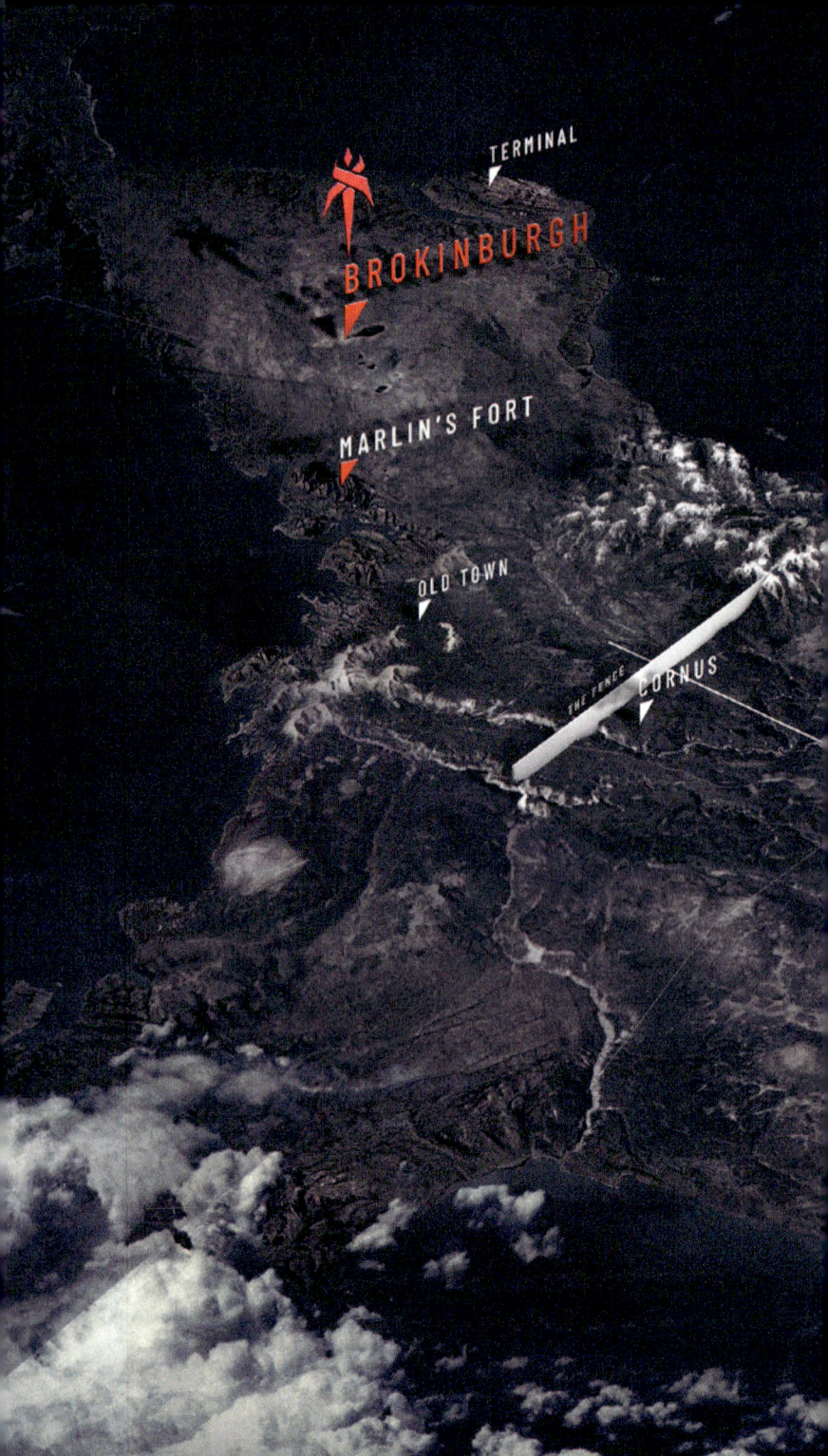

THE GREAT HIGHWAY

SERENITY
PORTUS PORTUS

ALTA REGINA

- Royal Citadel (court 0)
- Royal Tower
- Access to cliffside (Cascading gardens, Portus-Portus, Court 1, Glamtech)
- Upper Town
- Western pinnacle
- Court 3
- Military barracks

FLOAT
BUSH

BRUXELLES JE T_AIME
ANGÈLE

HOW TO BE EATEN BY A WOMAN
THE GLITCH MOB

IN BIRDSONG
EVRYTHING EVRYTHING

ALLES VERBOTEN
TRANS AM

NOW YOU GOT ME
INHALER

MACHINE STOP
DUOLOGUE

NIGHTCALL (DUSTIN N'GUYEN REMIX)
KAVINSKY

IN A SPIRAL
PHANTOGRAM

Printed in Great Britain
by Amazon